TRUE BLUE

Joe Thomas was born in Hackney in 1977. *True Blue* is the final novel in the United Kingdom trilogy, set in East London, following *White Riot* and *Red Menace*.

Also by Joe Thomas

THE UNITED KINGDOM TRILOGY
White Riot
Red Menace

THE SÃO PAULO QUARTET
Paradise City
Gringa
Playboy
Brazilian Psycho

STAND-ALONE
Bent

TRUE BLUE

JOE THOMAS

MACLEHOSE PRESS
QUERCUS · LONDON

First published in Great Britain in 2026 by MacLehose Press

an imprint of Quercus
Part of John Murray Group

1

A CIP catalogue record for this book is available from the British Library

HB ISBN 978 1 52942 343 3
EBOOK ISBN 978 1 52942 344 0

Typeset in Minion by MacGuru Ltd

Printed and bound in Great Britain by Clays Ltd, Elcograf S.p.A.

MIX
Paper | Supporting
responsible forestry
FSC
www.fsc.org FSC® C104740

Papers used by Quercus are from well-managed forests and other responsible sources.

Quercus
Carmelite House
50 Victoria Embankment
London EC4Y 0DZ

John Muray Group
Part of Hodder & Stoughton Limited
An Hachette UK company

The authorised representative in the EEA is Hachette Ireland, 8 Castlecourt
Centre, Dublin 15, D15 XTP3, Ireland (email: info@hbgi.ie)

Author's Note

Though set during certain factual events of 1978–1990, *True Blue* is a work of fiction. Where possible, and in the context of a work of fiction, I have used the recorded words of real-life figures, in some instances weaving these into my own dialogues, though the interactions and situations these figures share with my characters are imagined.

Acknowledgements follow the main text and include a comprehensive bibliography of all sources consulted and notes referencing all quoted material. The Acknowledgements itemise instances where fact and fiction meet, what happened and what I have imagined; I provide information as to which is which – as far as that is possible in the context of a work of fiction – as well as where further information can be found. A guiding principle: the scenes in which real-life figures appear are fictionalised versions of real-life events, or fictional situations created to deliver factual information based on their testimony and footage.

Where fictional characters appear in scenes set at recognisably historical events, these are fictionalised and used fictitiously. The police officers in the novel and their actions are entirely fictional. Whilst the Acid House promoters and events, the bands, the music and the magazines in the text are real, my characters are fictional and therefore the portrayal of their work and their interactions with those real people, organisations and groups is wholly imagined.

I'd like to thank Wayne Anthony in particular for his recollections of the period as immortalised in his explosive memoir *Class of 88*, which I reference and quote in the text. Thank you, too, to Mat Snow and *Q*, Luke Turner and *The Quietus* for permission to quote from a number of articles about Paul Weller and The Style Council. And, finally, thank you to John Eden at the Radical History of Hackney for his support; the archive has been invaluable for the trilogy. Simply, it wouldn't be what it is without the documents, articles and commentary that John writes and curates. I am extremely grateful.

Throughout the text, factual quotations are attributed and referenced in the notes. Quotations from the speeches and writings of well-known and less well-known figures, and from other texts pertaining to them, are a matter of the historical record and also cited in the notes; any conversations or interactions they have with my characters are entirely invented.

For my mum and dad

'For there can be no freedom without order, there can be no order without authority; and that authority that is impotent or hesitant in the face of intimidation, crime and violence, authority which is like that, cannot endure'

Margaret Thatcher, Speech to Conservative Central Council

'Crap into your Union Jack and wrap it round your head'

The Beautiful South, 'Have You Ever Been Away?'

You believe in the United Kingdom.

The United Kingdom has made your fortune. And you've raised your children in British robes.

You believe in the idea – the union; you believe in the system.

You believe that the sum is greater than its parts. And you've used this system, worked it inside and out.

Because, most of all, you believe:

You believe in –

You.

PART ONE
Black Death

1978

1

The Jackal Run

Stoke Newington High Street,
10 December 1978, one o'clock in the morning

Parker wistfully examines the Middle Eastern bulk of the Astra Cinema through the passenger door window.

Not that he's a fan of uncensored martial arts movies, or especially fond of softcore sex films, these being your essential offerings at the Astra, but it's freezing in old Bill Stewart's rusty motor, and he'd give anything to be inside.

He's heard a rumour some Turks might want to turn the place into a Mosque. You can see why, what with those domed twin towers, pillars all about the place.

Parker pictures a very different clientele to who's in there right now.

They're showing *They Call Her Cleopatra Wong* in the main screening room.

It's got a tasty-looking tagline:

She purrs like a kitten and makes love like a siren. This side of the Pacific, she is the meanest, deadliest and sexiest secret agent.

Parker thinking, ironic, now there's a girl after my own heart.

In his own first six months as an undercover, there hasn't been much lovemaking, sirens or otherwise.

Tart cards in a phone box and strippers in pubs is about as exotic as Parker's got.

This Cleopatra Wong, on the other hand, sounds like a real credit to the profession, in all fairness, a real *personality*.

Parker laughs, shakes his head, shivers.

The Astra doesn't advertise what's on in the smaller room – unless you count shifty-looking chaps in raincoats shuffling in as advertising.

Moody prints of Asian arthouse erotica. That's what they call it, anyway, *porn*.

'Rat Trap' comes on the radio, a number Parker's heard before. He doesn't remember the name of the group though, one of them punk outfits, he thinks, dirty hair and attitude.

Then the driver's door opens, and old Bill barges his way in, thrusting a wrapped kebab at Parker who stops worrying about 'Rat Trap's provenance.

'Get your laughing gear round this, son,' Stewart instructs, slamming the door, blowing into his hands. 'It's brass monkeys out there.'

Parker doesn't need a second invitation. 'Yeah, thanks, Bill.'

He tears at the greasy paper and buries his snout in the meat and in the sauce, crunches the onions, slurps the fat –

Stewart, mouth churning, says, 'You hear the one about the German coastguard?'

'The what coastguard?'

'The German coastguard.'

'I ain't heard it, no.'

Stewart wipes his face with the sleeve of his leather jacket, mops at his forehead. 'Bit much the state of this sauce, mind,' he declares. 'I'm fucking melting here.'

Parker chewing. 'Yeah, quality though, cheers.'

'Turkish gaff. Fair play to them.'

'You were saying.'

'German coastguard stationed on the North Sea, gets an SOS. He's a young lad, first day on the job, and there's someone yelling in English, I'm sinking, I'm sinking.'

'We all are, mate.'

'Right, good one. Anyway, I'm sinking, he hears, I'm sinking, and the young German's going, fuck me, and he gets on the radio, and he says, sinking?' Stewart pauses, swallows. He grins. 'Vot are you sinking about?' he says.

'Good one.'

'Yeah, it's funny.'

'Germans, eh?' Parker says.

'Yeah. Cunts.'

Parker eats his kebab, thoughtfully. 'Who's this singing? Not exactly a barrel of laughs, is it, the song?'

Something about being young and acting tough, about gasworks and meat factories, lamp boys who are coming on strong, a refrain: you've been caught, you've been caught, you've been caught –

'Boomtown Rats,' says Stewart. 'Singer's name is Bob Geldof. Irish lads. Dublin, I believe.'

'You're well informed.'

'Yeah, well, when you've sat in a car as much as I have, you start to become very familiar with the hit parade.'

Parker thinks he's been sitting in *this* car for quite long enough.

'What we doing here, Bill, *really*?'

It's not an unreasonable question given the circs.

Parker considers the last few months:

Brick Lane in September, his handler Detective Constable Noble's subsequent suspension, his fellow undercover officer Alan, beaten half to death by National Front thugs –

And now this.

'Getting you back in the game,' Stewart says. 'Tactical withdrawal followed by surveillance followed by re-engagement and redeployment. What we're looking for, ultimately, is *integration*. To have you integrated in the local community. You're switching sides; you need an in with the activists.'

'Not sure that answers the question, Bill. And integrated how?'

Stewart shifts in his seat, faces Parker, who sits side on.

Stewart places his kebab – lovingly, half-eaten – on the dashboard.

He gives it a prod. Obediently, it stays where it is.

Parker ain't surprised: with old Bill, you do what you're told.

Stewart nods. 'The Special Demonstration Squad,' he says, 'is both secretive and elite, and, as far as you're concerned, Parker, *I am* the Special Demonstration Squad. And integrated in any way possible, son. Make friends with the natives is one way. Powwow.'

Parker sniffs. Make friends. It's not school, though, is it?

Outside, the high street glows with cold. A bloke in a high-vis vest sweeps the forecourt of the car wash across the road. The Baptist Church is in darkness, tall trees and thick hedges. Stoke Newington nick a short distance up the road, cloaked in murk, Parker thinks, *wild east*.

The Astra's doing a bit of trade, but it looks mainly like people leaving, collars up and hats down, hands in pockets, whistling –

Not me, guv, is the look they're going for, Parker thinks. I'm just off home to the lady wife, me, I've not been watching a bluey, oh no, not on your Nellie.

Parker sees a group of black lads go in, laughing.

Teenagers, he thinks.

He counts six of them.

He can see them horsing around, joshing, ordering drinks from the foyer bar, bottles of pop and buckets of Slush Puppies, by the looks of it, friendly enough.

'But where do I fit in, Bill, is what I mean?' Parker says. 'Noble's not around, for now, so—'

'And why do you think Detective Constable Noble is not currently around, Parker?'

'Because of what we done, Bill, over the summer, because of Brick Lane.'

Bill smiles. 'No, son, it ain't exactly that. It ain't what *you* done, believe me.'

Parker thinks about what he done over the summer –

The summer of hate, seventy-eight.

He thinks about how he got on side with, how he *infiltrated* a National Front cell in Bethnal Green, fought running battles down Brick Lane and up Chapel Market with Anti-Fascists and the Bengali Youth League, among others, what he chanted, what he said, what he *did*. How his counterpart, Alan, was on the other side, how they looked out for each other as best they could in the skirmishes, how Parker couldn't help Alan, in the end, how he'd had to walk away.

The tactical withdrawal Stewart's talking about: less and less involvement over a period of time, loosening then cutting ties, growing his hair, new threads, moving house, changing telephone numbers –

And now this.

He's not yet worked out what he's achieved, Parker hasn't.

Noble using him as part of the Met Race Crime initiative – what's come of that, then? – but the violence and the murdering never stopped, did it?

Altab Ali, murdered, racially motived, 4 May, Whitechapel, just a few days after the Carnival Against Racism in Victoria Park.

Ishaque Ali, died of a heart attack in Hackney Hospital, 25 June, after a racially motivated attack by three white men, one of whom strangled Ali with his bootlaces, for fuck's sake. Detective Chief Superintendent George Atterwil told *The Times* that 'the motive here is theft and robbery'.

Parker's never questioned what he did, not really, he's just gone and done it, done his job, that's all.

What he remembers is the weeks he did inside to give him the credentials to do the job that he does. If he's been inside, then he's clean, is the theory. A hard few weeks. Prison is tough.

What Parker's done is *earned* this job.

And it was old Bill who picked him out from the recruits at Hendon, old Bill who arranged for the aggravated assault charge, the time and then the dismissal, old Bill who set the whole thing up with Noble, so, yeah, maybe Bill really is the Special Demonstration Squad as far as Parker is concerned.

'So, what is it then, Bill?'

'What it is, is that Noble wasn't flying straight with his superiors, all right. What you were doing, wasn't exactly what he said you were doing, so when poor Alan copped a brick in the canister, Noble copped one too, figuratively, of course.'

'What did he say I was doing?'

Stewart sniffs, shakes his head. 'It don't matter, *you're* still here.'

'I—'

'That's enough questions, son. Shut your noise and eat your food.'

Obediently, Parker does what he's told.

'Jesus,' Stewart says, tongue out. 'This sauce. It's *murderous*.'

Parker examines the street.

'How many more nights like this do you think, Bill?'

Stewart considers the question. 'Surveillance ain't exactly an exact science, to be frank. What we're doing is working out when to re-engage, when to re-deploy.'

'By sitting here?'

'Habits, Parker, we're establishing certain habitual behaviours, patterns.'

'The only pattern we're establishing is a late-night kebab habit.'

'You're a clever boy, anyone ever tell you that?'

'Habitually.'

'There's such a thing as *too* clever, young man.'

'By half.'

'Yeah, that's the phrase, work out what it means.'

Parker watches three of the teenagers pour out of the Astra, onto the pavement with their drinks, still laughing and messing about.

He wipes his hands on a piece of toilet paper. 'But who are we watching, Bill, that's what you've never told me.'

Stewart grins and starts to shake, mouth full again, he can't get the words out –

'When you see it, son,' he manages, 'you'll know!' Stewart laughing at this, spluttering and coughing, gasping. 'Here, pass me that bottle of water, Jesus.'

Parker fetches the bottle from under his seat.

As he hands it over, he hears shouting from the other side of the road, sees the teenagers freeze, look to see where it's coming from.

Parker sees three white lads.

Three white lads dressed in bomber jackets and boots.

Parker thinks, hang about.

The three white lads are shouting at the teenagers across the road.

They're shouting about there ain't no black in the union jack.

They're shouting about go home dirty nigger bastards.

They're shouting about peanut heads –

They're shouting –

NF NF NF NF NF NF

Nazi salutes and monkey chants –

Parker opens the passenger door.

'Stay inside, lad,' Stewart says.

Parker shakes his head. Stewart glares. Parker turns, slams the door –

He hears Stewart swearing, then Stewart's door opening –

Ahead, the teenagers are in conference.

They look scared, Parker thinks, and two of them retreat up the Astra stairs as Parker jogs down the street.

The white lads grunting quickly across the road.

One of the teenagers stays outside.

Parker's not quite fast enough –

And the white lads are on the black teenager, they knock him down, kick him once, twice, there's a glint of steel –

No, Parker thinks, no –

And then the three white lads tear off down the road.

Parker stretches his legs after them, sees the black kid bleeding, his friends crowding round, hears old Bill shouting, 'Get after them, get an ambulance.'

The white lads are off down Brighton Road, over a fence –

Parker cursing, swearing, and he turns and he's back onto Stoke Newington High Street just as the bleeding black teenager is carried up the road by his friends, old Bill yelling encouragement, beckoning Parker to get a wriggle on, Parker following up towards the nick.

Parker sees them stop by a phone box, hears them shout and yell, It's fucking been smashed in, and off they go up the road, Parker following, Parker hearing, Let's take him to the Babylon shop, that's where the nearest phone will be, let's go.

As he passes Bill –

And Parker's moving quickly, mind, he's a big boy, Parker, your basic *unit* –

As he passes Bill, Bill grabs him by the arm, stops him mid-stride, no mean feat *that* –

And Bill hisses, his breath wet in Parker's ear, 'You make sure they see your face, son, all right?'

'Eh?'

'You heard.'

And Parker's off again. *Who needs to see my* face? he's thinking.

It's pushing two in the morning, and Parker hangs back a touch as the lads half-carry, half-drag their friend up the steps and into the police station.

Parker follows.

Parker hears –

What do you lot want?

What have you been up to?

Yeah – what's going on?

Hold your horses, I want to know exactly what's going on here.

Parker watches the duty officer, watches another PC come in –

Watches the boys.

Shut up – now first of all, give us your names and addresses.

Keep quiet son, we'll attend to you in a minute. I've got to take a statement first.

Where was this?

Did you recognise any of them?

Parker watches a more senior officer approach the desk.

Parker hears –

What's going on here?

These boys have been starting trouble.

Watch your language with me, sonny. Now have you lot been in any trouble before?

So you started a fight, eh? Picked on some white boys, eh? Then you got the worst of it and come here with your lies about other kids?

Be very careful, son. Now what time did this so-called attack occur?

Oh yeah? And what were you little boys doing out at that time of night?

Just answer the questions.

Parker hears –

Just answer the questions.

A likely story.

Parker shaking his head.

I don't want no lip from you, Sambo. Now what street did this happen on?

What street's this then?

Who do you think you're bloody swearing at? Up against the wall!

You too, up against the wall!

You—

Parker hears –

There's nothing wrong with him, just a bloody scratch – you can't have us on.

Look, the quicker you tell us what happened, the quicker your mate will see a doctor.

So where were you when he got stabbed?

Where were you?

Have you been in trouble with the police before?

Where were you?

You could have been out nicking tonight for all we know.

Parker watching this unfold, this poor boy bleed out –

He steps forward, says, 'I saw what happened.'

The boys look at Parker.

The PCs smile.

One of them places a hand on Parker's shoulder. 'A word, son, in your shell-like.'

He leads Parker a few paces away from the desk.

He says, 'You sure you want to be involved, mate? You want to make a statement, do you?' He nods at the boys. 'For these lot? You sure?'

Parker thinks, statement, right, somewhat complicated given his current role within the Metropolitan Police.

'Nah,' he says, 'I won't be needing to make a statement.'

'Good lad,' the PC grins.

Parker clocks his collar number: GN224.

'How long 'til you lose a digit there?' Parker asks.

Meaning: when you going to get promoted?

The PC smiles. 'Mind your own, son, if I were you.'

Parker watching, the boys shouting, no ambulance called –

'What's your name?' Parker asks.

The PC looks over his shoulder.

He seems reassured that no one is listening, Parker thinks.

Reassured that his colleagues are busy not calling for an ambulance.

'Jenkins is my name,' he says. 'Police Constable Dave Jenkins. For now.' He jabs his finger into Parker's chest. 'And don't you forget it.'

Parker nods.

Jenkins says, 'Now on your bike.'

Parker nods, pushes past him. 'Call a fucking ambulance!' he tells the desk sergeant, who sighs and does so.

Parker leaves. He waits outside. He doesn't return to old Bill's rusty motor, though he can see it's still there, old Bill no doubt sweating rage.

Half an hour passes, perhaps a little more, then the siren of an ambulance.

Parker hopes it isn't too late.

Next day, Parker meets Bill in the pub for breakfast. Bill sits behind four pints of stout, untouched.

'Have a drink,' Bill says.

'I don't want a drink.'

Bill pushes a pint of stout across the table. 'Have a *drink*, son.'

Parker nods and has a drink.

'Better?'

'Considerably.'

Bill pushes a piece of paper across the table. On it, in typescript:

Michael Ferreira was born in Stanleytown, Guyana in 1959. In 1971 he emigrated to the UK to join his parents who had moved here a few years earlier. He was a pupil at Downsview School, Hackney, and left at the age of 16 to become a mechanic. Michael was still a teenager when he was killed.

Parker finishes the stout. 'I think I'll have another drink, Bill.'

Bill slides a second pint across the table.

Parker has a drink.

'There is a bright side, son,' Bill says, after a while. 'There's always a bright side.'

'Yeah?'

'Yeah.'

'Why don't you enlighten me?'

'They've seen your face now.'

'Who's seen my face?'

'The kids saw your face, the have-a-go-hero, you helped them out.'

'Hardly.'

'You did your best.'

'So what if they've seen my face?'

'It's an in, Parker old son, an in.'

Parker nods. He regards Bill's slab of Special Brew skin, *his* face.

'There'll be meetings, protests,' Bill says. 'You can go, get involved. Community action, all that.'

'For what, Bill?'

'It's your fucking job, Parker, that's for what.' Bill sniffs. 'You wanna remember how we got your identity, Parker, son, do you remember that? *That* ought to tell you everything you need to know about this job.'

Parker does remember.

They call it the Jackal Run, down in the archives at St Catherine's House, national registry of births, marriages and deaths, looking for a kid the same sort of age as him but who's dead, using that name, that identity, that *past*, then inventing your own history based on that real past, that was the idea, meaning if anyone ever did any digging they'd find something that looked legit, even if Parker's passport, driving licence and tax code are fake, in the name of someone who was once real.

'Now shape up and finish your drink. We've got work to do.'

Parker shapes up.

And Bill's right, of course.

'It's Christmas time, old son,' Bill says. 'It's not supposed to be good for your elf.' Laughing like a plonker at that one.

Parker leaves.

21 December: Parker attends a meeting of more than one hundred and fifty people who gather to protest the circumstances surrounding the death of Michael Ferreira.

A group is set up, the Hackney Black People's Defence Organisation.

Parker finds himself at several meetings, several protests, finds himself welcomed at these meetings, these protests.

19 January: Parker is part of the Hackney Black People's Defence Organisation presence at Highbury Magistrates at the second hearing of the white men accused of the attack on Michael Ferreira.

All black people entering the court are searched –

Parker is not.

The hearing is adjourned 'due to the large black presence', in the words of the *Hackney People's Press*.

This adjournment leads to outrage.

Michael Ferreira's mother shouts: 'We want justice!'

She is taken into police custody, 'manhandled and insulted'.

Winston James – a young black man – protests the treatment of black people in the court and is the victim of an unprovoked assault by police officers.

He is beaten and he is hit.

His testicles are grabbed.

He is charged with obstructing the police –

And he is charged with assaulting a policeman.

Parker sees this and Parker does nothing.

20 January: Parker attends Michael Ferreira's funeral.

It takes place on a Saturday. It is cold and it is snowing.

There are several hundred people gathered in Clapton, Parker one of them.

They are there to mourn Michael Ferreira, just nineteen years old.

It is east London's fourth racist murder in eight months.

There are no banners or placards, no chants, no papers are sold.

There is a solemn procession, equal numbers of black people and white people following a flower-lined hearse, with an enormous wreath reading SON.

Parker walks with his head down. One or two catch his eye, but he remains discreet, now is not the time, surely. Not that old Bill would say that.

They march slowly up Kingsland High Street. There are crowds of black people gathered at the end of Ridley Road market to pay their respects.

There are raised fist salutes.

'We shall overcome' is sung again and again.

A man standing by the side of the road asks: 'Who was he? Was it anyone important?'

Parker looks at this man, this man who sees a crowd of black people and of white people and is confused. Parker shakes his head at this man, this old, confused man.

'Will no one tell me if it was anyone important?'

The question is answered shortly after the funeral in the *Hackney People's Press*:

> *Of course Michael Ferreira was important. He had a family, he had friends and they have lost a nineteen-year-old son or brother, cut down in a cowardly attack. But there is more to his name now. By his death he has become a symbol of all that is wrong with our racialist society.*
>
> *This is why the Hackney Black People's Defence Organisation has been formed, to demand justice for the death of Michael Ferreira, and justice for the racialist oppression of black people everywhere.*

Two white men are charged with manslaughter and affray at the Old Bailey in connection with the killing of Michael Ferreira.

The one with the knife, the court hears, used to carry it around with him in case 'coloureds wanted trouble'.

The judge, Parker hears, dismisses any connection with the National Front.

The one with the knife gets five years for manslaughter and affray.

Michael Ferreira's mother says:

'There is no justice in this land for Black people ... I am completely flabbergasted with the sentence. I cannot see Black people given proper justice in the courts of this land. I myself felt like dying when I heard that the judge had sent that "murderer" down for just five years. I expected that he deserved to get fourteen years for killing my son.'

Parker hears this and Parker does nothing.

And Parker thinks about what old Bill said, what old Bill said about the community, about getting involved, about *integrating* –

He's shown his face at the meetings, at the protests, he's got himself involved, and it's working – to a point.

What Parker thinks is there's a way to *really* integrate:

Find the right woman.

Kiss the girl.

TEN YEARS LATER

PART TWO
Death of a Party

December 1989–January 1990

CRACKDOWN ON DRUG PARTIES

Police are cracking down on the drugs-related dance craze Acid House. A task force of investigators are working all-out to break a suspected ring of drug-pushers they believe are organising the illegal parties in Hackney.

Hackney Gazette, 21 October 1988

ACID HOUSE DRUG PARTY FEARS SPIRAL

Alarm about a growing drugs menace sweeping Hackney from the latest 'Acid House' party craze was expressed at the meeting.

But a drug squad officer explained there had been no large-scale seizures in the borough of the LSD-type hallucinatory drug known as 'Ecstasy'.

Hackney Gazette, 25 November 1988

POLICE HALT NOISY WAREHOUSE PARTY

Police swooped to close an all-night warehouse party attended by 400 revellers in the early hours of Sunday morning.

'It was not an Acid House party,' said Sgt Gerry Carroll at Dalston Police station. 'It ended peaceably with the minimal amount of disturbance.'

Hackney Gazette, 2 December 1988

NEW   NEW
YEARS   YEARS
EVE   EVE

YOU ARE INVITED BY

GENESIS
SUNSET

TO

'THE FINAL PARTY'
LEASIDE ROAD, UPPER CLAPTON ROAD.

TOP D.J.'S   **20K**
                               TURBO
Eddie Richards   **SOUND**
COLIN HUDD   PHIL & BEN
Terry Farley   **FAT TONY**

INVITE ONLY
10:00pm – 10:00am

THE MANAGEMENT RESERVE THE RIGHT TO ADMISSION
STRICTLY OVER 18'S | LIABLE TO BE SEARCHED AT DOOR

1

Kibosh

31 December 1988

Chequers, lunchtime.

She, Mrs Thatcher, is working. She thinks, I'm always working. Always toiling, always striving, always *here*, putting in a shift.

She smiles at this.

Say what you like about me, she thinks – and of course people do exactly that, they say *exactly* what they like about her – say what you like about me, she thinks, but I do put in a shift, I do put the hours in, I do *punch the clock.*

New Year's Eve and she's waiting to be bustled in front of camera and microphone to record her message for the nation.

New Year's Eve, a night of revelry and celebration, traditionally, though she has often felt, Mrs Thatcher, a sudden and uncharacteristic melancholy as the clock strikes twelve and rather than looking forward – resolutions and whatnot – she'll find herself reflecting instead on what she hasn't achieved, what she's lost, who she's lost, Brighton, for example, will spring to mind, Norman, Mrs Tebbit, she'll think of what she hasn't prevented in Eastern Europe, in Lebanon, in Belfast – not the Falklands, though.

Is that how we are doomed to measure our achievements, by what we fail to do, by our impotence?

Denis labours past, scowling. Speaking of impotence, she thinks, a touch cruelly.

'Dolled up yet, are you, Margaret?' he snarls, cheerfully. 'Got on your war paint?'

She, Mrs Thatcher, ignores Denis, as she does more and more.

Your average Joe constituent would likely find it hard to conceive of his Prime Minister's working and living arrangements, such as they are, that her husband can wander freely around in his dressing gown in her offices, the offices from which she runs the country, for twenty of the twenty-four hours in the day.

And, no, not yet, she hasn't yet *got on her war paint*.

She rather wishes Denis would leave off with the comedy. Besides, a pastel lipstick and a can of hairspray is all she needs these days, so there.

She examines the dregs of tea in her china cup, looks at her wristwatch.

She's waiting to talk to her favourite Chief Inspector, about revelry, in fact, about public order and how best to maintain it. A junior minister has not long briefed her on what he calls the Acid Rave movement, which didn't sound like much fun, she thought.

But something in this briefing piqued Mrs Thatcher, got her bloodhound nose sniffing.

Thousands and thousands of young people, young people of all creeds and backgrounds, mobilised by a few telephone calls to gather together and dance through the night.

Quite something, logistics-wise, she thought. Dangerous.

There is, the junior minister suggested, unity, unity and euphoria, at these gatherings.

Also, dangerous.

They are, he declared, defiantly apolitical. A celebration of life and love and difference, of togetherness, very much *not* political.

Well, we'll see about that, Mrs Thatcher thinks now.

She remembers the apparently *very* political musical movements she's dismissed in the past, feigned ignorance of, denied their existence, in a way, by avowedly never engaging with them publicly:

Rock Against Racism
Live Aid
Red Wedge

Yes, we'll see about that, thinks Mrs Thatcher, checking her wristwatch and picking up the telephone.

Divide and rule; know thy enemy.

Scotland Yard, afternoon.

Detective Constable Noble is in with Chief Inspector Young, operational head of the Special Demonstration Squad and now, in addition, a senior man in CIB2, Scotland Yard's Anti-Corruption Squad.

Which means that Noble is likely to soon be engaged by CIB2 as well as the SDS, where he's been for some time after performing well enough in the late-seventies in the cross-region Met Race Crime Initiative. Apart from that little hiccup, back in 1978, the summer of hate, though it's donkey's years in the past now, a previous episode, and Young had already earmarked Noble, made him his eyes and his ears, and he kept his faith. Noble's been seconded here and there – mainly Stoke Newington, or thereabouts – but he's only ever really answered to Young.

Noble thinks this is some sort of privilege, or at least acknowledgement of his ability, this independence. Not that it's reflected in his rank: it can't be, if he were any higher up the food chain he wouldn't be able to shoulder his way to the trough.

As per usual, he's now learning – or *not* learning more like – the nuances of his latest assignment.

It's about all he can do to get the headlines, he thinks, the level of insinuation, the nudge-nudge, wink-wink patter of the man. Makes subterfuge feel like a gossiping session at a Women's Institute meeting.

'Your undercover,' Young says. 'He's still in with the groups around Hackney, despite, well, despite the unfortunate business of that young associate of his.'

This unfortunate business of that young associate being the brutal, and as yet unsolved, murder of Parker's snout.

'He's still there, guv, yes,' Noble says.

'Hanging on then,' Young chuckles, *avuncular* the word Noble's after.

'Yes, guv.'

Young pushes a piece of paper across his desk. Noble sees that it's an advert for a New Year's Eve party in Hackney, a 'rave'.

'You've told me about this,' Young says. 'Your *other* job,' he smiles.

Noble's current secondment: a unit tasked with investigation and policing of the illegal rave scene. A *task force* as it's called. Those in the know call it the Acid Squad.

Noble nods.

'And your boy is involved, to a point?'

'He's going tonight, I know that, guv.'

'Jolly good.'

One of those heavy Young silences follows, the room muggy, thick.

'Now,' Young begins. 'What you're doing on your unit, what your UCO is doing full stop, is reconnaissance work regarding criminal or seditious activity, gathering intelligence.'

'Yes, guv.'

'That all goes on, you understand, as planned.'

'Yes, guv.'

'But what I need – what *we* need, you understand – in addition to this, is for your UCO to feed up intelligence on the logistical and political nature of this movement, under the guise of his criminal investigation.'

'In other words, don't tell him, guv.'

'Nail on the head.'

Noble nods. Noble thinks he can use Suzi for that; he can just ask her.

'There is, I gather,' Young adds, 'going to be something of a media storm about all this. Your unit will set up relationships with journalists. The headlines will scream about this ecstasy evil, this threat to civil society, to English values, *Conservative* values.'

Noble nods.

'That business at Wapping, the print dispute, you remember?'

Noble does remember. Parker involved there too, never quite knowing what he was up to.

'Well, the press – some of them – owe us a favour after Wapping, how that was policed. They owe *her* a favour. You won't have any trouble with the *writers*.'

Young stands. 'Just make sure you don't get *your* name in the papers.'

Noble nods.

'More anon on what you're to do in terms of CIB2,' Young says. 'This is the priority. For now, baby steps, what will be will be and so forth.'

Noble thinking, let sleeping dogs lie then.

'You know what I mean by anon, of course.'

'I did Shakespeare at school, guv.'

'Good man.'

Or, to put it bluntly –

We can tolerate what's going on behind closed doors at Stoke Newington and Dalston until we can't.

2

Genesis

Lower Clapton Road, Hackney, 7 p.m.

Suzi Scialfa sits in the back of a souped-up Ford Escort, wondering –

Am I too old for this?

She's thinking, I'm too old for this, everyone is so *young*.

And that's just in the car. God knows what it'll be like inside, inside this *rave*.

The lad in the passenger seat – and he's young, this lad, early twenties tops – turns to smile at Suzi. 'Nearly there,' he says.

'I know.'

'First lot of these events, we all met in the ice-rink car park, went from there. Gave the Old Bill the run around.'

'But not this time.'

'No.' The lad grins. He brandishes a flyer at Suzi. 'See? It's all legal now, park sensibly, thank you!' Laughing.

Suzi can't help herself – he's a funny puppy, this lad, infectious – and she laughs along with him.

'Why do they call you Roy, Lee?' she asks him.

He shifts in his seat. 'My name, innit? Lee "Roy" Wilson.' Making the air quotes.

The driver, a huge man called Big Danny – Lee Roy's muscle, his *bodyguard*, Suzi understands – says, 'Roy the boy. Wide Boy Roy.'

'Lee boy.'

'Wide Roy.'

'Which is the name of your production company,' Suzi notes.

'Yeah, Wide Roy Productions, what of it?'

'It's got a ring to it.'

'Well, you know, we're just starting out, this is just an early partnership.'

'And what do you bring to this partnership, exactly?'

Lee Roy's nodding now. 'Style,' he says. 'That's what it is. Style.'

'They pay you for this style, do they?'

'Handsomely.' Grinning again.

'You know what,' Suzi says. 'I think I might need a drink before we get there.'

'OK, nice one.' Lee Roy nodding away. 'Let's stop at the Prince of Wales, down by the canal, yeah?'

Suzi nods. 'Sounds good.'

She thinks, when did I last go to the Prince of Wales?

Christ, it might have been with the Rock Against Racism gang, one of those meetings they'd have, brainstorming. Would have been 1978, or thereabouts.

'You heard the lady, Danny.'

Suzi sits back and looks out of the window.

Lower Clapton Road hasn't changed much, she thinks.

Since moving to Shoreditch, she hasn't been *back* much; there isn't much to come back to. The squat that she and Keith lived in has long been under scaffolding. As has she and Keith.

It's been a year since she's seen him, more than two since they split up, since she left. It was she who left, in the end, despite Noble telling Keith a few things about what Suzi had done for him. Not everything, but enough to make Keith leave, though he didn't, and in some ways that was the final straw for Suzi, that passivity: how could he stay after what she'd done?

Well, he did, so Suzi left.

And the last time she saw him he seemed fine. Still working with The Style Council, though that seems to be winding up now, Suzi's heard.

Apparently, Weller's obsessed with Chicago house music, she's heard an early version of a track called 'Promised Land' – a cover – that attests to this obsession, and Keith has a taste for it himself now too. Christ, Suzi thinks, he might be there tonight –

'You get any older folk at these shindigs,' she asks, 'or is it just kids?'

'Yeah,' says Lee, 'there's loads of people your age, don't fret!'

'Charming.'

'I mean, you know, you'll fit right in.'

'That's what I'm worried about,' Suzi mutters.

'Eh?'

Suzi smiles. 'I said, that's what I'm hoping.'

'Yeah, nice one,' says Lee. 'Danny,' he adds, 'we're there.' Meaning the pub, the Prince of Wales, Lea Bridge Road –

Suzi climbs out of the car and looks down the canal. Her and Keith's old squat, currently being *developed*, it appears.

'Saloon bar all right for you?' Lee Roy asks, slamming the passenger door.

'I am a lady, after all,' Suzi says.

Lee Roy claps his hands, rubs them together. 'Danny boy, get the drinks in,' he instructs.

Canal, between Lea Bridge Road and Leaside Road, 8 p.m.

Parker bounding along the towpath away from Carolyn and Marlon and some of the others further ahead who are nearly up at the warehouse, and he looks across the canal into the darkness of the merchants' yard and there's torchlight, a few clowns in suits, and he's wondering: which jokers get to use the footbridge?

Why aren't we using the footbridge?

After all, Marlon is well in with the chancers who run this game.

Approved business supplier is apparently the terminology.

At least that's what it says on the moody business cards Marlon carries around.

Approved business supplier, Wide Roy Productions

What Parker's thinking is that the business supplies Marlon provides are very likely *not* approved in any legal sense.

Parker doesn't have any proof yet – he never has any *proof* – but he's confident that Marlon has got those chunky gold rings on his fingers in an impressive number of patties.

What Parker doesn't understand is how Marlon manages to present a respectable front, as if he wasn't directly involved in Shaun's arrest after the riots.

Shaun, Carolyn's little cousin whose spell in Feltham is shortly up, and who will be coming to live with Parker and Carolyn in their new digs in Hackney, idea being this will distance him from Broadwater Farm and all the trouble he got into there.

The thing Parker can't share with Carolyn and her family – and the thing Marlon *won't* share – is that the mob that got Shaun into all that trouble, weren't actually from Broadwater Farm at all, but holidaying up there from Hackney.

Parker hears the thump of bass and skitter of drum behind him –

The sound cutting in and out, start-stop, rewind, start-stop –

Disco lightshow in the mist and murk above the canal sludge and towpath graffiti, rusted bikes and shopping trolleys in a red-yellow flash.

Soundcheck.

At least that's what Parker gathers it's called.

Testing, testing. Check, one-two –

Marlon was insistent: we've got to get there in time for the soundcheck.

Parker still doesn't understand why. But he's legging it now and needs to be back with them again pretty sharpish –

The lamps are lit across North Millfield's Park, and there's a couple of pensioners walking the dog, but otherwise it's the sound of kids, of ravers. The Prince of Wales pub just behind him glowing and bubbling, a bit of a singsong and have a banana, Auld Lang Syne, thank you very much, the Ship Aground next to it darker, forbidding, a famously unpleasant place, what with its racist landlord and his racist rottweiler.

Parker clocks where he is exactly and thinks –

This is where they pulled Shahid Akhtar out of the water, full of whisky and heartache, they said, misadventure, they said, over ten years ago now.

Parker was newly Special Demonstration Squad back then, getting on side with the National Front, undercover, rucking in Brick Lane with lefties –

Nineteen seventy-eight, summer of hate.

And the reason he's now jogging away from Carolyn, away from Marlon, is he's just off for a quick chat with his handler Detective Constable Patrick Noble.

His handler then, his handler now –

'I need some fags, darling,' he told Carolyn. 'I'll be right behind you.'

Prince of Wales, same time.

'You see, that's what this whole scene is about,' Lee Roy's saying, two pints down. 'It's in the dancehall tradition, right, the Jamaican Soundsystem *tradition*. It's been going on for years, but all you lot—'

'White people?'

'Journalists, all you lot *journalists*, you think dance music was invented *this* year as that's when little England got on board.'

Danny grunts, 'Lee Roy's the blackest man in east London.'

'All right, turn it in,' Lee says. 'What I'm saying is, this rave scene, it's Dennis Bovell, right? It's outlaws, but fighting the good fight, we're like, who is it—'

'Robinson Crusoe?' Big Danny offers.

'Robin Hood, you plonker.'

Suzi smiles.

'Dennis Bovell,' Lee says, 'it all started with him.'

34

'I know who Dennis Bovell is, Lee.'

'Yeah, OK, but do you know what he done?'

Suzi uncaps her pen and opens her notebook meaning, go on.

Lee grins. 'This'll go in, will it, me telling this story?'

'We're on the record,' Suzi says. 'Just let me know when you want to go off it.'

'Carib Club, Cricklewood, nineteen-seventy-four,' Lee says. 'Bovell's Sufferer HiFi sound system is competing, and the place is shaking. It's been raided before, and on the night in question the police go in to, ostensibly—'

'Do you know what ostensibly means, Lee?' Big Danny interrupts.

Lee makes a face. 'To, *ostensibly*, arrest some lad for nicking a motor, right?'

Suzi nods.

'Anyway, the crowd aren't tickled by this intrusion, don't fancy one of their own in handcuffs in the toilets, so they free him, and the Old Bill end up barricaded inside the toilets themselves, all the while Mr Bovell is doing the business on stage.'

Lee pauses for, Suzi believes, dramatic effect.

The pub chatter is civilised, Suzi thinks, volume-wise.

The thick carpet and layers of wallpaper soften it somewhat, she expects, and the lights – too bright, too many – make the pub feel welcoming, but festive like your in-laws' front room on New Year's Eve –

Pass the Babycham, dear.

'So the OB get out the toilets and do one but then come back mob-handed, a hundred and forty officers and a dog team, seal off the surrounding, all that, laying into the rude boys with the old truncheons and boots, reports of one of their dogs chasing a woman down the road, tearing at her clothes with its teeth—'

'They used to sharpen them,' Big Danny says.

'You what sharpen?'

'The teeth, they'd sharpen them.'

'The dogs' teeth?'

'Yeah, they'd sharpen them, what I said.'

'They'd sharpen the dogs' teeth?'

'What I said.'

'*How?*'

'I don't know, some implement. Nail file perhaps.'

Suzi's laughing, Lee shaking his head –

'They make forty-odd arrests, right, but most of these arrests are old-fashioned fit-up jobs. One bloke they arrested wasn't even there—'

'How could they have arrested him if he wasn't there?' Danny asks.

Exasperated, Lee says, '*After.* They arrested him after. He signed a confession.'

'That he wasn't there?'

'Jesus, are you winding me up?'

'Is that a rhetorical question?'

'For a bloke what don't say much, Daniel,' Lee says, 'you aren't half gassing away tonight.'

Suzi, who knows the answer, says, 'What happened to Dennis Bovell, Lee?'

'Dennis Bovell was arrested.' Lee shoots Danny a look. 'Ostensibly for grabbing the mic and yelling "Get the boys in blue!" when the place was raided. Incitement to violence.'

'Ostensibly,' nods Danny.

'Mr Bovell pointed out that no black man was going to refer to the Old Bill as the boys in blue, now are they, all a bit Dixon of Dock Green that.'

Suzi says she thinks it's a fair point.

'Thing is though,' Lee goes on, 'they have him up as part of a gang, violent by proxy. They say that when the police went in, he put on "Beat Down Babylon" by Junior Byles, fomenting disorder. He got a three stretch, did six months, then they overturned the verdict in the Court of Appeal, and he was out. Word is Mr Bovell was a trade: the Old Bill gets the poster boy for the rapidly growing dancehall culture that is putting the wind up little England, and the Carib Club stays open.'

Suzi smiles. 'It's a good story, Lee. What's it got to do with tonight's shindig?'

Lee leans forward, eyes smiling. 'Everything,' he says.

So Parker nips into the Prince of Wales to use their cigarette machine and there's Noble stood at the quiet end of the public bar, two pints in front of him.

It's only Noble and old Bill Stewart who know what it is that Parker really does, Parker thinks, crossing the pub.

Noble points at one of the drinks and says, 'I hope you're thirsty.'

Noble now a part of this new task force working out of Dalston nick while they rebuild and refurbish fortress Stoke Newington, ready to put the kibosh on the rave scene –

Or at least lock up a few dealers, seize a bit of product, keep Little England sweet in terms of Maggie's position on immoral behaviour, is how Parker sees it.

Her ladyship needs to be seen to be doing something to prevent the nation's youth from being led astray.

It's a vote-gatherer, a *task force*.

Two most boring words in the English language, according to Noble, at least from a Met detective's viewpoint.

'So remind me again why you said yes to this?' Parker says.

'You think I had a choice?'

'I think you're cleverer than that, guv.'

'Flattery gets you precisely fuck all, long term.'

'I mean,' Parker says, 'there's likely more to it than a simple secondment, is my guessing.'

'Clever boy.'

'Is what I'm saying, guv.'

Noble smiles at that, brushes dirt from the sleeves of his recently acquired leather jacket.

Parker raises his eyebrows. 'You've got the threads, then, to be a Hackney copper. Drug squad chic.'

'Very funny.'

'What, you trying to fit in?'

'Present from the missus, so behave.'

'It looks expensive.'

Noble sniffs. 'Yeah, well.'

The pub is busy, mobbed. Locals out for the New Year and a younger crowd too.

Noble nods. 'This lot going to your party then?'

'I expect so.'

'Look, we can't hang about in here.'

Parker looks around, nods.

'I'm going to be there,' Noble says. 'Tonight.' He checks his watch. 'In about ten minutes. Giving you a heads-up is why we're in here now.'

'I'll save you a seat.'

'Don't be funny.'

'Wouldn't dream of it.'

'The chief from Stoke Newington is on his way to shut it down.'

'Oh, that's a shame, I was up for it tonight.'

'Except he ain't going to shut it down, not really, but it's an excuse for a couple of us to have a shufty on the premises, get our faces seen.'

'You want your faces seen?'

'Yeah, we'll be the ones being reasonable.'

'Right.'

'The chief's going to call in a fire officer, who'll declare it all kosher and by then I'll be in with the in-crowd.'

'Why're you telling me?'

'A heads-up, that's all.'

Parker nods. He knocks off the end of his pint. He says, 'How have they let *you* into Stoke Newington?'

'You think they had a choice? Anyway, we're based in Dalston for now.'

Parker laughs. He knows Stoke Newington nick is being done up, so it makes sense Noble's working out of Dalston now. 'But it's that same division, right, same mob?' he says.

Noble nods, leans close. 'You're right, son, course you are. This is what you might call a precursor.'

'Yeah?'

'Yeah. My senior officer, you know him, he wants me in place for when the reckoning happens.'

'That sounds theatrical.'

'Yeah,' Noble deadpans. 'It's fucking Shakespeare, is what it is.'

'Bravo.'

'It don't change nothing – for you, I mean, not for now, anyway.'

'No?'

'No.'

'All right,' Parker says, shaping up to leave. 'I'll go and get on with my job then.'

'Good lad.'

Noble angles his glass for another pint, watches Parker loping off, ponders –

I still don't know how he does it.

'Certainly, your highness.' From the barmaid this, sarcastic.

'God save the King.'

'Oh, you're a funny bloke then.'

'It's all in the timing, darling.'

'I'd've thought,' she says, handing Noble his pint, 'royalty might drink something more sophisticated than three pints of bitter.'

'Yeah, well,' Noble winks. 'Don't overdo it, will you, with the thinking.'

Under her breath. 'And a happy New Year to you too.'

Noble drinks, raises his glass. 'You know what they say.'

'Oh yeah?'

'Smile, it might never happen.'

'And what if it already has?'

'Here—' Noble leaning over the bar. 'You going down the canal to this do, later?'

'This "do"?' Laughing.

'You know what I mean.'

'You asking me out?'

'I'm just asking.'

'Dunno, might do.'

'Many of your customers going, you think?'

'Look around you, what do *you* think?'

Noble nods. It is more your knees-up Mother Brown sort of a crowd –

Across the bar, in the saloon, he spots Suzi with a couple of likely looking lads, laughing.

She made it then. He checks his watch. Meet with the chief at the warehouse in twenty minutes.

'I'll have one more,' he says. 'And have one for yourself.'

'Don't mind if I do.'

Noble sees Suzi slide out from her seat, put on her coat, finish her drink.

She looks a little pink-cheeked, he thinks, fair play –

Noble sees Suzi sees him, sees her hold his look a beat, the smaller of the lads elbows open the saloon door, and she's gone.

Back into the car, Suzi's thinking, I'm too old for this –

Lee's got the window down, chain-smoking, the air cold and sharp, the heater hissing dry heat that leaves Suzi parched, her tongue heavy, her head tight, and she's got that little pit of worry in her stomach, that mix of nerves, fear even, and anticipation too, *excitement.*

'We're going straight to the office, yeah?' Lee tells Danny. He turns to Suzi and winks. 'Bypass the crowds.'

Suzi smiles. The thing about her job: she hasn't had to wait in line at a musical event since she was a teenager, and, even then, she was normally plucked out and ushered in, Suzi Sweetheart, her nickname for a bit.

Danny pulls the car out onto Lea Bridge Road and turns right over the bridge up towards Walthamstow. He then does an immediate left into a building supply merchant behind which Suzi realises is the warehouse. Two big units in black suits lean into the car, see Danny and Lee, and wave them through. Suzi thinking, this doesn't feel quite right –

'I thought—' Suzi begins.

'Yeah,' Lee says, pointing, 'you're right, it's on the other side, but VIP parking's in here and there's a footbridge.' Lee grins. 'Bridge over troubled water.'

'A bridge too far,' Danny says.

'Burning bridges.'

'Yeah, let's hope not.'

Suzi sees shapes in the dark snaking their way along the other side of the canal, flames from cigarette lighters and matches, hears voices and laughter, the low beat of music from car stereos –

Lee opens the passenger door. 'Come on,' he says, 'the water's lovely.' Cackling.

Suzi takes a breath and slides out of the car.

Lee extends an arm. 'One thing, yeah, they'll offer you something, you know what I mean?'

'Will they?'

'They will, and if I were you' – grinning again – 'I'd take it.'

Suzi nods.

She's been thinking about this, about drugs, about *ecstasy*.

She and Keith became fairly heavy users of the old Bolivian marching powder, though Suzi never found it too hard to resist – or enjoy.

She's sort of knocked it all on the head really, but something about how close they are to her and Keith's old home, and how far she feels from their old life, has left her with that hunger to have a good time.

She smiles. 'I'll keep that in mind,' she says.

In her notebook, a line from Andrew Weatherall, writer, and producer, one of the Boy's Own collective, on this very subject:

'I went from listening to "United" by Throbbing Gristle to dancing in a field to "Josephine" by Chris Rea,' he told her. 'Which gives you some idea what a powerful drug ecstasy is.'

Suzi, to be fair, does enjoy the song.

'The French Edit, Andrew,' she told him. 'That version is just about acceptable.'

Though Boy's Own seem to be edging away from the scene, Suzi thinks, just as it's beginning.

Better dead than Acid Ted!

Screams a headline in their *Boy's Own* fanzine.

Suzi asked who Acid Ted was when he was at home.

New ravers in dayglo T-shirts shouting 'Acieeed!' she's told, the idea being they were like the old rockabilly, forty-something teddy boys.

In other words, well past it.

Already, Suzi thinks, I've only just got here.

Then again, Weatherall's partner-in-crime, Terry Farley, is DJ-ing later, so maybe tonight passes muster.

Maybe Andrew will be there even.

Suzi hopes so; she liked him.

Lee points. 'That's the warehouse.' Points again. 'And that's the office, where you're going to do this interview with them all.' Lee checks his fat silver watch. 'They're expecting us – quite soon, in fact.'

Suzi threads her arm through Lee's. 'Lead the way, squire.'

'Behave,' Lee says, grinning again.

On the towpath kissing Carolyn, Marlon corralling them to a side door for the VIP treatment, Parker thinking, this warehouse is fucking massive –

Thinking, I've only gone and forgotten the fags.

'Give us one then, hero,' Carolyn says.

'Steady on,' Parker laughs. 'Bit public, ain't it, even out here in the dark.'

'No, you wally. I mean a cigarette. Let's have one.'

Parker smiles, thinks –

'Course,' he says. He reaches into his jacket pocket, pauses, pats himself down –

'Oh fuck,' he says. 'They must have fallen out when I was running after you. I'll just pop back, shall I, find them?'

Marlon waves a packet of Dunhill in the air. Bows and hands it over.

'Nice one,' Parker says.

Marlon grins. 'That's nothing,' he says. 'I've got something for you, you're going to love it.' Laughing now, snapping his fingers.

Parker smiles. Carolyn shakes her head.

'Come on,' she says. 'Inside, the pair of you.'

3

Blag

Suzi's got her notebook out. The fellas whose idea this shindig was are quite something. Especially young Wayne Anthony from Genesis.

Wayne's explaining to Suzi how they secured this particular warehouse for their Christmas Eve party.

Something about a blagger with a sawn-off, an accusation of a stolen venue, and how they, ahem, saw him off.

The office is kitted out with a battery of portable phones, bin bags that seem to be quite rapidly filling up with cash, an unused safe, and a fair amount of cocaine in sprawling lines on a makeshift desk, a bookshelf laid across two piles of car tyres.

There are car tyres everywhere, Suzi thinks.

Wayne Anthony tells Suzi that he headbutted this blagger square on the nose, someone else whacking him over the head with a lump of wood. The negotiation was somewhat more straightforward after that.

Laughter, a bit of posturing, and Suzi says, 'And did he come back?'

Wayne Anthony opens his arms, opens his palms as if to say: I can't see him, can you, love?

Wayne Anthony's hand goes into his bomber jacket. From the inside pocket, he withdraws a folded piece of paper. He brandishes this piece of paper and hands it over to Suzi.

'This is great, this bit,' Lee says.

Suzi sees that on the piece of paper, smudged a little with oil and dirt – car tyres, no doubt – is a handwritten note from the legal owner of the premises explaining the terms of a venue hire contract with Genesis Sunset promotions for a private music event.

'See, it's all legit,' Lee says, bending over the desk, finger on a nostril, can of Red Stripe in the pocket of his own bomber jacket –

Lee gesturing, saying, 'You sure you're all right?'

Suzi nods.

'Let us know, later, yeah?'

Suzi nods and Suzi smiles.

Suzi scribbles, turns the page, scribbles some more –

'This is all on the record, OK?'

Nodding, shrugging, yeah, course –

'Let me know if there's anything—'

The consensus seems to be anything *goes*, Suzi thinks.

Lee now gabbing away about promotional behaviours, merch prospects and market pendulums, Danny over by the door –

Crackle over a radio. A voice –

'Dibble's downstairs.'

Suzi notes mild concern, eyes darting –

Suzi hands the piece of paper back to Wayne Anthony.

'You might be needing that,' she says.

Ayeleen. Lauren's mum's new house, Fletching Road estate, same time.

I'm not sure about tonight, but Lauren insists it's going to be amazing, and I do trust her, I always do, and she's normally right about this kind of thing.

'Get a move on, Leenie!' she shouts, knocking on the door to the bathroom where I'm staring at myself in the mirror. 'I'm going to wet my knickers in a minute.'

'You bloody better not,' her mum says, walking past. 'You're all right, Ayeleen!' she calls out. 'I've put down some plastic, so take your time!' Laughing.

'Mum!'

I smile. 'Just a minute, yeah.'

It's the lipstick, I never know about the lipstick, not sure that it suits me, and I know what Lauren's going to say, she's going to say slap on some lippy, Leen, and done with it.

'Leen,' Lauren says. 'I ain't kidding about wetting myself, so slap on some lippy and done with it!'

So I do. I open the door, and Lauren pushes past me and sighs in relief –

Her mum is picking up clothes from the stairs, filling a washing basket. 'How's *your* mum, Leenie?' she asks.

'She's well, thanks for asking.'

'Send her my best, won't you, love?'

'Course.'

'And you two have a good time tonight, yeah?'

'We will.'

'And if you can't be good,' she laughs, 'then be careful!'

I smile, tell her we will, and go back into Lauren's room, sit down on her bed. I flick through a magazine. Lauren comes back in, adjusting her top. She closes the door.

'Hang about,' she says.

She's got a bottle of Coke and digs behind the bed for the rum I know she keeps down there. The radio's playing a song by one of the bands we saw at Live Aid.

'This is U2, ain't it?' Lauren asks.

I tell her I think it is. 'Angel of Harlem' is what it's called, I tell her.

'What a day that was, eh, Leen!' she says. 'Your uncle really did the business there, didn't he?' She nods at the radio. 'They didn't do this one, though, right?'

Lauren's smiling now at the memory, her tongue sticking out the side of her mouth as she carefully tips the rum into the Coke.

'I honestly can't remember,' I say. And I can't.

'There.' Lauren holds the bottle up to the lightbulb. 'Gorgeous, look at that. Golden. Perfectly mixed.' She's laughing.

'What a connoisseur.'

'A rare treat, this, Leenie, a real degustation.' Saying it day-goose-station, and I'm laughing too.

'Here,' she says. 'Ladies first.'

I take a big gulp and it burns my throat a little, but it's smooth enough and it tastes OK.

I hand it back, and Lauren does the same. We smile at each other.

'What time is it?' Lauren asks.

'What time does it start?'

'Flyer's on the desk, pass it here.'

'Says ten.'

'Let me see.'

I give it to her. 'It says invite only,' I say.

'Well, what do you think this is?'

'There's only one of them. There's two of us.'

'Don't be soft, Leen, it's fine.'

'You sure?'

'Course I'm sure.'

I nod. 'OK, I trust you.'

'You bloody should!'

Then the song changes on the radio, 'Buffalo Stance' by Neneh Cherry and I'm grinning, and I say, 'Turn it up, Laur, they're playing our song!'

And she does, she turns it right up, and we're singing along, doing the voices, dancing around the room, on the bed, spinning each other around and around, and we can hear Lauren's mum yelling up the stairs for us to pipe down, turn that racket off, and we're laughing, and the song ends and we do.

Out of breath now, lying back on her bed, Lauren says, 'You do want to do this, don't you?'

'Show me again,' I say.

She nods at the floor. 'Lock the door, will you?'

I jump up. She opens her purse, and in the bit where you keep your coins she pulls out a little plastic bag with two small pills in it.

'They're not very big,' I say.

'They're called "Calis",' she says. 'The same I had on Christmas Eve. I got them from the same geezer too.'

I nod.

'I only had a half of one,' she says. 'That's what we'll do.'

'But there's two.'

'Well, if we're having a good time, we'll have the other one!'

'Don't, Lauren, I'm nervous.'

'It'll be fine, it's magic, honest, and look, we're only ten minutes' walk from there, so if you don't like it, we come home.'

'Yeah?'

'Course.'

'All right then.'

'Shall we go pub first? Don't want to be on our own in there!'

'Yeah, let's,' I say.

'Party, party!'

She's jumping up and down again, then she's trying to wrestle me onto the bed –

'Pack it in, Lauren!' I scream. 'Stop it!' But I'm giggling.

We're both out of breath and she says, 'Let's go then, yeah.' And picks up her purse.

'On the flyer, Laur,' – I point at it – 'it says liable to be searched at door. You're just going like that?'

'I'll stick them in my knickers in the pub, don't worry.'

'Well, no one'll look for them there.'

'Ayleen!' she says. 'How could you?'

I grin, wink.

I'm nervous, it's true, but this is our last year at school, exams and all that in the summer, then what we don't know yet, and Uncle Ahmet wants me in his new place on Chatsworth Road, but I don't know about that, maybe college, so I should really try a few new things and better I do it with Lauren, and she's right, it is only just over the road, it'll be fun.

*

Jon and Jackie Davies are in the 'family room' of the Prince of Wales, meaning a few tables and chairs pushed to the side in a corner of the pub that has been reserved by Jackie's cousin Chick to, Chick's words, quote unquote, bring the new year in, in style.

Jon's not seen Chick for a while.

In fact, if he's honest with himself, after the Docklands incident, Chick's syndicate's situation, asking Jon to look over those documents, and then Chick's hospitalisation and the quiet word in Jon's ear, Jon has been consciously giving Chick a wide berth.

And given the size of Chick, the *space* in which Chick operates, this means Jon has been quite a long way from Chick for quite a long time.

Jackie brings over some drinks for the two of them. A pint for Jon, a large G&T for herself –

'Cheers,' Jon says, smiling at her. 'Nice to be out, isn't it?'

Jackie pulls a face. 'Is that what we're going to talk about when we're out, how it's nice to be out?'

'Well, it's a start, isn't it?'

'We've been here hours, it feels like.'

Jon laughs. '*Two* hours, love, two.'

'You can calculate how much that means we've spent on the babysitter so far tonight in your head.'

Jon smiles.

One of Jackie's brood – a younger cousin? A niece? Jon's never quite sure – is looking after the boy and Lizzie, at least she's supposed to be.

More than likely, she'll be on the phone to her boyfriend and doing her nails, was Jackie's verdict when they engaged her.

To be fair, Jon thought her nails looked like they didn't need doing, at least not *again*, not yet.

He'd checked on the way out.

Well, the *family* is in full swing tonight, Jon thinks now.

He and Jackie stand to one side, watch as New Year gifts are swapped, a family tradition, Jon understands, and drinks are drunk in toasts to some very specific family outcomes.

'Still, it's nice to be out,' Jon says.

Jackie smiles. 'It is, love, it's nice to be out, with *you*.'

They say nothing for a little while and drink their drinks, mug for the cameras –

'Oh, look,' Jackie says, 'that's the girl from over the back, family's just moved in not long ago, at least I've seen the mother, Lauren her name is.'

'Oh yeah.'

'Oh, all right, Lauren,' Jackie says. 'You OK?'

'Oh, I'm fine thanks, Mrs Davies, Mr Davies.' Then hurriedly. 'We are eighteen, you know.'

Jon smiles and says nothing.

There's another girl just behind Lauren, the pub is packed by now, and Jon opens up a little space for her.

Jackie laughs. 'I should hope so too!'

'Yeah, we're old for our year.'

'Final year, is it?'

Lauren nods.

'Any plans yet?' Jackie asks.

The two girls look at each other, shrug.

Jon says, 'Early days still, girls.'

'Yeah, well.'

Jackie gives Jon an amused look. 'Well, we'll let you go and see your friends. Happy New Year!'

'Same to you, Mrs Davies!'

'Seem like nice kids,' Jon says.

'Yeah, the mum's nice.'

'Another drink?'

Jackie nods.

At the bar, Chick eases his way in beside Jon. It's hard to find any sort of berth at all, Jon thinks, squashed in, trying to get served, waving a tenner at the staff in hope more than expectation.

'I'll get these,' Chick says.

He clicks his fingers and yells, not so much at, as *towards* the barmaid. 'A pint of Special, darling, a large G&T, a drop of Scotch, three lagers and lime, two vodka tonics and' – turning to Jon – 'what do you want?'

'I—'

Laughing. 'I know what you want, Jon, I already said it!'

'You did, Chick.'

'Ice in all the short drinks, darling,' Chick adds. 'Except the Scotch, of course. I ain't a philistine, am I?'

The barmaid agrees that Chick is not a philistine.

'Got a tray?'

The barmaid shakes her head, touches her ear with her finger.

'A tray!' Chick shouts. 'Got a tray?'

Jon points. 'She's got the drinks on a tray already, Chick.'

'So she has, clever girl. You wanna Scotch? Have a Scotch.'

'I'm OK—'

'And a drop of Scotch, for my friend here,' Chick shouts. 'In fact, Jon, have mine, I'll have the new one, darling. Cheers.'

Jon takes the Scotch and sips at it.

'Quality, right?' Chick says.

'Cheers, Chick, kind of you.'

'Yeah, well. Cheers.'

Chick knocks their glasses together, gulps down the Scotch.

'Look, um, Jon,' Chick says. 'I appreciate what you done, you know that, right?'

'I do, Chick, course I do.'

'Good.' Chick gestures at the room, at the family celebration. 'We're moving on now, that's all over, that unfortunate business.'

'That sounds positive, Chick.'

'Yeah, positive, why not.'

Chick indicates the pint of Special, the large G&T. 'These are yours, I believe. Happy New Year. We'll talk.'

Jon thinks, will we?

Jackie's chatting to one of her cousins. Jon hands her the large G&T.

The cousin says, 'Well at least you've got Jon for when it's midnight, Jacks! Someone to kiss.'

'I've *always* got Jon,' Jackie says. 'Not just on special occasions. Try as I might, I can't seem to be rid of him.'

The cousin says, 'A puppy's not just for Christmas!' And explodes into laughter.

'Happy New Year, love,' Jon says.

Noble's enjoying watching the promoters try to convince his chief inspector that their party is all legal and above board.

'This is a genuine music business showcase for invited guests only,' says one of them.

Noble smiles at that.

He's shivering outside the front of this warehouse near the canal, his freezing hands buried in the pockets of his jacket, DC Dave Jenkins with him, another member of the Stoke Newington/Dalston task force.

'We have provided fire extinguishers, illuminated EXIT signs and crash barriers. We have made sure fire regulations are implemented and anything flammable has been removed or sprayed with fire-resistant chemicals,' the same promoter adds.

'I see,' says the chief.

Noble thinking, off the back of a lorry –

'We have one thousand specially invited guests from the world's music industry,' the other one chimes in, 'ranging from celebrities to major record company MDs. Stepping on our toes could lead to massive lawsuits and huge compensation fines.'

'Right you are,' says the chief.

Noble smirking.

'We have legal rights to be on the property with the landlord's full blessing,' the first one says. 'Here.'

He hands the chief a piece of paper. The chief hands it to Jenkins, who passes it on to Noble, handwritten and creased, but it does say what they say it says.

'In fact, we are quite within our rights to ask you to leave the building and only return with a court order or warrant.'

'You think that'd be sensible?' asks the chief.

The promoters share a look, consult their clipboards –

Celebrity guest lists, band schedules, contact information –

All snide, no doubt, Noble thinks.

The promoters tell the chief that, no, that wouldn't be very sensible and that what they would like to do is cooperate.

'I'm going to need to bring in a fire inspector,' the chief says. 'He'll make the final decision.'

The chief nods at Jenkins. 'Go and get him. It's only a five-minute jog.'

He nods at Noble. 'You go with one of these gentlemen' – indicating the promoters – 'and have another gander inside.'

Noble goes with the wider of the two promoters. On the door, boarded up, a sign:

WARNING

GUARD DOGS ON PATROL

Noble says, 'That true, is it?'

'Yeah, you should see them,' the geezer jokes. 'Six-foot something and martial arts experts, our guard dogs.'

'Gotcha.'

'Someone once told me,' the promoter says, 'your mob used to sharpen your police dogs' teeth. *That* true?'

Noble winks. 'Shall we go inside?'

'You know,' says the promoter. 'I was at a rave earlier this year when it was raided. To try and break it up, Dibble set off all the sirens on the vans to drive everyone out. Know what the DJ did?'

Noble shakes his head.

'He played a tune, "Can You Party" by Royal House, that has a sort of siren sound running through it.'

'Very clever.'

'Yeah, it was, the crowd loved it.'

'What's your point?'

The promoter holds open the door. 'We're enterprising,' he says.

'I'll give you that,' Noble says.

They've gone and tried with the warehouse, these promoters, Noble will give them that too, but it's not exactly the Hippodrome.

There are an awful lot of *tyres*, he thinks, some handmade banners, flags and so on. The security team are in suits and have radios. There are lights and there's a sound system.

But there's something distinctly Del Boy about the whole operation, Noble decides.

It's very long, the warehouse, like an aircraft hangar, he thinks, and with the yellow lines running down the middle of it, you could sort of imagine a private plane taxiing through and out along the towpath and up over the marshes –

Noble allows himself a moment to enjoy this thought.

There are metal pillars every ten steps or so, and each is protected by a circle of tyres.

From these pillars, strung across the ceiling, hang white drapes that look like Halloween decorations. Alongside building site materials, there are orange plastic sheets in grids of squares of the sort that wrap around roadworks, hanging like enormous hammocks just above head height.

A couple of neon signs. A banner spread across the side windows reads:

GENESIS

In yellow, black and red lettering, set inside two red lines.

Noble nods at it. 'Your little brothers do that, did they? Art project at school?'

'Don't be cheeky.'

Noble smiles. 'This is a genuine music business showcase for invited guests only,' he adds.

'All right, turn it in.'

Noble points at the plastic, the cotton, the rubber –

'Anything flammable has been removed or sprayed with fire-resistant chemicals. You sure about that?'

The promoter sniffs. 'That'll be up to the fire officer, I'd imagine.'

'Yeah, course. No need to get mardy,' Noble says. 'I'm just pulling your leg.' He sees a bigger pile of tyres at the far end of the hangar. 'What's that down there then?'

'The bar. You wanna drink?'

'You licensed?'

'Licensed to give them away, yeah.'

'Go on. I'll have a pint.'

'Very funny.'

By the DJ stand, which Noble sees is entirely built out of scaffolding, an inflatable gorilla balanced on a makeshift plinth – an old door balanced on top of another pile of tyres – behind a camouflage net, floor to ceiling, as if in a cage, or on a podium, ready to dance –

'Jesus,' Noble says. 'What happened to that gorilla?'

The promoter laughs. 'UV paint. Luminous under the lights. Well psychedelic.'

'Yeah, he looks like a real hippy.'

'Don't laugh at him, he's a big unit.'

On the other side, an inflatable skeleton behind more of the orange plastic, glow strings hanging from around it, Noble thinking, Halloween, knock-off –

'Where d'you get this lot,' he asks, 'a joke shop?'

'Yeah, exactly, it's all they had left.'

'You don't say.'

In the corner, bedsheets hanging lengthways from the ceiling, more of the painted, homemade designs:

Orange and pink splodges, hearts and question marks, alien faces glowing orange, sawdust on the floor –

By the bar, a much smarter mural, stencilled in gold lettering, two-feet high, across a brick wall painted black:

GENESIS'88

And a stencilled drawing of their trademark symbol, the geezer with the beard and the pixie ears and the flowers in his hair –

'Who's that then? Pan?' Noble asks.

'God of the wild.'

'You sure you've got the apostrophe in the right place?'

'What, you the grammar police?'

'No, just the ordinary police.'

'Let's get you that drink.'

At the bar – more doors and crates, more tyres, two fridges plugged into an extension cord that runs back towards the hum of a generator – Noble is handed a can of lager.

'Much obliged,' he says.

'Give us a sec, will you?' Pointing at a door behind –

'Knock yourself out,' Noble says.

'Much obliged.' Being ironic.

Noble gulps at his can. He's taken a fair bit on board tonight already. He shouldn't, really, but he'll be off soon enough, surely, then it's on to a little party where Lea will be getting involved in the kitchen disco and telling him to catch up, so he might as well catch up now.

He surveys the empty space, thinking that when the lights get going it'll probably be decent.

Then, from out the door behind the bar, Noble clocks Parker, and to the left of that, coming down the fire escape stairs, there's Suzi with the clowns she was with earlier in the pub.

The promoter's rubbing his hands, giving it the New Year bonhomie –
'Come and meet a special guest,' he's saying.
Noble smiles.

4

Go on then why not you're only young once

Suzi sees Noble propped against the bar and hesitates –

She keeps talking. 'So the piece I'm writing is based on that, based on what Lee Roy here was trumpeting earlier, Acid House as a natural development of the black Soundsystem tradition.'

'You *were* listening, girl!' Lee shouts, delighted.

'It's a thesis I'm aware of,' she says. 'Soul II Soul is the perfect example of how the scene has grown and is changing. They were firebombed out of blues parties in Hackney not long ago by the National Front.'

'And what's changed?' someone asks.

Suzi sees Noble watching her, listening to her performance, a bit of a smirk on him, him knowing it's a performance –

'Like Jazzie B said himself, something like, "White people involved in your sound system means different ideas, equipment, technology."'

'Which is why,' Lee declares, 'house music was invented in 1988!'

Laughter.

'When Jazzie B said that he was being interviewed by Lloyd Bradley—' Suzi drawing the crowd in now, 'and *he* said, "We grew up together, we had gone through school together, we chased the same girls together, we played football together – why not go to clubs together?"'

'Beautiful sentiment,' Noble says.

Suzi watches the group turn to him.

'This is a representative of Hackney's finest.'

'Honoured, et cetera,' Noble bows.

Suzi's eyes dart –

And there's Noble's stooge too, with his girlfriend, Carolyn, and wait, Suzi thinks, didn't –

Parker breathes in deep, goes, 'It *is* beautiful.'

He sees Noble, he sees that Suzi bird, he thinks, Christ, he feels –

He feels the group's eyes on him, Carolyn's eyes on him, Marlon giving him a wry look –

'Mate of mine owns a little club,' Parker says. 'He went on a bit of professional training, trying to learn the business a bit better. You know what one of his lecturers told him?'

Noble shakes his head, as if, Parker thinks, on behalf of not just the group, but the system, Babylon, as it were –

'My mate is told there are three golden rules of venue management, off the record, right? No blacks, no Pakis, no sportswear.'

Marlon laughs. Noble raises an eyebrow. Carolyn looks grim –

'Cheer up,' this bloke with Suzi says, gurning. 'You don't have to worry about all that in here.'

Parker thinking, go on then why not you're only young once.

'Have you heard the album yet, then?' This is Danny asking Suzi, who's feeling a bit fluttery, if she's honest, a bit knocked-sideways all of a sudden.

'Sorry,' she says. 'Album?'

'Soul II Soul,' Danny says. 'The album they've done.'

'They've done an album, of course they have.'

'But you've not heard it.'

'No, not yet. Just the singles so far.'

'You don't get some insider advance copy then?'

Suzi smiles, her insides tight, her head light – she smiles –

'I will, yeah.'

'Right,' Danny says, nodding.

'Would you like me to get you one, Danny?' Suzi asks.

'I would like that, yeah,' Danny says. 'That'd be sweet.'

Suzi smiles again. Suzi thinks, I'll do you that favour and you can do me one later too.

Suzi thinks, I'm going to try it, tonight, why not.

Noble looks up and sees his senior officer approaching with a tall, thin man who must be the fire officer, and the other lad, Jenkins.

The conversation around Noble quickly stops.

'They're planning some kind of party,' says the chief. 'We don't want it, and I'm sure it's not safe. Have a look. It's down to you.'

The fire officer nods at this. He doesn't look thrilled to be here, Noble thinks. Probably a decent piss-up down the station tonight, a buffet perhaps, shame to miss it.

The promoters don't look too chuffed neither, Noble thinks, and he can see why. The bloke must be fifty, neat, grey hair, very *efficient*-looking –

The wider promoter starts banging on about fire regulations and EXIT signs and fire extinguishers, and the fire officer sniffs and nods, not looking especially engaged.

'I'll have a nose around,' he says.

And nobody moves for a long moment.

And everyone watches the fire officer traipse around the room, poking at pillars and tyres, inspecting banners and drapes, peering closely into the gorilla cage –

Audibly muttering, what the bugger's all this about?

Still no talking, the promoters smiling, nonchalant, all in a day's work –

Then he's back. 'Everything seems fine to me,' says the fire officer. 'As far as I'm concerned, they can have their party.'

The chief nods. The promoters grin, slap hands. The chief looks at Noble. The chief nods at the door –

As they leave, he says, 'Make any new friends?'

Noble nods. 'Yeah,' he decides. 'I think I might have, guv.'

Jon's quite drunk now, but to be fair most of the party seem to be too, and he looks at his watch and thinks, when can we start ducking out of these things *before* midnight?

He watches Chick wrangling a couple of brothers into a conga line. Jon swerves *that* and shoulders the door, steps outside –

The cold is a relief.

The moon glows.

The canal shines.

The towpath is quiet.

Jon listens to the water lapping against the rubbish collecting alongside the bank, lapping against the sludge and the foam, that fizzing layer of scum –

When they come down of a weekend, they'll leave the kids at an outside table with their crisps and their Cokes, and the boy tells Jon they watch the rats pissing into the river.

This doesn't seem to stop the fishermen, or the fish, which look healthy enough when they're hooked out of the slime.

Jon's down the pub steps and onto the towpath, a few strides towards the bridge and he stops –

Remembering Shahid Akhtar, his neighbour, just a little further down, ten years ago it was. Jon peers into the murk. He sees white lights, red lights, blue lights, yellow lights, hears music, a dull thud.

New year, he thinks. He shivers, turns –

Back up the steps, back into the pub, the warmth and the cheering, thinking –

Back to Hackney Council as Borough Solicitor, new year, new role, new you –

Laughing.

*

Suzi examines the tablet in her palm, looks up at Lee, who smiles, nods, go on, he tells her, you're going to love it, and she smiles, bites it in half, slaps one of the halves into her mouth and washes it down with lager.

'How long, normally?' she asks.

'Doing it in halves is clever, girl,' Lee says. 'Less intense at the beginning, which can be frightening it's so good, but you time it right, and you'll be up as long as anyone else in here.'

'Very scientific.'

'In about forty minutes, you'll really start to understand dance music,' Lee winks.

'What about the other half?'

'One at a time, darling, know what I mean.' Laughing, Lee checks his fat watch. 'Well, it's nearly ten, so I think I'd be inclined to wait until about two. See how you feel.'

'And drinking?'

'Bit of lager, bit of water, just not too much of anything.'

'Everything in moderation.'

'See? You're funnier and friendlier already!'

Suzi feels a tingle, but it can't be anything other than psychological at this point, or, she thinks, just plain excitement.

Parker and Marlon in conference.

Parker thinking he's seen that other copper before, the lad with Noble, but can't quite place him –

Marlon shaking his head, saying, 'New face.'

Parker thinking he'll ask Noble next chance he gets, but that snide, narrow-eyed, ratty little look about him definitely rings a bell.

Stoke Newington, but from *when* exactly?

Marlon goes, 'Party's happening, then.'

Parker clocks Carolyn chatting to Suzi and wonders, what's going on *there*, exactly?

I'm tired of this, Parker thinks, I'm *tired* of this.

Marlon palms Parker pills. Parker nods –

Marlon winks.

Parker looks across at Carolyn, shrugs, raises his eyebrows, mouths, Well? –

Carolyn mouths, Yes, grins –

Parker slaps a pill into his mouth, necks lager. He watches Carolyn do the same.

He watches Carolyn and Suzi laugh, knock their cans –

Then:

Lights off. Music on. Lights red, lights white –

Doors open.

Noble waves as the chief leaves in a squad car down Lea Bridge Road, turns to Jenkins and goes –

'One for the road? Debrief?'

Jenkins nods.

'Prince of Wales suit you?'

Jenkins shrugs.

Lines of young people – and some older people too – pass on their way to the warehouse.

'Maybe we should've stuck around,' Noble jokes.

5

Can you feel it?

Ayeleen. We take our halves on the walk from the pub to the warehouse and then join the queue and I'm shaking with the cold and I'm feeling a little sick, but it's just the drinks and the nerves and the excitement and Lauren's here, so it's OK. The doors open and the lights inside pour out and we're waved in and Lauren shows our flyers and the security just smile and tell us to have a good night and then we're inside and it's massive, this place, and everyone's smiling, and it's all sorts of people, nothing like those clubs we've been up West, here it's the clothes you notice first of all, there are men and women wearing Adidas tracksuits and trainers, and others in Polo shirts and jeans, and sunglasses and T-shirts with smiley faces, and tie-dyed T-shirts, and T-shirts with slogans, and dungarees, and there's these topless lads, their T-shirts hanging from their belts. I cling on to Lauren, the bass is really, really thumping, and I tell her it's not doing my tummy any good, this bass, and she says, let's find a little corner and we'll start the night there, and we do, and it's a bit quieter, but not much, and she gets us a couple of cans from the bar and a bottle of water, and says, don't drink fast, just a little bit at a time, and then we spot some girls from school, friends, yeah, course, but not in our circle exactly, and they come rushing over, all smiles and hugs, and I'm pleased to see them, saying what are you doing here, and they've snuck in some mini bottles of spirits like what you get on aeroplanes, I think, and they pass them round and Lauren says, being ironic, are you all, you know, *on* one, and everyone laughs and nods, first time, Lauren asks, and it's yeses and noes, and I feel better, surrounded by friends and someone says, what's your name, where you from, what you on, and everyone laughs, really laughs, and the song's going, Can you feel it, over and over, and the bass and the drum and

Suzi's nodding and chewing the gum Lee's given her, she's really grateful, and the lager, which tastes amazing, really *cold*, and Lee's leaning in telling her, this is Mr Fingers, Chicago legend, listen, listen to this, *really* listen, come on, dum, dum-dum-dum, dum, dum-dum-dum, and they both shout, Can you feel it, and Suzi feels a tingle now, a definite *something* all over her face, and the low sort of organ sound comes right through the tune, and the cymbal and the bassline and the layers, that's what it is, the layers, and then it flattens out into percussion and a preacher declaring let there be house, and Suzi is smiling, eyes closed, and the track drops down, and she moves down with it, and the preacher's voice dies and then Can you feel it and whistles and cheers and clapping and everyone is smiling and the lights change from white to red to yellow to blue to green, and everyone is dancing and Lee says, where's your notebook then, eh, smiling and Suzi lifts her hands in the air, let there be house, she's whispering, let there be house, let there be house, can you feel it, can you

And Parker feels the track change into a fiddly Casio keyboard thing and he's thinking, some kid did this in his bedroom and it's winding around a bassline that becomes more and more insistent and he feels it, he feels it lift and lift and then someone's whispering over this track I can't let go, and Parker eases Carolyn out of her coat, and she's dancing with her black trilby and gold earrings and black top black skirt black sunglasses and their hands interlink and they lift them up, up, up and Parker slows, moves in time with the bass drum, hears body next to me, start to sweat, and Carolyn's got her eyes closed and she's licking her lips and Parker brings her closer and they move together and it feels like the whole place is moving together and Marlon in his blue shirt and jeans and a camo vest over the top his own gold glinting in his smile and he leans in and goes even white people can dance to this and Parker smiles and Parker thinks it's true and it *is* true and there's a jerky woman in a blue and white cap with a hoodie unzipped over a pink vest and pink shorts sort of shuffling and their group are bouncing about and close by there is a handful of geezers in terrace casual who are chewing and nodding along and jogging on the spot, their hair cropped, and Parker's thinking, not long ago this lot would be after our lot and one of Carolyn's boys is moving like a mime I can't let go and that promoter Marlon knows is waving and opening up his arms and then he's introducing Parker to the casuals calling out their names hearing Harris Sparky Half-Inch Spoon and these lads are yelling out Acieeed! and Parker's grinning, he's grinning, and Carolyn is swaying and shimmying and Parker feels

Ayeleen. We find a little tunnel and there's three bouncy castles in it and we all sit down all of us nodding and all of us bouncing a little and I'm still feeling a little tight in the stomach and I'm clinging on to Lauren's hand but we're all happy, we're all dancing, even when we're sitting still we're moving, even when we're sprawled over each other we're dancing and then 'Love Sensation' comes on and Lauren's pulling me up and we're into the main room again and we're dancing in a circle and everyone's cheering again must be the disco and then the DJ moves into something else or it sounds like something else sounds like the same but different

Suzi thinks, I've heard this before it's by someone like Black Box an Italian producer and it's a sample from Loretta Holloway and she's telling Lee he's nodding like he cares and then Carolyn's right next to Suzi and she's dancing like she's swimming and Suzi is bobbing and moving from foot to foot and she eyes Parker and she wants to tell him something but she can't she shouldn't but she really wants to tell him something, really wants to tell Carolyn something just to say you know here we are and so she says this is Lee, he's involved and Parker smiles, and the circle widens a bit and Suzi's thinking, it's all about the space we're in and the space we're in is what it's all about and she looks good Carolyn like she's got some glamour about her like no one else looks like she does and Suzi thinks, what about that other half then, too early, and she asks Lee and he says I've done mine already Auld Lang Syne in a minute and Suzi nods and digs into her pocket and swallows it down and Parker's smiling and he

Noble kisses Lea. Happy New Year, darling, he says. She reaches her hands around his neck. I love you, she says. Now take me home

Jon and Jackie fall in through the front door of 99 Mildenhall Road. Jackie's niece or cousin, Jon still doesn't know, says something about a taxi and Jon's handing her a tenner then another and then the cab arrives and she's off and Jackie says, don't get any ideas, lover boy, I'm in no state

Parker's saying to Suzi, isn't that your old fella, pointing to the side of the DJ platform, and Suzi looks

Suzi looks around at everyone in the place with their hands in the air singing along and she realises it's that song The Style Council are covering 'Promised Land' by Joe Smooth and everyone in the place is singing about brothers and sisters and peace and doves and being free arms in the air *inside* the music all of them and then she hears a slight shift and it's Weller's voice now, she's sure of that, the DJ cutting it in and out of the tune and she hears Parker saying I'm sure that's your fella and then she sees Keith and he's grinning handing records back and forth to the DJ and fiddling with knobs and pressing buttons and Suzi thinks, course he's here course he is and she waves and smiles and he does the same and makes a sign like give us a minute love and I'll be right with you and Suzi's happy to see him and Lee seems to know him all right grandad he goes and it's lovely to see him actually yeah really lovely

Parker kisses Carolyn and he feels the crowd swell and his heart swell and he's grinning at Suzi and he's grinning at Marlon and he's even grinning at this cockney chancer Lee and he's thinking hold tight son hold tight this is going to be OK one way or another it's going to be OK

6

Source of life

1 January 1989

Mrs Thatcher listens to her New Year Message, as she does every year, with whisky and notepad and pen.

She's pleased, overall, with what she's delivered.

The theme, the *balance*.

The need to insist that triumph can come from disaster, indeed *does*.

Denis, reading the draft, told her he was moved to tears.

'Crying with laughter, Margaret!' he said, howling and red-faced. 'Sobbing!'

She could hear it too, this laughter, when he wasn't busy flushing the lavatory.

New Year's Eve, and she, Mrs Thatcher, sits upright, listens to her own voice.

> *The end of 1988 brought tragedy and hope:*
>
> *The tragedies of earthquake, train crash, and air disaster.*
>
> *The hope which came from the generous response of people every-where. Barriers were forgotten as the needs of humanity were put first.*
>
> *But hope sprang also from the great events and achievements of the year:*
>
> *At home, from the highest standards of living we have ever known, lower taxes, lower unemployment and far more jobs.*

She pours herself another measure of Scotch. She wonders what the plebs think New Year's Eve is *for*. There's an entropic lust in the English, she decides, to use these folkloric occasions to dissolve, usually with alcohol, present into past.

She can hear Denis's guffawing, so she knows he's listening.

And she knows why: mention of the Soviet Union, of Mikhail, what Denis will call obfuscation, or, as he put it the other day, 'They're stupider than their children, your *electorate*. Just make sure you're in the right bloody photograph when the wall comes down.'

From a man, of course, who was watching cricket at the Oval when his own children were born.

'I just wished the little buggers had been drowned at birth,' he'd said not long ago, and not joking.

The two most boring words in international politics, Denis is wont to offer: Soviet Union.

She wonders which number gin and tonic he's on, and if his second packet of cigarettes has yet been breached.

She reminds herself that the trick to these New Year Messages is *not* to say what you *are* planning to do in the coming year.

And what of 1989 – the closing year of this decade, this great reforming decade? The prospects are better than at any time this century.

As our people have become more prosperous, so they have become more generous towards others.

As they have earned more, they have begun to build up their own capital and enjoy the sense of independence it brings.

As business has become more flourishing, so it is more active in the community, in the inner cities, in cooperating with universities, in building close contacts with schools, in sponsoring the arts, and in contributing to all good causes.

As Britain's wealth has grown, so we have the best ever Health Service, better pensions and better housing.

So, she, Mrs Thatcher, does not mention the community charge, the dissolution of the rates, or the imminent privatisation of water services, a public, stock market flotation –

No, she does not mention any of this, of profit and change and counting pennies and getting rich.

She takes her pen, writes.

Of course, we all require higher standards in the quality of water and that will mean increases in costs and, therefore, in prices, and the same would be true whether water remained in the public sector or was privatised. There is far more likely to be increased capital spend on the improvement of water quality if the industry goes into the private sector. France, a country which has nationalised many things, has specifically kept water in the private sector because it provides a better service than would a nationalised water service.

She thinks, make it a 'major green initiative', perhaps.

She thinks, why is it such an unpopular idea, privatising water?

Food is just as much a basic commodity and not even Labour are suggesting that there should be government bread and jam.

Water.

It taps into – oh, Margaret, she thinks, forgive the pun – some sense of divine right, as if, falling from the sky as it does, it's bestowed on one, heaven-sent. The source of life.

Maybe it *is* a gift from heaven, but it still needs trapping, collecting and storing, and then purifying and delivering to the customer.

Industry, then, free market trading, *competition*, something the government, in Mrs Thatcher's opinion, should encourage and facilitate and not much more than that.

Truly it is a world which needs us all to pull together as we scan the horizon for the future that is to be.

And I assure you that Britain will be at the forefront in these great endeavours in the coming year.

Float water, she smiles. On cue, the lavatory flushes.

The night pours on. Suzi watches hours race by. The feeling is still there as it approaches dawn, but they're chasing it, the crowd, and Suzi can feel *that*. Lost in music. Lost in. Lost. The sun creeps in through the warehouse windows, the art deco warehouse is grimy in the soft light. The feeling is still there, the unity, the vibe, the togetherness, sure, Suzi feels that, but no one's really smiling anymore, they're moving, yes, always moving, and nodding, and sipping water, sipping water, sipping the source, and sipping cans of lager and cans of pop, but it's winding down for a good chunk of the crowd, while some are seeking more drugs, more hours, more time.

Suzi thinking, where next then, where next, where –

Parker nods at his new friend Lee Roy. Parker notes the chunky silver timepiece on Lee Roy. Parker taps his wrist, raises an eyebrow. Lee – bobbing, nodding, gurning – mouths six o'clock. Lee lifts six fingers in case there's any doubt –

Six meaning four hours to go and Parker's flagging a touch. Marlon's got a bit of pill on a palm and Parker laps it up. The DJ has Carly Simon on now, Parker's sure of it, 'Why', and it's a touch slower and there's a bit of a reggae feel to it, the piano chords insistent.

La di da di-dah

Sings Carly Simon

And then it's some bird doing that Neil Young song and Parker's laughing and Carolyn says what, she's smiling, saying what love, and Parker just goes, not exactly cutting edge is it, and Carolyn's whispering only love can break your heart, hero, and then Marlon's saying two hours and we're off, right, and Parker checks Lee Roy's wrist again and eight o'clock and that little bit did something then, Jesus

7

Up the canal

Jon's been awake and groaning for about half an hour before he realises the kids are up and yelling for him to get their breakfast.

It's a need for water that drives him downstairs in the end. The children are quite capable of not eating breakfast without him being there and getting stressed about it, is the reasoning. Jackie is snoring, happily. Just after eight and she doesn't look like surfacing any time soon. Jon remembers he promised her a lie-in, told her he'd take the kids to the park first thing, let her start the new year on her own terms, an hour or so for *her* –

Booze, it's the promises you make that'll kill you, Jon thinks now, staggering down the stairs, all rough skin, puffy cheeks, greasy hair, dressing gown seeming to have shrunk in the arms, he thinks, Y-fronts askance –

'Happy New Year, Dad,' says the boy. 'Was it a good party?'

And Jon can't help but grin at this, the sheer grown-upness of it, the fact that a minute ago the boy was mewling and bawling and already look at him sitting at the table with his hands in his lap keeping an eye on his sister as she plays with yesterday's newspaper and it's not the hangover that's causing Jon to rub his eye, no, it wouldn't be, he's still drunk.

'Yeah, it was,' Jon says. 'How was—'

'Jocelyn.'

'Yeah, Jocelyn, that's her name. All right, was it?'

'She let us stay up until …' and Jon sees him hesitate. 'Nine,' the boy says. 'She let us stay up until nine.'

Jon mutters something about we should've paid her for half the hours then.

'What did you say, Dad?'

'Nothing.' Smiling. 'What do you fancy for breakfast? Fish and chips?'

'Dad.'

'Fair point.' Jon looks down at his daughter. 'You all right down there?'

Lizzie nods, says, 'I need more paper.'

'What are you doing with it?'

She holds up the side of a cardboard box. 'Gluing it to this. It's a shield.'

'A shield?'

'For a knight or a princess.'

'I'll make us some eggs, shall I?'

And Jon takes the non-response as a form of tacit agreement and ducks into the fridge.

He breaks six eggs into a mixing bowl and gives them a quick whisk.

It proves an exertion too far, and he leans down on the countertop, presses his cheek against the cool tiles, lets his thick tongue loosen –

Tea, he thinks, orange juice –

Water and sugar.

He boils the kettle, turns on the radio.

The boy's reading his *Shoot!* magazine – again, Jon thinks, he's had this one for *months*, when's he going to outgrow it, eh, he's a bit old, isn't he, Jon's not sure – Lizzie still gluing.

'She hasn't got today's there too, has she?' Jon asks the boy, meaning Lizzie and the newspapers.

'Nope.'

Must be on the doormat, then, if they've delivered it all.

Jon thinking about the match report, West Ham's goalless draw at Charlton, Jon relieved the boy hadn't forced them to go all that way for that –

Tomorrow, Wimbledon at home, and Jon's worried about it, worried about it all, to be fair, relegation doesn't look a million miles away, doesn't look as unlikely as it should after 1986 and all that, though the last couple of years haven't exactly lived up to their little success, and the worst of it is how's the boy going to cope, West Ham haven't been relegated yet, not for him, he'll be devastated.

Jon takes a deep breath and slaps butter into his big frying pan.

Radio news is on, the headlines, and Jon cocks an ear:

Mrs Thatcher has warned against a revenge attack on those responsible for the Pan Am disaster. As the search for evidence continues, the police denied her husband's accusation they'd taken too long to deal with the bodies.

Thanks, Denis, Jon thinks, for that insight.

And in Rio de Janeiro, over a hundred New Year revellers are drowned or missing after a pleasure boat sinks.

Bloody hell, Jon thinks. Well, at least he didn't fall into the canal, look on the bright side.

He pours the egg into the pan, folds it, pushes it around –

He pops toast, butters it. Plates, knives and forks, glasses –

'Table,' he says.

They eat.

Twenty minutes later, hair washed in the sink and dressed, Jon is wrapping a scarf round Lizzie's neck and sending the boy back upstairs to put on some tracksuit trousers.

They amble down Mildenhall Road. It's crisp and fresh and damp and Jon's got his mouth open and his eyes wide, encouraging a bit of life back into him.

The boy dutifully with the football under his arm, Lizzie clutching tennis racket in one hand and tennis ball in the other. When they reach Chatsworth Road, their tradition –

'Go on, Dad,' the boy says.

He tosses the football to Jon.

Jon punts it high over the road, quite far, into Millfield's Park.

He hopes it avoids the usual stray dog shit as it rolls through the grass.

Not that stray, he thinks. Great big bulldogs and rottweilers pulling their owners all over the gaff, crapping.

The boy hares off after the ball. Jon takes Lizzie's hand and follows –

Towards the pylons, the estate, the astroturf, the canal –

The pub. Jon thinking he's not quite timed this right for a livener, hair of the dog, thinking, let's push on up the canal to the marshes, watch a bit of Sunday League.

They pass the Prince of Wales, under the bridge, the towpath busier now with joggers and walkers, and Jon hears thump, thump, thump as they approach the footbridge and there's, what's the word, *partygoers* out and about now too, looking a little worse for wear, but smiling, certainly happy.

Jon tells the boy to come here, and he takes his hand, that little protective instinct, and they cross the canal, the music louder, *demanding*, Jon thinks, must be a hell of a racket in there, relentless, twelve hours of *that*, and the boy races up the hill towards the football pitches, and their wheezy, red-faced men yelling 'time, Clive, time' and 'referee!' and Jon smiles, Lizzie laughs and the boy has the ball under his foot now, watching.

And Jon looks down at the water behind, the industrial estate on the other side making the Anchor and Hope pub, not a hundred metres away, inaccessible, and he thinks that tomorrow's new job might have something to do with the construction works he can see down there and further up towards Enfield, connected to the Thames Water Ring, the Leaside Project, Jon remembers it's called, and he wonders if Godfrey Heaven has anything to say about it.

Jon suspects he likely has.

The week before Christmas Jon telephoned Godfrey to give him the good news that he, Jon, was coming back to Hackney Town Hall as Borough Solicitor.

'And how do *you* feel about this, Jon?' Godfrey asked. '*I'm* delighted, of course.'

'Of course you are, Godfrey.'

Jon said nothing for a moment. Then, 'I think it's a role to aspire to, if you know what I mean.'

'I think I do, Jon. Now that you've accounted for all of Docklands, I suppose.'

Jon wasn't thrilled by this assessment. 'You don't sound convinced.'

'It doesn't matter what I think.'

'We'll be working together again.'

'And all the other experiences we shared went swimmingly, of course.'

'We did our best.'

'Yes, we did.'

'I feel like this time,' Jon said, 'I can make a difference.'

'As Borough Solicitor?'

'As Borough Solicitor.'

'Power, then.'

'If you say so, Godfrey.'

'Heavy is the head and all that.'

'Yeah, I've been thinking the same.'

'It's the *compromise*, Jon, that you won't like.'

'I'm not that principled, Godfrey.'

Jon felt Godfrey's sigh. Godfrey said, 'The Borough Solicitor is an instrument of the council, which is an instrument of local government, which is an instrument of, and so on.'

'What's your point?'

'I don't have you down as a pen-pushing lackey.'

'I'm flattered.'

'I'm glad to hear it.'

'Any advice, you know, anything to keep on my radar?'

'Water, Jon.'

'Water?'

'Water.'

'Oh yeah?'

'Privatisation and what it'll mean for our residents.'

Jon nodded. 'The Lea Valley, Thames—'

'It's a political decision they're making, not a philanthropic one.'

'OK.'

'It should be opposed. Or at least examined.'

'Thanks for the heads-up.'

'I'll look forward to seeing you, Jon, in a couple of weeks.'

'Likewise,' Jon said.

And tomorrow, that couple of weeks is up, Jon thinks.

He turns again to the Leaside works.

He thinks, construction, meaning money.

He thinks, seeing Chick last night brought it all back a bit, *Docklands*.

He thinks, Geraint Thomas –

I never really looked into that, Jon thinks.

Ayeleen. We leave the warehouse. I'm leaning on Lauren and it's cold and crisp and sunny and she lights a ciggie and we share it on the towpath. It's quiet and it's peaceful and I feel a bit sick but really happy and I say to Lauren, 'That was—'

'Yeah,' she says. 'It was. Let's go home.'

We walk under the bridge, past the pub and over the park, and there's families and dogs and Lauren spots her neighbour, the bloke we saw in the pub, and she keeps her head down but we reckon he's likely too hungover to notice, and anyway he's chasing his daughter behind a tree, we laugh, it's sweet, but not too loud, and, for a little while, I don't think about school and our exams, I don't think about my mum and how she is, what's wrong with her, and I don't think about Uncle Ahmet and his promise we can come and work for him permanent when we leave, and I really don't think about how he got the café back in Stoke Newington, don't think about that, don't want to know –

And we get back to Lauren's and creep up the stairs, and her mum yells, 'I don't wanna know!'

And we lie down together, barely taking our coats and scarves off, Lauren giggling, mumbling something about we need to do this again, *soon*, and I'm smiling, then –

Sleep.

8

There's no way that this can last

Suzi tells Keith, yeah, I'll come back, why not, all this lot are going then, yeah, and Keith tells her, yeah, course, afterparty at my new gaff, like the good old days, the good old bad old days, Suzi says, and Keith goes it weren't like that, you know, and Suzi says, it was.

Keith's new 'gaff' is close by, literally metres away, and it's big, industrial-sized, not much smaller than the warehouse when they get in there with just the half-dozen or so, Suzi and Lee and Danny and Carolyn, a couple of her mates, a classic 'Keith friend', in the industry in some form, Jed the Head his name, Parker and that Marlon character on their way.

'How'd you swing this then?' Lee asks, and Keith explains:

'It's an artists' and makers' premises, crafts and whatnot, and I live here unencumbered by rent.'

'No rent?'

'The way they tell it, I'm the friendly face of the Leaside Workrooms – managing the studios and office facilities and handling the application process. Part of this regeneration,' Keith sniffs.

'Sounds like a free lunch.'

'Hackney, your thinking man's Venice!'

Keith grinning now, administering lines on a long table. 'We provide affordable studio space and in-house business support to talented makers.'

'Turn it in,' Lee offers.

Keith winks. 'We're an award-winning social enterprise, home to dozens of independent creative businesses in London.'

'What's a maker?' someone asks.

'Craft, innit?' Keith explains. 'There's no one else here on a weekend, so turn up the music. Beers in the fridge over in the corner by that loom.'

Laughter.

'Turn right at the kiln,' someone shouts.

Suzi's on the sofa in her coat, cosy. Carolyn next to her. They're both smiling and chatting, not saying much.

Suzi runs her hands over her arms, her face, it feels good, it still feels good –

'When does it finish?' she asks. 'When does it leave off?'

Carolyn laughs. 'First time?'

'Yeah.'

'Me too.'

'It's nice now, isn't it, calmer?'

'It is.'

They survey the room. A few people drinking cans of beer round a long office table, Lee and Danny round the record player comparing notes, Keith generous with his supply –

Suzi hears Keith's performance, his *analysis*, and it's nice to hear it again, really, it is, of course he was there, of course he's a part of *this*.

He's saying, 'So this track, it's a *track*, that's the point. Listen to it.'

And the room stops to cock an ear.

'"Jack Your Body" by Steve "Silk" Hurley,' Keith says. 'Now, house music has come to have two distinct strands, *already*. That's what's amazing about it, it's the future and it's here now. This' – Keith gestures at the room, towards the warehouse, gestures at their night, their *experience* – 'is something. It's really something, it's political.'

'Two strands, Keith,' Lee Roy says. 'Don't lose focus.'

'Two strands, *tracks*, like this one, and *songs*, like "Promised Land" with which we brought in the new year, and which has been covered by my boys The Style Council.'

'What's the difference?'

'Deep house is songs, musicians, humanism; tracks is machines, repetition, liberation through trance-dance. At least that's what some writer told me.'

Laughter.

'All strings and succour, like gospel, and that's what appeals to our English soul boys like Weller, right? It's Martin Luther King, 'Promised Land'. But this *track* is what they're calling a 'jack track' and it's keyed into what we're doing on the dance floor. This is what's next and it's already here. It's political, mark my words, my brothers and sisters, someday we *will* be free, and this is how!'

A round of applause, some cheering and laughter, Keith bowing –

Suzi warm, happy, pleased to see he hasn't changed, worried too that he hasn't, but don't dwell on that, not now –

'Where's your bloke then, and his pal?' Suzi asks Carolyn.

'Still at the warehouse,' Carolyn says. 'Helping out or something.' Making the air quotes.

'What, they clearing up?' Suzi jokes.

'I think they're counting the bin bags full of money.'

Suzi laughs.

'I'm not joking.'

'Lucky you, then.'

'Oh, I'm not involved. Marlon is, some sort of supplier.'

'Right.'

'Oh no, it ain't nothing like that. It's something legit.'

Suzi smiles. 'Either way.'

She wriggles further into her coat.

'You wanna beer?' Carolyn asks.

Suzi smiles, nods, *grins* –

'I really do.'

Carolyn levers herself upright and pushes off towards the fridge.

Suzi sinks further into the sofa, lets her ears settle on Keith pontificating, Jed the Head in attendance, the others drifting off –

'It's like Weatherall told me,' Keith's saying, 'and this is a quote, right, I've only gone and memorised it.'

'Fair play,' decides Jed the Head. Suzi smiling –
'I wrote it down, hang about, I'll find it.'
Keith locates his own notepad –
'So, he tells me this.'
Keith clears his throat, reads:

Everyone that was involved in the early part of the scene has made some sort of success, or has done something that they wanna do, because they went to the Shoom, or they went to Spectrum, they went to Future, they then went round to someone's house and, like, came up with mad hare-brained schemes, let's do this, let's do that, let's do a record label, let's set up a T-shirt company, you know, the clubs always been the catalyst and they're full of energy at the moment.

Carolyn hands Suzi a beer and settles back into the sofa, nestles in next to her.

They open their cans. 'Cheers,' Suzi says, smiling.

'Cheers.'

'It's been a while,' Suzi says. 'I guess Clapham Common was the last time I saw you, well, properly, anyway.'

Carolyn nods.

Clapham Common, Festival for Freedom, June 1986.

Suzi there with Keith, The Style Council special guests, not listed on the bill. Suzi scored a bunch of passes, and she and Carolyn took some of the kids from Broadwater Farm, the youth club.

'How's your cousin doing?' Suzi asks. 'Shaun, isn't it? He was interested in my camera, if I remember rightly.'

Carolyn nods. Gives Suzi a tight smile. 'He was.'

'And what's he up to now?'

Carolyn shifts forward in her seat. 'He's—'

'Yeah?'

'He's in Feltham, young offenders.'

'Oh, Christ, I'm so sorry, what happened?'

Carolyn smiles, puts a hand on Suzi's arm. 'You know what, let's not talk about it now, let's not ruin the night, yeah? I'm having too nice a time.'

'OK. But if you ever—'

'Yeah, you know what, that might be good actually.'

'OK. You know how to find me.'

'I do.' Carolyn smiles. 'We'll talk.'

Suzi smiles. 'I'd like that. Cheers,' she adds.

'Yeah, cheers, Happy New Year.'

Marlon tells Parker he needs to pick something up from the promoter and then they'll head over to the afterparty.

Parker nods.

He's buzzing, still buzzing, his jaw working, his skin flushed, his eyes pricked –

'Sounds good, mate,' he says, nodding, nodding, nodding.

Marlon grins broad. 'Loved up!' he says, snapping his fingers, laughing.

The warehouse empty now, security team gone, the promoters in the back office with two geezers, and he and Marlon go through and they're counting pound coins into ten-pound stacks and Parker thinks there must be three grand in here.

He nods at the blokes who smile and give Parker the thumbs-up, gesture at the table where there are lines of coke, and Parker has a big sniff and thinks, woah there, but in a good way.

Marlon's in the corner with the promoters and then he's back carrying a small sports holdall.

'We good?' Parker asks.

'Very.'

'Let's do one.'

Marlon's turning and waving goodbye to the lads and Parker's doing the same and then there's voices coming from the corridor and everyone in the office looks up, Old Bill, is it, a note of concern, so the two geezers go out the door and Parker hears them saying, this area's out of bounds, and then a voice – angry, agitated – going, we're looking for the promoters, and someone's saying something that Parker can't hear and the others in the office are grabbing weapons now, iron bars, knives, a lump of wood, knuckle dusters, and Marlon gives Parker a look, gestures at the holdall, gives Parker a look that means, shape up, and Parker shapes up.

Then a tall, skinny geezer piles into the office and one of the promoters hits him with an iron bar and he goes down.

Parker clocks three more of them outside the door, and he puts himself in their way, gets involved, another intruder gets an iron bar in the canister, a call goes out to security, and the blaggers are pushed back and out, they're running running running and Parker and the others are after them and then they give up, laughing and wheezing, and Parker's thinking, fuck me that happened quick, but he's all right and they wait for the security team who check the perimeter but find nothing, no one, and everyone leaves, buzzing.

Parker and Marlon bouncing down the towpath, newly brothers in arms, Parker thinking, that's some easy money if they'd been tooled up and he says, 'Where's the rest of it then?' meaning the money and Marlon tells him it was divvied up hours ago and stored in separate safe houses close by, and Parker thinks –

This won't last. There's no way this can last.

Noble wakes up, unentangles himself from Lea, and makes tea.

He puts bacon into a pan, cracks eggs, toasts bread.

He thinks –

We've never done it like *that* before. What are the chances she's up the stick already?

Good-to-firm, he hopes.

Suzi slips out of Keith's bed, gets dressed –

Keith says, unhappily, 'I can't believe I've woken up with you.'

Suzi says, 'I'm going to imagine the tone you took there was unironic.'

Keith laughs.

She walks straight home, head clear, thinking –

I need to do something about all this.

Thinking Noble blackmailing her *still*, thinking spycops and the truth, thinking deep cover, thinking –

Why not?

Parker wakes up, his head in Carolyn's neck, he breathes her in, he pushes himself closer, pushes his knee between her legs, wraps his hands round her legs, her bum, her hips, she moans gently, rolls over, they make love, sweaty, slow, do it, she says, just do it

Shaun. Sixty-three days done. Twenty-seven days left. New Year's Day on my bunk, looking at the ceiling. Most are watching some film but I'm not.

There's a screw who's all right and he's told me that this new version of Feltham is called the 'New Generation' of prison design. I tell him, what, they *designed* this place, and he thinks that's funny and goes, look out the window there's trees everywhere, but I reckon he's joking as all the walkways are covered and the windows have bars so yeah you might be able to see a bit of a tree but that's all.

Feltham A: boys.

Inmates in small groups so they can be more naturally and continuously supervised without the need for the alienating patrols common to more traditional blocks.

Is what I'm told by this screw.

Two groups of nine housing units, each triangular, with cells along two sides and large windows on the third, overlooking the communal space. A central 'street' running through trees and lawns.

I tell the screw, I've taken the tour, and he finds this hilarious and he's good to me for a bit, looks out for me, settles me in after my stint on Lapwing where they put you when you first arrive for introduction, filthy and miserable, like they set you up to feel it ain't nothing but this for the next however many days weeks months years –

Then he calls me that coloured comedian to some other lad and I'm wondering why he'd be snide, mug me off, and think probably best not to think about it so I don't.

Here, you're always inside, always.

Even the walkways have roofs and bars. I'm ready to go mad, I'm all in my head and I just want to get outside, get out, the boredom, the isolation, the pettiness.

And day after day, no association – no time out the cell. I ask why: cuts, I'm told. Cuts? Staff shortages, sick leave, unlucky.

A few days like that, twenty-three and a half hours in the cell and you feel you don't want to go out, just shut the curtain and pretend. Lie here and shut off, shut down. But even that's impossible. I hear everything now. Even when I ain't listening. And right now, it's quiet, some film on but I ain't interested. New Year treat. Twenty-seven days left.

That screw says to me last night, Happy New Year, not long left now, we'll keep your bed warm for you.

I been lucky. Three months for holding and there's enough of them boys from Hackney in here that I know I ain't going to be touched. A message from Marlon came sharpish to tell me this. Head down, it said, safe trip. No one touched me and no one tried to get me involved, so, lucky, yeah, kept myself to myself, really lucky.

Week one and I saw two kids going at it in the yard, really going for it, but it weren't nothing, it turned out: it was a diversion so the screws didn't see another kid being shanked in his cell.

Man comes in bit before Christmas. Fifteen years old, got six months for setting fire to a shed, meaning he ain't from London so a long way from home. His mum can't afford to visit him. His gran carks it after he's been in a month. Social services tell him he can't go to the funeral, too far, too complicated. A screw finds him in his cell, crying his eyes out. So he's a risk, so they keep him in his cell pretty much all day every day. Until they find him hanging from one of the bars in his window.

So, yeah, *lucky.*

PART THREE
Exodus

February–July 1989

1

The Hackney Riviera

You think: given water is the source of all life then you need to get involved.

Stage one: make yourself useful.

You achieve this by providing funds through Compliance Ltd, and are awarded construction contracts taken up by a subsidiary company of your own Excalibur.

The project:

A tunnel connecting the Stoke Newington site of the proposed Thames Water Ring Main to the Coppermills Water Treatment Works.

The thinking:

Water may well be the source of all life, but it needs to be clean.

True blue is the colour.

Stage two:

Work out how you can benefit most from the potential flotation and subsequent privatisation of the water industry, a flotation and privatisation that your political chums describe as 'imminent'.

Stage zero:

Land grab – the Lea Valley.

How to make land cheaper, is the question.

And how to buy it and how to own it and how to have *it.*

Not always the same things.

You sit in your office, and you ponder these questions.

Water.

It's one possible answer.

Noble dreaming about the past: *nostalgia ain't what it used to be* –

Telephone ringing and ringing, not yet 5.30 a.m., Noble dry swallowing and groaning, Lea sighing, moaning, rolling over, Noble telling her not now, darling, and out of bed, into the kitchen, the telephone ringing and ringing –

'Get your arse into work, son,' Jenkins says. 'Tip-off.'

Noble gets straight on the Euston Road towards Dalston nick, east through Islington, then east again –

Again, here he is again –

In he goes, up the stairs, down the corridor, into another smoke-filled room, another room that reeks of stale booze and coffee, of takeaway curry, of body odour and grease, another tired, strip-lit room, just like their old room, that same room, up the road at Stoke Newington nick.

Here he is.

The place has been redecorated, but you'd never know it.

The task force is all present and correct:

DC Dave Jenkins, DC Barry Fife, PC Johnny Bond.

They're dressed in going-out gear, Noble notes, rubbing his eyes.

Jenkins tosses Noble a set of keys. 'You're driving, Hollywood.'

And out they go, one by one, one by one they leave the smoke-filled room, the reek of stale booze and coffee, the smell of the food and the smell of the sweat, the black mould and the stained carpet, down the corridor, down the stairs and out the side entrance this time, out the side entrance and into the car park, into the car park and into a squad car, into a squad car and Noble keys the ignition.

Jenkins pops the siren, points at Fife and Bond and says, 'Follow that car.'

Just gone six and Jenkins mopping his brow, his breath wet, his breath on the glass, moist in the air –

Noble cracks the driver's window and puts his foot down.

They're heading north up Kingsland Road, then right towards Hackney Downs, left again, then right, there's the park and rearing up alongside –

The Nightingale Estate.

Noble remembers it well, remembers sitting at the foot of it in a car with Parker and his grass Trevor, telling it like it is.

Noble remembers –

Noble's been here before.

Noble clocks squad cars flashing lights, silent, a dozen uniforms in riot gear –

Out the car, Noble looks up at Rachel Point, across the road, into the estate –

Noble remembers:

The lift stinking of piss, but it works.

Fourteenth floor –

Here we go again, Noble thinks.

Noble looking right, left, right, eyeing the floorplan –

Here we are again:

Remembering:

Down the narrow path, front doors still peeling, the odd pot plant still dying, again, the rusting bicycles still with one or no wheels, the threadbare mats still insisting Wipe Your Bloody Feet, the housewives still twitching net curtains, the shouts of kids on the ground drifting up, the washing hanging in the arches –

Noble's been here before.

Jenkins nodding.

Noble knowing what he's going to say –

'This one.'

He gestures for Noble to ring the bell. Uniforms gather either side.

Ding-dong.

Noble's been here before, been to this flat before, here he is again –

Again

Sound of shoes clipped and sliding –

The door opens.

A woman peering around the door. Impassive, resigned, she raises her eyebrows at Jenkins, she nods.

The uniforms pile in.

Noble and Jenkins behind them.

Fife and Bond keeping an eye on the walkway, keeping an eye on the door.

Noble hears:

Get down hands behind your head

I didn't do nothing, I didn't do nothing, where's your fucking warrant, pig cunts

Noble hears:

I said get down

A young black man – head down, topless, tracksuit trousers, unlaced trainers, gold jewellery – handcuffed, led through a poky corridor outside into the light.

A uniform hands Jenkins a sports bag.

'All in here, guv.'

Jenkins nods.

That ain't mine, I never seen that before in my fucking life.

Jenkins grins. 'My life now, your life,' he says.

Nodding at the uniforms and the young man carted off –

'Time of arrest?' Jenkins says.

Fife checks his watch. 'Five forty-five a.m.,' he says.

Jenkins nods at the woman. 'You'll corroborate that, love?'

She nods.

Jenkins points at Fife. 'You bring the bird in too, all right.'

Fife nods, gestures with his chin for her to follow, which she does, head down.

Noble checks his own watch: 6.17 a.m. Six being the cut-off for over-time pay.

Jenkins smiles. 'Overtime, pal. First rule of this squad is overtime.'

Noble sniffs.

'Johnny'll show you how to do the forms when we get back to the nick.'

Noble nods. He looks at the front door of this flat, this flat he has been to before, he thinks –

Say nothing, and so he doesn't.

Dalston nick.

Two hours later. Noble at his desk. Chewing a pen, tongue round his teeth –

Cold coffee and the remains of a bacon sandwich, white bread crusts and thick strings of fat.

Johnny Bond comes in, nods. Noble notes Dave Jenkins and Barry Fife exchange a look.

Noble scribbles on his overtime form, sticks it in his desk drawer.

Noble leans back, spins on the chair.

'Just popping out,' Jenkins says. 'Anyone need anything?'

Noble points at the remains on his desk. 'Champion's breakfast,' he says.

'Full Irish.'

'No need to be racist, Dave.'

Jenkins laughs. 'You punched in your overtime form yet?'

Noble points again at his desk. 'One step at a time, Dave, you know me—' snapping his fingers, wagging one, pointing. 'Methodical.'

'Right you are.' Jenkins shrugging on his leather jacket, middle finger in the air as he departs. 'See you later, ladies.'

Noble coughs.

He turns a biro through a few circles in his fingers. He watches Barry Fife and Johnny Bond for a bit, both of whom are apparently engrossed in their fraudulent paperwork, their timesheets.

He gathers up the leftovers, the plate, the mug –

'I guess I'm on washing-up duty then. Here.' Gesturing for the plates and the mugs on Barry Fife's desk, on Johnny Bond's desk, on Dave Jenkins' desk.

Ketchup smears and milky skin –

'Lovely jubbly,' Noble jokes.

The pair of them grunt and Noble's out into the corridor, down the corridor and into the kitchen, dumping the plates and mugs in the sink, back out into the corridor and down the stairs, down the flights of stairs into holding, where he sees Jenkins with the young man they lifted only a couple of hours earlier.

Jenkins handing the young man a zip-up tracksuit top.

Jenkins handing him the sports bag they confiscated only a couple of hours earlier.

The young man opening the sports bag, peering in, gesturing, saying, It's fucking empty, come on –

Jenkins smiling.

Much obliged, Noble hears.

Noble turns, back up the stairs, into the main foyer of the nick, making for the front desk, over his shoulder aware of the young man leaving via the side exit.

Noble smiling at the young plod on duty. 'Second thoughts,' Noble says. 'I'll be back later.'

Then he's up the flights of stairs, down the corridor and into the kitchen and that's where Dave Jenkins finds him, washing up.

Noble sniffs. 'We got any budget for rubber gloves?' he says.

Jon Davies has been Borough Solicitor for Hackney Council for two months and has achieved not a great deal in his own, precise, estimation.

The radio's playing 'Belfast Child' by Simple Minds and Jon isn't sure why he hasn't turned it off. It goes on a bit, the song, reminds Jon of that old Tory joke:

What are the two most boring words in the English language?
Northern Ireland.

Looks like it's still Maggie one, Irish Republican Army nil, though, overall, after Brighton and all that, Bobby Sands and the H-Blocks.

Would you like a chicken supper? sung at the football north of the border.

You filthy Fenian fucker

Elegant, as ever, that particular sectarian rivalry.

Jon doesn't like to think about it too much, to be fair, it's all very uncomfortable, in that sense of it's only over the road and it's only families like mine and how did it end up like it has, doesn't bear thinking about, so Jon doesn't.

But Simple Minds make it hard.

It's very long, Jon thinks, for a number one.

Where's the radio edit, when it's not at home, eh?

Someone should have a word, make sure these pop stars know the three-minute rule.

Every song on the album is called something serious like 'Biko' or 'Mandela Day', titles that scream five minutes plus.

Simple Minds, Jon thinks, are the very definition of early stuff, as in, I like their early stuff, and it's one band Jon thinks, fair enough, it's spot on, that description, too often it's men, well, it's men like him, demonstrating their superior knowledge, their superior taste, and Jon doesn't usually abide that.

He makes an exception for Simple Minds, though, as a rule.

He's in a bigger office now though, Jon, in the town hall, big enough that 'Belfast Child' echoes about the place, the size of the windows providing a landscape view of the tops of the buses trundling up and down Mare Street, four floors up and close to the seat of power.

It takes Godfrey Heaven five minutes just to climb the stairs, heaving himself through the door, puce and wheezing.

Course it means it takes a lot longer to get rid of him too, if Jon needs to get rid of him.

First there's the sitting down and the heavy breathing, the blood pressure drop and the whitening of the face, then the recovering of the composure, the scratching of the head, the rifling of the inside pockets of the tweed jacket for the folded and torn memo or minutes, then the memory – the *aha*! – and then the meeting.

On cue, a knock at the door and John waits a beat, calls out come in and Godfrey's head appears, and he shuffles into the space, coughing, waving envelopes bunched in his fist.

'Post!' he splutters. 'Brought it up for you.'

He collapses into a chair.

'They don't get any easier, then, the stairs?' Jon asks.

'The stairs are the same as they've always been, Jon,' Godfrey says. 'I'd say it's down to me how easy or hard they've become.'

'That's philosophical.'

'Age, Jon, it's a great leveller.'

'Depends how you set about it.'

'Age?'

'Life.'

'Now *that's* philosophical, Jon.'

Jon smiles. 'I had a lot of time to myself over in Bethnal Green.'

'Less of that now.'

'Much less.'

'People endlessly traipsing up to see you, I expect.'

'Always something for me to sign.'

Godfrey Heaven nods. 'The fate of the party bureaucrat.'

'I work for the borough, Godfrey.'

'Course you do. Here.'

Godfrey slaps the envelopes onto Jon's desk.

'What can I do you for, Godfrey?' Jon asks.

'The like-minded existential banter not enough?'

Jon smiles. 'I thought that was extra.'

'The community charge, Jon, is why I'm here. The poll tax.'

'Pledging your support, I suppose.'

'Very funny.'

'What of it?'

Godfrey Heaven sniffs. 'There's a strong feeling around the place' – leaning forward, conspiratorial – 'that we're likely to have, in the *borough*, a very high amount of non-compliance.'

'Can't pay, won't pay sort of thing.'

'That's the catchphrase doing the rounds north of the border.'

'What's your point?'

'Our position, as a council, within a borough of high non-compliance, legally speaking.'

'As in what is our position?'

Godfrey snaps his fingers. 'In a nutshell.'

'And in a nutshell, I don't know. Not yet anyway.'

'Party position not clear then?'

'At some point' – Jon stretches, sighs – 'I'm going to start getting fed up of your insinuations, Godfrey, old son, all right?'

'Crystal, Jon.'

Jon fans the envelopes out on his desk in front of him, waits.

He notes one of these envelopes is addressed by hand, a wobbly biro by the looks of it, a little untidy, sellotaped down at the back.

The rest are typed, stamped, sealed –

'Go on, Godfrey, I'm all ears.'

'How we respond,' Godfrey says, 'as a borough, as a council, will have some consequences, repercussions.'

'All ears.'

'There's a feeling, I gather, higher up in the party, that Mrs Thatcher's policies are now essentially irreversible.'

'OK.'

'And this feeling is beginning to be shared by certain leaders of the labour *movement*.'

'Miners' strike, Wapping and all that, I suppose. Not a great run of results.'

'Indeed. Point being that the Labour Party's best bet now after the trouncing at the last election is what they're calling "capitalism with a human face".'

'What I think you're saying is that the poll tax might well be a fait accompli but we shouldn't lose sight of the struggle?'

'More widely, yes, that's exactly what I'm saying.'

'So, non-compliance might serve a political end, as well as a bit of bothersome protest.'

'It might.' Godfrey wrestles himself upright in his chair. 'The Tories have gone to war with local authorities, Jon, as you've seen. Cuts in services by slashing rate support grants which, in turn, are to force councils to increase domestic rates, or privatise services, and either way your borough resident suffers.'

'And I work for the borough.'

'You work for the borough *residents*, Jon. In a sense. Protect their interests, ensure fair treatment, legally speaking.'

'Non-payment as a delegitimisation of the Thatcher project.'

Godfrey stands, shakily. He pulls a piece of paper from an inside pocket, course he does. 'I quote, Jon, the Conservative Manifesto from 1987: "We will legislate in the first session of the new parliament to abolish the unfair domestic rating system and replace rates with a fairer Community Charge. This will be a fixed rate of charge for local services paid by those over the age of eighteen, except the mentally ill and elderly people living in homes and hospitals."'

'We knew it was coming then.'

'Might be the shortest suicide note in history, if you get my drift.'

'Crystal, Godfrey.'

'How are the kids, Jon?'

'Thriving. Unlike their parents.'

'Selfless, Jon.'

'Thankless more like.'

Godfrey smiles and makes for the door –

'Don't forget to write,' he says.

Jon shakes his head, smiles.

He thumbs the handwritten envelope into his hands, opens it –

The letter has been typed on a typewriter, complete with Tipp-Ex corrections and crossings-out. He reads for gist, it's short, confusing, an elderly couple on a council-owned low-rise row not far past Springfield Park, canal-side –

Complaining of taps not working, plumbers nonplussed, in the Lea Valley –

Jon thinking, *what*?

Next day, two more handwritten envelopes, same street address, same typed text, same *content* almost, like members of the community have got together and drafted a missive, as if no one else is doing anything about it so they've taken matters into their own hands.

The Leaside Project, Jon thinks, is close by.

The Hackney Riviera, some jokers are calling it.

Near the Robin Hood pub.

He could take the boy on a bike ride at the weekend, have a shufty.

2

Promised Land

Suzi's watching *Top of the Pops*.

It's been quite a mix of music, she thinks, so far. A real snapshot of the state of it all as the decade comes to a close. She's jotting down her sardonic – but not unreasonable – thoughts in her notebook, preparing for a TV write-up piece, on assignment.

'Rocket' by Def Leppard (ripped denim, hair, pointy guitars) followed by 'Belfast Child' by Simple Minds (monochrome, earnest) followed by 'Can't Stay Away from You' by Gloria Estefan (dry ice, perched on a stool, live vocal) followed by 'Every Rose Has Its Thorn' by Poison (hair) followed by Top 40 Breaker Clips for Edie Brickell and the New Bohemians, Pop Will Eat Itself, and Debbie Gibson (American gimmick, weekender, America's sweetheart) followed by 'I Don't Want a Lover' by Texas (drive-time) followed by 'Stop' by Sam Brown (frock, lipstick, string quartet, prominent jewellery), and then 'Stop' by Sam Brown is followed by –

'Promised Land' by The Style Council.

Why Suzi has been watching.

And her first thought is:

It's a little bit of a pointless cover, isn't it?

Then:

Great version, *great* song –

Soul, gospel, four to the floor –

Paul Weller and Mick Talbot sit at upright pianos on opposite sides of the *Top of the Pops* stage.

Dee is front and centre in a fitted red blazer and a big hat, billowing trousers, dancing –

There is not a microphone in sight. Not even the slightest attempt to pretend that they're not miming, which feels very Style Council.

Honorary Councillors Mary and Benita on backing vocals, trouser suits and disco ball handclaps –

Mick Talbot has a beard, Suzi notes. That's new. Bit of an Amish vibe, Suzi thinks, what with the weight of the beard focused on the chin. Double-breasted jacket and cravat completing the ensemble.

Paul Weller mouthing the words in zipped-up bomber jacket, gold cross over black T-shirt, slicked-back hair –

Looking sharp, when does he not –

And that's it, really, performance-wise.

And then the crowd are clapping, some technician turns the track down slowly, and Mark Goodier or Andy Crane is introducing this week's number one, 'Something's Gotten Hold of My Heart' by Marc Almond and Gene Pitney, and Suzi takes the opportunity to have a wee.

When she's finished, they're playing out with 'Hey Music Lover' by S'Express, the video something of a kitschy in-joke, but Suzi likes the track.

And that's it until next week, folks.

Suzi sighs. She wonders what they're *doing*, The Style Council.

She noted two early reviews of the single. *Melody Maker* or the *NME* – she didn't write down which, doesn't really matter which one it was – declared it to be:

'Horribly drum heavy and is the kind of fake-soul/pseudo gospel that 80s people dance to in order to get off with each other in sordid night clubs to the aroma of lager and Blue Stratos. I'm sorry but I hate it.'

Which is clear, at least. *Record Mirror* used a bit of irony to show its support, how clever of it, Suzi thinks now:

'It's a career move that may just work, simply because they've been rendered unrecognisable. The best TSC single ever, by default.'

Suzi knows there's a best-of out next month, *The Singular Adventures of The Style Council*, and after that the rumours she's heard are all about a house record, *Modernism: A New Decade*, is what it's supposed to be called, and the title sounds about right.

Paul Weller told Suzi in *The Face* the year before:

'It is about making records. The rest is all crap. I spend my life trying to make records, trying to better myself and the band through the songs I write and the records I make. When I read the article afterwards, I think, why did I bother doing that?'

There's been some back and forth with the label after the commercial disappointment that was *Confessions of a Pop Group*.

Suzi's a bit worried about the band if she's being honest.

But she won't write that down.

Instead, she ends the piece with more Paul Weller:

'I just thought it was a good song. It always sounded like a gospel song to me, the chords and the way the voices were. We didn't change it that much really, but we just made it more inspirational, more "up".'

Suzi nods at this, smiles.

Then the phone rings. Carolyn.

They swap some pleasantries, catch up –

'You said you'd be happy to talk,' Carolyn says.

'Of course.'

'How about tomorrow, go for a coffee or something?'

'Sounds good.'

They decide on a place and Carolyn hangs up.

Next day, and Suzi's in a café on Chatsworth Road, fidgeting.

She looks up and sees Carolyn come in, stands.

They embrace, smile.

A waitress appears. Carolyn points at Suzi's mug.

'I'll have what she's having,' she says.

Suzi smiles. 'It's just a white coffee.'

'Perfect.'

They sit quietly for a moment.

'Thanks for coming to meet me.'

Suzi smiles again. 'Of course.'

'Thing is, Shaun is coming home soon, and I thought I should explain, just in case, you know.'

'Of course.'

'What happened to him is what happened to a lot of the boys on the estate after the disturbances.'

'I remember.'

Carolyn sniffs. 'Well, you had some idea, yeah.'

Suzi nods. The waitress delivers the white coffee. Carolyn adds sugar, stirs –

'Cheers,' she says, ironically.

'Cheers.'

Carolyn blows on her drink, sips carefully. 'I was also thinking you might be able to talk to him, when he's home.'

Suzi thinks, hang on a minute.

'About your camera, I mean.'

'Of course.'

'I don't know what he plans to do, but at least—'

'I understand.'

'Thank you.'

'Do you want to tell me what happened?'

'OK.' Carolyn takes a breath. 'After the disturbances, and you helped, I know you did, I know how much evidence you collected, collated, you know that.'

Suzi nods.

She'd been pretty involved at Broadwater Farm after the uprising, typing up interview transcripts, using her shorthand knowledge, but it had only really been clerical work, she wasn't doing the interviewing, she wasn't an activist. She was helping, doing what she could.

Carolyn continues. 'So, of course, you know that hundreds of people were arrested, that the police were all over the estate, any excuse. And of this first wave of arrests, over half were kids.'

Suzi nods.

Carolyn goes on. 'You'll also remember the complaints that were being made by the estate residents that kids were being deliberately targeted, held incommunicado, given no access to solicitors. Or their families.'

'Awful.'

'And those families that *were* notified, they were often given misinformation as to where their children actually were.'

'Yeah, this I know, awful.'

'So desperate to get an arrest, they crossed a lot of lines.'

Suzi knows all about *this*.

So desperate, a witness to the killing was conveniently found.

Three kids charged with murder.

They were aged 14, 15 and 13 years old.

Interrogations, and these kids admit to involvement, though they later denied that anything they'd told the police was actually true, that they were led, persuaded.

Suzi remembers this. The youngest kid was arrested for looting, initially, then held for three days wearing nothing but his underpants and a blanket.

Similar stories for the other two, and the judge having none of it. The three kids were acquitted, unreliable confessions and an unreliable witness, so there you go.

This was all widely reported, and Suzi had kept an eye on it. The Clapham Common festival was a way to brighten everyone's lives, and it had done, so what happened to Shaun?

'There were arrests being made for other things too,' Carolyn says. 'Shaun was seen with a bag, you understand?'

Suzi nods.

'He was a courier, I suppose, a mule if you put it another way.'

'I'm sorry.'

'Thank you.' Carolyn smiles ruefully. 'The ringleader, some lowlife called Trevor, apparently, he was found dead, murdered, around the same time Shaun was arrested. A couple of kids got the same treatment as Shaun. The judge was one of them zero-tolerance types, I believe.'

'Huh.'

Carolyn nods. 'Anyway, he's coming home soon.'

'I'm glad.'

'You know what,' Carolyn says. 'It's not too early to go for a drink, is it, celebrate?'

So they go for a drink and Suzi says she'll happily talk to Shaun about anything at all, if it's helpful, but she doesn't hear anything from Carolyn.

3

The Hackney Community Defence Association

Set up in the summer of 1988, the Hackney Community Defence Association is a campaigning organisation which works in Hackney to challenge police attacks against the community. HCDA holds regular meetings on alternate Wednesdays, where all aspects of its work are discussed.

There are five main areas of HCDA's work.

Legal defence: HCDA takes up cases of people who have suffered police injustice.

Police monitoring: HCDA monitors police activity in the area.

Public events: HCDA engages in political activity by raising the issue of police injustice in the community.

Paralegal support: HCDA provides paralegal support to campaigns who are likely to find themselves in confrontation with the police.

Community Defence: HCDA seeks to build confidence and strength within the community so that people can readily challenge police injustice.

If you want to learn more about HCDA write to HCDA, the Family Centre, 50 Rectory Road, London, N16 7QY. Or leave a message on the answerphone on 071-249 0193

1 January 1989 is the day the Hackney Community Defence Association start to monitor cases of injustice in the Hackney and Stoke Newington divisions of the Metropolitan Police.

Of course, Parker and Carolyn – both useful wheels in the Association's cog – were not exactly compos mentis on 1 January 1989, given they were well into their second day of raving on that particular date, and so weren't monitoring anything except their somewhat erratic heartbeats, Parker now reflects.

He's based at 50 Rectory Road again, HCDA headquarters.

He's adding notes to a file. He's adding notes to a file and he's thinking about Shaun. He's thinking about Shaun, who is – Parker checks his watch – due out any moment.

Parker's been there – albeit on an SDS fix – and he knows what Feltham is like and he knows what it's like to get back out.

So, while he's thumbing through paperwork, while he's placing newspaper clippings in chronological order, while he's annotating and highlighting, shuffling and tidying, Parker's thinking about Shaun, thinking about Shaun coming to live with him, live with him and Carolyn, and what the fuck that means in the bigger picture.

So Parker does what he always does in these situations, does what he always does when he doesn't want to think about things, when thinking about things only creates a mess of contradiction and impossibility, the tension from which causes his nut to hum and to buzz, a humming and buzzing that gets louder and more insistent, a throb in his neck and shoulders, a pulse behind his eyes –

What he does is not think about it, box it.

He doesn't think about it, and then he boxes it.

He sticks it in a box, sticks it in a box to think about, to think about later.

Instead of thinking about Shaun and what the fuck it all means big picture-wise, he records the first case of police criminal violence taken up by the HCDA from an incident on 15 January. Civil action proceedings taken out against the Metropolitan Police almost immediately. The case requires anonymity at this early stage; Parker notes that the plaintiff is 73 years old and a great-grandmother.

He refers to her as Woman A for the file; Man A is her husband.

They don't discriminate, the Met, when it comes to brutality.

Anyone is fair game. Parker knows this much already.

The facts of the case seem clear enough:

Woman A and a family friend are in the family car, the family friend driving, when they have a minor traffic accident.

Nobody is hurt, so they return home to report the incident.

Parker's not sure quite how minor the accident was given the phrasing in the accident write-up – 'veered off the road, crashed through the railings and ended in a pond' – but still, benefit of the doubt and all that.

Man A is subsequently arrested at home, despite not being involved in this minor accident, on suspicion of drink-driving.

Man A, it turns out, is diabetic, and Woman A tries to deliver his pills and a jug of water as he is led off in long johns, vest and socks by Hackney's finest.

Woman A is pulled to the ground and restrained by three officers, then taken off herself to Hackney nick.

Woman A is then searched and charged with assaulting a Woman Police Officer.

Smashed the jug over one WPC Martin, so it is claimed.

Two days later, the charges are dropped.

Woman A intends to sue for assault, wrongful arrest, false imprisonment, trespass and malicious prosecution.

Parker reads on, Parker joins dots –

Parker cross-references HCDA bumph.

Bingo, here's the kicker, he thinks –

Woman A and Man A are the grandparents of one Trevor Monerville.

Parker thinks back.

Parker reads the same statement he read to Noble not six months ago –

1 January 1988:

Trevor Monerville, a young black man, arrested and held incommunicado at Stoke Newington police station.

On 8 January he has emergency brain surgery to remove a blood clot from the surface of the brain.

The Family and Friends of Trevor Monerville is set up to campaign in support of justice for Trevor.

New information:

Trevor Monerville is arrested on a number of occasions in murky circumstances.

In 1988 Trevor Monerville is cleared at Snaresbrook court of attempted robbery and assault on a police officer.

Nine other charges against him are dropped.

There's no such thing as coincidence, dear boy, Parker thinks.

Parker looks at the telephone.

It's still not ringing.

It's still not ringing to tell him that Shaun is home, safe and sound, safe and sound with Carolyn, Parker's Carolyn, safe and sound, Shaun is, in his own cousin Carolyn's flat.

Parker's flat.

What happened after Broadwater Farm:

Shaun's arrest, the connection with Marlon suddenly clear – to Parker, at least, though what that connection actually *meant*, what Marlon was actually *doing*, very fucking unclear – and the only reason Parker said nothing to Carolyn at the time, beyond comforting her and being a *brick*, is that Marlon ain't stupid and Parker knows Marlon's eyes are wide open to all and sundry around him and about the place and Parker knows that when his grass – the other Trevor, Parker's ear on the ground – was found with his tongue pulled through his cut throat, the news leaked that someone was doing something in Stoke Newington and every half-arsed rude boy started thinking about who's who and what's new.

Trevor then revealed as grooming Shaun and the other kids, which was helpful to Parker, kept the questions to a minimum.

Trevor's involvement pure fiction, of course, evidence supplied by someone higher up than Parker, than Noble even, and what it did was keep Parker safe. But, of course, the trade-off was that poor old Shaun has had to do some difficult time at Feltham Boys.

Parker's kept his head down since, and Noble's left him well alone, mostly, but now Noble's back at Stoke Newington, back at Dalston, Carolyn's cousin is jibbing over, and Marlon seems to be in cahoots with these white soul boy ravers.

Parker's feeling like his head might soon be back above the battlements.

And he ain't too happy about it.

Domestic bliss has been exactly that.

4

Hype text

It took Suzi three days to tell Noble that, yes, she was in, yes, she'd do it, she'd get on the inside of the Genesis Sunset rave crew.

'Good night then, was it?' Noble winked.

'Business and pleasure,' Suzi said.

'Cash. Weekly envelopes. Nice and formal, you know, *official.*'

Suzi nodded.

That was January.

Two months later, and Suzi's been to a few more raves, there's that at least.

The first obstacle in the Genesis Sunset push for world domination was that they had to move venue; the warehouse for the New Year's Eve do turned out not to be owned by the geezer who provided the hand-written permission slip at all.

What a surprise.

The Police Chief popped round to inform the promoters that this chancer was not in a position to lease them the building given he didn't own it.

Not just didn't own it, Suzi later told Noble, but was a squatter and had no rights at all.

Just a blagger, the promoters shaking their heads in disbelief.

Takes one to know one, lads, Suzi said.

So it was all about finding venues that were usable –

No cunt's going to rent us a warehouse, after all, was the feeling.

And Genesis Sunset had a bit of class, a bit of quality, so they were on the sniff for something safe.

Minimal risk to the punters was the key phrase.

Not that it was especially about concern for the punters, more like if they're safe we'll be all right, legally speaking.

Suzi went along on a couple of the house-hunting expeditions, as they became known.

Crowbars and gloves, windows on latches, doors hanging from hinges, a plastic bag of poisoned meat in the unlikely event of guard dogs –

It wasn't an exact science.

After a venue was identified, Suzi sourced estate agent literature, property-for-sale lists, that kind of thing, any piece of paper with a logo on it.

'Truth is, Suzi,' they'd say, 'you're the only staunch person with a typewriter we know.'

So Suzi covered whatever was written on the piece of paper with a blank white card, photocopied it about ten times, then typed under the logo:

This document is to confirm the use of (Venue Address) as a location for private music-business functions. The project manager is (Name) who represents the (EMI, or Sony, or Virgin) recording company. For further details please contact this department during office hours only, or consult the project manager for a full brief of events. Yours sincerely, Special Projects Department Manager (EMI, Sony, Virgin) (Estate Agent)

'You've really crossed the line, now, Suzi,' Noble told her. 'Snide licences, theft, *fraud* even.' Noble grinned. 'Impersonating an estate agent is a serious crime.'

'I'm not sure where your scruples end and your morals begin, detective.'

'You may mock.'

'It's all above board, in its way.'

'Oh yeah?'

'The Public Entertainment Act of 1982.'

'OK.'

'Keeps us within the law. Licensing of private parties.'

'Us?'

'Deep cover. I need to be careful. Clearly.'

Noble rolled his eyes. They were in their usual drop spot: the saloon bar of the Prince of Wales pub.

'Might as well meet where it all started!' was Noble's reasoning.

Noble finished off his pint. Stood. As he shrugged on his leather jacket, he said, 'You do know why I wanted you inside all this, don't you?'

Suzi nodded, settled back into her seat, her own pint still half full.

Noble turned to leave. 'Why don't we have some progress on *that* next time, eh?'

What Suzi did next was take the envelope of money and deposit all its contents in a dedicated building society account. She hasn't – and won't – spend a penny of it.

And the other thing she's not going to do is feed Noble any info on where the significant numbers of ecstasy tablets consumed at the Genesis Sunset raves come from.

No one's told her, and she's not sure if asking is the done thing, really.

She imagines the networks, the connections, the legit/not-legit business associates –

There's a lot of overlap. No one wants to be too specific about their role in it all.

And, anyway, it likely wouldn't help her grievance against the Metropolitan Police if she were to end up doing any policing, inadvertent or otherwise.

The tablets are there, and it's a part of the scene, there's no denying that, and Suzi can do as much music journalism in inverted commas as she pleases but there's no questioning the relationship between the drugs and the warehouse.

Even across these first few months of 1989 Suzi's noticed the DJs seem more intent on delivering a musical experience that suits the drug experience.

She thinks her DNA may have been profoundly changed by this combination of experiences; she never used to like dance music much.

Now when she attends, she does so clean, and she enjoys it, just not until halfway into the next day.

What she has noticed is heavier people in the office of whatever warehouse they've blagged for the night.

Holdalls and suitcases full of cash rather than bin liners. Sharp-looking men in suits. Thick-necked men in suits –

It seems, to Suzi, that if this enterprise is going to last until the summer, then they need to go legit, or at least as close to that as they can.

At the same time, the muscle and the finance seem further and further removed from the vibe the promoters are trying to create.

'Membership scheme,' she hears one day. 'It's a loophole.'

The idea being some outfit called Pasha has found an east London venue and it'd be nice to do more than one night there.

Suzi's roped in for the narrative.

'We're going to make an announcement on the next flyer and we want to project good vibes so there'll be a short story on one side,' Suzi's told, 'the *hype*, and all the details on the other.'

'OK.'

'Young Minds Entertainment.'

'It's better than Wide Roy,' Suzi notes, to laughter.

The hype reads nicely:

The Genesis chapters began in a small, deserted London street, where three young minds pulled together in the hope of bringing a new light to the world of entertainment, calling this form of entertainment Genesis.

For the support and encouragement from you, the people who make everything possible, we are truly thankful. We offer to you our very own exclusive limited Members Club and promise the struggle will continue!

Summer of Love
Winter of Joy
Year of Genesis

She tells Noble all this, laughs with him at the aliases the promoters use when talking to the Old Bill – Claude Ferdinand, anyone? – laughs at the gullibility of your average dibble, to use Claude's word, when presented with a moody leasing arrangement, a thousand people, and a cocksure kid who thinks he's a pop star.

She tells Noble all this, which is telling him nothing, really, and she does nothing with his money, and she waits, she waits.

5

Lairy Dave

The acid squad down the pub.

What they're doing there is something Dave Jenkins has termed *networking*.

Dave the rave.

Networking meaning meeting like-minded professionals working in an overlapping sphere and sharing notes, *collaborating*.

Meaning lunchtime drinking and a fair bit of –

You didn't hear it from me, mate, all right?

Noble isn't too fussed about the terminology.

And he's tired, Noble, he's exhausted.

The theory is that society's interests are best served by a combined effort of law enforcement alongside other guardians of the peace.

In practice this means Jenkins feeding scare stories about drugs and violence, the horrors of the rave scene, to the national media.

They're installed in the back room of a grimy Wapping boozer, a pool table's green cloth stained brown, fruit machine chatter –

Dave the rave, Noble, and journos from three of the country's biggest-selling publications – two tabloid, one broadsheet – now working full-time in the area thanks to the move east from Fleet Street a couple of years ago.

Local colour is the theme.

They're talking about a certain DI Goddard who works out of Bethnal Green.

Jenkins bending ears, roaring –

'That cunt? Talking to him you have to bring your own eggshells, am I wrong?'

Red-faced and panting, the journos laugh.

Goddard is known for being cooperative with the press, meaning he's a leak and/or a pushover.

It's clear that Jenkins doesn't hold him in the highest regard, and Noble's not sure why not.

Noble watches spit fleck in the corners of mouths, lukewarm lager crawling down throats, filling bellies, heads swimming –

'I mean,' Jenkins goes on, 'he's a bit bloody sensitive. It's not like he stuck his own head in the oven, is it?'

Jenkins laughs at this, loudly. Noble notes the journos exchange looks –

Noble thinking, who stuck his head in an oven?

Thinking, that Welsh scribe, *Socialist Worker*, Geraint Thomas –

'Be fair, Dave,' says Steve Sidney. 'It was pretty messy.'

'I bet it was!' Laughing and spitting, Dave is now, coughing and wheezing –

Steve Sidney smiles thinly.

Steve Sidney, Noble remembers, is the broadsheet journalist who covered the tragic accident that accounted for Geraint Thomas.

'Yeah, well, it wasn't pleasant.'

Jenkins finishes his pint and waves his empty glass. 'My round,' he says. 'Same again, darling!' he shouts at the hatch that opens into the main bar.

Steve Sidney presses on. 'Point is, Dave, Goddard ain't as bad as you'd have him.'

'No, he's a lot worse,' Jenkins concludes. 'Now turn it in and have another drink. You bloody lot have gone soft.'

'I'll bring them over,' Noble offers.

'Shorts too, all right, we're working, after all.'

Noble nods, shakes his head, smiles –

This lairy Dave performance is just that, a performance, and it works, puts a bit of distance between them on the task force and the Fourth Estate, makes the journos a tiny bit worried that old Dave here might be a loose cannon, and who knows what a loose cannon in the Met is capable of.

At the bar, waiting as the barmaid fills five glasses, Noble thinks, and not for the first time –

What am I doing here?

They're not exactly stopping the parties, after all, but they're not exactly *not* stopping the parties, neither.

They're not doing any of the heavy work – it's Territorial Support Group units that break things up, a new iteration of the discontinued Special Patrol Group, the heavy mob, an Inspector with a few vanloads – and it *is* heavy work, largely, there's not much to justify a task force of senior-ish detectives.

What happens is a rival promoter rings the hotline installed in Dalston nick and does the old anonymous tip-off routine, meaning one shuts down while another starts up.

This keeps the scoreboard ticking over and the headlines coming and everyone's happy.

Jenkins told Noble just the other day, 'This rate suits us for now, trust me, we don't want any more, not yet.'

'Not yet?'

'Not yet.' Jenkins sniffed, got right up into Noble's ear. 'Who gives a fuck about a bunch of kids having fun?'

Noble shrugged.

'We need them to keep on having fun,' Jenkins said. 'Until we know exactly where that fun is coming from. You know what I mean?'

Noble does know.

He's working the same angle himself, except Suzi ain't exactly coming through for him, not yet.

Jenkins doesn't know about Suzi, of course.

No one does.

Noble now listening to Dave the rave telling the little story he knows about the pub, the anecdote rolled out every time, Noble running it word for bloody word in his head as Dave's spiel unfolds.

'In 1811, right, the pub once again took on a new identity and became known as Town of Ramsgate, in which, of course, you now all stand. Ramsgate, as in the fishermen of Ramsgate who landed their catches at Wapping Old Stairs just down there.' Pointing at the door. 'And the fishermen of Ramsgate landed their catches at Wapping Old Stairs just down there to avoid the taxes not long earlier imposed higher up the river close to Billingsgate Fish Market, all the way up there.' Pointing at the other door.

'That right, Dave?'

'That is right, yes. Oldest pub on the river.'

'I thought that was the Prospect of Whitby.'

'You thought wrong, son. This one, this one here, 1545, known as the Red Cow, it was.'

'Named after a barmaid,' suggests Steve Sidney.

Jenkins likes that one. 'Very good, Steven.' He splutters and coughs, slaps his thigh. 'Very good indeed.'

'Funny 'cos it's true.'

'Give over.'

'Straight up.' Sidney points at the bar. 'You should ask *her*. She'll tell you. There's a leaflet.'

'Course there bloody is.'

The barmaid nods at Noble. 'There *is* a leaflet,' she says.

Noble smiles. 'I know. We've one framed back at the station.'

The barmaid laughs. 'Shorts, the usual?'

Noble nods. 'You know the drill.'

And she does indeed know the drill.

Three whiskies for the writers, two measures of tap-water vodka for the coppers.

'Don't drink too much, will you,' she winks.

'I'm doing my best, darling, believe me.'

'We all are, love.'

Noble grins. 'I'll see you back here in a minute.'

'Missing me already.'

Laughing, 'Now, now, settle down, I'm spoken for.'

'Lucky lady.'

Noble turns, addresses the back room. 'Sarcasm won't get you nowhere, sweetheart.'

Drily, 'So I've been told.'

Noble laughing. 'Toodle-pip,' he says.

He brandishes a tray, hands out the lagers, the shorts, the packets of crisps –

'Yeah, cheers,' says Dave, raising a glass. 'Your good health.' Giving each of them a look, a nod, tips it back –

The journos do the same with their whiskies, gasp and shudder, wince and smile –

'Full Irish that,' says Steve Sidney. 'Very healthy.'

Laughter –

Noble thinking, I've been on about my health a fair bit of late –

What with Lea's ongoing efforts to get herself pregnant.

Theirselves.

It's been a long year, disappointment-wise, already.

They're trying, what a terrible phrase that is, been trying since the very first day of this year, and it *is* trying, Noble thinks, sipping his drink, wiping his mouth, it is very fucking trying, what with all the cycles, the times of the month, what with all the moods and the needs, the constant fucking *needs*, and what's it all for, anyway, this whole palaver, which will pale into nothing when the little bugger eventually gets born, of course, Noble thinks, this is all nothing, *this* bit.

Thing is, it was his idea, something *he* wants.

At least he supposes he does.

Careful what you wish for –

With kids you can never know what it's really like until you have one.

And if you decide you don't fancy it, after all, it's a bit late.

It's a clever fucker, Noble thinks, evolution.

Only way to get good at parenthood, then, is to do it.

Bit like fighting, in its way.

Noble shakes his head, clears it, sniffs –

Jenkins announces, 'Right then, ladies, to business.'

The journos take out their pens, their notepads.

Jenkins says, laughing. 'And next time, don't use that line about "Ecstasy Wrappers", all right. They're pills, you plonkers, tablets!'

Scotland Yard.

Next day, and Noble's in with Chief Inspector Maurice 'Special' Young.

'There'll be a formal op,' Young says. 'Soon. Down the road.'

Noble nods. 'OK.'

'But it *will* happen, the formal operation.'

Noble thinking, the lady doth protest and all that –

'Point is, you're there for a reason, right, we've put you there for a *reason.*'

'I know, guv.'

'It's worth pointing out.'

'Yes, guv.'

'This thing you're doing' – waving his hands in the air now – 'is nothing, an illusion. We don't care about it, the thing you're doing, OK?'

'Yes, guv.'

'You will be placed in CIB2, Scotland Yard's anti-corruption squad, to investigate the most serious case of corruption in the Metropolitan Force in twenty years.'

'Yes, guv.'

'This is all off the books, you're still in SDS, effectively, it's another unique secondment on my authority.'

'OK, guv.'

'That work you did with your UCO, back in 1983, well, it's borne fruit.'

Noble thinking, it's about bloody time.

But this time perhaps it *is* an internal police investigation, an inquiry. I'll believe it when I see it, Noble thinks.

'The task force, guv, I—'

'You're still on it. And for form's sake you need to get involved a bit. And if you do, you're protected, and it might help too, in the longer term. Do you get my drift?'

Noble nods. 'Yes, guv.'

'You can see yourself out,' says Young.

Noble nods and Noble leaves.

First then, this need to get involved a bit. Young meaning: make sure you're one of the chaps.

Noble thinking, that shouldn't be too hard given Jenkins' approach, which is hardly on the subtle side.

Terry comes to you one day and tells you that the brothers want to see you.

'Again?' you ask.

Terry tells you they've had one of their ideas and you go, those boys and their ideas, eh, Terry, and Terry laughs and Terry tells you that this idea is a good one, or it seems to be, and you think back to the other ideas that the brothers have had over the years and the pattern has been all right, all told, they do the work, they keep shtum and you make money.

You've kept the brothers at arm's length since the strike in Wapping ended and the brothers are still using those East London Logistics vehicles to ferry their product across the three boroughs, as you've lately taken to calling your patch –

Newham, Tower Hamlets, Hackney.

To the manor born, you were, you sometimes think.

'You'll give me the gist, will you, Terry?' you ask.

Terry gives you the gist, and it doesn't sound like you've much to do, which is how you like the arrangement with the brothers and their schemes; in the end it's respectful to secure your blessing, is what it's really about.

What Terry tells you is that the brothers and their brothers are moving in on the illegal warehouse party scene, intending to use the excuse of free love and all that malarkey to shift some of their units.

The theory, according to Terry, is that running the parties creates layers of monopoly that means pure profit.

'Monopoly is the enemy of free trade, Terry!' you cry.

Terry wonders at this, the hypocrisy.

'I've my principles to think about!' you add. 'A principled man of business!'

Terry smiles. 'I'll tell them green light, shall I? Give them your blessing?'

'Do just that, Terry.'

You've read the papers, the hysterical national press, the fear our country's teenagers will be made permanently immoral thanks to this dance music craze, this drug –

And it occurs to you that you might be able to leverage some influence or other if you're clever about this.

'What we need to do, Terry, is arrange a sit-down.'

'Right.'

'A sit-down: get the Canning Town brothers in here and someone on the payroll up where they're doing these events, these concerts.'

Terry nods.

'And tell the brothers to do some maths.'

'OK.'

'How much do they stand to lose if a night goes pear-shaped.'

'Pear-shaped?'

'You win some, you lose some, Terry. How many nights can they afford to lose.'

Terry nods.

Noble in the kitchen, splashing wine into glasses, Lea softly crying, Noble saying it's all right, darling, nothing to worry about, sit down, here, have a drink, it's only the one, take the edge off, Noble massaging her shoulders, her sitting at the kitchen table, pasta sauce bubbling, windows steaming, Noble thinking, when did it all become about this, only this, nothing else mattering, the tiniest little setback triggering *this*, this despair, this fear, and all he really wanted was to be a dad, that's all, if it worked out, and if didn't c'est la vie, but it don't feel like that no more, it all feels a bit over the top, the desire, or something like that, a bit overwhelming, like they've set themselves up and whatever happens next ain't going to match the emotional toll of all this preparation, or whatever you want to call it, and Noble can't say nothing, not now, he's committed, and he ain't that bloke anyway, he's sure of that at least, he ain't going nowhere, no chance.

6

Killed by Babylon

Shaun sulking, Parker keeping an eye on him for the afternoon – again. Carolyn telling Parker, 'Look, he's depressed, course he is, and I need you to be patient. Please. I love you.'

No answer to that, of course.

Staring at the telly, daytime crap on, Shaun sullen and sofa-slumped, reaching into a bin liner of crisps and pulling on a two-litre bottle of pop.

'You sure you don't want a piece of fruit with that, mate?' Parker asks.

'You're still funny, hero.' Shaun not smiling.

'Suit yourself.' Parker levers himself up out of the armchair. 'Lovely day. What about a breath of it, a little walk or something?'

'I'm watching this.'

'Watching what?'

'Telly.'

'It's a repeat.'

'Well, I didn't see it first time round, did I?'

'If you say so.'

'I was inside, weren't I?'

Parker sighs. 'I don't think you were inside when this was first on, son, believe me.'

'Well, I've never seen it before, have I?'

'What's with all these questions, Shaun? Or are they rhetorical?'

'What do you think?'

'Yeah, well played, very good. You're still funny too, son, didn't lose your sense of humour inside then.'

Shaun chews and swallows, drinks. 'If you lose that you got nothing,' he says, finally.

Parker nods. He thinks that's probably true.

He also thinks there's got to be a better way than this, though, it's been a month he's lain here farting and eating, lip curled –

'What about your old friends from up the road?' Meaning Tottenham, meaning Broadwater Farm, meaning, the good old days. 'What's his chops? Anton, yeah? I bet he'd love to see you.'

'He could of seen me, but he didn't.'

'To be fair, there's some parents that won't have it, visiting and all that, bad juju.'

'He could of come on his own.'

'Yeah, and you could go see him on *your* own.'

'It's complicated. I can't go up there, not now.'

Parker nods. 'You're all right, you know you didn't do nothing, no reason not to hold your head high, believe me.'

'Yeah, you said.'

'What?'

'Believe me. You've just said it, twice now.'

Parker mutters, 'Give it a fucking rest, eh, just an hour or two, give me a fucking break.'

'What was that?'

'You heard.'

Shaun changes the channel, watches the adverts for a bit.

Parker sits back down in his chair. 'If you keep this up,' he says. 'You ain't gonna fit into your tracksuit.'

Shaun's fistful of crisps an inch from his face –

'Baby steps,' Parker says. 'I've got to see a man about a horse. Get dressed, come with me, we'll be back in half an hour.'

'Where?'

Parker smiles. 'Good boy.'

*

Suzi's at The Style Council rehearsals for a summer gig at the Albert Hall, the plan being to unveil the new deep house direction of forthcoming LP *Modernism: A New Decade*.

Weller's old mate Paolo Hewitt is providing Suzi with a few choice quotes on the influences, 'groups such as Blaze, Phase 2, and producers like Marshall Jefferson and Frankie Knuckles.'

Suzi nodding. *Everyone* nodding, in fact. Hard not to, given the drum machine.

Paolo Hewitt saying: 'Through their work, Weller has seen how contemporary RnB can be shorn of its increasingly slick nature and returned to its roots with a modern sound and feel. This is where he now wants to take The Style Council.'

Suzi holds a copy of the set list.

She doesn't recognise many of the songs.

She's pleased to see the puns are still in there:

'Mick's Blessings', 'Mick's Company', still funny –

It's a Mick's bag, she smiles, listening to Paolo Hewitt, not quite daring to make the joke to him herself.

Keith's there, behind some equipment, head down.

At some point, Suzi thinks, she'll go and say hello.

He won't believe that she wants to see him, wants to say hello, he'll tell her she's only talking to him in case he's got some inside track, which is partly true, she'll admit that, then he'll give her some inside track, then tell her not to write about it, and she won't, and they'll both part, a bit sadder, a bit relieved –

Paolo Hewitt is smiling and offering his hand, and Suzi makes a wry little remark about The Style Council film *Jerusalem*, and this ends their interaction nicely, and Suzi examines the set list and frowns at the stage, trying to work out which number they're playing, then folds the list and pops it into her handbag, and sighs, listens, she listens, really listens.

*

Shaun's started to accompany Parker into the HCDA office on Rectory Road on a pretty much daily basis.

Parker thinks having him there can't hurt, he's definitely keeping an eye on him this way, and the kid's doing some photocopying and filing, answering the telephone and making the tea, so it's a bit of a banker, this, for the old Curriculum Vitae, a definite head start when it comes to applying for gainful employment, not that that's the best way of selling it to Shaun, of course. The kid wants no thought of his future, he's made that clear.

Back to school? It ain't easy with the previous – Parker knows all about that – but vocational college or something like that might be doable, and, again, this is doing no harm.

So that's Parker's game: get Shaun along on the basis of keeping Parker company and, by increments, turn him into a reformed and model citizen.

After a week or so of helping out, Shaun asks, 'What we doing here, exactly, hero?'

'We are continuing a long tradition of resistance to police injustice in Hackney.'

'Meaning?'

'We're a self-help group for the victims of police crime. We investigate allegations against the police, provide mutual support for victims, and coordinate campaigns against police injustice.'

'Where does it say that?'

'Here.' Parker throws over a leaflet.

Shaun examines it. 'But what are *we* doing here?'

Parker nods. 'Well, we ain't interviewing any prisoners, and we're not private dicks, are we, as they say across the pond. What we are is admin staff.'

'You what?'

'It means we're sorting out the records, the paper trail.'

'Right.'

'I'll give you an example.' Parker points at a lever arch file on a shelf. 'See that? Case One. Next to it, Case Two. And so on. You get my drift?'

'It's complicated stuff, hero.'

'We are recording and gathering all the important details regarding allegations against the police, instances of police misconduct.'

'When did you start sounding like a brief?'

Parker gives Shaun a look. 'Slow down, *chief*,' he says. 'Don't be cheeky.'

Shaun lifts his palms.

'Case One, for example. The allegation against the police is planting. The verdict is no evidence. And the outcome is a civil action against the police.'

'A result then.'

'One–nil us.'

Shaun smiles.

'Case Two, not so good. The allegation against the police is planting and theft, but the verdict is a conviction, and four and a half years for our man at Her Majesty's pleasure. Case Three, planting, no evidence, no outcome. Case Four, corruption and threatened, the verdict is another conviction and a two-and-a-half-year stretch for our fella. I can go on. And it will go on.' Parker makes a face. 'So you get my drift now, then?'

'I think so.'

'Good boy.'

'So that's what I'm copying, then, records?'

'Yep.'

Shaun nods. 'Cup of tea?'

'Thought you'd never ask.'

Parker watches as Shaun disappears round the corner to the kitchen.

While he's gone, with the kettle hissing and steaming, Parker gathers photocopies of recent file additions.

He places these in an envelope.

He places the envelope in his backpack –

Off to see Noble first thing.

Shaun calls out, 'You want sugar?'

'Three, please!' Parker yells. 'It's the afternoon, after all!'

When Shaun comes back from the kitchen, Parker tosses him a book.

'Have a gander at this,' Parker says. '*This* is what we're doing here, son.'

The book is a new publication:

Policing in Hackney 1945–1984, A report commissioned by The Roach Family Support Committee, Produced by an Independent Committee of Inquiry.

'You remember Colin Roach?' Parker asks.

'Yeah.'

'Well, this is what you might call community action. Read what it says on the inside cover.'

Shaun reads aloud:

'We believe this document is important. It is certainly unique: to our knowledge, it is the only study to collate so extensively the experience of the policing of one community. Yet, although a specific study in that sense, we also believe it is of much wider significance, touching as it does on the ever more crucial issue of the policing of the inner-city.'

'Very eloquent,' Parker says.

'So what? Everyone knows what happened to Colin Roach.'

'And what's that then?'

Shaun shrugs. 'He was killed by Babylon.'

Parker sniffs. 'Yeah well. Look, give it here.'

Shaun hands back the book. Parker thumbs pages.

'Hang about,' he says. 'Here it is. Listen: "The Report presents a wealth of evidence, independently collected and fairly summarised. It will strengthen the political will of people in Hackney and elsewhere not simply to accept as gospel what those in power say and do, just because they are the powerful ... In the absence of a public and official duty to discover the truth at whatever cost, it is at least some comfort that ordinary people are still willing and able to take action for themselves."'

'Who said that?'

Parker reads again. 'Professor Stuart Hall, Adviser to Independent Committee of Inquiry into Policing in Hackney.'

'And you think this will make a difference, then?' Shaun asks, hopefully.

Parker considers this.

He doesn't know, if he's honest.

But the book is in his hand, and that alone is a triumph of something, though of what he's not exactly sure.

He smiles at Shaun.

'Well, it ain't gonna hurt,' he says.

7

Spoon feeding in the long run teaches us nothing but the shape of the spoon

4 March, lunchtime

Mrs Thatcher is in the Connaught Rooms in London preparing to talk to journalists, preparing to make a speech at the Conservative Local Government conference. She is thinking about local elections, about privatised and state industries, about local government, the community charge.

It feels, she thinks, presently, that she's *always* in a room preparing to talk to a journalist.

Always having to speak to defend herself, her policies, her government, to justify what are, she thinks, quite reasonable approaches to government, to running the country.

She thinks didn't they vote for us to do exactly that?

She inspects her handwritten notes.

As it always feels that she is preparing to talk, it also feels that it's always she, Mrs Thatcher, who ends up doing all the bloody writing and the bloody note-taking, all the bloody *work*.

How hard is it, she thinks, more and more often these days, to write a bloody speech?

It's not often she swears, not even in thought.

They – all the bloody speechwriters and aides and staff – they all call her mother when she's not around.

Mrs Thatcher sighs and inspects her notes, her handwritten notes.

She inspects her notes and wonders about the community charge, again, this poll tax, and the wisdom of it.

She shakes her head. No, there is wisdom, there is sense, there is always sense in her policies, in her governance. She mustn't let herself doubt *that*.

The community charge will make every Council accountable, is the point.

And this is why Labour campaign against it.

It is the fairest system of paying for local government that we will have ever had.

She knows this, Mrs Thatcher, believes this.

On average 75 per cent of money for local government comes from the taxpayer and businesses.

And on top of this equitability, for the first community charge, 9.5 million people will secure a rebate because they can't afford to pay. Half of those will pay nothing.

Something else Labour wants to believe isn't true.

Her notes are clear:

The times require a new kind of Council.

Councils who make it possible for others to exercise responsibility in the provision of local services & jobs.

Councils which welcome enterprise and work with the private sector to deliver better services.

For as E.M. Forster said, spoon feeding in the long run teaches us nothing but the shape of the spoon.

May I thank you for your stewardship – may it be renewed and extended in May.

She looks back at this last line, the word *stewardship*.

It's a word she likes, a word that feels right, a word that represents her –

Stewardship: the careful and responsible management of something entrusted to one's care; stewardship of natural resources.

Entrusted to one's care –

Natural resources.

Yes, she thinks, quite so.

[Independent Radio News Archive: OUP transcript, 4 March 1989]

IRN Journalist

As is her custom, Mrs Thatcher went for attack as the best mode of defence and she admitted plainly and clearly that the line – her line that is – does need a bit of defending just now.

MT

I know that the subject of privatisation of water has not in fact been handled well or accurately.

IRN Journalist

Of course, said her aides, this is an attack on media not ministers, but as Mrs Thatcher and her aides know perfectly well, the media go for the best and the pithiest lines, so if they're getting them out of the opposition rather than the government, whose fault is that one may ask? Mrs Thatcher, one suspects, has come to her own private conclusions. Certainly she set out to rectify any deficiencies there may or may not have been on the part of her team by providing plenty of bullish bites of news herself, like this one about her comrades who begin at Calais.

MT

France has a socialist government. That socialist government nationalised things left, right and centre. There's one thing it dare not touch: water. Water is in private hands and they dare not touch it because the standard of efficiency excels *anything* which they could have as a nationalised industry.

IRN Journalist

A gesture of any kind of solidarity between Mrs Thatcher and any kind of pinkos, especially French ones, is indeed a rarity, proof positive that she knows she's got a fight on her hands. However, the tone varied from the conniving we've just heard to the soothingly reassuring. Private water is nothing to worry about, she purred, in fact really it's nothing new.

MT

Twenty-five per cent of water has been provided privately for a very long time *indeed*. There is nothing new about it, it's as old as the hills or very nearly. The hills are older than ... well there were private water services when the hills were created, *[laughter]* but 25 per cent of water services have been provided privately for ages so there's nothing new about it.

IRN Journalist

However, for those good loyal Thatcherites who recognise the value of sound money and notice when their bills go up, Mrs Thatcher reverted to her customarily confrontational mode.

MT

Now it's going to cost money. Of course, we also have to get the nitrates out of the water, which is a comparatively new thing because of the run-off from the fertiliser. You simply cannot have higher standards without it costing money. That increased cost is not due in any way to privatisation. Privatisation will be more efficient. That increased cost is due to higher standards.

IRN Journalist

And it's dishonest of Labour to pretend otherwise, she added. Still worse for the government if the punters get to believe it and, given the Tories relatively flagging state in the opinion polls, Mrs Thatcher's clearly decided that now is the time for all good men to come to the aid of the party, and if they fall down on the job, it's down to the good woman.

8

Ark

Law is good, law works.

Law clarifies, cuts through, and captures the essence of the evolutionary spirit –

Thinks Jon Davies, smiling to himself, how clever I am, he thinks –

The Gordon Gekko of local government, then.

Borough Solicitor and pestered by Labour councillors about what to do should Hackney residents decide not to pay the poll tax.

'A party that believes it will be soon in power, and responsible for legislation, cannot repudiate obligations under the law. You cannot argue for the rule of law when the right people are in charge, and have the luxury of picking and choosing when they are not. The party which takes this course forfeits.'

Godfrey Heaven sent this helpful quotation in a memo to Jon not long ago, timed to coincide with the national demonstration against the poll tax in Glasgow when 20,000 people shivered through the rain, chanting.

'Break the law not the poor, Jon,' was Godfrey's sign-off.

It's a headache.

Day after the Glasgow demo, another note from Godfrey:

'We cannot afford to wait three years for the next Labour government, because we need a mass campaign against the poll tax to make sure we get a Labour government.'

Hear, hear, the sign-off this time.

Jon in his office, hearing whispers of a march down the road in Walthamstow.

He thinks it doesn't affect him, wrong council, and realises that it's reached that point already, work defined by role not by value or importance.

A sad state of affairs; the beginning of a career in management.

He should ask Godfrey what he thinks.

Godfrey who keeps sending these notes. Today, from Prime Minister's Questions, apparently:

'When water is privatised, the duty of regulation and policing the standards of water and of rivers will come either under the National Rivers Authority or under the Director General of Water Services who will also be able to control the prices. That will be a great advance in addition to the extra efficiency that we will get from privatisation. It will be a good deal for the consumer.'

Godfrey signing off in his enigmatic way again:

'If you build it, they will come.'

And then:

'Two by two.'

Jon's been receiving more letters about water, or lack of it.

He hasn't visited the estate up by the Leaside Project yet, but if the correspondence is anything to go by then the drought is still on and the taps still off.

He looks at his diary. There's nothing urgent in it all morning. He sniffs, nods. He stands, shoulders on his suit jacket and clips his trousers. He locks his office and heads down the stairs. His heels click and echo. Ever since he started working here some fourteen years ago, he has considered this click, he has considered this echo.

As he's noted many times, it's the click and echo of institutions, of court, of power, of public baths, of head teachers' offices, of empty warehouses, of textile factories, of unfurnished council flats, of underground car parks –

He thumbs the code into the door, the door that takes him down into the underground car park. He unlocks his bicycle.

As he does every day, he bicycles up the ramp from below Hackney

Town Hall and turns left, past the Britannia pub, past Graham Road, past the old Woolworths, and then left again, past Hackney Central station, past the disused toy warehouse, past the pet shops and knock-off white goods stores on his right, and he circles round towards Hackney Downs before turning right past the Pembury Tavern and up Pembury Road, the Pembury Estate still flanking either side, still looking ominous and vast and warren-like. He carries straight on past the Seven Sisters pub, down Cricketfield Road and past the Cricketers pub, the West Indian takeaway to his left, and then out onto Lower Clapton Road, and onto the Lea Bridge Road roundabout, taking a right towards Walthamstow and down to the canal and onto the towpath by the Prince of Wales and then north as far as he can go, right up to the edge of the private industrial estate, where he crosses the footbridge over the canal and to the marshes, stretches his legs, the air crisp, the sun streaky, the Anchor and Hope, the Robin Hood, Springfield Park, the Leaside Project all on the other side, flashing by –

Back to the other side again, over the bridge by the rowing club –

And then he heads south, back past Springfield Park, back past the Robin Hood, back past the Anchor and Hope, to the Leaside Project fences and gates, the barbed wire and security portacabin, beware of the dog and smile, you're on camera!, which he skirts, off the towpath and onto Bakers Hill, wriggles through a car park onto Leaside Road, under the railway bridge, past the warehouse where they had that New Year's Eve party, the Leaside Project fences now on his left, Jon slides onto Riverside Close, slows down and finds himself on the low-rise council estate where the letters have come from and he thinks, Christ, the lawns look a bit parched.

Then again, they're so close to the canal you could just dip your watering can. Bit murky though, to be fair, Christ knows what's in there, that old game Jon and Jackie used to play walking to the pub –

Bike, shopping trolley, boot, fishing rod, football, plastic bag

Then one day they pulled Jon's neighbour Shahid Akhtar out of the murk and the game wasn't quite so funny.

Jon examines the first letter, reads the sender's address on the back of the envelope.

He looks up, looks down, looks up –

There it is.

He identifies the house, wheels his bicycle towards it.

9

Black boys on mopeds

Ayeleen. Every weekend and every evening I work in Uncle Ahmet's new place, another café-bar but this time on the Lower Clapton Road, opposite the pond, just down from Chimes nightclub, and we're doing what Uncle calls 'brisk business', and he keeps it open late for the after-party kebab trade, a takeaway counter as you go in through the door, the restaurant seating at the back, fast food, but *quality*, he says, but he won't let me work late, 'too dangerous, darling' – shaking his head – 'black boys on mopeds.'

'Cousin,' Mesut tells me. 'That's my shift for a *reason*, yeah, you get me?'

Lauren snorts at that. 'Big man, yeah? Please.'

Mesut shifts his weight from foot to foot, and I see him blush, blush just enough for me to see, Lauren won't notice, but he's smiling too, knowing Lauren is always the same, always chatting shit to him, to Uncle Ahmet, to me –

Just about the only people she's not chatting shit to is customers, so Uncle Ahmet puts up with her.

That and of course 'cos she's my best friend and what chance me leaving to go and work somewhere else if she does, a pretty good chance, he knows that, and that'll leave *him* well in my mum's bad books so here we are.

'Customer service, girls! That's what it's all about!' Uncle announces.

'This is what I'm telling you, Uncle Ahmet, customer service.' This is Lauren, reminding him: 'I'm blessed! It's a gift I'm blessed with. You say one thing you want us to sell this week, drinks, food, whatever it is, and I can guarantee you that on my shift, on our shift, we'll shift it.'

Uncle Ahmet claps his hands. 'A challenge!' he says.

And he disappears into the kitchen to find something to add to the menu.

Mesut's saying now, 'And on *my* shift, you girls won't be here.'

'Like you said, Big Man.'

'No, *you* said that.'

'Implied, Mesut, it was *implied*.'

'Well don't imply me, yeah, say what you mean.'

I'm shaking my head now, laughing, wiping down empty tables, mid-afternoon it is now, and quiet.

'What I'd ask you, Mesut, is where you are when it kicks off up the road.'

Mesut opens his palms, puffs his chest. 'I'm here, that's where I am.'

Lauren looks serious, impressed. 'Like security, you mean, protecting the family business?'

Two of the cooks bring out all the onions and peppers and chillis and salad and tomatoes and all the rest of the prep for the takeaway counter, breads already sliced and wrapped in paper, chicken skewers and lamb skewers and pork skewers in trays covered by cling film and foil, and they line up the veg on the counter and make it presentable and slide the meat into the fridges beneath.

I see them listening, and I try and catch the younger one's, Tariq's, eye but he's too smart, knows you can't take the piss out of the boss's fam, whatever silliness there is and however much it might be justified.

'There are,' Mesut explains, 'several places in this family business which might be vulnerable to attack, to violence, and to crime.'

Lauren nods solemnly.

'Think about it,' Mesut says. He counts with his fingers. 'One: till. Two: office safe. Three: customers. Hear that? *Customers*.'

'Customers,' Lauren nods.

Mesut's got his palms open again. 'A precious commodity. And we protect precious things.'

Tariq is turning the meat for the doner kebabs, making adjustments to the heat, cleaning out the grease tray – and I can see he's biting his lip, trying not to laugh.

Lauren says, 'We protect our commodities.'

'Business, Lauren, that's what business is.'

Lauren smiles. She starts to say something when Uncle comes back from the kitchen clutching a tray of what I think is dondurma.

I know it is, in fact, as I know what Uncle is about to say.

'Lauren, a challenge. Dondurma, battered dairy ice cream.'

'Ice cream, Uncle Ahmet. Easy peasy.'

'Wait, my darling, listen to this.' Uncle waves a piece of paper, the tray in one hand, wobbly, he might drop it, I'm thinking. 'Here is your challenge,' he says. 'You sell it and you *describe* it when you do, understand, my darling?'

Lauren nods.

He puts the tray down on the counter and reads.

'Dondurma. Traditional Turkish ice cream. Famous, as the purveyor of this particular ice cream, is wont to joke with customers when he or she sells it. The most traditional essence is damla sakızı, or, for western palates, we can translate this as, wait for it: gummy bears. In Greek society it's known as the Tears of Chios. Both refer to the mastic taste obtained from the mastic tree.'

'Sounds delicious.'

'A challenge, Lauren! You are blessed. I think this is what you told me.' He pulls a spoon from his pocket. 'Now taste it!'

Lauren's looking dubious, bit like she does when she doesn't fancy doing something, like it's physically a little bit repulsive to go there, do this, talk to that person, like an inconvenience to Lauren might actually make her sick. She's always been like that.

'Thanks,' she says, taking the spoon, not meaning it.

'Blessed!'

Mesut has his arms crossed and a look on his face that says, who's laughing now, Lauren, and she gives him a look, sticks her tongue out and says –

'Cheers.'

Everyone sort of waits for her like she's about to do some athletic feat or a magic trick or something, and I'm looking at Uncle and he's grinning, and I think this clown act of his, it's new, isn't it, and why, exactly, is he always playing the fool, 'cos he is, ever since we moved on from the place in Stoke Newington, ever since it was obvious we weren't getting the licence back, ever since then really, he's been acting a bit of a wally, at least in front of me, in front of the staff.

He always made such a big fuss of being the astute businessman, and he must still be, so what is it about, this change?

After we watched that film round her mum's, Lauren said Uncle used to be like Gordon Gekko and now he's more like Del Boy, but she didn't mean nothing by it.

I mentioned it to Mum the other day and all she said was, 'Protecting himself, Leenie, that's all. That's what he's doing. Protecting himself.'

I don't really know what *that* means, but I suppose if you're not ambitious, you'll never be too disappointed, which is one way of going about things.

I smile thinking about that now and thinking about what Mesut said, protecting our interests.

Then Lauren has a spoonful of the dondurma in front of her, and I'm laughing, and then the bell goes as the door opens and that black boy who used to come to Stoke Newington, used to pick up there, chat with us a bit, what's his name, Shaun, that's it, Shaun walks in, and I think –

Bloody hell.

Lauren sees him, but she's got a gobful of traditional Turkish ice cream, and she snorts and it's up her nose and she's coughing, and Uncle says, 'Perfect sales pitch, Lauren!'

'Hello,' I say to Shaun. 'I remember you.'

His eyes dart around the room. 'Yeah?'

'Yeah, course.' I smile. 'You eating?'

He nods.

'Staying here or takeaway?'

'I'll stay, if that's all right.'

'Be our guest,' I tell him and show him to a table in the corner.

'Nice spot,' he says. 'Like the old place.'

He's right.

The decor in the restaurant is lifted straight from it, the climbing plants like vines, the pictures on the walls, paintings of Turkish land-scapes, old photos of family, even the furniture – wooden chairs and chipped tables – *authentic*, Uncle says, by which he means old and dif-ficult to clean, but it does still feel like a restaurant and a lot of these kebab shops really don't.

'Formica and plastic you will never meet in my establishment!' he announced, me cursing over a washing-up bowl and dirty flannel. 'Elbow grease, Ayeleen!'

Lauren hisses at me. 'Leenie,' she goes. '*Leenie*, look who it is.'

'I can see who it is.'

She nods at him. 'I'll let you get his order, shall I?'

I smile.

She raises an eyebrow. 'I'll take that as a yes then.'

'Yes then.' I give *her* a look. 'You go and clean that cake off of your face.'

I take Shaun a plastic menu. 'Same food, basically, as the last place, plus doner kebabs.' I point at the sweating meat, Tariq still tending to it, that's what he calls it, *tending*, like it's a flock of sheep and not a dead lamb upside down on an electric grill. 'They're good, fresh, you know.'

Shaun smiles at that. 'Fresh?'

I'm grinning, I can't help it. 'Straight off the boat.'

'I'll have a doner, small, lots of onions, some cucumber and lettuce, no tomato, and a portion of chips.'

'Chilli sauce?'

'Go on then.'

'It's spicy.'

'Do you have it on yours?'

'I have it on everything.'

'Then yes, please.'

I take the menu. 'Coming right up.'

I give Tariq the order, who slices meat, then prepares the pitta, shakes the fryer, sets the chips going.

Lauren's back from the bathroom, smirking. 'Well?' she says.

'Well, what?'

'Well, what, is my question, Leen.'

'How long since we seen him, you think?'

'Got to be Stoke Newington. Never saw him nowhere else, did we?'

I shake my head.

I go back over to his table. 'You want something to drink with the food?'

'A Coke.'

I nod, go over to the fridge, take out a bottle, then fill a glass with ice, pour, take it over to him –

'Bottle?' he says. 'Classy.'

He takes a sip, smacks his lips, really enjoying it, I think.

I say, 'Looks like you've never had it before.'

'Not like this,' he says. 'Been a long time I ain't drunk it in a glass, with ice, in a *restaurant*.'

If he's taking the piss, I don't feel it.

I smile. 'Glad to be of service.' Tariq waves me over. 'I'll fetch your dinner.'

'I can't wait.'

I watch Shaun eat.

He's quiet, methodical, good manners, uses his hands, but delicately, uses his knife and fork too. Wipes the plate clean of chilli sauce with pitta bread.

Lauren's in the office with Uncle Ahmet talking about the ice cream, the *strategy*, apparently, and there's no one here, not at this time.

When he's finished, Shaun leans back in his chair, whistles low, sighs.

I'm about to go over and clear his plate, but the bell goes again, and I turn, and an older man comes in.

'I'm here to see Ahmet,' the man tells me. 'You can tell him it's Marlon.'

I see this Marlon look over at Shaun, and I see Shaun look at him, and I see them both do a double-take.

There's a look in Shaun's eyes, they widen, then he smiles, but he doesn't look exactly happy.

I see this quickly, but before I can say anything, Uncle is bustling out from the back, Lauren behind, and he's dropped the act, and he says to this Marlon, serious, 'Let's go to the office.'

I watch Marlon wink at Shaun as he goes past. 'Bon appetite,' he says.

'You're supposed to say that *before* a meal,' Lauren mutters.

10

Get involved

Suzi hasn't been spending too much time with the Genesis crew but it's no bad thing as she *has* heard reports of their parties being busted, it's happened a few times already.

Suzi wonders if the bubble hasn't burst.

Then she gets a call with a date and a place and an invitation.

'Come down,' she's told. 'Get involved. Write about us. This one is not to be missed.'

Suzi thinking, oh go on then.

'Acieeed!' Yelling down the phone, laughter.

Suzi hangs up, makes a note of the particulars.

It's not a Genesis party, some new mob, apparently, but they'll all be there.

Noble at his desk.

Doing nothing, nothing doing.

This is Noble trying to get involved, as he's been instructed by Chief Inspector Young. Get involved. It shouldn't be too hard. Jenkins is as bent as a nine-bob note, that's as clear as day, but Noble ain't sure *where* exactly, how. Jenkins is on the sniff for something, but who is he working with, and until Noble knows any of this, it's pretty difficult to get involved.

The overtime scam is a non-runner, that's for sure. With those half-wits Johnny Bond and Barry Fife doing the paperwork, there'll always be an excuse:

It's a fair cop, guv, I only went and wrote the wrong time. I can't read a digital watch.

No, it's not enough. And as for seeing Jenkins and the lad they nicked and their exchange over an empty sports holdall, there's nothing there neither:

Returning personal items upon release.

Noble at his desk doing nothing.

Fife reading the newspaper at his.

Bond snoring in his chair, hands behind his head, feet on the desk, yellowing stains under his arms, white shirt straining –

Lunch: three pints at the White Hart and a hand job across the road at the Thai massage place.

No wonder he's tired, Noble thinks.

Fife's phone rings. He answers it, talking too quietly for Noble to hear what he's saying, and after a minute, he hangs up. Then he stands up, stretches, yawns, nods at Noble.

'You wanna coffee?'

'Not after three p.m., Barry, ta.'

'Suit yourself.' Fife shoulders his way into his jacket, indicates Bond. 'I'll leave you in charge, shall I?'

Noble laughs.

'Need anything from the outside world?' Fife asks, not waiting for Noble's answer.

Noble watches him leave. Bond snores on. The room getting that odour again.

Noble rolls his neck, cracks his knuckles –

Then a voice in his ear:

'You're nicked, me old beauty.'

'All right, Dave?'

'Pukka. You?'

Noble indicates the room. 'Slow.'

'Well, that's about to change, son. Get your coat, you've pulled.'

'Eh?'

'Come on, we're going out.'

Noble stands. 'Where we going?'

'A meeting.'

Noble shrugs on his coat. 'What sort of meeting?'

'A meeting with the Queen, what do you bloody think?'

'Keep your hair on, I was only asking.'

Jenkins tosses Noble his car keys. 'You're driving.'

'Where to, guvnor?'

'Wapping.'

'Wapping? Not that old pub again.'

Jenkins shakes his head. 'Intelligence, DC Noble, we're acting on intelligence.'

Noble points at Bond, now drooling. 'Shouldn't we bring him with us then?'

Jenkins sniffs. 'Best idea is you don't tell either this clown or his bum chum fat Fife about our meeting at all, all right?'

Noble nods –

Get involved.

11

You do what you can

On the Riverside Close Estate, Jon Davies looks at a third envelope, double-checks the address and, for a third time, wheels his bicycle to the front door of a house that has quite clearly, and not long ago, been vacated.

Jon pats his jacket pocket: three more letters, all addressed by hand, typed text inside.

Jon locates each of these three addresses – it's a small estate, low-rise, tidy, canal-side and family-friendly, it looks like – and quickly visits each to find the same thing:

Empty, and apparently recently.

In each of the letter boxes of these three addresses is a communication.

Jon scans the leaflet.

It has been prepared by a water management infrastructure company calling itself Thames Water.

Jon thinks, privatisation hasn't happened yet.

Yet clearly being the word.

Godfrey, Jon thinks, will have an opinion on this.

The literature concerns the building of what this company is calling the Thames Water Ring Main, which will 'carry drinking water from water treatment works in the Thames and River Lea catchments for distribution within central London and the surrounding area'.

Jon notes the confidence of this missive, the fait accompli.

The building of this Thames Water Ring Main has already begun, clearly.

But if privatisation hasn't happened yet, then who might be paying for it?

Jon reads the other side of the leaflet, does a double-take:

A connecting tunnel is under construction from Coppermills Water Treatment Works in Walthamstow to Stoke Newington, a little way up the canal.

Jon recognises a logo at the bottom of the page:

Compliance Ltd

They get around then, he thinks. He thinks about Geraint Thomas –

He doesn't recognise the names of the building contractors or other listed partners.

He notes no mention of the Leaside Project, despite its proximity.

Jon pockets the literature and looks around, thinking, what next?

The estate is quiet, but it's mid-morning on a weekday, it'd likely be quiet even without these recently vacated houses.

It's likely, in fact, designed to be quiet *all* the time.

Sand-coloured, one-up one-down houses, ample parking in marked spaces, greenery, a little yellow and dry admittedly, and private access to the towpath, which is currently under development and fenced off for now, though it won't be long, Jon's heard.

It's quite nice, really, Jon thinks. Well-established, it's been around for a good while, the estate.

So why have at least six families relocated?

Jon decides to walk the length of it, three horseshoes of houses, must be a dozen units *at least* in each –

Must be someone around.

He goes along the towpath side, gaps in the fence making the canal visible, and it does look low, Jon thinks, it does look *thick* –

Pipes, spaced at intervals of every fifty metres or so, trickle sludge.

It's not completely dry, then.

Jon hears birdsong, shouts and whistles from the football pitches across the canal, the whirr of bicycles along the towpath.

It is pretty idyllic here, he thinks. And idyllic is, *almost*, the right word for it.

Then, the sound of a car braking hard, a door slamming, a voice, loud –

Jon turns and realises it's he, Jon, that this loud voice is directed at.

'The fuck are you doing here?' the voice asks.

'I—'

'Well? Fucking answer me, cunt.'

'I—'

'You're from that fucking water company, I know you are, snooping around again—'

'I—'

Shouting now in the general direction of the estate –

'There's another one of them cunts from the water company! Come and have a look if you don't believe me, I said they'd be back!'

Front doors open, Jon hears, perhaps two or three.

'What's going on?'

'What's all this racket about, Ray?'

Ray, then, Jon thinks. Jon sees that this Ray has a steering wheel lock in his hand.

Ray says, 'I've come out to talk to this fella to find out how they're planning on mugging us off *this* time.'

Ray's wearing a suit, though his tie is at half-mast, flapping about, and his shirt is untucked. He doesn't look good, Ray, Jon thinks. His face is red and crumpled, collapsed in on itself, scowling. What's left of his hair is shaved to, well, about a millimetre of its life, and Ray looks a good three-quarters into his own, and it's not been a long or happy one, by Jon's estimate.

'Ray,' Jon says, his hands up, palms out. He takes a step towards Ray, a step towards the steering wheel lock.

A man in overalls holding a rake has joined them. 'Who's this clown, Ray?'

'Ray,' Jon says again.

'Water company stooge, is what this clown is, I expect.'

'You don't know then, Ray?'

'Listen, Ray—' Jon says.

'Well, let's clump him now and ask questions later, Ray.'

'I don't work for any water company, Ray.'

'No, we'll clump him after, I want answers to my questions, after all.'

'I'm not with the water company, Ray.'

'Well, I'll go and put this away then.' Meaning the rake.

Jon looks at both men, palms up again, makes a face to say, easy lads, pulls one of the letters and the Thames Water literature from his pocket.

'I'm from the council,' Jon says. 'I've come to find out what's going on here.'

'What's going on here?'

'Yes, exactly.'

'He's come to find out what's going on here, Ray.'

Ray sighs. 'I know, H., I heard him too.'

H., Aitch, Jon thinks.

H. says, 'So what is going on here, then?'

Jon nods. 'Well, that's why I'm here, H., if I may?'

H. shrugs. 'You may.'

'I've had letters about your water supply.'

'Too right you've had letters about our water supply,' Ray says.

'Did you write these letters, Ray?'

Ray shakes his head. 'No, I did not write those letters, or any other letter.'

'What about you, H.?'

'H. can't really write, to be fair,' Ray says. 'Can you, H.?'

H. shakes his head. 'I work with my hands, always have, never really seen the need.'

'No need for your life story, H.,' Ray adds.

'I'll go and put this away.' Meaning the rake. 'Back in a jiffy.'

Jon nods, smiles. 'I'm not from any water company, Ray.'

Ray nods. 'You look like you are, though, to be fair.'

'How's that then?'

'You're here. No one else ever comes.'

'How often they been here?'

'Three, four times in the last, what, let's see, last six weeks or so, I reckon.'

'And when did the water shortages start, Ray, roughly?'

'Have a guess.'

'Six weeks ago, or thereabouts.'

'Bingo.'

'And what did they tell you when they were here?'

'They told us about that.' Pointing at the literature in Jon's hand. 'And they told us there might be a little disruption, a little *temporary* disruption, yeah, that's what they called it, a little temporary disruption.'

Jon nods.

'Then they told us how we might go about buying shares in their company, the face on them.'

'OK.'

'*Then* they reminded us of our right to buy as council-housed residents and offered to help us buy and then sell our homes.'

Jon whistles.

'Then the water stopped working.'

'Six weeks?'

'Barely a drip.'

'And, what, some families have sold up and left?'

Ray nods.

'And you don't know who wrote me these letters?'

'If I knew, I'd tell you.'

Jon nods.

Ray crosses his arms. 'Now if I were you,' he says, reasonably, 'I'd fuck off before H. gets back wanting to give you a slap. He's a bit slow on the uptake.'

Jon nods. 'That's helpful advice.'

Ray gestures with his chin. 'That way's quickest.'

Jon gets on his bike, then gets on his bike. 'I'll be seeing you, Ray,' he says as he cycles away.

At home that evening, as he comes in the door, Jackie calls down to Jon that the kids have eaten and are getting ready for bed, then 'we're having a takeaway and watching a film, it's been a while!'

Jon shouts up the stairs, 'What film?'

'*Chinatown*,' Jackie shouts down. 'It's on the box and I've not seen it yet.'

Jon smiles.

Over the next week or so, Jon receives another four letters, handwritten addresses and typed text, just like the others, and he pops up to the Riverside Close Estate and checks the addresses, and each one is vacant, just like before, and he pokes around for half an hour and it's even quieter this time, and he doesn't see Ray or H., wonders which houses *they* live in.

But he does see the words *Compliance Ltd*, and this gets him thinking about Docklands and Wapping and old Chick, Jackie's cousin, who accidentally got involved with some heavy people and asked Jon to look into the legalities of certain land deals as well as the economic realities of the right-to-buy scheme, Chick ending up in hospital with his jaw wired shut and Jon wished a very happy Christmas by a very scary man.

Jon did what he was told, left it alone, and with his secondment in Bethnal Green coming to an end, it was easy to do so.

Now he thinks about the parallels, and he thinks about what Geraint Thomas was doing exactly, chasing a story for *Socialist Worker* about, what, property irregularities, was probably the gist of it.

So Jon decides to visit the town hall archives and dig out the newspaper coverage of Geraint Thomas' death.

There's not much, to be fair.

Well, Jon supposes, given the political leanings of much of the Fourth Estate, it's perhaps not a surprise that a journo for an agitating left-wing rag isn't exactly top of the pops on the obituary pages.

What Jon does note is that pretty much all of the coverage appears in a certain left-*leaning* broadsheet, and that the articles are all written by the resident crime correspondent, Steve Sidney.

There doesn't seem to be a great deal of investigative reporting, but it's respectful enough and just *sceptical* enough of the coroner's verdict of suicide to satisfy Jon that it's worth contacting this Steve Sidney.

Jon thinking about Colin Roach in 1983. Dead by gunshot wound in the foyer of Stoke Newington nick. Coroner's verdict: suicide, despite a good deal of evidence that suggested otherwise.

Jon was very pleased to see the report that the family had commissioned into policing in Hackney published as a book just this year.

Course, soon after this verdict, the jurors write a letter to Mrs Thatcher's new home secretary, Leon Brittan, a letter that explicitly criticises the police handling of the case, and specifically police treatment of the Roach family, especially Mr and Mrs Roach.

A week or so later, Leon Brittan – the youngest home secretary since Winston Churchill, in fact, Jon remembers – replies to the letter, indicating that it will be referred to the Police Complaints Board.

The Police Complaints Board. Hardly an independent inquiry, hence the Roach family-commissioned report.

Jon's not sure what progress since.

So, to Geraint.

Problem Steve Sidney recognises in his articles is the present and compelling evidence of suicide, as well as very little to suggest otherwise.

Jon does note that one of the articles states that a van was seen by neighbours in the area close to Geraint's flat at about the same time.

The company:

East London Logistics.

Steve Sidney doing some doorstepping then. The police certainly weren't.

In the next article, however, a clarification:

The van was engaged in a series of deliveries to local businesses, and the manifest confirms this, as do witness accounts at these local businesses.

At the end of each article, a number: Steve Sidney is happy to hear from you.

Bringing the mountain to Mohammed.

Jon scribbles this number into his notebook, then goes back to his office and calls it.

An answering machine.

Jon says, 'Hello, Steve Sidney. I'd like to talk to you about Geraint Thomas. I'm Borough Solicitor for Hackney Council and can be reached at the town hall. I knew Geraint, personally. I hope to talk soon.'

Jon hangs up.

It's not often he plays the Borough Solicitor/town hall card, but he figures most journalists are looking for an inside track of sorts, so it'd be an added incentive.

Couple of hours later and the switchboard puts through Steve Sidney, and an hour after that Jon's in the Britannia pub on Mare Street, next door to the Hackney Empire, a hop, skip and a jump from his office.

Not that Jon uses this pub much, murky as it is inside, pickled onions and tripe on the bar, a bit much, Jon thought all that palaver was safely in the past.

Then again, as his eyes get used to the murk, Jon sees it's not just old soaks with betting slips in one fist, halves of mild in the other, a short on the bar to go with.

No, there's a younger group, flashier, pinstriped and booted, lairy ties and loud laughter.

Maybe the tripe is for a ye-olde-east-end kind of vibe.

It's working.

Jon orders a pint and finds a quiet table near the door.

After a few minutes, a man comes in, orders a pint, looks around –

He sees Jon, nods, and sits down across from him.

'Jon Davies?'

'Steve Sidney?'

'Cheers.'

'Yeah, cheers.'

Steve Sidney sniffs. 'Nice in here.'

Jon smiles. 'You should see it first thing.'

'I bet the tripe is good then.'

'It walks in from the kitchen and climbs up onto the bar itself in the mornings.'

Steve Sidney laughs. 'No wonder it's looking so tired then.'

'Very good.'

They drink their drinks.

'Looking forward to the World Cup next year?'

'Not really,' says Jon. 'I'd rather West Ham won a throw-in than England win a match.'

'That's not very patriotic of you.'

'I don't feel very patriotic anymore. This season we didn't win much more than throw-ins, to be fair.'

Jon still with the hump at West Ham being relegated after eight years in Division One, nearly winning it only a couple of seasons ago. Jackie's told Jon to shape up about it more than once, but he's been stewing and has had a bit of a mood on for a few weeks, if he's honest.

'But you did?' Steve Sidney asks. 'Once feel patriotic?'

'Once upon a time.'

'Yeah, fairy tales do come true.'

'Be careful what you wish for.'

'Spoken like a true West Ham fan.'

'You're not one then?'

'Charlton Athletic.'

'Could be worse.'

'Yeah, Millwall was taken.'

Jon smiles. 'Right, now we've got to know each other, how about we talk.'

Steve Sidney nods. 'Let's.'

'You wrote a few pieces about Geraint.'

'I did.'

'Why?'

'Let's call it professional courtesy.'

'Slow week then, was it?'

Steve Sidney makes a face.

'I mean to say,' Jon adds. 'You're here, aren't you?'

Steve Sidney sighs. 'I am, yeah. I'm here because I'm tired. And I'm curious too.'

'I'm curious about your snooping, Steve. East London Logistics, specifically.'

'What about it?'

Jon opens his palms, nods. 'You know.'

And Steve Sidney does know, and he tells Jon about how, yes, he did indeed pop down to Geraint Thomas' neighbourhood to ask a few questions, and that was because a friend of a friend of Geraint's told Steve Sidney that he didn't think Geraint was the sort to take himself on a long walk off a short pier, and Steve Sidney learned a little of what Geraint was up to and thought, where's the harm?

Well, the doorstepping didn't achieve much exactly, and neither did talking to the police officers who were on duty the night of, or even the Detective Inspector, Goddard, who confirmed the self-checkout diagnosis.

'Apparently,' Steve Sidney tells Jon, 'young Geraint had something of a chequered relationship with the old booze.'

'Hard not to,' Jon says.

'Empty bottles of Scotch in the kitchen, very high levels in the blood, pretty much open and shut, is what Goddard told me, mentally unbalanced, has a few and takes the easy way out. Inside a gas oven.'

'And what about East London Logistics?'

'My editor sent someone else down there to follow up.' Steve Sidney shrugs. 'Which is when they got the clarification regarding the manifest, printed it straight after.'

'Your editor?'

'Yeah, and his boss told him, and *his* boss told him, I gather.'

'Professional courtesy, like you said.'

Steve Sidney finishes his pint. 'You want another?'

Jon nods. 'Why not?'

Steve Sidney goes to the bar and Jon thinks, I should go and have a word with this DI Goddard.

So he drinks his pint quickly and he asks Steve Sidney, 'Where's this DI Goddard based?'

Steve Sidney snorts, nods at the door. 'Up the road. Hackney nick.'

Jon smiles. 'I've looked in there before,' he says. 'Though it's been a while.'

And Jon goes straight up to Hackney nick, emboldened by his swiftly drunk two pints, and he asks to see DI Goddard, telling the duty officer that he's from the council and it's important and he's shown straight through.

Not that it does Jon much good.

'Coroner's verdict was conclusive,' DI Goddard tells him. 'It was reviewed, higher up.'

'Independently?'

'In a manner of speaking.'

'Bit like the Police Complaints Board then?' Jon offers.

'Case closed, was the instruction.'

'Instruction?'

'I'm sure you're very busy, Mr Davies.' DI Goddard stands.

Jon agrees that he is.

Walking his bicycle home later that afternoon, Jon reflects that he is very busy, it's true. He wonders about this, about how his life might have got in the way, regarding Geraint Thomas, regarding Chick too, come to think of it. Jon thinks that perhaps he's let himself accept things that he might have pushed harder against. In the end, he thinks, you're a parent, and there's a priority: and it's your family. There might not be any other way to look at it, he thinks. You do what you can.

12

East London Logistics

Noble parks the car outside what looks like an industrial estate, a glorified scrapyard.

Jenkins points. 'This is us.'

At the gate, Noble nods at two large men in suits.

One of them says, 'This way, Mr Jenkins. They're expecting you.'

Noble thinking, *Mr* Jenkins?

'Yeah, cheers, lead the way,' Jenkins says. Turns to Noble. 'Come on then.'

Through the gate and into a large forecourt.

Portacabin offices and warehouse space.

Shipping containers.

Vans parked in a line.

White paint covering old lettering, logos.

Noble makes out:

East London Logistics

A skip overflowing with building material.

'Right on the river,' Noble says. 'Aspirational.'

Jenkins grunts. 'Welcome to Wapping,' he says.

Their guide ignores this. 'Just down here.'

Into a warehouse hangar, eyes adjusting to the dark, an office to the left, three men sitting round a table, another man standing –

'In there.'

The door's open and they're ushered in.

'Gentlemen.' This is the elder of the seated men. 'Join us.'

He indicates two seats at the table.

'Terry,' he says to the man standing up. 'Will you kindly fetch our guests some refreshments?'

Terry nods and disappears.

'You'll know who I am,' the man says.

Jenkins nods. 'Course we do.'

Noble's not sure *he* does.

'Good.' The man pushes back in his chair and stands. 'I'll leave you with the brothers then. Important you know they have my blessing, that's all.'

Jenkins stands. Noble stands.

'Much obliged,' the man says, bowing. 'I do hope you enjoy our hospitality.'

He ushers Terry back in. 'Chop, chop, Terrence, everyone's thirsty.'

And then he leaves, this man that Noble doesn't know.

Terry's carrying a tray: a bottle of Scotch and four glasses.

There's a naked light bulb above the table, a filing cabinet in the corner, cardboard boxes, and bin liners full of something or other, spilling fabric and string.

Terry pours.

The brothers aren't smiling, but they're not exactly unfriendly either. They're both dressed in smart tracksuits, jewellery.

'Cheers,' one of them says. 'Your good health.'

Everyone drinks.

Terry's lurking in the shadows, Noble notes.

He sits tight, Noble, says nothing for now.

Jenkins says, 'Thanks for the invite, boys.'

'No problem. I think we can help each other out.'

'I think we can.'

The brothers look at each other, nod.

One of them says, 'We're doing security for an up-and-coming sound system, you know, warehouse parties, *raves*, all that.'

Jenkins nods. 'And you know what we're doing, of course.'

'We do,' says the other brother. 'And it'll suit us if one of these parties gets shut down, you know what I mean?'

Jenkins nods.

'There's currency in it,' the other brother says. 'And we need to lose certain elements of the competition.'

'OK.'

'We mean you don't nick any of ours, you follow?'

'I do.'

'There'll be plenty to choose from, we'll make sure of that. Plenty of product too.'

Jenkins looks at Noble, then at the brothers. 'Key thing for us is timing. We get there too early, and there's no result; too late, and there's nothing we can do.'

'The venue's perfect in that regard.'

'Go on.'

'A warehouse not far from here, just the other side of Docklands. Only one road in or out.'

'What about the meeting point?'

'Bit further east. There'll be a convoy, effectively, and your mob can wait out of sight until we give the word.'

'And you'll kettle the group you want lifted?'

'We're in charge of security, we can do what we fucking like.'

'Just make sure none of yours go down the tunnel.'

'We'll keep them out of it.'

Jenkins sniffs. 'And what do you propose we get out of this?'

The brothers look at each other. 'Two things.'

One of the brothers nods at Terry. Terry brings over a holdall.

'This is the first thing, a deposit, if you like.'

'OK.'

'Second thing is they'll have an awful lot of tablets, the people you'll be nicking.'

'We'll have to log some of them.'

'And you can sell the ones you don't to us.'

Jenkins looks at Noble. 'Sounds reasonable.'

Noble nods.

'You can use our connection up there in your manor, you know him.'

'Yeah, he does some work with us too.'

'Good. He'll be there on the night. Don't fucking nick him!' Laughing.

Noble thinking, Trevor?

Noble thinking, here we go then.

On the drive back to Dalston nick, Jenkins says, 'I'll bring you in once it's done, all right?' Patting the holdall in his lap.

Noble nods.

'Safer that way,' Jenkins adds. 'For you.'

Here we go then, Noble thinks.

Next thing Noble does is get on the blower and arrange a meet with Parker, usual spot.

Lunchtime at the Prince of Wales.

'Food in a pub,' Noble says to the barmaid. 'Whatever next, eh?'

'Stranger things have happened.'

'It's the future.' Noble gestures at the empty saloon bar. 'Though I don't see too many yuppies in here yet.'

The barmaid pours drinks. 'Anyway, we don't call it food. It's pub fayre.'

'All's fayre in love and football. What are the specials?'

'Crisps.'

Noble laughs. 'I'll be back to order the fayre in a minute.'

'Take your time.' She smiles. 'There's loads left.'

Lunch:

A pint and a ham sandwich for Noble. A pint and a mixed grill for Parker.

'You'll expense this, right?' Parker says, tucking in.

Noble nods, eyes Parker's plate.

Bacon and liver, two sausages, two eggs, mushrooms and a grilled half-tomato, onion rings and chips –

A thick-cut steak to add some class, Parker sawing away at it with his knife.

Parker says, 'Can't argue with this, guv, quality *and* quantity.'

'Her indoors not feeding your properly?'

Parker stops chewing. Gives Noble a look. Spears a sausage, works his mouth. 'Your other half expecting yet?'

'Don't be cheeky.'

'I'll be the first to congratulate you.'

Noble pushes a piece of paper across the table.

Parker wipes brown sauce from his mouth, wipes his hands on his trousers. 'What's all this then?'

'A party, the meeting point, the venue, dates and times.'

'What of it?'

'It's going to get turned over.'

'By you?'

'By us.'

'Interesting.'

'Yeah.'

'What do you want me to do?'

'You're going to be there.'

'A night out, eh? What a line manager.'

'You've said that before.'

'I meant it then too.'

Noble smiles. 'There's a link between the organisers and the Stoke Newington mob, and there's someone who connects them. And I reckon there's a link with that someone and what happened to your Trevor.'

Noble watches Parker for a reaction. Nothing, he stonewalls it.

'Right.'

'Any ideas?'

'Maybe.'

'See what you can find out.'

'Roger wilco, guv.'

'First thing is though, get yourself invited.'

Parker grins. 'Me? I know people, not a problem.'

Noble finishes his pint, stands, points at his ham sandwich. 'You can have that too, for your afters.'

Parker picks it up, uses it to wipe egg yolk and condiment from his plate, bites into it. 'Much obliged, guv.'

Noble shakes his head, smiles.

And the next thing Noble does after that is pay Suzi a visit. He gives her an envelope; he gets her report –

Of course, what she tells him is the date and venue of this party Noble knows all about already. And, no, the crowd isn't a political one, I've told you that before.

Noble doesn't tell her *anything*. Keep me posted, is the vibe.

Let's see what shakes out, he thinks, need-to-know basis, ignorance is bliss.

13

Customer's always right!

Shaun. After that first kebab, I was smiling the whole way home.

Ayeleen said, 'Come and see us again.'

Her mate Lauren giving me a funny look.

'Just remember,' she told me as I walked out the door. 'You have a kebab every day, you won't fit through *that*.'

Meaning the door.

'Lau-ren!' I heard.

'What?!'

Grinning, happy.

I went back two days later.

'You again.' That was Lauren.

'You liked the food then?' Ayeleen said.

I nodded. 'Something different today, though.' I pointed at the door. 'Yeah?'

They laughed and Ayeleen told me about their healthy options, a menu her uncle was designing to attract more women and families into the restaurant.

'Thing is,' she said, 'this place just *looks* different to the last one, it's less elegant, I suppose. Takeaway, mainly.'

The healthy option was pretty good.

Lamb shish, plain yoghurt, cucumber, onions –

No chips, though.

I thought about what Anton would think of that, no chips, you're having a bubble, bruv, no chips.

Lauren asked, 'Did you know we'd moved here then? Where you been?'

'Nah,' I said. 'I just moved here myself, living with my cousin now.'

'So it's a coincidence.'

'I like Turkish food, I come in.'

'Yeah, OK,' Lauren said to that, tutting, smiling.

Truth is, I saw Ayeleen and Lauren in Clapton a little while ago, after school, I suppose, and I watched where they went – I didn't follow them, just watched – so that's how I knew she was working there.

From the back, I heard, 'Customer's always right, Lauren!'

What I was doing when I saw them was walking.

I been doing a lot of that, walking, up to the office on Rectory Road helping Parker out, then walking, walking –

That day I seen them, I went to Hackney Downs, crossed the park and just kept going.

I knew about this place, Granny's, that was somewhere around there, Parker used to bang on about how the food was like my own granny's, and so I went looking for it, up by the pond, for something to do, really, and there they were, that's all, and I saw where they went, that's all it was.

It took me a few days to get my courage up to go in, though. I was nervous. I'd barely chatted to anyone except Parker and Carolyn, and I could tell they've been fed up of my moods.

It's difficult to say that you're feeling lonely, I've learned. Inside, it's not something you can even let yourself *feel*. I guess what you do is you say you're alone.

And I feel like I've been alone for a long time now, no friends, no school, no social life, just trying to keep my head down, that's what the fam is telling me, at least, just keep your head down, Shaun, things will look up.

'Let's have a look at one of them vocational colleges,' Parker keeps telling me. 'Apprenticing, that is, basically.'

'Doing what though?'

'Whatever you want, that's the point, you learn.'

'I don't know.'

He's doing his best, Parker. He said, 'Let's go and have a look at one, that's all I'm saying. Apply now, start in September, if you *want* to.'

'I ain't got much in the way of qualifications.'

'You've got enough.'

Which was sort of true. I did three O-Levels inside, passed them all.

'You just need a bit of confidence, that's all,' he said after that. 'Believe in yourself, son.'

'What, 'cos no one else will.'

'Oh, give over, Shaun.' He threw his hands in the air. 'Enough of this tiny violin business, yeah, you're in good shape, son, we'll go to the college and have a think, just that, a start, OK?'

I said, OK, and Parker set it up and picked up a brochure for me, and we're going and I'm thinking about the courses they got there and what I can do. Art, Craft and Design, I like the sound of, Sport and Fitness, maybe Motor Vehicle.

'You can't even drive, mate!' Parker said when I suggested that.

'You don't need to,' I sniffed. 'I got the grades.'

'The grades! To be a mechanic! You're having me on, son.'

'I ain't having you on, that's what it says.'

'What is the world coming to, eh.'

'This was your idea.'

'Yeah, I was thinking more, you know, give me that brochure.'

I watched him study it for a bit.

'See? Creative Media and Game Design. That'd suit you.'

'Maybe.'

'Or what about Catering and Hospitality? You like food, I think we've established that, and you could certainly mind your manners a bit better.'

'I don't know.'

Parker smiled. 'I'm joking, son, you do what you want.'

'I don't know whether, like Design, or something more practical, you know, Electrical, or Construction and Building Trades, Painting and Decorating.'

Parker taps a page. 'Plumbing, then, that's the badger. There's always work for a plumber.'

'Work with your head down a toilet.'

'Yeah, maybe.' Parker sighed. Nodded, looked me in the eye. 'You're right, son, you are absolutely right, but them are the choices, basically. What you need to ask yourself is where you want to work, where you want to spend your days, in a poncey office with a load of cunts who studied Media, whatever that is, or outside with your head in a motor or down a cement mixer.'

'When you put it like that.'

'I'm only joking, Shaun, I'm just playing devil's advocate, making you *think*.'

It did make me think, to be fair to him.

'If you were going to vocational college,' I asked Ayeleen, 'what would you study?'

Lauren snorted. 'Plumbing,' she said.

'Lauren.'

'Well?'

'Catering, cooking, something like that.' She pointed at the back. 'My uncle would then rope me into the family business and that'd be me.' She thought for a moment. 'Actually, he'd probably I rather did Business, become our accountant.'

'But you think this ...' I waved my arms about, at the restaurant. 'You think this is a good trade?'

'Trade!' Lauren laughing.

'I think it can be, yeah, course.'

'Food for thought,' I said.

'Very funny. You're funny.'

'But you don't wanna do it, right, get roped into the family business?'

'I'm roped in now.'

'I mean later.'

Ayeleen sighed. 'I don't really know what I want to do later,' she said.

'That's why I want to go college, find out, I suppose. Maybe that's what you should do.'

I thought if I did something in Catering and Hospitality, what's to stop me helping out here.

But I didn't say nothing then, maybe I won't.

Day of the college visit, Parker tells me to scrub up, put a jacket on, a tie.

'I don't have nothing, except my old school uniform.'

Parker gives me a look.

'I thought it didn't matter what I wear, is what they said.'

'Don't listen to all that rhubarb, son, you can borrow my suit.'

It went well at the college.

They showed me round, told me I had the 'credentials' with my three O-Levels, Parker showed them the references from the Hackney Community Defence Association and another one he said was a bit moody, but it'd do, headed paper, some friend of his who does a bit of import export, food and that, relevant.

Because what I've decided to do, I think, is the course in Catering and Hospitality, Culinary Arts, an introduction to the business, effectively.

'Do you want to be a chef?' they asked.

I told them I didn't know, but I thought so, and I wanted to find out.

'This is the course for you then,' was the feeling.

There was no mention of Feltham; it didn't seem like there was any need. I thought maybe Parker said something in advance or cleared it with them, I don't know, and he says he didn't.

'Thanks, hero,' I told him.

'And don't you forget it.'

After I sent the forms in, I told Ayeleen.

'That's wonderful,' she said.

From across the restaurant, Lauren shouted, 'We should celebrate.'

I looked at Ayeleen, shrugged.

'Our exams finish next month.'

'And there's a party happening! A big one near Docklands!'

'We're all going to go, you should come.'

I nodded. 'Yeah, all right, that sounds good, I'd like that.'

'It's a date!'

'Lauren!'

It felt good to be invited to a party, even if it is one of them big warehouse things and we'd just be going all together, it still felt good. Nobody's invited me to nothing for time.

'We can all get ready at mine, my mum won't mind,' Lauren said. 'You can come over when we're all made up, all right?'

'When is it?' I asked.

'July first.'

'Summer of love!'

'Pack it in, Lauren!'

'Good luck next week,' I said, meaning the exams.

'She won't need it!'

And little while after that I got confirmation: I had a place at the college to start in September.

We had a little party at home, Carolyn and Parker, some balloons and the ingredients to make a curry.

'Go on then,' Parker said. 'Get on with it, this is your first lesson.'

It went all right, I think.

The first time I saw Marlon since getting out, I felt a mix of sadness and fear – and relief.

Which is exactly what I told that screw who'd been friendly with me for a bit.

He was being kind, then, and he was talking about reoffending, about how so many do, and it's all down to the environment, he said, all down to *your environment*, which means the people you see in the place where you live, the people you can't avoid 'cos they're from the neighbourhood too.

But Marlon ain't from my ends, so I weren't scared of that, weren't too worried, really, about my *environment*.

What I told him was I was scared of seeing Marlon 'cos I didn't know what he'd want from me.

Sad 'cos it meant I was still in exactly the same place I always was.

Relieved 'cos, well, here we are then, I been waiting for this and here we are and what's next.

Course it wouldn't be my environment until Carolyn told me where I was going to live when I got out, all decided, family all in agreement, she said.

Just a matter of time then, weren't it, Clapton just down the road.

So I wasn't sad, not in that way, I *wasn't* in exactly the same place I always was, no –

But I was sad 'cos I was in Ayeleen's place that first time and I was happy to be there, to have found her again, and I couldn't have him ruin *that*, couldn't have him ruin that for me, that wouldn't be right.

He's said hello a couple of times after that, but nothing else.

14

Deep cover

Suzi's writing a piece. I'm *always* writing a piece, Suzi thinks. And there's something about this that feels reassuring – and something else that feels deeply sad.

A job's a job though.

This job: The Style Council's new direction and imminent Royal Albert Hall performance in early July.

Paul Weller remains staunch; Suzi's been looked after, she's been given access, *again*, and there's no sense of quid pro quo, no expectation of the position she's going to take –

There's never had to be.

She's always admired what they're about, is the point.

And, anyway, first and foremost, Suzi will always be thought of as a photographer.

Another sadness, it doesn't matter how much she writes, how many *pieces* she writes, she'll always be the bird with the camera in the industry's eyes.

Not the case with Paul Weller, she knows that, but she wonders how respected her pieces really are, on the scene, as it were, how many people dismiss them as fluff, essentially, a few good images and a bit of fluff to pad out the pages. Lifestyle vibe.

Maybe she's being hard on herself. Maybe she's not being hard enough. Maybe –

Maybe what Suzi is, is lonely.

Maybe that's what she's feeling, at home, alone, writing pieces: lonely.

Interviewing pop stars and going to gigs is only so satisfying when it comes to a personal life, a social life, a *sex* life, let's be honest.

She doesn't need *that* reputation on top of everything else she's coping with.

She smiles to herself: her next photoshoot and interviewee is Australian soap opera actor and teen heartthrob Jason Donovan, for *Smash Hits*.

Kiss and tell?

She shakes her head, smiles again: she doesn't need the money – or the aggro.

She stands, stretches, goes to her window, looks out at building sites reaching into the sky all across east London.

She pours tea from a pot, splashes milk, folds and twists her hair, pony-tailed, into a band.

The piece starts with a reappraisal of The Style Council's last album, *Confessions of a Pop Group*, which was not especially well received, and which has not sold well, not done the business the record label, Polydor, would have wanted.

And it's this anxiety that Suzi wants to address; it's an album that deserves a critical reappraisal.

It's really very good, basically, is Suzi's thinking.

She's just not sure they got the track listing right.

Suzi hits play on her Dictaphone, transcribes.

'There was a sense our time was up,' says Paul Weller. 'It wouldn't have mattered what we put out, it would have bombed. So we thought, if this is going to be our last time, we better make sure it counts.'

Disillusion post-Red Wedge, Labour's election defeat, Maggie's landslide –

Confessions of a Pop Group was the result of all this, representing the death of hope, in its way, no longer trying to effect change, instead writing about the state of things.

Not unreasonable, Suzi thinks, given the circs.

'A creative burst,' Paul Weller says, 'written as poetry then set to music. We were aiming high. We knew we were being ambitious, doing something new. We knew it might have consequences, might lose our audience but that wasn't a consideration. We had to do what felt right.'

'There was a sense that Santa doesn't exist anymore,' says Mick Talbot. 'How could we have been that naïve?'

Piano ballads and blue-eyed soul smuggling into the lyrics some pretty bleak messages.

'Iwasadoledadstoyboy': the title straight from *The Sun*, an actual headline printed in the newspaper.

'This was how ridiculous it had got, it was just pure propaganda for the Tories,' says Paul Weller. 'It felt like we were just another state of America. We no longer had our own voice. It didn't matter what we did or said, nothing would change. The rich would get richer, the poor poorer, it didn't matter what you believed in, it wasn't going to happen. We set out to document the dismal times but at the same time we wanted to elevate pop to an art form. Sometimes it's important to do that and I think we succeeded in both.'

Suzi thinks about these words, Paul Weller's words, and they give her pause for thought, as they often have, over the years.

We better make sure it counts
It didn't matter what we did or said, nothing would change

Suzi asks herself what she's doing, asks herself what *she* believes in. Revenge.

This deep cover switcheroo is her own *Confessions*.

What is she doing?

She looks at her Dictaphone.

Keeping Noble's money proves what exactly?

They've had her over a barrel for years, anyway.

She's a journalist; she knows what an editor will need to be able to publish.

A half-cocked story and a building society account won't be enough.

Her Dictaphone is state of the art, runs quietly, picks up from a distance, not too much background noise.

Her and Noble are always hunched over each other in the pub, discreet, probably closer than she'll ever have to get to Jason Donovan.

If she has something of use, of *real* use, something he *actually wants*, he might say something *she* can actually use.

This party in July, a few days before The Style Council Albert Hall gig.

Suzi stands, goes to the fridge, uncorks an unfinished bottle of Sauvignon, pours what's left into a tumbler, drinks it down –

Bites her lip, has a little think.

Yes, she thinks, nodding. *This.*

She telephones old Lee Roy on his Wide Roy Productions line, leaves a message that she wants to meet, wants to interview him for the piece.

15

Iron lady, iron fist

House of Commons, PMQs, 4 May 1989, Mrs Thatcher's ten-year anniversary as Prime Minister, the first British Prime Minister in the twentieth century to reach this milestone.

Mr Kinnock
Would the Prime Minister be good enough to recall for us today the prayer of St Francis of Assisi?
The Prime Minister
I think that one has achieved that prayer and brought a great deal of harmony where there was a fantastic amount of discord under the last Labour Government.
Mr Kinnock
It bears repeating:

'Where there is discord may we bring harmony,
Where there is error may we bring truth,
Where there is doubt may we bring faith,
Where there is despair may we bring hope'

Can the Prime Minister tell us why, in ten years, she has failed to live up to a single one of those principles?
The Prime Minister
Perhaps the right hon. Gentleman will remember the discord in the winter of discontent of 1979, when, under Socialism, there were strikes in the hospitals and one could not even get the dead buried. Perhaps the

right hon. Gentleman will realise that there is now faith in Britain over-seas – *[Interruption.]* – and perhaps he will realise that the social services are at a level of efficiency and generosity which has brought hope and a higher standard of living than people have ever known before.

Whitehall.

Mrs Thatcher is on her red telephone, meaning a discreet conversation, which today is with her favourite Chief Inspector.

Ma'am is what he calls her when he's feeling deferential. There's something about types like his, MI5 and MI6 bods too, if she thinks about it, the *men.*

Looking like they've climbed straight from their cricket whites into their dark suits.

But he's her favourite Chief Inspector thanks to his loyalty and sympathetic position.

One doesn't need to spell things out.

'What one needs,' Mrs Thatcher is saying, 'is understanding of priority.'

'Yes, ma'am.'

'I gather friends of yours in east London have been cooperative before.'

Mrs Thatcher, despite the discretion of the red telephone, is always careful quite what she states explicitly and what she doesn't.

'Yes, ma'am. We have, shall we say, associates in certain places.'

'Worth communicating that for these associates business-as-usual is tolerated while the scourge of our youth is addressed and brought properly to order.'

'Yes, ma'am.'

'Dependent on continued cooperation, in this particular matter.'

'Of course, ma'am.'

'And, worth communicating, the level of policing to remain unrestricted in this particular matter.'

'Understood, ma'am.'

'That'll be all,' says Mrs Thatcher.

Iron Lady, iron fist, I may as well be both, she thinks.

The approach threatens to court further popularity, certainly with the chaps, anyway.

No harm, no foul, a collateral consequence, and not an undesirable one.

'All this drugs and sex we're hearing about,' Denis remarks drily. 'We get enough of that at home.'

'Yes, dear, quite.'

'One can but hope!'

'You're quite right, dear, one can always hope.'

'Once more unto the breach!' Denis cackles. 'Room for one more on top!'

Mrs Thatcher sighs. She addresses her desk, her pile of paperwork.

Clearly this Acid House movement, if it can even be called a movement, will have nowhere to flourish, nowhere to *breed* and develop, like bacteria, if it has nowhere to go, nowhere to multiply, to spread.

There's talk, she knows, of legitimate events, and that's entrepreneurial, after all, distinctly in her lexicon of social activity.

Stopping illegality is fundamental.

There are compromises and duties that one takes on when one enters into a social contract with the state, with *her* state.

Young people have been having fun for centuries, running away from reality for a brief, heady day or two; this is hardly new.

Do it within the confines of the law, she thinks, and any threat to the fabric of society is cushioned, minimised.

The way, of course, to stop it: money.

As in: take theirs.

She makes a note to poke Geoffrey into proposing a Private Member's handout Bill to increase the penalties for illegally organising the events and to make the profits of such events liable to confiscation.

That and noise disturbance, public nuisance, fears for the safety of attendees.

These are tangible consequences and, in the eyes of the public, unarguable priorities in terms of law and order and so on. Yes, much better to address these concerns than to enter into any hysterical tabloid discourse.

Virginia for this, perhaps.

A look into the operation of the relevant noise provisions of the Control of Pollution Act 1974, into the licensing law that governs public entertainment, into Section 14 of the Public Order Act, and into the common law powers of the police to prevent public disturbance.

That ought to do it.

Hitting the profits will discourage the craze. Penalties, confiscation, the tightening of public entertainment licensing law will be the justification to action.

She remembers a recent report:

The police should be quietly encouraged to use their intelligence to stop illegal parties taking place, working in conjunction with the local licensing authority. No amount of statutory power will make it feasible for police forces to take on crowds of thousands on a regular basis. We cannot have another drain on police resources equivalent to policing football matches.

Well, she knows very clearly how we're going about *that*.
And all part of the same thing, of course, the Tory project –
The Thatcher project.
She quite likes that, makes a note.

16

Squat party

Dalston nick.

'Dress rehearsal,' Jenkins is saying. 'Preparation for the big one on July first.'

Noble watching Bond and Fife. The war room strip-lit and stale. A smell of sour milk and armpit, fried bread.

'We've had a tip-off about an illegal party in Dalston,' Jenkins goes on. 'Smallish, but still in our remit.'

Nodding, coughing, Bond and Fife sucking on their John Player Specials.

'We'll have the heavy mob with us to do the dirty work. A fired-up Territorial Support Group unit. Don't be surprised when they take the numbers off of their epaulettes.'

There is a good deal of smirking at this, Noble notes.

'They won't want to be identified any more than you will, so keep your heads down and hang back.'

Fife says, 'Who's our intermediate?'

Jenkins sniffs. 'You'll remember we paid a visit to the Nightingale Estate, picked up a young man.'

Nodding.

'He's being very cooperative.'

More smirking.

'I'll deal with him myself,' Jenkins adds.

Bond asks, 'When?'

Jenkins consults his timepiece. 'Tonight, so get a bit of shut-eye this afternoon. Shouldn't be too hard for you two.' Meaning Fife and Bond.

'Pub lunch then?' suggests Fife.

'Be back here by eight, latest. Class dismissed.'

Noble gets on the blower and leaves a message for Parker, who calls him back.

'Dalston, tonight. Heard anything about that?' Noble asks.

'Nope.'

'Well if you do, steer clear, savvy?'

'Crystal, guv.'

'We'll catch up after, debrief.'

'For you or me, guv?'

'Fair point. Can't really debrief you if you weren't there.'

'Looking forward to it.'

'Don't be cheeky, son.'

Hangs up and redials. Same conversation with Suzi.

'It's nice you're so invested in my social life, detective,' she tells him.

Women, Noble thinks, putting the phone down, always the last bloody word with them.

Later, Noble stands by a police van and watches the numberless Territorial Support Group unit swarm into a Dalston squat. Within moments there is the sound of breaking glass. Dozens of partygoers pour out the front door, hands over their eyes, some of them bleeding from head wounds. The uniforms start mopping them up, collaring any they can get their hands on and shoving them, handcuffed, into the paddy wagons. Two burly TSG lads carry out freshly damaged stereo equipment, in pieces. Bond and Fife smoke and laugh, direct traffic. Noble drifts off and round to the alleyway at the back. A line of uniforms barricades the exit. Noise and smoke, shouting, the sounds of violence and anger. Noble clocks topless youths, eyes popping on ecstasy, rage-filled and drug-crazed, bouncing and jumping at this thick blue line. Noble slides into the doorway next door, slips in behind the industrial bins and waits. He hears leather shoes on broken glass. Jenkins and the lad from the Nightingale Estate in conference. Jenkins points at a piece of paper. 'These three, we've got, right?' The lad nodding. 'And these?' The lad indicates with his finger, jabs twice at the piece of paper. 'They're not yours then?' The lad shakes his head. 'Where are your lot, Simeon? Can you tell me that?' Simeon says something Noble can't hear. 'And they've got it all, have they?' Jenkins says. Simeon nodding. 'How much?' Again, Noble can't hear. Jenkins nodding, 'Good. That's a result. Our friends in Canning Town *will* be pleased. Where is it?' Simeon hands Jenkins a piece of paper, which Jenkins pockets. Noble notes which pocket. Jenkins says, 'We need to set up shop somewhere, something more permanent. An empty flat or something. A safe house. Or a house with a safe at least.' Laughing at this, the clever cunt. 'You done sterling work, Simeon,' Jenkins adds. He slaps him on the back. 'Now do one.' Noble waits. Glass crunches underfoot, then nothing. He edges out from behind the bins, down the alley and to the barricade. Spots Jenkins consulting with a uniform. Noble says, 'We got what we need?' Jenkins grins. 'And some.'

Back at the nick, the Acid Squad celebrate a good result. Whisky and cans. Noble slips off to Records. Date and first name are what he has, and he delivers this intelligence to the chap on duty. He potters off to the archives and is back, pronto. 'This the fella, is it?' he asks. Noble opens the file and sees a mugshot of Simeon. He nods. He pulls a twenty-pound note from his pocket. He lifts the polaroid and leaves the cash tucked into the file. 'What photograph?' says the chap. Noble rejoins the party. Jenkins' leather jacket hanging over the back of a chair. Radio on and the whisky bottle half-empty, cans crushed and dripping onto the threadbare carpet. It'll have to wait, he thinks. 'I'll get a round in then,' he says, pulling on his own jacket. 'Good man!' shouts Bond. Noble takes the stairs two at a time, leaves via the side entrance, into the car park, key in the ignition –

Home.

17

We're on the same side

'See what we're doing, it's more than just legal, right, it's, it's emotional too, it's *support*, it's giving someone an arm to lean on and a shoulder to cry on.'

In a café in Hoxton, Parker's telling Noble a bit more about the Hackney Community Defence Association.

Parker's thinking, it's not just leaflets and court papers, it's community.

'What it is, is *community*, right,' he says. 'That's literally what it is. A network, a support network for people who don't have anyone to support them.'

Noble shrugs and then nods. 'Yeah, I get it.'

Parker grimaces, says, 'And we've recognised two things, two key things, and this is important.'

'We?'

'You know what I mean.'

'Go on.'

'First bit of analysis has led to this finding: a tendency for officers to charge their victims with criminal offences in an attempt to conceal or justify their wrongdoing.'

'Makes sense.'

'Second, there's no point using the police complaint process, doesn't lead nowhere.'

'Not a surprise.'

'Instead, the route we're going – sorry, guv, *they're* going – is civil proceedings as a remedy to police wrongdoing.'

'And how's that working out for you? I mean, *them*?'

'It's slow, is one way of putting it.'

Noble snorts. 'What isn't?'

'Mostly, the point of it all is providing something for people who have suffered psychological trauma and want nothing to do with the police at all, right?'

'I'm starting to see the pattern here.'

'They need someone they can trust who can act as an intermediary.'

'As well as?'

'Solicitors with certain expertise in police litigation practices. It's still very early days, guv.'

'You say that like it's a bad thing.'

'What you need to know, guv, is that this thing ain't going nowhere, and it's helping people.'

'That service you're talking about, support for people who don't have any support?'

'Yes, guv?'

'That sounds like a form of protection racket, in principle, anyway. The pitch, I mean.'

'No one's paying no one nothing, guv.'

'You know what I'm saying.'

Parker doesn't especially like the tone of all this. 'Community action.'

Noble says, 'And what have they got on *us*, specifically?'

Parker nods.

Bacon sizzles, chips bubble, kettles steam. Cutlery on cheap plates.

Some old codger mouthing off about Hillsborough and the Scousers.

Parker hasn't decided how to answer Noble's question.

The truth is that they're building a database of plods who have misbehaved, whether it's wrongful arrest, or assault, or planting, or straight-up theft, anything at all.

And this database is recorded on the two computers they have in the office.

And there's only a very small number of people who have access to these computers, Parker being one of them.

He makes a decision.

First off, he's got to look out for himself.

Noble's on his side, at least he always has been, but Parker doesn't know what Noble does exactly with what Parker tells him.

No one else is looking out for Parker, he's pretty sure of that.

Down the line, it's another story, but for now, this –

'Nothing – or no one – specific,' he says. 'It's about the victims, guv.'

Noble nods. 'And the other night? Dalston. Anything?'

Parker shakes his head.

'Likely too soon.'

'Word is that at the close of play it was only the dealers who got nicked. Young ones, bottom-rung-of-the-ladder types.'

'Something like that.'

Parker says, 'We're on the same side, aren't we, guv?'

'Course.'

'I mean, isn't this what we've always been trying to do?'

'Yeah, that's right. That's still the priority.'

'I just—'

'What?'

'No, it's nothing.'

'Go on, son, you can tell me.'

Parker takes a breath. 'I don't know what it is you do with what I tell you, I suppose is my point.'

'I suppose you don't.'

'Yeah.'

'Parker, son.'

'Yeah?'

'You just got to trust me. What I'm doing, I can't tell you. What you're doing is helping that, right?'

Parker nods. He doesn't feel exactly reassured by this. 'We're on the same side,' he says, again.

'We are, son.'

Parker sniffs. 'I do trust you, guv.'

'Good,' Noble says briskly. He takes a photograph – a mugshot – from his inside pocket, hands it to Parker. 'You seen this fella about the place?'

Parker examines the photograph. A young black man. 'I haven't.'

'What about in the files, Rectory Road?'

'I don't think so.'

'Keep that.' Meaning the photograph. 'Check, all right?'

Parker looks around. Pensioners, a couple of young mums, babies asleep in prams, mid-morning quiet. Outside, a group of labourers in boots and hats finish their cigarettes and shape up to come inside. A council estate cloaked in scaffolding through the misted glass –

They stand.

'What about the party?' Noble asks. 'Any progress?'

'I'm on the guestlist.'

'Not what I meant.'

Parker's thinking about Marlon, thinking he might offer his services, muscle, given what happened New Year's Eve, Parker doing the business.

Muscle for what, he's not sure.

'I'm getting there,' he says.

Outside, Noble turns towards Liverpool Street. 'Be lucky,' he says.

Easy to say, Parker thinks.

He mooches north, Carolyn waiting for him. Lunch with her and Shaun in some Turkish gaff near the house.

Apparently, Shaun's got some bird on the go. About time.

Parker crosses into Haggerston, down onto the canal path.

Cyclists, joggers –

Leather-faced fishermen, sitting on their tackle boxes, staring out at orange tips in the thick green water, waiting for a twitch, cane pole rods on rests, like lumber.

Narrowboats line the path. Rusty tugs and rowing boats, rotting.

Ahead, approaching Broadway Market, Parker watches canoeists in wetsuits negotiating a lock gate. A couple and a shivering teenage girl. The couple keeping their patience admirably, Parker thinks, not raising their voices despite the noise of the water.

The girl's got a face on and she turns away as Parker smiles.

'You look like you've done this before!' he calls out.

The dad smiles, shouts, 'There's an art to it, looking like you've done it before!'

Parker enjoys this. 'Be lucky!' he says, arm in the air bidding farewell as he bounces off.

Up the steps and onto Broadway Market, past the pubs and the caffs, the butchers and the pie and mash, all the way to the end then across London Fields, out onto Mare Street, onto a 106 bus, up the stairs, top deck, front seat –

Breathes in, eyes closed, breathes out, eyes open –

Out the window, the town hall and the Hackney Empire, Woolworths and Hackney Central, the Pembury Tavern and the Pembury Estate, Hackney Church and Hackney Police Station, haven't been in either of them for a while, Parker thinks, Hackney Baths and the Round Chapel, off the bus at the pond and into this Turkish restaurant.

Parker greets Shaun from across the room. 'Where's my other half, then, eh?'

Shaun shakes his head. 'On her way, your *better* half.'

'Yeah, yeah, very good.'

Parker's over to Shaun's table in three big steps. Still standing, he scans the room, nods at the young bird behind the takeaway counter, smiles. 'You do Efes here, do you, darling?' he asks. 'I bloody love Efes.'

Parker notes the eyeroll.

'One Efes coming right up.'

Parker sits. 'Make it two, I'm thirsty.' Winking at Shaun, another shake of the head.

The bird delivers the drinks on a tray.

'Thanks, darling.'

'It's Lauren,' she says.

'Thanks, Lauren.'

Lauren smiles, pouts. 'My pleasure.'

She fiddles with a bottle opener, looks at Parker, does a little double take, narrows her eyes. 'Wait a minute,' she says. 'I know you.'

Parker's turn to shake his head. 'I don't think so, sweetheart.'

'No, I do,' she insists. 'You used to come in the old place we had, over in Stoke Newington.'

Parker smiles. 'I used to go a lot of places, to be fair.'

Shaun snorts.

'Leave it out,' Parker tells him.

Bottle open, she pours it into a glass, still looking at Parker with knitted brow.

'You'd come in for an Efes or two with a gentleman called Trevor.' Nodding. 'I remember *him*.'

'Do you?'

She smiles. 'Course. He was, well, he was charming, weren't he? Asked me out once, in fact.'

'Did you go?'

She shakes her head. 'Nope. I never saw him again.' She makes a gesture with her thumb and forefinger. 'Bit of a drinker. Brandy, if I remember right.'

Parker nods. 'You do.'

Parker thinking –

Hold steady.

He says, 'I ain't seen him myself for a while, a good couple of years, come to think of it.'

'Say hi from Lauren if you do see him.'

'Old school friend, you know how it is.'

'Anyway.' Lauren turns on her heel, makes to leave them alone. 'Enjoy the drinks, the food's the same, so you'll enjoy that.' She points at Shaun. 'He certainly does.'

Off Lauren twirls, sniggering, at least it looks that way from Parker's vantage point.

'She's not your one, is she?' Parker asks, Lauren out of earshot.

'Give it a rest, eh, Parker.'

'I'm only being friendly.'

'Just be nice, yeah?'

'Course.'

The door goes and for a moment the noise and the dust and the exhaust and the voices from Lower Clapton Road drift in, intrude, then fade. Both Parker and Shaun look up. It's Carolyn, who smiles, waves.

'You nervous, son?' Parker asks quickly.

'No. Why would I be?'

'And she's your girlfriend, is she, this bird we're going to meet?'

'Not exactly.'

'Not exactly? What does that mean *exactly*? I thought this was the big reveal, the red carpet, all that.'

'Hang on, yeah—'

Shaun stands to give his cousin a hug. Parker waits, stands himself, kisses Carolyn, offers her a seat with a chivalrous sweep of the arm, bowing for added effect.

'All right, gorgeous,' he announces. 'I've got you an Efes, they're bloody delicious.'

Carolyn sits down, relieves herself of coat and bag, which looks a bit of a struggle, Parker thinks, it's the problem with your longer summer coat, the tails of the thing getting stuck everywhere. She smiles at Parker, Carolyn, a touch tightly to Parker's keen eye.

Nodding, she says, 'No, thank you, though, but I'll have sparkling water, I think.'

'Oh, all right.' Parker looks up, around. 'When young Lauren returns, I shall order you one.'

Carolyn smiles again, and it really is a tight one this time, and Parker decides he might dial down his act a touch, her attention is on Shaun, that's obvious, and quite right too, why not, that's why they're here, after all.

Carolyn smiles at Shaun, warmly, a *thick* smile, Parker notes. 'You OK, love?' she asks.

'Yeah,' Shaun says. He checks his watch. 'She'll be here in a minute.'

'Ayeleen, that's right, isn't it?'

'Yeah, Ayeleen.'

Lauren reappears. 'And I'm doing her shift.' She winks. 'Can I get you anything while you wait for her ladyship?'

Parker grins. 'A sparkling water for *her* ladyship.' Thumb pointing at Carolyn.

'How about some of those little cheese things, you know, the starters?' Shaun asks.

Parker snorts. 'You'll need better lingo than that come September.'

'Sigara borek, Shaun.'

'That's the one.'

'Right you are. I'll bring a generous portion.'

Parker sips his lager. Then the door goes again and in walks Ayeleen, least that's who Parker assumes it is, given the speed with which Shaun is out of his seat and Parker thinks, yep, I know her, will she remember me?

Course Ayeleen's done a number on the food order and they're all tucking into pretty much everything on the menu and a good chunk of stuff that ain't.

'Anything for friends of Ayeleen!' announced the owner, her uncle.

Parker remembers him too. Parker remembers the holdalls that came through their old gaff and wonders if that's still a feature here.

He doesn't think so; it feels more *naïve*, is the word. Maybe the old fella's putting it on, but he's certainly being very *uncle* all about the place.

They eat and Parker takes down a few delicious Efes and Carolyn fusses over Shaun and it's all very wholesome and if Ayeleen knows Parker from Adam then she's doing a good job of hiding it, though Parker tells himself – *reminds* himself – that there's nothing wrong with going to a Turkish café for a beer with an old mucker.

Nothing wrong with that at all.

Yeah, someone you don't know, he rehearses telling Carolyn.

Bit of a loose cannon, you wouldn't like him, but he's a mate, you know how it is, I've not seen him for donkeys.

She's nice, Ayeleen, Parker thinks, very sweet.

'We're going to celebrate,' she tells them as they leave. 'My exams and Shaun's place at college.'

'That's nice,' Carolyn says.

'At a party, all my friends will be there, down near Docklands, it is.'

Parker thinking, *what*.

'Sounds good. When?' he asks.

Ayeleen is smiling. 'July first.'

'That's quite soon.' Parker makes a face. 'If you can't be good, be careful!'

'That's really nice,' Carolyn says. She looks at Shaun. 'You can go by the way!'

And everyone laughs.

18

I just want to be an H2Owner

Hackney Town Hall

Jon Davies and Godfrey Heaven having a conversation: the poll tax and water privatisation.

'I just want to be an H2Owner,' Godfrey says.

Jon smiles. 'We'll come back to that, Godfrey,' he says.

And they will.

Jon's been on the phone to this company Thames Water for days and no luck talking to anyone about Riverside Close and what's going on at the Stoke Newington end of the Thames Water Ring Main.

All anyone tells him is how lucky he is to have the opportunity to become an H2Owner.

For now, while he's got Godfrey in with him, Jon's more interested in the poll tax and the effects it looks like having on the borough residents.

The gist of the discourse, in Jon's understanding, and there has been an awful lot of discourse flying about, is that the poll tax is Mrs Thatcher's attempt to finish off local government, and Jon's quoting here, 'as any kind of progressive instrument of wealth distribution'.

Standard enough strategy from the big woman: capped spending, enforced privatisation of services, the working class turn against the Labour-run councils, mop up the votes –

Pretty snide. Standard.

'I've got a leaflet, here, Jon,' Godfrey says. 'A draft, I should say. Have a read.'

Godfrey's made a paper aeroplane out of this leaflet, this draft, and he sends it Jon's way, across Jon's desk.

It lands nose first.

'Is your mode of delivery a reflection of your opinion of this draft, Godfrey?'

'I'm thinking of you, Jon. You're going to be right in the middle of all this.'

'How so?'

'Her upstairs,' meaning MP for Hackney North and Stoke Newington, Diane Abbott. 'Her upstairs is very much against it. But she will doubt-less, *officially*, not encourage non-payment. And yet.'

'And yet?'

Godfrey smiles. 'Do what I say not what I do.'

'That's what I tell my son.'

'Does it work?'

'No.'

'Well then. That answers your question.'

'Right.'

Jon unfolds the leaflet, straightens it, examines the draft.

Hackney Against the Poll Tax Federation newsletter
YOU, THE POLL TAX AND THE LAW
The Poll Tax will be stopped by non-payment.
The Tories and the mass media will be putting out lies to try and frighten people into paying up. These are the facts about Poll Tax and non-payment. Please read it carefully, photocopy it and pass it on.

Jon looks quickly at some of these facts.

He's not sure about the veracity of some of the legal assertions. The one that says you can't go to jail, for example, not sure that's true, he thinks.

'They might ask a solicitor to look this over,' Jon says.

'I'll tell them you're offering, shall I?'

Jon shakes his head. 'Best not, Godfrey, I think.'

'What I'm saying, Jon, is when it comes to it, you'll be the one filing the non-compliance paperwork. *Militant* is already talking about Hackney being the borough with the best non-payment record, when it comes. There's talk of a league table.'

'Jesus.'

'It won't matter what you think about it all, you're going to be the villain.'

'And her upstairs?'

'She'll distance herself from the Borough Solicitor who acts at the behest of the council and whose role is in no way political.'

Fuck, Jon thinks. He's right. He's always bloody right, is Godfrey.

'So what you're saying, Godfrey, is I'll be doing the Labour Party's dirty work.'

'That's very astute of you, Jon, putting it like that.'

'The Labour Party won't condone non-payment, and the Labour councils will have the highest instances of non-payment and will have to chase these to demonstrate the Labour Party's commitment to the rule of law.'

Godfrey stands. 'I think my work is done here.'

'No, it ain't, sit down.'

'Keep your hair on, Jon.'

Jon sniffs. 'You still friendly with the new Planning Committee types?'

'I am friendly with everyone, Jon.'

Jon smiles – thinly. 'Can you ask them about Riverside Close for me?'

'What about it?'

'Applications, land sales, that sort of thing.'

'Timeline?'

'This year.'

'Consider it done.'

'Cheers.' Jon picks up the leaflet. 'Can I keep this?'

'It's all yours, Jon.'

Jon screws the leaflet into a ball and, deftly, throws it into the bin on the other side of the room. Godfrey raises his eyebrows, impressed.

'You can go now, Godfrey,' Jon says.

19

Say nothing, act normal

Parker takes the photo Noble gave him to 50 Rectory Road.

The office is empty and Shaun's not with Parker as much these days and Parker certainly didn't invite him today, that's for sure.

Parker takes lever arch files from shelves. He pulls all the files of recorded instances of police malpractice this year. There's a fair few, and it's not even half-time in 1989, though it's getting closer and closer.

Parker flips pages.

Each file is fastened by paper clips, the thicker of them with crocodile clips, photos in the top right corner, on page one, of each file.

Parker flips and Parker skims.

Nothing.

He puts aside a handful of files: young black men in the photographs.

He places the photo Noble has given him next to each in turn, a double-check, to measure resemblance.

Nothing.

No photo of this chap, Parker thinks, satisfied.

Next stop, the computer database that Noble doesn't yet know about.

Parker boots it up, which takes a while, so he pockets the photo and puts the kettle on.

The kettle whistles. The computer beeps, gives it that static sound. Parker hums along to the radio, Soul II Soul's 'Back to Life', thinking, back to reality, what's that then?

Parker then shelves this thought alongside the lever arch files. He's no right to it, is his latest coping mechanism, don't think, just do.

Like poor old unfortunate Trevor used to preach: say nothing, act normal.

Do your job, son.

Parker prepares his tea – two teabags into the mug, a good slug of water, a splash of milk, stew to a rust-tinged brown, three sugars, teabags stay in – and addresses the computer, which is now ready for him.

Key issue here is that the files are presented in the reverse manner, i.e., they document coppers, not victims, and there aren't always images in the files, so it's a bit of a turkey shoot.

Parker decides, with this in mind, to kill two birds, and he takes a notepad and jots down the names of all the plods that stand accused.

No Noble, which is something, he thinks.

The name Jenkins pops up, and Parker squints, thinks, do I know him, and from where?

It'll come back to him.

He clicks and he squints, he squints and he clicks. And he takes names, scribbled in pencil on the back of an envelope.

Which is apt, given the number of envelopes some of these bad apples are most likely pocketing.

Course this database isn't about all *that*, but Parker expects that there would be a hefty overlap of 'wrongful arrest' and 'on the take'.

He clicks through the files and sniffs.

Nothing.

He swallows the end of his tea, takes his mug into the kitchen. It doesn't look too clever, the inside of Parker's mug, and he leaves it to soak.

Maybe he should bleach it, he thinks.

Tomorrow, he'll have a look at it then, consider the extent of the staining.

Next stop, the pub, to meet Marlon.

He's thinking, Parker, about showing Marlon this photo, though it's a risk.

Where'd you get that? is the obvious first question.

Why'd you get it, is the next one.

Anyway, it's a silly thought.

He's telephoned Marlon, given him a sense of what he wants, and the meet is really a firming-up of his offer.

In other words, Parker's put in the application and he's about to find out if he's got the job.

Parker bounces across Hackney Downs, then Clarence Road, Cricketfield Road, then into the Cricketers pub –

Which, Parker remembers, is notoriously unfriendly.

And the elders certainly give big Parker the once-over.

Parker striding up to the bar –

Two younger bredren getting out of their seats, Parker notes, vests and chains –

'Half a Guinness,' Parker says to the landlord. 'Top of the morning to you.'

The landlord, a fifty-something Rasta who likely hasn't smiled since West Ham won the FA cup, raises an astonished eyebrow.

Parker grins.

One of the younger bredren is about to speak, his hand perilously close to Parker's shoulder.

And that's when Marlon heaves into view.

Marlon jerks his thumb at Parker. 'He's with me.' He distributes cash with the same thumb. 'I'll have the same.'

The landlord shrugs –

Marlon ushering Parker to a table by the fruit machine.

At which sits the young man in the photograph in Parker's pocket.

'This is Simeon,' Marlon says.

Parker smiles. 'Top of the morning to you.'

And the three of them have a good laugh about that.

'So, hero,' Marlon says when they've settled down to their halves of Guinness. 'Simeon here, he's your security detail.'

Parker's got the job then.

'What you do is escort him to the party as it kicks off, see him safely to the promoters' office, then avail yourself of a good time.'

Parker nods. 'I can do that.'

'Simeon has the use of a vehicle.' Marlon slides over a piece of paper with two addresses on it. 'Top one is where you pick up the motor. Bottom one is where you pick up Simeon.'

'Gotcha.' Parker looks at the first address. He recognises it, a garage. He swallows, his mouth suddenly dry, his lips cracked, has a drink.

'Here's to a job well done,' Parker says.

They knock glasses, Marlon grinning.

'Your missus coming, hero?'

Parker shakes his head. 'She didn't fancy it.'

Marlon gives him a look.

'Her cousin will be there, though,' Parker says. 'You remember Shaun. With his new bird. I'm the chaperone.'

Marlon smiles wide, all gold teeth, joyful –

He says, 'The lickle something in that Turkish place?'

'Not the one you're thinking of, you perv. You're old enough to be her ancestor.'

'Either way, good for him,' Marlon says. 'Truly happy for the boy, bless.'

Parker nods and says nothing for a moment.

Marlon sniffs.

'I best be off,' Parker announces, standing. 'Simeon, it's been one.'

Simeon nods.

20

Wide Roy Productions

Suzi is set to meet Lee at his office, which is a broom cupboard above Regal Records on Lower Clapton Road.

In the shop, there's a heavy vibe, music-wise, dub rattling the windows, pounding the ceiling –

Suzi's been here before.

Across the hall from Lee is Robert 'Ribs' Fearon of Unity Sounds.

Suzi's written about him, about the singles he put out earlier in the decade. 'Watch How the People Dancing', 'Pick a Sound', probably the biggest, certainly the two Suzi remembers.

Ribs was a great interviewee, and Suzi pops her head in, but he's not there.

She smiles, thinking of Lee and his Dennis Bovell story. She remembers Ribs saying something about Dennis Bovell too.

She pauses in the corridor and looks again at her Dictaphone. The tiniest piece of black tape covers the red light that shows it's recording. She runs her thumb over it, a fingernail, and it feels smooth, and surely you wouldn't notice it if you didn't know it was there, she thinks, and takes a deep breath.

Lee's on form. When's Lee *not* on form?

Garrulous, would be a good word, Suzi thinks, and jots it down. The garrulous Lee of Wide Roy Productions. A natural storyteller. A twinkle in his eye. A crisp fiver in his pocket. A bullshit artist. A man of the people. Serious wide-boy energy.

Take your pick.

'See, what I'm telling you, Suzi,' Lee's telling Suzi, 'is that we are

Thatcher's children providing for the disenfranchised.'

We, being the lads – and it's always lads – that are creating and developing (Lee's words) this Acid House scene. The disenfranchised being the muggins who swallows the price and swallows the drugs (Suzi's prose).

'And what you call that, Suzi, is a false opposition.'

'I think it's more like a paradox.'

'Nah, false opposition. Contradiction in terms.'

'That's not what false opposition is, Lee.'

'Let's not split hairs, it sounds good,' Lee grins.

Suzi smiles. She thinks, everything Lee says *sounds* good.

'The future, though,' Lee says, 'will be in a legit warehouse scene, or equivalent, right. This business with the Old Bill and the moody licences and all the rest is getting in the way too much. If you wanna make serious moolah, then you got to do it straight. Too much to lose if you're nicked. Look at what happened in Dalston the other night. Chaos. Money down the toilet. Well, not literally, but where do you think the takings are then? That's right, in Old Bill's pocket. So, yeah, change, that's what I'm about. Innovation.'

Suzi nods. 'Go on.'

'There's a few of us talking about it, the future, the next level. Imagine: venues outside the M25, huge fields, huge hangars, you know, *aircraft* bases, whatever it is, you rent the space for tuppence ha'penny, charge through the nose for tickets, get the biggest sound system you've ever heard, the top DJs, and, voila, you're printing money.'

'You sure you want this in the piece, on the record?'

Lee pouts. 'It's a fair point. Maybe the vision but without the capitalist motivation of it all.'

'Why will people pay any more than they do now?'

Lee leans forward. His gold bracelet lands on the desk with a clunk. 'This is the good bit. If they're legit, they'll definitely happen, your night is a dead cert, *guaranteed*, and that's what the people want above all else: assurance. What people want, Suzi, above all else in this life, is certainty.'

Suzi nods. He's right on that front.

'Anyway,' Lee says, 'I trust you to make me sound good.'

She smiles, sees the opportunity.

She picks up her Dictaphone and makes a show of switching it off, though she doesn't.

She shifts in her chair, leans in a little closer.

'Off the record,' she says. 'If it's legit, what about, well, what about the—'

'The drugs, Suzi, what about the drugs?'

Suzi nods.

She's been careful here not to say anything, let Lee speak.

She can scramble his voice and he'll be anonymous; she'll protect her sources as she always does, but even so, off the record is one thing and entrapment something else.

And she knows that what she's doing is bang out of order.

Lee nods. 'Well, the thing with going legit is you need backing, and there are serious organisations with legitimate business interests who, well, let's just say that they are not averse to diversifying their portfolios.'

Suzi nods, raises an eyebrow.

'I mean to say,' Lee says, 'that an organisation like the sort I describe will soon be calling time on your amateur, illegal warehouse rave supplier.'

'OK.'

'A takeover, mergers and acquisitions, you know.'

Suzi nods.

'Decent security and relationships with hooky cops is a good start.'

'Any names you can share?'

Lee considers this request. He shapes up in his seat, he sniffs. He gives Suzi a look like he's weighing her up, but Suzi knows he likes her, they've had some good times.

'Between friends,' Suzi adds. 'Satisfy my curiosity, that's all it is.'

Lee nods. 'No, I know, between friends.'

Lee considers this some more. His flick from side to side, to the door.

'Look, Suzi, I shouldn't, I don't really know nothing anyway, it's really not my area of expertise.'

'Fair enough,' Suzi says, 'I respect that. I just thought we were friends, that's all.'

'We *are* friends, Suzi,' Lee says, a bit sharp now. 'And friends don't ask friends questions like this.'

'You're right.' Suzi gathers notebook and pen, puts them in her bag. 'I was just being nosy, curious, that's all.'

'You fancy going for a quick drink, then, celebrate the article?'

'I can't,' Suzi says.

'Oh yeah?'

Suzi nodding. 'Yeah.' She gives Lee a thin smile. 'Thanks for your time though, very helpful.'

'You'll come to the party?'

'In a professional context, I will.'

Lee looks disappointed. Breathes, makes a choice. 'All right, fuck it,' he says, 'everyone knows anyway.'

'What's that?'

'I can tell you this. Look into East London Logistics, that'll get you somewhere.'

'I said I was nosy, that's all.'

Lee sighs. 'I may well be an awful lot of mouth, Suzi, but I'm not stupid.'

Suzi frowns, nods softly.

She looks at Lee, weighs what he's saying, there's a hint of sadness to him, as if he knows his whole performance is exactly that, a performance.

She understands how he feels, of course.

For Suzi, living alone, working in this world – music – this world that is dominated by men, wondering, too, when her own performance will end, if it ever will, and if it does end or if it doesn't, wondering if she'll be happy, when it does or doesn't end.

'Course you're not, Lee.' Suzi smiles. 'I'll see you at the party. Course I will.'

'Not if I see you first,' Lee winks.

Suzi picks up the Dictaphone, shaking slightly.

She's careful not to audibly switch it off.

As she places it in her bag, she coughs, loudly, just in case.

'You know what,' she says, smiling, 'let's have that drink.'

'Smashing.'

Back at home, Suzi tinkers with her recording.

She transcribes the quotes she'll use in the piece, makes Lee sound good, then fast-forwards to the end of the tape and transcribes separately the incriminating part of his testimony.

Next job is to protect the source and, more importantly, herself.

Years ago, Keith gave her a 2-track recording deck, which she uses to transfer her Dictaphone material. She remembers his spiel well. Classic Keith.

'Your birthday present, my dear,' he told her, 'is work-related, I'll admit that, but it will help you to back up your interview recordings, as well as provide a foolproof way of protecting your sources, should you ever need to.'

'Sounds unlikely, love.'

'Let me explain.' Keith grinned.

They were in bed, a Sunday morning, Suzi's birthday in 1982.

Breakfast was a bacon sandwich and a bottle of bubbly.

Keith said, memorably, 'We'll have a go at this, a roll in the hay, and then a bit of kip before lunch. Happy birthday.'

'Go on then,' Suzi said. 'Explain.'

'In nineteen eighty-one,' Keith began, 'Tascam launched a two-header model Tascam 124 AV, equipped with a two-track combination recording/playback head and the corresponding eraser head.'

'I'm with you.'

'The deck is not metal capable.'

'Heavy metal?'

'Don't interrupt.'

'Not another word, I promise, love.'

'The deck is in fact intended for operating slide projectors, the lower track used to ensure a lack of dropouts, in other words, stable performance. The deck is capable of full stereo recording and playback. I have modified it too, to suit your purposes.'

'How?'

'You let me worry about that when I show you how to use it.'

'What about this protecting of sources?'

A glint in Keith's eye at that. When was there *not* a glint in Keith's eye, Suzi thinks now. Too much glint might have been his problem.

'Even without my modification, recordings made on this deck are fully incompatible with the standard cassette format.'

'So?'

'So you can't play them on anything else, is the essence, Suze.'

'You mean destroy the original and there's only this version.'

Another glint.

'Exactly,' Keith said. 'I mean it's not entirely foolproof, as one might procure another modified Tascam 124 AV model and play it on that, but I suspect that's at the unlikelier end of the spectrum, events-wise.'

Suzi now connects the Dictaphone to the 2-track.

She then does what Keith showed her so that Lee's voice, when recorded onto the tape of the 2-track, becomes unrecognisable. The words are clear, but, as Keith put it, you wouldn't know from Adam who's spoken them.

Next, she takes the Dictaphone tape and mangles it, then stamps on it until it breaks in two. She takes one of the pieces and places it in the rubbish bin. The other piece she pockets to dispose of outside. She knows she's being paranoid, faintly ridiculous – she's not bloody James Bond, after all – but she has a feeling Noble won't be satisfied with the transcript alone, he might need a little more than that, and if he's going to listen to the interview, he's going to do so on her terms.

She calls the latest number Noble has given her, leaving a message telling him she wants to meet.

Then she has a little lie-down.

21

**And if you don't know what you want,
we'll give you what we've got!**

Jon's examining the files Godfrey pulled for him: this year's planning applications and land transactions involving the Riverside Close Estate.

'They're approving them faster than the amanuensis can keep up,' Godfrey told Jon.

'I'll give you the nod when I'm done.'

'They're not all signed off, Jon, so they're on loan.'

'For how long?'

'Give or take ...' Godfrey shrugged. 'Tomorrow.'

So Jon's working quite hard.

Radio's on, playing Jason Donovan singing 'Sealed With a Kiss', and Jon thinks, this was rubbish the first time around, Brian Hyland in 1962. Then he thinks, hang about, nope, that was the *second* recording. The original was released in 1960 by the Four Voices. Rubbish then too. Rubbish again when Bobby Vinton released a version in the seventies. Hard to see the point of another version, in fairness.

Then he wonders: is this why Jackie fell in love with me? This sort of thing?

It's charming, in a way. It's *distracting*. Jon thinks that Jackie might not be all that interested in him at all, really, at this point. She certainly likes things quiet in the evenings, a bit of space for herself, as she calls it. So they sit quietly with their books, or Jon with his headphones on recording vinyl LPs onto cassettes, or one of them watching television with the sound low. They eat dinner together, they talk about the children, about the family calendar, and Jon's in bed and asleep by ten, Jackie in later.

The thing is, Jon doesn't want space for himself.

He wants his Jackie back.

Jon rubs his eyes.

The applications are complex and, really, he's interested in what's going on at Riverside Close.

Jon thinks back to his cross-council role and the government's Right to Buy proposal. He remembers it is council-run and therefore he should be looking out for the interests of council residents. Jon remembers the Land Registry, the funny little fella who explained it all to him, Jon's key question being, what is the obligation to register property and who exactly is obliged to do what.

Jon remembers the carpet having a real pong about it, very musty feeling to the place.

Jon was told that compulsory registration was phased in across the counties in a piecemeal fashion, meaning that the Land Registry itself was – and likely is – still in the process of trying to work out exactly which bits of this country of ours are owned by who. Or *what*, Jon thinks.

What Jon had no idea about was voluntary registration being an option, and it very quickly became clear why you might go through the hassle of the admin to voluntarily register.

Jon remembers the Land Registry chappie telling him that if your *holding*, your land, is registered as yours, registered as *owned by you* according to Land Registry records, it's much easier to dispose of it, much easier to sell it.

And if a council property is bought up privately and the sale is registered, future sales are simpler as a result too.

The Land Registry holds the records of registered Right to Buy purchases.

'And if you don't know what you want, we'll give you what we've got!'

A snappy line, no wonder Jon remembers it.

And Jon made an appointment and asked for a list of council home Right to Buy purchase registrations in the tri-borough area of Hackney, Tower Hamlets and Newham, and the problem, he remembers, was that they're registered by name, not location.

He remembers that it was council houses rather than flats that were mostly purchased in the initial flurry after the policy went live. He thinks that Riverside Close would have been an obvious place for that to happen, given the relative calm of the place, the quiet, the size of the units, the location.

It would be worth knowing how many – if any – units were purchased before the issues with the water, and how many have been purchased since.

What strikes Jon now as it struck him before, is that voluntary registration is conversely a very useful principle if something murky is going on.

Hiding in plain sight.

Or, to put it another way, not actually breaking the law.

Right to buy means right to sell, of course. Jon might well believe he is acting in the best interests of the council residents, but they are allowed to make their own decisions.

He goes back to the planning applications.

He scans the documents looking for any that might be reliant on the principle of adverse possession. Adverse possession being defined by the ability to *prove* occupation of land. To have occupied land without permission and then prove it.

Not as hard as it sounds, Jon knows.

The bigger a city gets, the more it's developed, and, exponentially, the more profitable it can be to own land. People seem to decide they own something when other people become interested in close quarters.

One useful marker Jon's looking for in the applications is that, legally, the adverse possessor only becomes the property's new owner if the property's previous owner does not exercise their right to recover their property. So, there is a quid pro quo of sorts.

A second marker is company names in applications protected by standard confidentiality agreements, i.e., we're not telling you who's fronting the cash.

Equally, multiple companies acting as syndicates in which the actual spread of interest and ownership is complicated by the number of individual or collective holdings within each company – or syndicate.

Jon's role in this is complicit, he knows, and it troubles him.

He signs off, as Borough Solicitor, on legal elements of these applications. Yes, it's to protect the interests of the residents of the borough. In theory.

In practice, Labour-controlled councils regulate certain land, take part in its sale to outside interests, which undermines those of their residents.

It's surprisingly easy to issue bearer instruments, via offshore nominee directors, to enable anonymous investment.

And this is what Jon is looking for. And there's a lot of small print. It's taking him ages.

Jon's been reading applications all morning and is getting nowhere quite slowly.

He looks again at the files and makes a decision.

He takes them to the copy room.

He shouldn't do this, he knows that, but he needs more time.

He doesn't want to be coated off by Godfrey, or worse, by anyone else, especially not her upstairs.

It's a risk, that's for sure.

He who dares, Jon thinks.

Suzi hears from Noble.

Time to get ready.

Suzi dusts off another of Keith's innovations. A tiny lapel mic modified to work with the Dictaphone. It's powerful too.

It's a touch seasonal to wear a heavy coat and keep the Dictaphone in an inside pocket so Suzi opts for a flowery summer dress and a nice big handbag with a zipped compartment. She connects the mic then zips the Dictaphone into this compartment. The mic's cable is thin and black, the same colour as the bag. She draws the cable out and threads it along the handle, attaching it on the inside. It's small and neat and looks a bit like a hairclip if you look too closely, but, again, if you didn't know it was there, you wouldn't see it.

Now then.

What Suzi needs, she thinks, is Noble on tape proving that she's gathering intelligence at his behest.

Criminal intelligence.

She likely needs nothing more; she's unlikely to *get* anything more, knowing Noble and how close to his chest he stores his cards.

Now then.

Suzi arrives at the Prince of Wales ten minutes early and gets herself a gin and tonic – a double, steady the nerves – and a pint for Noble.

She finds a table in the corner in the saloon bar, by the window, the frosted glass giving the canal-side location an aspirational, riviera feel.

She places her bag on the table with the mic towards her. She changes seats, briefly, ensures that Noble wouldn't be able to see it. She changes back and hits the record button.

Bang on time, Noble saunters in.

Deep breath.

Now then.

Back at home, listening to the tape, Suzi thinks –

Nailed it.

Noble saying, 'So you've found something out for me that's useful for a change.'

Silence, background pub chatter.

Keith was right, it *is* powerful.

Noble again. 'East London Logistics is a drug front, is what you're saying.'

And again. 'And you have this on the record from an associate.'

And again. 'At some point I'll need more than the transcript, Suzi, you must know that.'

The bell goes for last orders, ten to three –

And again. 'Here, take this,' Noble says on the tape. 'Don't spend it all at once.'

Back at home, Suzi fingers the envelope.

Then she transfers the recording to the 2-track, this time *not* scrambling the voice.

Then she goes through the same routine with the Dictaphone tape.

Now then.

You're in with your financial adviser and he's talking paperwork.

Paperwork, that's all it ever is anymore, since your portfolio of interests widened to include legitimate business activity.

Technically, what you're doing – what you do *– is all legal, all above board, legit.*

The end product, that is.

How you get there is questionable, in some instances, or would be, in the eyes of the law.

Your financial adviser isn't interested in any of that, of course, he's simply a numbers and paperwork man.

'What we've heard,' he's saying, 'is that the government intend to cancel all the long-term debt owed by the current water authorities and then inject cash into the new companies in what is being touted as a green dowry.'

'Which means?' you ask, not for the first time.

'Which means that the net proceeds to the Treasury, even after selling the companies for a total of seven point six billion pounds, will be roughly zero.'

'And how does this help me exactly?'

'What this means is that there will be a quick stock market win for your smaller investor. The prediction is about a twenty per cent rise in the first month.'

'You could be an H2Owner.'

'That's the idea.'

'So, the advice for the smaller investor is sell at the end of the first month, January?'

'It's sensible advice. The companies are going to be sold much too cheaply.'

'And the consequences of that?'

'There'll be further investment. We can anticipate extra profits which will likely be ploughed into diversifications, dividends, boardroom pay.'

'Which is what we want.'

'I expect money will be invested in infrastructure, improved drinking water.'

You nod.

'I'd get involved, if I were you,' your man says.

You nod again.

'One day it'll all be sold down the river, forgive the joke, to a foreign investor who'll strip it to bits. You might want to be part of that sale, eventually.'

All this suits you, you think.

You say, 'I'm going to need you to process a lot of share purchases. Small investors.'

'OK.'

'There'll be quite a number of them.'

'Taxpaying is the only criteria. That OK?'

'In a manner of speaking.'

You write down a name and a telephone number, give it to your man. 'Call this number in a month and you'll get what you need.'

'The flotation is happening in December.'

'I told you, there will be a lot. You'll have time.'

'I'll make it.'

'Good man,' you say. 'Cheerio then.'

Terry's in with an update. 'The brothers say there's just the two units left holding out on Riverside Close.'

You nod. 'Turn the taps off again,' you say. 'Same drill.'

Terry nods. 'Planning applications being processed as we speak.'

'Good,' you say. 'Tell the brothers there's an extra incentive.'

Terry nods.

'Alongside each of the loans we give them, there'll be shares in Thames Water too. Which we'll buy off them in January.'

'That's all the units?'

'All the units up there, and down in Wapping, Docklands, Limehouse. We need names and tax details for the lot.'

Terry licks his little bookie's pencil, makes a note of this in his little book.

'You've got a month,' you tell him.

Terry says, 'The brothers, they've asked for one, a unit, you know, to use in the meantime. That all right?'

'Deniability?'

'Total.'

'Slice?'

'Considerable.'

You nod. 'Tell them the terms, though they bloody know them already.'

'Right you are.'

And you are right –

You know that.

22

Rabbit out of the trap

Saturday, 1 July

Saturday first thing. Noble – bleary-eyed, confused, still in some of his clothes after a late shift – needs a piss. He climbs out of bed and staggers to the toilet. He unzips, shoves open the toilet door.

'Oh shit, sorry, love,' he says to Lea. 'I thought you were in the kitchen.'

Lea's looking flushed, sitting on the bog with something wet in her hand, grinning.

Noble, eyes wide, flies undone, tongue halfway out, asks:

'Is that what I think it is?'

Lea nods.

'Bloody hell,' Noble says.

He leans down and kisses Lea, holds her, tells her he loves her, wipes away her tears, sheds one or two of his own, the sheer relief.

He kisses her again. 'I do really need a piss, though,' he says.

Lea screaming with laughter.

Saturday and Jon's got the kids to himself, which means finding them something to do.

His first thought is to spend the day watching Wimbledon on the box given the boy is all about Stefan Edberg – who's going well again, of course, that lovely sense of time and space, real class – and the boy's even got himself a tennis shirt like the one Edberg's wearing this year, which he won't take off, God knows when Jackie bought that or where.

A couple of weeks ago was the Hackney Show, which they missed as Jackie didn't fancy it, didn't fancy drinking warm lager and stepping over dogshit all afternoon, she said, and Jon thinks now that it would've been perfect for today, as he picks up the leaflet advertising it, still in the kitchen.

Key words:

Children's funfair creche dance beer

They make a good case, Jon thinks.

King Rudder and his big band
Charlie Roots
Romi and Jazz
King Pleasure and the Biscuit Boys
Compere: The Ranking Miss P

Jon does like a bit of all that.

Live PAs and Top DJs with Madhatters Trevor, Steve Jackson, Paul 'Trouble Those Decks' Anderson from Kiss FM

Sounds from Pyramid Arts Development featuring Gemi Magic, Genus Sound, Company Soul Sound, Dub Bug

All this and lots more ...

Not today.

There's an argument, Jon thinks, that as a senior figure in the council, he should have been in attendance.

Bit late now.

Jackie called out goodbye half an hour ago and they haven't really made any progress since.

Night before, over dinner, Jon had a bit too much to drink.

Had himself a bit of a rant about the system and the failure of capitalism based on a conversation he'd had with Godfrey not long ago.

Banged on about the need for state rent control, the dangers of privatisation and the difficulties young people face –

'Capitalism's not working, though, is it, love?' he said. 'In the past, right, you became a part of the system based on an exchange: get a job, pay tax and expect affordable housing, reliable healthcare, and utilities and infrastructure that actually function.'

Jackie gave him a thin smile and forked pasta into her mouth.

'These are the rights of a citizen in a capitalist democracy. If that exchange is no longer realistic, then what?'

'You should protest, Jon,' Jackie interjected, drily. 'Why don't you protest? You have done before.'

'Protest achieves very, very little, *ever*,' Jon said.

'If you say so.'

'Look,' Jon, feeling the booze, trying to tone it all down, but once the rabbit's out of the trap and all that. 'Poll tax non-payment will be a form of protest that *might* work, but I have to work *against* it! What are the answers?' Jon counting them on his fingers. 'One, a form of social capitalism. Two, an overhaul not a revolution. Three, it's the system that's rotten. Four, it's the system that needs changing. Five, oh, I don't know.'

Jackie got up and left the table.

At the kitchen door, she turned and said, 'What's this really about, Jon?'

Jon's not sure. What am I doing, he thinks again.

He sighs.

Jackie wasn't too mardy with him this morning, but she wasn't going to miss him today, was his feeling.

'What do you reckon?' Jon asks Lizzie.

Lizzie looks up from the kitchen floor where she's playing with two dolls and she smiles.

'Good answer.'

Jon decides that a good use of the morning is to sort all the crap that's accumulated in the outside loo, in a manner of speaking.

A little chain gang going, Jon to the boy to Lizzie –

Damp tennis balls, buckets with broken handles, a plastic cricket bat with a hole, spades soiled by the garden, all of it into a black sack ready for the tip.

'Dad,' insists the boy. 'Wimbledon starts in a minute.'

'No sweat,' Jon says. 'We'll be done in time for Edberg.'

Suzi's pacing the flat, nervous.

She's writing everything down; and writing everything down is making her nervous.

Hence the pacing.

The writing and the pacing, the pacing and the writing.

Gordon Bennett, she thinks, quoting Keith.

Bloody Keith, I miss him, she thinks.

I bloody miss Keith, not that he'd be any help, of course.

About as much use as a chocolate watch, she thinks. Which is what he'd say, quoting him again. It's chocolate teapot, anyway, she thinks, how many times did I tell him that?

Later, she readies herself.

Make-up and disco gear laid out on the bed. Nice bottle of wine in the fridge.

She decides to do what she always does when it all gets a bit much.

Suzi goes for a walk.

She leaves the camera at home for once and joins the canal towpath near the junction of Cambridge Heath Road and Mare Street.

She follows the canal all the way down to Hackney Wick. She crosses to the other side and keeps walking until the Prince of Wales pub.

There, she orders a pint of bitter shandy – a criminally underrated tipple, Keith's assessment – and takes it outside to a table overlooking the canal.

She sees that the seafood stall is open and considers getting something to eat. For Keith it was always cockles drenched in vinegar, of course it was, and Suzi would have a tray of prawns, sometimes an oyster or two, whelks if they were feeling adventurous.

She's not sure she has the stomach for any of that today, what with the nerves she's feeling.

She takes a big gulp of her drink and assesses these nerves.

She's going tonight for research purposes, to help with the article she's been doing on the evolving Acid House scene. It needs a party, after all, a set piece to pull all the threads together.

She'll take her notebook, her camera, she'll have Lee Roy introduce her around –

It's work.

On the river, a family of ducks floats past a fisherman's line. Joggers and cyclists on the towpath.

Suzi has another mouthful of shandy.

She reminds herself that what she's doing, the writing down of everything that has happened to her, everything that she has done with or *for* Noble, is, really, a question of documentation at this stage, that's all.

She's simply recording what's happened, what she has been a part of, like a diary or journal of her experience. At this stage, there is nothing to fear, she has done nothing wrong. Her Dictaphone recordings have been transferred and are safe; she could even, quite easily, put all that down to an error on her part, and she can still destroy anything she likes, at this stage.

She can still decide exactly what it is she wants to do.

Hold tight, she thinks.

It's all to play for.

*

Parker asks Carolyn if she knows what Shaun is up to.

'Party tonight, remember!'

Carolyn smiles. 'Look after him and have fun.'

'That's the plan, darling, believe me.'

Carolyn smiles, proudly Parker thinks, but he doesn't know why, and he doesn't ask. It's nice enough as it is.

Mid-afternoon, he locates Shaun.

Tells him, 'Meet me at this address at eight. Tell your missus you'll see her at the shindig itself.'

Shaun starts to say something.

'No buts, mate, you're coming with, end of.'

Shaun nods.

Parker thinking, I need to keep an eye on him, all told, for his own good, as well as mine.

The address: the one Marlon gave him for the vehicle. After that, fetch Simeon and on to the meet.

If Shaun's close by him, Parker reckons, there's a lot less danger of him inadvertently getting himself into any trouble.

The last thing Carolyn says to Parker before he leaves the flat:

'You take good care of Shaun tonight, all right?'

No good deed goes unpunished, is Parker's other thought.

'You sure you don't fancy it, darling?' Parker asks.

Carolyn smiles, really *smiles*, her eyes with that twinkle he hasn't seen for a bit, that he's missed, if he's honest, that he's been a little bit too busy to help provoke.

That's twice now today she's given him that look of love.

'I'll be here when you get home,' she says.

You're in with the brothers, Terry taking notes.

'Now,' you say, 'I've just been on the blower to one of our senior friends in the Yard.'

The brothers nod.

'Your little logistics company front is in the frame, it appears.'

Terry sniffs.

'I'm not at liberty to disclose how my friend knows this as he is not at liberty to disclose that information himself. That's not how the relationship works.'

The brothers nod.

'Tonight,' you go on. 'Tonight is confirmed, as you know, you arranged it.'

The brothers nod.

'And I'm glad you did. Here's the new information: any vehicle with the words East London Logistics will be examined – closely. Do I need to tell you what that means?'

'No,' says one of the brothers.

'Well, I'm going to be more specific,' you decide. 'We allow the police to bust this party of yours on the condition that they leave alone the pre-existing trade in which you are engaged with my blessing and my slice. Certain casual dealers will be arrested; your associates will not. And I'd think about that intel on the vans, if I were you.'

The brothers nod.

'My instinct in these matters is to tell no one,' you advise. 'Experience has taught me that this sort of inside knowledge is best kept inside, away from all associates. Using it to try and establish whether or not anyone is iffy' – you smile – 'generally fails. Besides, you're more likely to know one from the other if you're holding all the cards. You get my drift?'

The brothers nod.

You make a face.

The brothers nod again.

'Here is the arrangement which I have brokered with our senior friend: police shut down a public nuisance and protect children from the evil scourge of this drug, which is a feather in the cap for them.'

Terry pretends to give a round of applause.

'What we get from allowing this to happen is the continued arrangement in which you are engaged. Once again, you get my drift?'

The brothers nod.

Noble at the Yard. He's been summoned out of the blue. Irregular, certainly, for a Saturday.

In with Chief Inspector Young.

And he's distracted, understandably, Noble. Not really a surprise that, he thinks.

And not that he can say anything, Christ on a bike, no.

Young thanks Noble for his intel on the logistics company.

'Not from your usual source, I gather,' Young adds.

Noble nods.

'Don't share this with your task force, or anyone else, is the word from upstairs. Your UCO, for example. The metaphorical flush, as it were.'

Meaning accountability, meaning look after number one.

The metaphorical flush being an opportunity to see if there are any leaks.

Noble thinks about Parker. If he tells him, Noble will be deliberately disobeying Young. Young's asking where Noble *did* get the intel, of course.

Noble sniffs, thinks it's not worth it.

Parker will be all right, Noble decides, and nods. 'Understood, guv.'

Young says, 'You should find it a straightforward evening, Detective Sergeant.'

'Yes, guv.'

'As it pans out, don't get too involved. Role is to observe, take note, report back, to *me*. And me only.'

'Yes, guv.'

'I'd expect a media presence, so low profile, head down. There's political capital to gain in a story like this.'

'Understood, guv.'

'Your UCO.'

'Yes, guv?'

'If this, and subsequently what occurs *consequentially*, goes according to the book, we'll be thinking about where to send him next.'

'Makes sense, guv.'

'He doesn't need that information at this time.'

No, he bloody doesn't, Noble thinks.

It's been a bit of an afternoon for Jon, all told.

After the great outside loo clean-up, they sat down to watch Wimbledon for half an hour and spent the rest of the day in front of the television. The boy was delighted, watching on his knees on a couple of cushions about a foot from the screen.

'Becker looks good, Dad,' he said at one point. 'They're saying it'll be him and Lendl in one of the semis.'

Jon grunted in general agreement with that assessment.

He likes Lendl, admires his chutzpah, this reinvention of himself as a robotic serve-volleyer in a most likely doomed project to win the championships at all costs.

'Edberg wins in straight sets!' the boy called out, waking Jon up properly. 'You missed it all, Dad.'

He's seen it all before, or a version of it, of course. That's what it is really, sport, repetition:

You really have seen it all before, once you've seen enough of it.

Lizzie played quietly – mostly – at the other end of the living room, and Jon fell asleep in his chair.

At six o'clock, Jon made them all breakfast for dinner: bacon, egg, beans and chips, fried bread and an apple for dessert.

Went down well, he thought.

He gave Lizzie a bath, read her a story – abridged, too many pages – and tucked her up.

She did that thing where she cries out 'Daddy!' once or twice, then hummed to herself, then grunted a bit, then slept.

He let the boy stay up a bit later than normal then got him upstairs and into a bath then bed with the promise he could read with his bedside light on as long as he liked. He'd be fast asleep within ten minutes.

It's funny how a little bit of agency can smooth out his temper, meaning the boy. Funny, too, how he's a lot easier when it comes to bedtime when his mum's not there. Fewer buttons to press, Jon supposes, and the boy's got a lot of fingers.

23

Eyes wide open

Eight on the dot and Parker's outside a garage behind Green Lanes, Shaun in tow.

Parker's been here before. Parker remembers this garage very well.

A big Turkish lad in a vest opens the tradesmen's entrance, pokes his head through and burps.

'Parker?' he asks.

'The one and only.'

'Stand back,' the lad sniffs.

He turns away from Parker and presses a button and the garage door clunks heavily into action.

'Open sesame,' Parker says.

The lad hacks and grunts, coughs a laugh. 'You'll need a magic wand to get into third gear in this motor,' he says.

Parker ducks his head. 'Wait here,' he instructs Shaun.

Inside the garage is a smallish van, room for three on the front seat, and several pieces of bulky furniture in the back, though it's empty of course. Two thin roof rack rails on top, and the side emblazoned with the words:

East London Logistics

Course it is, Parker thinks.

He's got form with East London Logistics vehicles, going back to Wapping and the dispute with the print unions, then tailing them up to this very garage, his snout Trevor keeping an eye out from Parker's old gaff round the corner.

Didn't end well for poor old Trevor, throat cut and his tongue pulled through it, the word 'Grass' on a handwritten sign hanging around his neck.

Parker abandoned the reconnaissance job straight away and never looked back; orders are orders.

But now he's thinking, Canning Town and Stoke Newington –

He's thinking –

Eyes wide open.

The Turkish lad was right: the van isn't exactly James Bond-ready, and Parker shunts and huffs their way south and east to the address in Clapton where Simeon awaits.

They arrive at eight-thirty or thereabouts. It's a closed-down establishment by the looks of it, all shutters and boards, the words *Clapton Café* faint under a recent paint job.

Simeon stands at the door with a cardboard box and two holdalls at his feet, smoking.

'Help the man with his luggage,' Parker tells Shaun.

To Simeon, he says, 'Hop in. And I hope you know where we're going.'

Simeon smiles and crushes the cigarette under his white high-tops. Before going to the passenger side, he hands Parker a piece of paper.

'Another one,' Parker grumbles. 'What's this one then?'

'Phone number,' Simeon says. 'We call it from a phone box, answer machine gives us the address. Wapping way.'

Parker thinking, that's the first time I've heard him speak. He also thinks that he hadn't expected to have to find out where to go like any other punter. Safety first, he supposes.

Shaun and Simeon clamber back in.

Parker turns in his seat. 'Simeon, old chum, do you know of any local phone boxes that are yet to experience the firm and exuberant application of neighbourhood youth vandalism?'

'I do not, boss.'

'Right you are,' Parker says. 'Hold on to your hats, gentlemen.'

Wapping meaning south.

Parker's thinking, Mare Street, Cambridge Heath, Bethnal Green, Mile End, pretty much a straight shot.

They can find a phone box on the way.

Suzi's in a car again with Lee Roy and Big Danny for 'the full experience from start to finish' as Lee puts it, roaring with laughter.

'Straight to the venue, though,' Lee tells her. 'None of that 0898 number and secret meeting place.' He grins. 'You can make that bit up in your article.'

'Can you tell me again how it works?' Suzi asks.

'Course.'

'Hang on a minute,' Suzi says, 'I'll record you if you don't mind.'

'Not at all, madam.'

She fishes her Dictaphone from her handbag. She winds up her window to block out the white noise of the street. The traders and shops of Commercial Road are closing.

C. BERNARD & CO. Sussex

Cousins and Sons Modern Furniture Purchased

Eastern Fruiterers

London Co-operative Society Self-Service

That vast pub lettering speaking straight to Suzi's heart:

TAKE COURAGE

Shutters and grilles, white lettering on red posters proclaiming:

SALE SALE SALE SALE SALE SALE

'All right,' Suzi says, pressing record. 'Good to go.'

Lee turns in his seat. 'So,' he says, 'first up is you flyer outside all the clubs up west and in Camden at the like-minded nights, you know, the Palace, Astoria, Heaven, Shoom, all them.'

'What's it say on the flyers?'

'Date and name of the firm. And the number of an answering machine service.'

'So, July first, Genesis, for example?'

'Tonight's not Genesis, Suzi. Fact check!'

'As an example, she meant, Lee Roy,' says Danny.

Lee sniffs. 'Yeah, fair, it works as an example. Probably have the logo on it too, bit of class, bit of branding. Everyone knows Genesis now, to be fair, so you might not even need the name. Just the logo and the date.' Lee pauses, nods to himself. 'It's a good idea that, in fact. I might suggest it. It'd look quality, well enigmatic.'

'Visionary,' says Danny.

'Yeah, yeah, Dan, leave it out.'

'And the answering service?' Suzi asks.

'That has the meeting point address info.'

Suzi nods. 'And that's all the promo then?'

'If you've got the wedge then you might do an ad for the pirate stations, same sort of principle, lots of hype without too much in the way of details.'

'Makes sense.'

'Secret location, size of the rig, who's playing, all that.'

Suzi nods.

She looks east towards the river.

Grey pebbledash towers, red-brick low-rise estates. Street lamps that are yellow and dim.

Up ahead, Docklands at dusk, the outlines of urban construction: cranes suspended in the gloom, hooks hanging from wire lines, trucks and diggers mushrooming rubble, portacabins and hazard lights, plastic sheets wrapped around scaffolding, flapping softly in the wind.

Suzi thinks, Gotham, future world of London.

'But *you* know where we're going?' she asks.

'If you're in the know,' Lee winks, 'you're in the know.'

'Any clues you'd like to share?'

Lee makes a serious face. 'We're going to stick a hood over your head in a minute, Suzi, purely for your own protection, you understand.'

'Very funny.'

'He ain't joking,' says Danny.

Suzi smiles ironically.

'Course I'm joking. I wouldn't joke like that with you, girl!' Lee grins. 'Limehouse Basin, near there. An industrial estate which can only be accessed from a private road, I believe.'

Suzi nods. 'When are the punters furnished with this information? If they're not already in the know, I mean.'

'And very few are.'

'That's what I thought.'

Lee checks his hefty timepiece. 'About now, in fact.'

'Very precise of you.'

'Yeah, they turn the phones on in the command centre at the venue when everything's set up and ready to go. Lights, sounds, action, you know. And they have to do that last minute given how these venues are acquired.'

This bit, Suzi knows.

Breaking and entering, blagging with moody licences and snide leases, estate agents selling the keys to vast properties that are soon to be re-let.

'I mean it's a balancing act, right,' Lee says. 'You can't start anything up too early or you risk getting spotted and shut down. Get a thousand or so people inside though, and the Old Bill will listen a lot more carefully to your claims that this gathering of souls is a private music industry event.' Lee grins. 'They don't want all them people knocking about in their cars and whatnot, intoxicated and pissed off, looking for a party.'

'So they turn on the phones.'

'And that's when—'

'That's when the organisers give out the venue details to the meeting-point people. *They* pass that on, and the convoy rolls!'

Suzi laughs. 'Very subtle.'

'Nah, it's clever this bit. Meeting points have to be somewhere cars can slow down without disrupting traffic. Wind down your window, you're handed a folded flyer with a map and an address handwritten on it, and bob's your uncle.'

'Can we have a look at a meeting point, you know, for the article?'

Lee turns again in his seat. 'Research purposes. Daniel?'

Danny considers the question. 'I think probably best not, given the one-way system round here. We don't want to get stuck.'

'You sure, Dan?'

Danny takes a moment, seems to visualise the route, weigh up the possible pratfalls, then nods. 'Yeah, it's the right move to go straight to the command centre. Besides, if we're too long, parking will be a nightmare.'

'Can't argue with that.'

Suzi thinks, fair enough then.

A Pizza GoGo moped swerves in front of the car, wobbles and rights itself.

Danny honks the horn, mutters, 'Cunt.'

Suzi closes her eyes, opens her eyes.

She wonders how much more of all this.

From the river, the long, low blast of a foghorn. Above, the chop and clatter of a helicopter. Danny slows down and allows a sleek black car to overtake, which it does smoothly, expertly. The road curves towards Limehouse Station. Train tracks on a bridge. A red beacon flashes at the top of a council block. By the bridge, faint light from the open doorway of the Railway Tavern. She imagines the rainbow rolodex of a fruit machine, the chime then chunter of change, the stumble and laughter of men out on the steps holding their pints and fags. Cars parked under arches. In front of the boarded-up derelict warehouses are jagged piles of wood and bricks, half-ringed by graffiti-covered corrugated iron fencing, rusting and sharp, posters advertising musical events – legal, Suzi supposes – slapped on at rough angles.

A dog barks.

Suzi looks up at the noise. She sees orange and purple lights in the bruising sky. She hears a stop–start beat. The repetitive flash of a strobe being tested.

Danny slows down and turns onto a slip road. There is the soft crunch of gravel under the tyres.

'Back entrance,' Danny grunts.

Ahead, an open gate. Two men in black suits with hi-vis wristbands stand either side, holding clipboards.

Lee winds down his window.

One of the men sticks his head in. 'Brother Lee Roy!' he says. They bump fists. 'You can park over there in the yard.' He points. 'VIP treatment, brother!'

Lee makes a face to say what else? 'Main entrance on the other side, is it?'

'Yeah, brother. There's about fifty inside already, rest on the way, I gather.'

'Nice one,' Lee says, offering a fist. 'Be lucky.'

Danny ghosts through the gate and slides into a parking space. He looks satisfied, Suzi thinks. Danny sees her little wry half-smile and nods.

'We can make a quick getaway from here,' he says. 'Not that I anticipate we'll have to.'

Doors slam.

'I asked that last question for your benefit,' Lee tells Suzi. 'For your bit, I mean.'

'You're like a research assistant, Lee. My work-experience boy.'

Danny laughs at this.

'Yeah, well, I'm not getting any royalties!'

It's Suzi's turn to laugh. 'There isn't much in the way of royalties writing for magazines, Lee.'

Suzi slips on her coat, notes the cooling air, how it feels nice after being in the car.

'Come on,' Lee says. 'Let's put you to work.'

Suzi raises an eyebrow at this.

'I said you'd take a few photos,' Lee explains.

Suzi indicates her shoulder bag. 'I've come prepared.'

'Dib-dib dob-dob,' Lee says, doing the Boy Scout gesture.

Suzi shaking her head, laughing again.

*

Noble rings Dalston nick and gets Fife.

'My missus isn't great,' he lies. 'Tell Jenkins I'll meet you at the rendezvous.'

'He won't like it.'

'He hasn't got much choice,' Noble mutters.

He smiles at Lea. 'I'm all yours for another hour at least, love,' he tells her.

'All *ours*,' she says.

'Soppy moo,' Noble jokes. 'I love you.'

'Yeah, you're not so bad yourself.'

Noble leans in for a kiss.

'Steady on,' Lea says. 'One's enough in there, isn't it?'

'I'm not sure biology quite works like that, darling.'

'Well perhaps it should evolve.'

Noble grins. 'Come here.'

Thinking, if we're quick I can be in Wapping in half an hour.

Parker pulls over near Mile End and Simeon gets out and makes the call.

He comes back after a few minutes. He climbs in and smiles, says nothing.

'Well?' Parker asks.

'Oh, sorry,' Simeon says. 'Elf Row is where we meet. It's the back road off of an estate near Cable Street.'

Parker nods. He remembers old Bill Stewart's joke about Christmas not being good for your elf. He wonders about old Bill's own bill of elf, thinks he's certainly getting on a touch.

'Gotcha,' Parker says. 'Do furnish me with the A to Z, Shaun, there's a good fellow.'

Shaun hands it over.

'On the correct page, you wally,' Parker says.

'How do I—'

'Jesus,' Parker says. 'Young people these days. Give it here.'

He locates the correct page and studies it.

Elf Row is a little no-through road running between two estates, it appears.

There are at least two car parks directly off it, for residents, no doubt, and what might or might not be a way out at the other end, though it's unclear.

Parker thinks, pull in, get the address and or the map from whoever's in position, turn round in one of the car parks and pull out. Given that these meeting points are chosen so as not to disrupt traffic, there must be plenty of space. The whole transaction, if that's even the word, should last about a minute, two tops.

This, Suzi can do. She has the various promoters and DJs and other types up against the wall, and she's snapping away. Industrial chic.

They're all laughing and sniffing, clad in Adidas trainers and sharp bomber jackets, upmarket leisure wear, baggy jeans and T-shirts, flat caps and woollen hats.

Suzi's giving orders. 'You and you both turn to the right. You and you put your hands up to your faces. You two look in that direction over there. Ignore me doing this.'

Laughter.

The sound system is being warmed up, the light show is in effect, the enormous warehouse has gaggles of ravers in various corners, there's a bit of trade at the bar, though the place still feels pretty empty.

Suzi snaps away, the lads pose and joke. Then she hears the radio crackling.

Two of the men confer. 'I'll go and see what they want,' says one of them.

'See what who want?' Suzi asks.

'Dibble.'

'Can I come with you?'

The man gives Suzi the once-over. 'Yeah, why not. Might be a good photo op, the local constabulary give their blessing, that kind of thing.'

Suzi smiles. She's thinking there might well be a much better picture than that, though she hopes it won't be the case.

'Follow me,' the promoter instructs.

They walk across the hangar. There's a twitchy energy in the space, Suzi thinks. Smiling eyes and nodding heads and it's not even got going properly yet. Sipping at big bottles of water. Smoking cigarettes through pursed lips. Sunglasses and sports gear. Dry ice and smoke machines. Glow sticks and whistles.

They're through the main doors and into the courtyard when Suzi understands quite what's going on. A semi-circle of police vehicles. A dozen or so uniforms and a chief inspector.

'Are you the organiser of this event?'

The promoter nods. 'That's right, I—'

But before he can start on his spiel and get out his paperwork, he's in handcuffs.

'You're under arrest and coming with me.'

'You can't arrest me. What are the charges? This is a perfectly legitimate event.'

Suzi takes a step or two back and eases her camera from her bag.

The security team have quietly closed the doors behind them and gathered in front, not quite squaring up to the police.

Suzi fires off a few frames of the stand-off.

'If you'll let me, I can show you the lease,' the promoter says.

'Where is it?'

'Inside pocket.'

The chief inspector removes it, pockets it without reading it. 'Come on,' he says. With the help of two uniforms, he leads the promoter towards a marked car. 'We're taking a drive.'

Several of the security team block their path to the vehicle. One of them steps forward. 'With respect,' he says, 'if you want this party stopped, the geezer there in cuffs is the only one who can stop it.'

'That's true. You let me out of these,' the promoter reasons, 'and I'll go and stop it right away.'

The chief inspector considers this. One of the uniforms, Suzi sees, shrugs as if to say, it's probably worth a try, guvnor.

'All right,' the chief inspector decides. 'You're still legally under arrest, mind, and in serious trouble. But you get in there and tell them to stop the music and pack up all the equipment and then you come straight back out here, and we'll have that chat. Understood?'

The promoter nods. 'Scout's honour.'

'Don't be cheeky, son. All the surrounding roads are blocked. No one's going anywhere until we say so.'

The promoter nods. The handcuffs are removed. The promoter bounds back inside. Suzi follows. The music stops. Suzi watches the promoter explain what's going on. She hears cursing and anger. She swaps her camera for her notebook, tries to get down the gist. She writes, 'Fuck the Old Bill, let's stand firm and confront the bastards.' She writes, 'There are thousands of people about to arrive, the streets are crammed. We're not standing for this taking of liberties, again!'

She writes, 'They're here to shut us down and no discussion. It's wrong!'

The promoter says nothing. Suzi watches as he weighs all this. She feels the indignation and the frustration. She feels the perceived unfairness, the sense that this crowd, this happy crowd here to have fun, together, all together, are being persecuted by the police, persecuted by the state.

Suzi senses a shift, a slight shift. She writes, 'Come on, let's fucking do it.'

The promoter closes his eyes and takes a deep breath. He shakes his head. 'No, we're not fighting the police,' he says. 'That's not what Acid House is about. It's not about resorting to violence. It's about love. It's about loving our comrades.' He nods and claps his hands. 'Go home, everyone. It's over for tonight.'

Suzi writes this all down.

The promoter beckons Suzi over. 'Listen, darling, you reckon I might be able to fit in Lee Roy's boot?'

'I imagine you might,' Suzi tells him.

Ayeleen. All I can see down the road are police officers and flashing blue lights, people running this way and that, shouting, and I'm feeling suddenly sober and scared, but we're not there yet, not quite, we can still get off the bus, turn around and go home and Lauren says:

'I think we should get off here and go home.'

I turn to her, she's biting her lip, looks nervous, and Lauren never looks nervous.

'Yeah,' I say. 'We should.'

'I'll get rid of the pills first.'

She puts a hand under her skirt and then edges it back out and stuffs the tiny package down into the gap in the seat.

We stand up, wobble down the aisle, grip the railing going down the stairs. The conductor calls out, 'You can't get off here, it's not a stop!'

But we ignore him and hop off the platform at the back and walk quickly towards Wapping High Street, sticking to the main road.

'We'll be fine,' Lauren says. 'Head down and keep walking, we've done nothing wrong, we're visiting my family, anyone asks, all right?'

'Yeah, course.'

'We'll be back to mine in no time, I promise, Leen.'

'Yeah.'

'We've got money for a taxi, remember, from my mum, so keep an eye out.'

I nod. 'What about Shaun?'

'Leen,' Lauren says, firmly. 'He's with his cousin's bloke, isn't he, he'll be fine, don't worry about him.'

'OK,' I say. 'You're probably right.'

'I am right, Leen, I know I am. Look, there's a cab across the road.'

Lauren sticks her arm in the air and yells, 'Taxi!' like in a film, and the cabbie sees us, the light goes off and he pulls out, does a U-turn and stops right next to us.

Lauren tells him her address, and he tells us to hop in.

'You're very lucky girls,' he says. 'I've been chocka all night!'

We don't say anything.

'Suit yourselves,' he mutters, drives us back in silence.

At Lauren's mum's, I try Shaun on the phone and his cousin answers.

'Oh, hi love,' she says. 'You've not found him then? They're not back yet.'

'No, we couldn't get a lift, in the end,' I lie. 'Decided not to go. Can you ask him to call me tomorrow?'

'Course, love.'

'Thank you.'

I put the phone down and go upstairs to Lauren's room.

'Everything all right?' Lauren's mum calls out from in front of the telly.

'Yes, thanks, all fine!' I shout back.

Lauren's lying on her bed, shoes still on, fully clothed.

'Well,' she says. 'That was close. Probably for the best too, don't want to make a habit of all this before uni, do we?'

I smile, nod. 'Yeah,' I say. 'Let's not do it again, eh?'

Parker pulls off Cable Street and onto Brodlove Lane, then does a sharp right onto Elf Row. It's a narrow road between two estates. On one side, a car park and garages below a block of flats. The gate is open. A man and a woman stand in the entrance both wearing hooded tops. They point for Parker to keep going. On the other, a row of stationary cars but there's plenty of space for the van.

Parker kills the headlights, it's still not quite dark, drifts down Elf Row.

On the left, overflowing bins in an alley. Graffiti stating, simply:

A sign ahead:

Welcome to the Shadwell Estate

Pigeons perch on sand-coloured brick. A CCTV camera hangs from a lamppost, smashed given the angle, frayed wire just about holding it up.

On the right, washing hangs limply over railings. Scaffolding and container units.

Another sign:

No ball games

There's a patch of grass and trees in bloom, green leaves bursting over the fences. Kids running about, throwing things. Parker glides another twenty metres or so down this cobbled alleyway. The van rocks a touch from side to side. Shaun and Simeon are silent. Parker sees another hooded figure, who signals for Parker to turn right into the estate, which he does through an open gate.

He slows to a stop. It's a dead end.

He thinks, three-point turn then on our way –

In the rear-view mirror, he sees the hooded figure close the gate, skulk off.

Then a police van screeching to a stop.

Four men pile out, two uniforms, two in plainclothes. The two uniforms hang back.

Parker thinking, fuck.

He turns to Shaun and Simeon. 'Sit tight and say nothing, all right.'

Parker climbs out the driver's seat.

He closes the door and turns, his hands in the air.

Noble.

'What the—'

'Round the front, quick,' Noble says. 'Get the bonnet open.'

Parker does what he's told.

Parker hears the other plainclothes. 'Right, you two, out. Backs against the van. Hands on your heads.'

Then: 'Get our geezer oh the radio to consult on these clowns. Though I know you, Simeon, don't I? You don't look too clever, son, if you don't mind my saying.'

Parker hears the hiss and crackle of police radios.

Noble says, 'Stay still, son.'

'I would love to know what the fuck is going on, guv.'

'All in good time.'

'You all right over there, Chance?' This is the other plainclothes.

'Yeah, golden. Reading him his rights.'

Parker hears laughter. Parker hears this other plainclothes on the radio, saying, 'Gotcha, nice one. Stay on the line.'

Noble tells Parker to hold tight.

The other plainclothes pops his head round, nods at Parker. 'Tell him to do one, he's only the driver. Tell him he's walking home. Unless he wants to take a detour with us via Leman Street nick.'

'Tell him yourself,' Noble says.

The other plainclothes looks at Parker. 'You get all that, pal?'

Parker nods. The other plainclothes nods, goes back to the other side of the van.

Noble points and hisses at Parker. 'Get behind those bins and wait for me.'

'I don't understand.'

'Just do it.' Noble cranes his neck. 'Now.'

Parker moves quickly and gets himself well hidden.

Through the windows of the van, he can see the backs of Shaun's and Simeon's heads.

The bins reek of rotten meat. Smells like *wound*, Parker thinks. Or there's a dead dog in there, a fox.

Something's on the turn.

Bags of soil, splitting and leaking, dumped on top of a No Parking yellow grid painted onto the road. Cracked paving stones, shoots of green growing between them. The sky darker and heavier like a blanket.

Parker thinking, they cannot arrest Shaun.

Thinking, Noble must know what he's about.

Thinking, that other plainclothes, I know him from somewhere, I'm sure of it.

The radios spit noise. Parker sees Noble and the other fella in conference.

Simeon and Shaun haven't moved.

Parker holds tight.

How many times, he thinks, have I been in exactly this position, figuratively speaking if not an actual physical reality.

Come on, he thinks, come *on*.

He sees more sirens flashing at the Elf Row turning, hears car horns and revving engines.

Party's over then.

He sees Simeon and Shaun ushered away from the van. The other plainclothes climbs into the driver's seat. He guns the engine and completes the three-point turn Parker wasn't able to tackle earlier. Plainclothes leans over and opens the passenger door and Simeon climbs in.

One of the uniforms opens the car park gate. The van moves off slowly back down Elf Row, followed by the two uniforms in the police vehicle, which dawdles, the engine running.

Shaun and Noble left alone.

Parker scrambles out from behind the bins.

He looks at Shaun. He looks at Noble.

'You all right, mate?' Parker asks Shaun.

Shaun nods.

Noble addresses them both. 'You two get yourselves home. This is your lucky night.' He points at the police vehicle. 'I'm afraid we can't give you a lift.'

Parker nods.

Noble stares at Parker, and, just for a moment –

A look crosses Noble's face.

A look Parker's not sure about.

Well, Parker thinks, I best be patient then, with regard to any answers.

And then Noble's into the back of the police vehicle, which pulls quickly away.

Parker turns to Shaun. 'What the fuck just happened?'

'Search me.'

Parker snorts. 'Did they?'

'No.'

'That's a relief, I suppose.'

They stand for a moment in silence. Parker points at where they came in.

'It sounds like there might be a bit of bother over there still.'

Shaun nods.

'I reckon we go out that way,' Parker adds. 'Through the estate. Just to be sure.'

'OK.'

'Come on. I'll buy you a kebab on the way home.'

Shaun sniffs. 'What about Ayeleen?'

'Don't worry about her, she and that Lauren can look after themselves, that's for sure.'

'You think?'

'Listen.' Parker grips Shaun by the shoulders. 'They're not after nicking young women, it's not a good look. They just want to stop the party, that's all.' He breathes out deeply. 'At the very worst, they'll have been moved on. Trust me, you can't put thousands of people in the back of a van, however big it is. However much you want to.'

'I suppose.'

'I suppose is right, son. Now let's get a wriggle on, eh.'

They walk quickly through the estate.

A dog barks and Parker's neck snaps round to the noise.

A car backfires, same thing.

Christ, he thinks, it's the nerves that get you.

They come out on Cable Street and Parker looks right and left –

No sign of the Old Bill.

Parker flags down a taxi and tells the driver Clapton Pond.

Safely inside and on their way north, Parker says, 'We'll drop in at Ayeleen's uncle's place for our kebab, make it known we're all right.'

Shaun thanks him and Parker smiles, meaning it. He feels a tremendous relief, if he's honest.

We *are* all right, he thinks, but only just.

Jon's watching telly when Jackie gets home.

'Anything good on?' she asks.

'I don't know.'

'You don't know?'

Jon smiles. 'I've not really been watching it.' He looks up and sees Philip Hayton talking in the BBC newsroom. 'The news, I mean. I just turned it over.'

'You just woke up, didn't you?' Pointing at the beer bottle at Jon's feet. 'Chin-chin, glug-glug.'

'Yeah, I drifted off.' Jon rubs his eyes. 'Long day.'

'I'm sure it was.'

'How was yours?'

Jackie nods. 'It was nice.'

'Good.'

Jackie smiles. 'Well,' she says. 'I'm off up to bed. I'll leave all this to you, shall I?'

Gesturing at the bottle of supermarket-brand French lager – Jon's fourth – the glass, the empty bowl of crisps, the dog-eared *Radio Times* sprawled on the carpet.

Jon grunts good night. Jackie nods, gives him a tight smile, and leaves him to it.

He inspects his watch.

The athletics is on after the news.

According to Jon's *Radio Times*, which Jon now picks up and re-examines, there is a tremendous evening in prospect in Oslo, culminating in the Dream Mile, which features Steve Cram and two of his greatest rivals Said Aouita and Abde Bile. Also in action tonight, Carl Lewis in the 100 metres, Derek Redmond against Butch Reynolds in the 400 metres and Colin Jackson versus Roger Kingdom in the 100 metres hurdles.

It does sound good, to be fair. He always enjoys watching Colin Jackson.

Jackie will likely still be awake and reading when it's finished, but *The Naked and the Dead* is on BBC Two later if he feels up to it, let her get some kip.

Next morning, Jon's first into the kitchen mixing porridge for the kids, a bit bleary-eyed if he's honest, that dry hangover taste and the old head feeling both empty and thick. Jackie and the kids still asleep at least, so he's got a little time to himself to recover.

He woke up with a resolution of sorts.

During the night, he remembered the other day, remembered thinking about how you do what you can, about how he might not have always done what he could.

What can he do, Jon woke up thinking.

He woke up thinking about those files Godfrey acquired for him on a short loan: this year's planning applications and land transactions involving the Riverside Close Estate.

Jon, of course, copied these without telling Godfrey, without telling anyone.

He's already returned the originals, as per their agreement.

And he hasn't really done anything yet with the copies. There's a lot of paperwork, in fairness.

Now, as he stirs the milks and adds a sprinkle of sugar, a smear of jam, he makes a decision.

Jon decides that, starting tomorrow, first thing, he'll go through all this paperwork, as long as it takes, and find out exactly what has happened to all those houses – those *homes* – on Riverside Close. Who sold what and to whom and why, if there is a why.

He can't tell anyone for now, but once he's established what's happened exactly, he can take it to her upstairs, perhaps, or go more widely than that.

It's Jon's suspicion that the water shortages are not a coincidence.

Nothing ever is.

He hears the boy murmuring to himself on the toilet, a flush. He smiles to himself.

Do *this* first, he thinks, Sunday.

Tomorrow can wait.

24

Anger is an energy

Suzi wakes up in a stranger's flat next to a naked man she doesn't know. Light pours in through curtain-less windows. She's also naked and there's a smell of dried sweat in the air, under the covers: sex. She checks her watch: just after midday. She can't have been asleep for more than a couple of hours, and she doesn't feel too bad, given the circs. The man is snoring lightly and looks happy, she thinks, what *is* his name? After it all fell apart down in Docklands, and after they smuggled the promoter out the back entrance in the boot of Lee's car, Lee and a couple of others told her they were going somewhere else, that it'd be great for her story if she came too. So she went, and she was so relieved that nothing had gone wrong – well, that nothing had gone wrong for *her*; in fact, given the angle of her article, it'd all gone really quite *well*, lots to report – that she went and she had fun, first in a basement on Clink Street and then under some arches in Vauxhall and she happily took what was offered, and she danced and she laughed and she forgot all about everything outside of what she was doing *right then*, and she can't really remember if she met this bloke at the first or the second place, but she knows why she went on with him to some friend's after-after party and she had a good time, that much she *does* know. She feels that lovely pins-and-needles tingle all over her. She looks at him now and thinks about waking him up but realises she's very hungry and very thirsty and instead she slips out of the bed they're in, dresses quickly, picks up her bag in which her notebook and camera remain, pops the door a crack and sees at least three bodies passed out on sofa and floor, she tiptoes around them and opens the front door of what she now understands is a first-floor council flat, and she's out onto the walkway, down the stairs and away –

It takes her a minute to realise she's in Shoreditch, just north of Old Street, so she heads south then east, makes for Columbia Road, what she needs is a pub lunch, get her head together, jot down some notes, the Royal Oak will be just the ticket.

A couple of nights later, Suzi peers over the balcony of the VIP section of the Royal Albert Hall as The Style Council perform material from their new album, *Modernism: A New Decade.*

In the stalls and in the seats, she sees people tearing up their programmes, leaving in what looks like disgust.

In the stalls and in the seats, she sees people dancing, moving in time to this new music, euphoric and ecstatic.

She thinks, we're not even hearing this in the clubs yet.

A realisation that this is what pop music will sound like in a year or two.

Which might well be too late for The Style Council.

She closes her eyes and feels a deep-seated melancholy.

Since the weekend, since the shutdown of the party, since her big night out and her one-night stand, something permanent-feeling has nagged at her, something existential, threatening. It's felt, these last few days, like her leg is being tugged as she tries to swim to keep her head above water. Flashes of the basement, the arches, grinning and laughter, lights and sound, a living room and cans of lager, a bedroom and a man, flesh and bone, hot breath.

She's standing stage left, just above, and when she opens her eyes, she can see Keith below at the mixing desk.

He looks up, sees her, and waves.

She begins her piece on Acid House.

Not for the first time, Suzi writes, the young people of this country are fed up with being told what to do.

She locates in her notes a quote, fellow journalist Bill Brewster:

'Protest is not the right word, because it is expressed in a completely different way … it is about creating an alternative society away from the mainstream.'

It's not about conflict, she thinks, remembering the promoter's words on Saturday night, it's about loving our comrades.

Good choice of word, *comrade*.

Just because a manifesto is unspoken it doesn't mean it's not there.

Eleven years of Tory government, maybe that's it, pent-up frustration.

Anger is an energy, after all.

And Suzi's angry too, of course.

She alternates between working on her piece and typing up her report for Noble on the night of the party bust.

She makes this report clear, unambiguous.

She distances herself from it in her mind; she's objective in this approach.

It's become something of a mantra, these last few days:

She can still decide exactly what it is she wants to do.

Hold tight.

It's all to play for.

25

The blade runner

Shaun. I never wanted to go to the party in the first place and only said I did 'cos Ayeleen was going and I didn't want her to go without me. Well, I wish I'd stayed at home, now, don't I, what a wally, to use Parker's favourite word for me.

'Look,' he told me the next day. 'It worked out all right. There's no need to let on to your cousin too much about what happened beyond we were turned away and came home, agreed?'

I nodded. 'Course.'

Fact is I'm not letting on to *him* now, neither.

On the Wednesday after, I'm in Ayeleen's uncle's place and I'm helping out a bit behind the counter. The lads there are showing me a few tricks, how to chop an onion, how to *slice* an onion, how to deseed a pepper, how to mix a raita, all that.

'Useful stuff, the basics of knifework,' as Tariq puts it. 'Not that we have our own set of knives here, but you student ponces might get some.'

I say, 'I don't know yet, innit, that's you not me.'

Tariq laughs, he always laughs at whatever it is I'm saying, to be fair, not really sure why, something to do with me 'being soft on Ayeleen' to use his words, I expect, though I don't know why he doesn't just call her my girlfriend, probably for her uncle's benefit, at least I hope it is, I don't want her telling people I'm soft on her, do I, I wouldn't sound too smart in that context, and it ain't true anyway, she is my girlfriend, at least that's what she tells me she is.

'Next week,' Tariq says, 'we'll give you the blade runner and you can have a crack at the meat.'

The blade runner being the motorised carving knife – though sword might be a better word – that they use on the sweating hunk of whatever meat it is that turns in the window.

'Shouldn't it be the person holding the knife that's the blade runner,' I point out. 'Not the knife itself.'

'What?'

'I mean, if you're holding it, you're the one running the blade, right?'

'The questions from this one.'

'I'm only saying.'

'Well don't. It's the blade runner, the knife is, always has been, always will.'

'What meat is it, anyway?' I ask.

'Meat, innit.'

'Yeah, but what kind of meat, is it red meat, white meat.'

'It's like brown and grey, innit, bit red in places.'

I shake my head. 'That's not a colour of meat.'

'No?'

'No.'

Tariq waves his knife. 'What do you see, young Shaun, that I do not?'

'Are you putting me on?'

Tariq smiles, does a Zorro move with the knife. 'Whatever can you mean?'

I never know if he's joking or taking the piss. I shake my head.

'All right, Shaun, I'll let you into a trade secret.'

Tariq holsters the knife and wipes his hands. He addresses the sweating leg, fingers spread, like he's about to measure it with a handspan like you would a horse, I suppose.

He looks at me. 'Come closer, young Shaun.'

I take a step towards him. The heat of the thing, no wonder they all look so filthy by mid-afternoon, all that perspiring they must do.

In a whisper, Tariq says, 'Don't be afraid, you mustn't be afraid.'

'I ain't afraid, Tariq, it's a kebab.'

Tariq shakes his head. 'Oh no it's not, Shaun, not yet.'

'Leave it out, eh.'

'They say,' Tariq still whispering, 'that when the pupil is ready, the master appears.'

'Oh they do, do they?'

'They do, yes, they do say that.'

'Well I'm ready, Tariq.'

'I—'

And that's when Marlon walks in.

He smiles at Tariq and points at a table and sits down at it. He gestures for me to go over, and I look at Tariq, who says, 'It's not like we're paying you, is it?'

So I go over.

'Sit down, yeah,' Marlon tells me.

So I do.

And that's when Marlon lays it all out.

It was him that stopped me getting nicked. It was him that made sure I was all right, I *am* all right.

The way he tells it, he knows everything about what happened, and he definitely weren't there.

I heard a voice on that copper's radio, it could've been anyone, so it could've been Marlon. It all sounds straight-up.

'And you're going to do me a little favour in return.'

'I don't know,' I tell him. 'I can't get in any trouble, you know that.'

Marlon smiles, his big gold teeth and his eyes sparkling. 'Nothing like that, Shaun.'

'Yeah?'

'Yeah.'

I breathe in and out.

'It's what's called quid pro quo, Shaun, my man.'

'What's that then?'

'I've scratched your back and now you're going to scratch mine.'

'And it's legit, you promise?'

Marlon stretches back in his seat. 'You ever have any trouble at Feltham?'

'Not really.'

He smiles again, grins. 'You see? I look out for you, always have.'

'But it's legit?'

He nods. He waves his arms about a bit. 'You going to be working here, then?'

'Not really working.'

'But this is where I can find you.'

I nod. 'Yeah, or at least leave me a message, you know.'

Marlon leans forward and rubs at his chin, nods. He gives me a little dig in the ribs. 'Tell your pal up there I'll have my usual.'

I stand up.

'Where's your little girlfriend got to?' he asks.

'She's in the office.'

Marlon sucks his teeth and flicks his wrist, snapping his fingers. 'Yeah, man,' he says.

I go back behind the counter and tell Tariq Marlon's order.

'Pussy only likes it medium hot,' Tariq mutters.

I try not to laugh. 'I'm going to trip, yeah?' I tell Tariq. 'See you later.'

We bump fists. I slide off the apron I've borrowed and hang it up. I go to the office and tell Ayeleen I'll be back later, maybe we can do something.

'Always distracting her!' Uncle Ahmet laughs.

Then he says, 'Anyone in?'

I tell him that Marlon is there, otherwise it's empty but it is only mid-afternoon, after all, and he bustles out to see him, thanking me more than once as usual.

Ayeleen kisses me goodbye, and I leave out the back way, go home.

Carolyn and Parker are sitting in the front room holding hands looking all misty-eyed and whatnot.

'We've got some news, Shaun,' Carolyn says.

'Oh yeah?'

'You're going to be an uncle.'

'Or an aunt!' Parker laughs.

I must look surprised, as Parker tells me to pick my jaw up from the floor and hug my cousin.

'An uncle?' I ask.

'Cousin, technically,' Carolyn says. 'But you'll be more like an uncle.'

'So that's why—' I start.

They're both nodding.

Parker says, 'I only found out myself an hour ago.' He grins. 'She's a clever one, your cousin!'

I say that I know she is.

And I'm thinking there's no way I can tell them about Marlon now, even if I wanted to.

Which I don't.

Parker stands up. 'Here,' he says. 'There's bubbly in the fridge, let's have it. You can practise your hospitality, Shaun.'

I go into the kitchen and find the champagne.

I choose some glasses, nice ones, give them a rinse and dry them –

Then we drink a toast to what Parker calls 'the new addition'.

I'm happy for them, course I am, but I can't help wonder about the living arrangements, what's going to happen next, 'cos something'll change, there ain't no doubt about that.

26

Politics

Mrs Thatcher decides that the outcome her chief inspector has relayed to her is promising, both in terms of the immediate result and the continued shutting down of this 'rave scene', but also in terms of getting her poll tax into action and functioning properly. Of ensuring blanket compliance, mass *payment*.

No, we don't like breaking the law, in general, we English, she thinks. And non-payment is against the law, after all, lest we forget.

She's calling the community charge that now, *her* poll tax.

Her state, her tax.

'It'd be a feather in your cap,' Mrs Thatcher tells her favourite chief inspector, 'if you were able to make an example somewhere along the line while maintaining the status quo as previously discussed.'

'An example in my work with CIB2, ma'am, I assume.'

'Without upsetting the apple cart.'

'No, ma'am.'

'Let's not throw the baby out with the bathwater.'

'Yes, ma'am.'

Mrs Thatcher smiles. 'Geographically speaking, this example would work best if local.'

'Yes, ma'am.'

'To extend the apple analogy, it's bad apples we want to expose, not a rotten core.'

'Very good, ma'am.'

Mrs Thatcher, briefly, wears a quizzical expression. 'You mean that you agree the idea's a good one and you'll carry it out, or that you approve of the wordplay?'

'Both, ma'am.'

Mrs Thatcher smiles. 'Very good,' she says.

Terry tells you he's had word that one of the two big hitters on your payroll at the Yard wants to have an even-handed conversation. You tell Terry that you're all ears.

Terry passes this on and receives in response an invitation to meet. The time, date and venue are scribbled on a card. You know the place, course you do.

'Once upon a time,' you tell Terry, 'one would meet one's contacts in the constabulary in the upstairs rooms of West End pubs with friendly landlords. What's the world coming to, eh?'

Terry shakes his head and agrees that he doesn't know what the world is coming to neither.

Precisely half an hour before the appointed time, Terry readies the car.

As you climb into the back seat and settle your briefcase and overcoat, you furnish him with an anecdote. 'Talking of what the world is coming to, Terry.'

'Yes, boss.'

'These fancy modern cars, engines start at the drop of one.'

'They do.' Terry then aptly demonstrates the ease with which the motor turns over.

'My point is that once upon a time a man could get himself a little peace and quiet before an outing.'

'Oh yeah?'

'That's right he could.' You sniff. 'My old man would mumble something about warming up the car a good three-quarters of an hour before departure.'

'That seems a little bit excessive.'

'Not if you knew my mother, Terry!'

Terry laughs politely, not too hard, it's your mother, after all.

'Let's take the temperature of the streets, shall we, Terry, the climate.'

'Scenic route then?'

'We don't want to be late, but, yes, of a sort.'

Terry lets the car drift on the breeze a little. Canning Town, Limehouse, Wapping, Tower Bridge all seem to float by in the plush comfort of the back seat.

'River's looking nice and full,' Terry remarks.

You nod. 'Important, water, as we know.'

'We do know that.'

'Indeed we do.'

'Just a few minutes.'

'I should hope so, Terry, given the time.'

You know the place, of course you do, but not many people know the place.

It's something of a privilege, you think, just to know that it exists, let alone get inside it. Very exclusive, years-long waiting lists, secret listing, all that palaver, but of course you've been invited in before.

Terry parks as close to London Bridge as he can.

You walk on the east side.

On the left, just before the bridge itself, a locked, wrought-iron gate and a Tardis-like lift behind it, a buzzer.

You press the buzzer. There's the intercom crackle, a long beep.

You're expected, of course you are, and the gate springs open.

Terry activates the lift and in you both get.

Down you go, down under the bridge –

The lift doors open –

You find yourself in the foyer of the Marylebone Rifle and Pistol Club, which shares the premises with the Stock Exchange Rifle Club.

The range is beneath the southern footings of the bridge, though you're not expecting to have to shoot anything.

'Or anyone,' as Terry noted when you told him.

No, you're thinking a drink and a spot of lunch will be excitement enough.

A club lackey in a blazer approaches.

'This way, gentlemen.'

He leads you through the empty foyer into the carpeted dining area. A young, butlerish type polishes glasses and nods at the lackey. At a corner table, by the fire – fire, you think, it's fucking July – sits your Yard big hitter nursing a short drink.

You point. 'I'll have what he's having,' *you tell the lackey.* 'Terrence?'

'I'll wait at the bar.'

The lackey nods.

You slide off your coat and ease yourself onto a stool at the table.

'I was just telling my associate,' *you say, gesturing towards Terry,* 'time was one would meet one's contacts in the constabulary in the upstairs rooms of West End pubs with friendly landlords.'

'Times change.'

'Don't they just.'

You clear your throat and smile. Your drink arrives. Whisky, by the looks of it.

You lift the glass. 'Your good health.'

'And yours.'

You roll the drink in your mouth for a moment before swallowing. 'Decent.'

'It's all right here.'

'Certainly has its charms,' *you agree.* 'Now what can I do for you, Chief Inspector Young.'

'Straight to the point as ever.'

'I'm like a marksman in that regard.'

'Very good.'

You smile. 'I know you're a busy man, I don't want to keep you.'

Young shifts in his seat. 'Firstly, let me emphasise our gratitude for our ongoing relationship.'

'*Ongoing* informal *relationship.*'

'Quite.'

You make as if to stand. 'Well, it's nice to be needed. Shall I—'

Young smiles. He circles a finger for more drinks. 'One for the road?'

You nod and settle back down.

Young says, 'In your area of concern, north-east, a young man and his grandmother have recently been registered as official police informants.'

'Sounds iffy.'

'Which means, of course,' Young says quickly, 'that they can legally participate in criminal activity.'

'Like I said.'

'Criminal activity in collusion with police officers.'

'Surely not.'

'I'm afraid so.'

You smile. 'I was being sarcastic.'

Two more whiskies arrive. You thank the lackey and sniff at your drink, take a thick sip.

Young says, 'We think that there might be some overlap of this activity with your own interests, or at least with certain associates of yours.'

You think of the brothers. You think of the unit on Riverside Close.

You nod.

Young goes on. 'If you're able to establish that this is the case, we'll be grateful.'

'Even more grateful.'

Young nods.

'Have any details you've got delivered to Terry over there in the usual fashion and I'll see what we can do.'

Young nods again.

You stand. 'If you'll excuse me, Chief Inspector.'

Young smiles. 'God bless,' he says.

Noble waits for Parker at their usual spot, public bar of the Prince of Wales pub.

He's standing at the far end of the counter with two pints of Guinness in front of him, a tray of cockles soaked in vinegar from the seafood stall outside, two wooden forks, and a packet of Salt 'n' Shake, for luck.

Noble arrived early to mull over what Chief Inspector Young has told him about the next steps, and what exactly he needs to communicate to Parker.

What Young told Noble was that a young black man and his grand-mother had been very recently registered as informants in the Stoke Newington/Clapton area of Hackney. Young showed Noble the file: Noble recognised the young black man, has had very recent contact with him, in fact, indirectly at least.

Simeon.

'Police informant meaning in this case, we believe, sanctioned and protected criminal activity in collusion with police officers.'

Noble nodded.

'Use all resources necessary to insinuate yourself into said activity, observe, record, report. We're looking at a name or two only, and clear, corroborated evidence of their involvement by around March next year. Understood?'

Noble nodded at that too. Get involved is the gist, and he's halfway there.

'And by resources, I include your UCO, of course.'

'Of course, guv.'

'Deploy as and where you see fit. You'll have him until April or May, I'd say. Then, well, things will likely change. We'll be looking at a new posting.'

Which is precisely what Noble is mulling over.

Given he doesn't know exactly what the next steps are, it's best he doesn't tell Parker that his current position might be under review.

It'd be wrong to speculate, that's for sure.

Noble doesn't much like it, doesn't like keeping Parker in the dark.

But it's for his own good, need-to-know basis, and ignorance is bliss.

Noble doesn't much like it at all.

He sighs, heavily, feels it all weighing down on him, this line he's treading, all these people encroaching, feels it deeply, etched inside somewhere.

He sighs again.

On the other hand, he needs Parker's help and they've both got a job to do, haven't they.

Parker bobs in, ducking and diving to the bar.

'What's all this then?' Indicating the spread. 'We having some sort of Irish wake?'

'Celebration.' Noble hands Parker a Guinness. 'Your good health.'

Parker gulps down about half. 'Celebrating what?'

Noble smiles shyly. 'Her indoors. We're in the family way.'

'*We* are?' Parker grins, clearly delighted. 'How very new man of you, guv.' He grins, offers his glass in a toast. 'Nice one, this is very good news indeed. I'm very happy for you.'

Noble reddens a bit. 'Yeah, cheers.'

Parker winks and looks down. 'Must be a relief, you know, the old swimmers and that.'

'Turn it in.'

'I'm not being funny, guv, I just mean, you know, it took a little while and you don't know, do you?'

'I suppose you don't.'

'Yeah.' Parker knocks down the rest of the pint. 'You don't know until you know. Then you know.'

'Another one?'

'Go on then, to the expectant couple.'

Noble smiles. He can't help himself.

He's excited, he wants to smile, he wants to share this good news, this very good news, but it's Parker too. The lad *makes* Noble smile, that enthusiasm, that cheek, that naughty face on him.

Noble gestures for two more pints. 'Have a cockle,' he says, pushing the tray towards Parker. 'They're a delicacy round these parts.'

Parker spears a couple and chews thoughtfully. 'I always liked that little bit of grit you get in these,' he says. 'When I was a kid, my old man used to say it weren't the sand or the sea salt or nothing like that.'

'No?'

'No.' Parker runs his tongue over his teeth. 'No, he always said they added it after, at the pub.'

'Right.'

'Yeah, from the car park!'

Noble spluttering and coughing, vinegar going down the wrong way, heaving.

Not 'cos it's that funny a story, but the idea of little Parker eating cockles, pulling a face, his dad slapping him on the back with a hearty only joking, son!

Noble steadies himself with a mouthful of Guinness.

'She doing all right, then, old Lea?' Parker asks.

'Yeah, less of the old, though, she wouldn't like that.'

'Figure of speech.'

'She's doing great, she's happy. *We're* happy.'

Parker nods. 'Me too, guv.'

Noble smiles, nods, then clears his throat. 'Right, well, we don't have all day.'

'Speak for yourself.'

'I've had some instructions that you need to know about.'

'Go on.'

'You might see me around a bit. Or hear about me at least.'

'You joining the dark side, are you?'

'Something like that.'

'So, in my role as part of the Hackney Community Defence Association I may encounter complaints directed at Detective Constable Patrick Noble and I should proceed forthwith.'

'You might, you might not,' Noble reflects. 'You might hear about me in another context an' all.'

Parker nods.

'I'm still on the same team,' Noble says. 'Meaning yours, meaning *ours*.'

'Gotcha.'

'I need to deliver a name, or names. And I need to be involved to do so.'

'And what do you want me to do, guv?'

Noble smiles and has another long drink of Guinness.

He nods to himself.

Yes, he thinks.

'Nothing, son,' he says. 'You carry on.'

Parker smiles, raises his glass. 'Aye, aye, captain.'

Noble raises his own glass, and they see off their pints.

Parker heads to the door.

'Oh, and Parker, son,' Noble calls after him, picking up the packet of Salt 'n' Shake. 'Catch.'

PART FOUR

Simeon

1

I think this is nice

July

Simeon sits up in the van saying nothing as Jenkins drives them away from Elf Row and the Shadwell Estate.

'I imagine, Simeon old son, you might be wondering exactly where we're going,' says Jenkins eventually.

Quietly, to himself, Simeon recognises that this is true. 'Yeah,' he offers.

'Well, sit tight, you're in for a surprise.'

Simeon rests his eyes on the dim cityscape, which floats by. He thinks about Parker and he thinks about Shaun and he thinks about how did they get home. He thinks about that other copper, Noble his name, he thinks, and decides that he must be in on all this, all this with Jenkins, he must be.

The van is draughty and rusting and smells of petrol. There's an echoing clunk when Jenkins changes gear, which is a lot.

They pass through Bethnal Green then arrive in Clapton. Jenkins pulls over roughly on the main road.

'Wait here,' he tells Simeon, who nods.

A few minutes pass.

Marlon climbs into the driver's seat. 'Where to, guv?' he jokes.

Simeon looks at Marlon's smile, his gold teeth, his red eyes, hooded –

He thinks that you never know where you are with Marlon. He's not particularly surprised to see him. He turns up, Marlon, he's always around. What Simeon's gran calls a bad penny.

Marlon guns the engine, which sputters and then catches. 'Home,

James,' he says, laughing. He turns violently into the traffic, honking on the horn.

At the Lea Bridge roundabout, they turn off the main road and wriggle through a few backstreets before turning into a low-rise housing estate next to the canal.

Marlon kills the engine. 'Grab those two bags out the back and follow me.'

Simeon does what he's told.

They walk past houses that look empty and are dark. Marlon stops every so often to check the numbers above the letter boxes. At the end of one of the rows, close to the fencing and close to the water, he stops outside a red front door.

There is a faint light somewhere inside on the ground floor. Net curtains. No noise. First floor pitch black.

Marlon fumbles in his pockets. Simeon stands watching, holding a bag in each hand. He doesn't put either of them down on the ground. A habit of his gran's, that. You never know where that bit of ground has been, she always says. Simeon realises that he's hungry and thirsty. He didn't expect much from the party, but he didn't expect this. The sound of children playing drifts towards them. Not that close. Maybe Springfield Park but it's a bit of a stretch. Nighttime summer air and it can travel though. Simeon hears pub noise, chatter and glasses, deep laughter, that low hubbub. Something like a fairground ride starts up, faint, then cheering. Fruit machine jackpot.

Marlon raises an eyebrow at this.

He shoots Simeon a friendly look as if to say it's someone's lucky night, then, all right for some. He locates a key ring. He checks over both his shoulders. Satisfied that they're all alone, he opens the door.

Gesturing politely with his arm, Marlon says, 'After you.'

Simeon steps inside. The corridor is narrow. He puts down the two bags. To the left, a kitchen with the lights off. At the end, stairs in darkness. Before that, an open door leading into a sitting room, television on with the sound down low. Simeon goes in. In the half-light, a figure sitting quietly in a reclining chair.

'Gran,' he says, startled.

He turns back to look at Marlon.

'Welcome home, son,' Marlon says, grinning again.

Marlon goes out to get them something to eat and gives Simeon and his gran a chance to catch up. 'Play happy families for a bit,' he says.

Simeon has a nose around first.

He takes the two bags upstairs.

There are two bedrooms, a large suitcase in each. All Simeon's clothes from their place on the Nightingale Estate are in one of them, his room, he supposes. He unpacks his toothbrush and razor. His trainers. A few magazines. He thinks that he doesn't really have very much stuff and wonders if he should have more. It doesn't feel very grown up. There's a bed and a wardrobe with a few hangers in and that's it. White walls and vinyl flooring. He stores the bags in the corner. At least the bed's been made, he thinks, his gran didn't have to do that.

The bathroom is pretty basic. A stained bath with a shower head and a toilet. The sink has one of those lights above it where you can plug in your electric shaver. He turns it on. The lightbulb is giving out, he thinks. Dirty yellow murk. He flushes the toilet to check it works, which it does.

Downstairs, the living room is the television and two easy chairs. A dining table and stools. No shelves, nothing like that. Bare walls and empty space. In the kitchen, he sees some of their old pots and pans and cutlery, a few plates.

There's milk in the fridge but not much else.

'What happened, Gran?'

'They came when you were out and brought me here.'

'Who did?'

'Two of the coppers who've been round before, I don't remember their names.'

'Can you look at me, Gran? The television will still be there when we've finished talking.'

His gran looks up at him and smiles. 'It's nice here, not having all those stairs. You know, the lift was always broken, wasn't it. I think this is nice, better.'

Simeon shakes his head. 'What are you watching anyway?'

'Oh some rubbish, I'm not even sure.'

'Right, well, I'll get some plates and things for dinner ready, it's late.'

Marlon brings back a curry. Simeon and his gran sit at the table and eat theirs in silence. Marlon takes his on a tray in front of the box, eyeing the athletics.

Simeon watches as he mops up korma with a naan bread, dips his hand into the poppadom bag at his feet, crunching through them.

Afterwards, Marlon offers the chair to Simeon's gran, who sits down gratefully and changes the channel.

Simeon walks Marlon out to the van.

'This is the new set-up,' Marlon says. 'In your bedroom, there's a safe under the bed.' He hands Simeon a scrap of paper. 'Combination. Learn it and bin it. Put what's in the bags in the safe.'

Simeon nods.

Marlon grins, his eyes sparkling. 'And await instruction!'

Laughing, he climbs into the van and drives off noisily.

Simeon goes back inside and tells his gran he's going to bed.

He finds the safe, which was hidden by the valance, his gran's handiwork, and if she saw it, she wouldn't say nothing, probably pretend to herself that she hadn't.

Into it, he stacks first cash and then bags of pills.

When he's finished, there's still loads of room inside.

He undresses, turns off the light, and gets into bed. It takes a while, but he falls asleep in the end.

2

A simpler option

August

Jenkins is round every Monday afternoon. Simeon lets him in and follows him upstairs, Jenkins bustling and joking about something or other, some muggins he's had in the station over the weekend, some fella who owes him a favour, the usual chatter. Simeon watches as Jenkins takes cash from the safe, adds packages, gives Simeon his instructions for the week.

As he leaves, he hands Simeon an envelope.

'Per diems,' he likes to say. 'Don't spend it all at once!'

And then he's off again.

Simeon takes the notes out of the envelope and places them carefully in a biscuit tin that he keeps in a kitchen cupboard. Enough money for his gran to do the shopping that she likes to do every day, down at the butchers on the high street, groceries from the market, pulling her rickety caddy and chatting with the elders, each week Simeon putting a little aside, which they use for a bit of furniture or something to make the place a bit more homely. So far, he's found them a nice coffee table and a couple of standing lamps at the second-hand place on Church Street, the front room much improved as a result. He's put a deposit down on a bicycle and in a couple more weeks he'll have that, which will help.

Marlon comes over on Thursday mornings to 'take the temperature' as he calls it, licking a forefinger and holding it up in the air, 'which way is the winds blowing, eh?', laughing like a drain.

He's always happy, Simeon thinks, or at least that's how he fronts up.

They'll do a little inventory – 'a stock check' – and Marlon makes a few calculations, checks the ledger where Simeon enters the week's take, the sales. There's a steady enough stream of customers when the shop's open, which is only at certain times of the day, clearly established, and generally respected. 'Corporate wholesale' – one of Jenkins' little jokes, Simeon assumes – is out-of-office hours and Marlon likes to be on the premises to oversee these larger transactions, which tend to happen on Friday and Saturday mornings, perhaps for obvious reasons. Marlon's little joke each time:

'Something for the weekend, sir?'

Simeon has noted it's the same faces each time, one or other of two white cockney blokes with tidy haircuts, dressed in smart clothes, chunky gold bracelets. Simeon thinks they're brothers, more than likely anyway. He fetches them a cup of tea, sometimes a snifter from the bottles of rum or whisky that Marlon keeps under the kitchen sink, sometimes both. They pay Simeon little heed, but they ain't unfriendly, always very polite, in fact, and the last time one of them was over he'd brought one of them clock gadgets that makes you a hot drink when the alarm goes off in the morning, for Simeon's gran.

'Give yourself a bit of a lie-in, son,' he'd winked.

Simeon's gran loves it, to be fair, and she's made a Jamaican rum cake as a thank you, wrapped tight in cling film and waiting on the kitchen counter.

This Thursday both Marlon and Jenkins show up in different cars, which is a first. Simeon opens the front door and waits.

There are three other plainclothes in Jenkins' car, Marlon on his own.

Marlon winds down his window and calls Simeon over.

'Get in, you're riding shotgun,' he tells him. Then: 'Buckle up, buttercup!', laughing again.

Simeon puts on his seat belt.

Jenkins' car in front, they leave the estate and head towards Lower Clapton.

Marlon has his music on loud. 'Don't touch my settings, Simeon old chap!'

Simeon doesn't touch anything, doesn't say anything.

He wonders where they're going and why but doesn't want to ask.

They follow Jenkins into Homerton.

Near the hospital, Jenkins stops in the middle of the road. A police van pulls out of a side street. Simeon notes the half dozen or so in uniform inside. Marlon lets the van cut in and the three vehicles move off in convoy.

They turn right towards the canal.

They skirt Mabley Green, the grass yellow and the air thick with smoke and laughter, kids playing football, two topless men holding cans of strong lager, arguing, their dogs barking and crapping everywhere. Pylon buzz.

They turn right onto Lee Conservancy Road.

On their left, low-rise estate blocks, two floors, a flat on each, Simeon thinks.

Jenkins turns into the car park of the second.

The van next.

Marlon doesn't follow them in.

Instead, he slows down and dawdles, pulls over at the side of the road, hazard lights on and the engine still running.

Simeon watches as Jenkins and the three plainclothes pile out. He spots Noble, yes, that's him, Simeon thinking, I knew it.

The uniforms follow.

The door to the ground-floor flat opens and Jenkins and two of the uniforms push their way in.

There's some shouting, the sound of women crying, young and old.

Simeon knows what this is like, he knows what's next.

A few kids mooching past stop for a peer at what's going on.

A uniform gives them the unceremonious heave-ho and on your bike, and they scarper sharpish.

Jenkins comes out the flat with two decent-sized holdalls.

The two uniforms block the doorway.

Jenkins winks at the other plainclothes as he carries the bags through the car park and out to Marlon's motor.

Jenkins opens the boot and delivers the two bags. He leans inside and says, 'You know the drill!'

Marlon checks his mirrors – for once, Simeon thinks – and pulls away.

Simeon turns in his seat and sees a man in handcuffs being dragged into the police van. He's not shouting or resisting, Simeon notes, he's just made himself a deadweight, given up, and it looks like he's a tough one to shift, a big unit. No, not a small fellow, Simeon thinks. He sees a uniform carrying another holdall and depositing this in the van.

Simeon settles back into his seat.

Marlon drives them back to Riverside Close and they unload the contents of the bags into the safe, bricks of cash and bricks of drugs, all wrapped in cling film, like his gran's Jamaican rum cake, Simeon thinks.

Marlon does an inventory and logs it all in the ledger.

He gives Simeon a look as if to say, don't touch!

But he's obviously pulling my leg, Simeon thinks, he knows I ain't touching nothing.

Marlon leaves after this. 'See you at work tomorrow, dear!' he shouts over the engine revs.

Simeon thinks, he wants to mind his engine if that car's going to last.

His gran cooks some rice and peas and fries some pork for their tea.

They eat it watching *Eastenders*.

Simeon wonders where they get their storylines from, his life ain't nothing like what they get up to in Walford.

After their food, Simeon makes them both a hot drink.

He sips at his and thinks about the man in handcuffs.

He'll be banged up for a few hours in Dalston nick, the custody sergeant taking possession of that other holdall and logging it as seized evidence. Then he'll be released on bail only to come back in a day or two to be told there are no charges.

That's the more complicated way of doing it.

It's what happened to Simeon, leading directly to his current predicament.

There's a simpler option: they don't bother logging the bag, the lad released without charge.

Either way, his drugs and money are upstairs in Simeon's safe.

Technically speaking, Simeon thinks, it's very likely someone else's drugs and money, just like it's someone else's safe.

Simeon hopes for the lad's sake that, whoever really owns this drugs and money, he's the understanding sort.

3

Hackney's colourful history

September

Marlon brings Shaun with him one Thursday morning. Simeon remembers him from the busted party, the van, that big fella, Parker.

'You remember, Shaun, course you do,' Marlon says.

Simeon nods.

'Shaun's helping me out on a project. He'll need access.' Marlon grins. 'You grant it, yeah, Simeon?'

Simeon nods.

Marlon slaps Shaun on the back. 'Come with me and I'll show you to your office.' Laughing.

Shaun turns up once a week after this. He fills a little backpack with something from the safe then off he goes on his bicycle.

He's friendly, but they don't chat much.

Simeon thinks that it's probably sensible not to get too pally.

Neither of them is happy about what they're doing, that's obvious from the carry-on whenever Marlon is on site, and talking about it is only going to make that feeling worse.

So they don't. It suits Simeon. His gran likes to make them some food, get the two of them to sit down together for a bit, chat. She seems to think that as they're not so different in age maybe they could become mates.

'It never hurt to mek a friend,' she says. 'An ally. You never know when you might need one.'

Simeon's always been a bit of a loner, and that's OK.

He likes his own company is all it is. He never really enjoyed the chatter of other boys at school. He was too shy, often found it intimidating, wasn't quick enough to keep up with the jokes, the insults. He was happy enough being around the other boys, playing on the football teams and that, but he never said much.

They had a nickname for him: Big Mouth.

It wasn't a piss-take or nothing, just a funny name 'cos he never opened *his*. Neutral, really.

'Oi, Big Mouth!' in the changing rooms, on the football pitch in the pre-match huddle, in the corridor after class. 'Pipe down, won't you?'

They used to joke that he'd be the perfect criminal accomplice. This was at Hackney Downs school, across the park from where Simeon and his gran lived on the Nightingale Estate.

On Mondays, there used to be a swimming club for little kids and their mums held in the school pool, though it wasn't for the Hackney Downs pupils, whether they could swim or not.

One day, some of Simeon's mates smashed the windows of the cars parked in the school playground while they were inside and made off with a couple of stereos and a handbag.

Simeon was walking past just as this was discovered. Tears and shock. The headteacher fuming and embarrassed.

'You,' he hissed at Simeon. 'What do you know about this?'

Simeon said nothing; he didn't have nothing to say.

The headteacher dragged him off to the office and gave him a good going-over. Nothing he *could* say, so Simeon said nothing.

The boys who done it were quietly appreciative. They still called Simeon Big Mouth but with a little bit more respect.

It was a good lesson.

Marlon turns up unexpectedly with Shaun in the passenger seat. Simeon sees them from the kitchen window. It's a wet Tuesday afternoon and Simeon's gran is asleep in her chair in front of *Sons and Daughters* on the television with the sound down low. Shaun knocks once and comes inside. Simeon gestures at the living room as Shaun heads upstairs. 'Try and keep it down, yeah?' he tells him.

Shaun nods. He comes back downstairs a few minutes later with his usual backpack and indicates that Simeon should follow him outside.

Marlon opens the passenger door. 'Get in,' he tells Simeon, who does what he's told.

Shaun slides onto the back seat.

They head down towards Homerton and pull over near the Kingsmead Estate.

'We ain't getting *too* close,' Marlon snorts. 'Hissing Sid not long gone away.' He kisses his teeth. Mutters something Simeon doesn't catch.

Course Simeon knows what he's on about. Hissing Sid is Sidney Cooke the ponce and child killer, leader of the Dirty Dozen paedo ring. Used a flat on the estate until Hissing Sid was invited to spend the rest of his sorry life at Her Majesty's pleasure.

Marlon is shaking his head, mumbling something to himself about here's hoping he gets sliced quickly enough inside. Talk about how to give a place a bad name, another proud moment in Hackney's colourful history. Sighing, though it keeps everything else a lickle bit under the radar. Still.

Marlon lights a cigarette and offers Simeon the pack and lighter. Simeon takes one and lights up, winds down his window.

Marlon shifts in his seat and narrows his eyes. Simeon puffs away happily enough.

'It's a quality smoke,' Marlon insists. 'Tek your time with it.'

Simeon examines the filter: Dunhill. It's all right, he thinks.

An unmarked car passes them and pulls over, stops, engine running.

Simeon sees three men inside. Leather jackets, meaning Regional Crime Squad, meaning Jenkins and his cronies, though he can't make out whether it's him or not.

Marlon flicks his cigarette out the window. He sniffs and coughs. Simeon does the same.

A few minutes go by slowly.

Another car leaves the estate, signalling left, and turns towards the canal.

The unmarked car's tyres squeal and it jumps forward, turns sharply in front of the other vehicle.

The three leather jackets – Jenkins and Noble, Simeon notes, one other – are out and all over the chap driving, who they pull out and handcuff, stick his face in the bonnet, arms behind his back. They toss the keys onto the pavement.

'Now,' Marlon says.

Shaun is out the back seat quickly and Simeon follows close behind. Shaun bends down and picks up the keys, hands them to Simeon.

'Open the boot,' Shaun tells him. 'Quietly, yeah.'

Simeon does what he's told.

Shaun drops the backpack into the boot.

'Lock it and put the keys back,' he says.

Simeon does what he's told.

All the while the plainclothes are yelling, the chap with his face in his own bonnet is yelling, and Simeon and Shaun slip back quietly into Marlon's motor, no one the wiser.

As Marlon pulls away, Simeon sees Noble pick up the keys from the pavement and open the boot.

'Bingo!' Simeon hears.

4

Rude boy

October

At the end of one of his Monday morning visits, Jenkins tells Simeon he's coming with.

'So get your coat!'

Leaves floating in puddles. The sun in the canal. Tarmac slick and shiny, new-looking.

Simeon climbs into the passenger seat. Jenkins leans over towards him, rough-skinned and day-old booze breath, sunglasses on a bright autumn day, hair thin on top.

'I need you to watch the motor while I do the rounds, all right?'

Simeon nods.

And so the morning unfolds.

Three stops on Kingsland High Street, two of them at Turkish drinking clubs, one at a clothes retailer, Jenkins disappearing down the stairs and out of sight. Each time coming back with an envelope which he adds to a briefcase that he keeps under his seat. Grunting to himself as he does. Simeon keeping his eyes averted. After that, it's two places on Sandringham Road, a café and a bookies. Then to Lower Clapton Road, working their way east: a chip shop, then a barbers, Hackney Baths, and finally two takeaways.

'Fruit machines,' Jenkins explains. 'VAT. Pays out twice.'

Simeon doesn't question this. All he's done is sit in the car.

'Any traffic wardens, you scare them off, son,' Jenkins told him. 'You can do that, a big black boy like yourself.'

Simeon reckons he could of, sure, but there weren't any need.

'We'll take luncheon at my club,' Jenkins announces.

He parks by the pond.

They cross the road at the lights and go into a Turkish restaurant. Jenkins nods at the blokes behind the counter in the front and points to the tables further back, where they sit down.

Jenkins removes his sunglasses and rubs at his eyes.

A young woman arrives and delivers menus. 'Anything to drink while you make up your mind?' she asks.

'I'll have an Efes,' Jenkins croaks thirstily. 'Simeon, would you like an Efes?'

'I'll have a Coke, I think.'

'Very sensible. An Efes and a Coke, darling.' Jenkins rubs his hands together. 'And two large doners, the works. All right, Simeon?'

Simeon nods.

The waitress makes a note and starts to wander off.

'Don't forget the chips, darling!' Jenkins calls out after her.

She turns slowly and smiles. 'Course not.'

'Good stuff.' Jenkins clears his throat noisily. 'They're all right in here. And look.' He points. 'Fruit machines.' Laughing now.

The food comes and they tuck in. Simeon realises how hungry he was, thinks that he's always hungry, really, always in need of a square meal, as his gran says.

There's a ding as the door goes, and Simeon looks up. His blood, for a moment, freezes. He swallows. His forkful of chips in mid-air, his mouth open.

Shaun.

They see each other, eyes darting. Simeon gives a very quick, very slight shake of the head, which Shaun acknowledges, though no one would notice this exchange.

Jenkins looks up from his plate, sees that someone has come in, grunts and settles back to his food.

Simeon breathes out slowly.

They finish eating and Jenkins pays the bill.

Outside on the pavement, Jenkins points. 'I'm going that way, Simeon old chap. See yourself home, all right.'

Wednesday. There's a knock at the door on what is normally a quiet morning for Simeon.

It's that other copper, Noble. Simeon opens the door.

Noble says, 'We'll talk outside.'

Simeon nods and follows him across the car park to the edge of the estate overlooking the canal. The water like glass in the autumn sun.

'I expect you're surprised to see me, Simeon,' Noble says.

Simeon nods, though in truth not much surprises him anymore.

'I'm going to lay something out for you.'

Simeon nods.

'The thing is,' Noble says, 'as soon as I tell you what I'm going to tell you, then you're complicit, you're a part of it and there ain't really any going back.'

'OK.'

'You understand what I'm saying?'

'Yeah.'

'And you still want to hear what I've got to say?'

Simeon nods.

'All right,' Noble says. 'Here it is.'

Noble tells Simeon that he is in the process of observing and recording Jenkins' criminal activity. He tells Simeon that this involves observing and recording the criminal activity of Jenkins' associates. 'If you get my drift.'

Simeon nods.

'There's a way out,' Noble says. 'And it's simple.'

Simeon nods. 'Go on,' he says.

'You keep shtum about my visits here.'

'What visits?'

'That's the spirit.'

'No, I mean, what visits?'

282

Noble grins. 'Today, and other visits in the future.'

'OK.'

'You let me in, you let me do whatever it is I do, and you tell no one.'

'OK.'

'You keep your gob shut, son, and I'll make sure you come out of this on the right side, all right. You become my snout, effectively.'

'You can do that, can you?'

Noble grins again. 'I ain't quite what I appear to be, Simeon old chum.'

'And I just have to trust you?'

Noble sniffs. 'You ain't got no choice. You tell Jenkins and I disappear, he won't touch me. And then he disappears, until he comes back with a warrant, and you find yourself in an awful lot of trouble, given the criminal activity out of this gaff of yours. A rude boy pushing dope.'

Simeon swallows.

'So you see, you ain't got nothing to lose by keeping quiet.'

Simeon nods. He says, 'That other lad, Shaun. You do the same for him, and we have a deal.'

Noble looks impressed. 'I think that's the most words I've ever heard you say at once, Simeon.'

'Well?'

'Yeah, why not. Nice to see the comradely warmth too, there ain't a lot of it about these days.'

'What sort of thing do you have in mind?' Simeon asks.

'Put it this way,' Noble says. 'After I pop upstairs, don't say anything over your blower you wouldn't want your gran to hear, you know what I mean?'

Simeon nods.

'Good man.' Noble slaps Simeon on the back. 'Now if you wouldn't mind showing me where the telephone sockets are.'

5

Lemon

November

A sharp, insistent knocking on the door wakes Simeon from a well-earned nap. He comes down the stairs and sees a man making a visor with his hand, his face all scrunched up, trying to peer into the kitchen window. He doesn't look much like a customer, Simeon thinks, or one of the brothers' firm, neither. He's wearing a suit that's not quite flash enough for that, one leg has got a bicycle trouser clip on it, and he's carrying a briefcase.

Simeon opens the door and coughs.

'Oh, sorry,' says briefcase. 'I didn't think there was anyone in.'

'Is that why you were looking in the window then?'

Briefcase smiles, embarrassed, by the looks of him. He wipes a hand on his suit jacket then offers it. 'Jon Davies, I'm from the council.'

Simeon sniffs and nods and then shakes Jon Davies' hand. 'Oh yeah.'

Jon Davies nods. 'Yeah.' He looks around, over his shoulder, gestures at the estate. 'I've been here before.' He smiles. 'Well, not *here*,' meaning Simeon's unit. 'But other houses, you know, knocked on doors.' He smiles again. 'And here I am.'

'What can I do for you?'

'Water's all right now then, is it?'

'Pardon?'

'Your water, the taps. No problems at all?'

Simeon shakes his head.

'Oh,' Jon Davies smiles. 'That's good to hear. There were some issues not long ago. Some of the residents wrote to me at the town hall, about the water shortages.'

Simeon nods and says nothing.

'But it looks like it's all fixed now then, the problem.'

Simeon nods again.

Jon Davies smiles and nods. He turns as if to go then turns back and frowns at Simeon. 'I can't see that there's anyone else living here at all anymore.'

'I live with my gran.'

'I mean ...' and he gestures again. 'The estate is empty.'

Simeon thinks that Jon Davies seems a little bemused by this state of affairs.

Simeon cranes his neck and decides to have a look for himself. 'Yeah, maybe.'

Jon Davies narrows his eyes. 'How long have you lived here?'

'Few months.'

'Right, a few months. And no issues with the water?'

'None.'

Jon Davies is nodding now. 'Is it, well, is the house yours?'

'We live here, yeah.'

Jon Davies smiles. 'That's not quite what I meant.'

Simeon sniffs again and runs his tongue over his teeth. He thinks about what he should say to Jon Davies. He thinks that he should say something that's true even if it's not quite *the truth*.

'We're council tenants,' Simeon says simply.

'Of course.'

'By the way,' Simeon adds. 'Do you have any credentials, you know, identification?'

Jon Davies raises a palm. 'Oh, I am sorry.' He smiles, his hand in his inside pocket, rummaging. 'I was just following up on some correspondence, I'm not here to see you specifically.' He waves an envelope at Simeon.

'OK.'

Jon Davies returns the envelope to his pocket. 'Well, cheerio, then,' he says. 'Thanks for your time.'

Simeon nods and closes the door, goes back upstairs.

'I assume you know your way around a motor, Simeon, old boy?' Jenkins asks next time he's over.

Simeon nods.

'Good man. Grab your driving gloves, you're coming with.'

Jenkins hands Simeon a piece of paper. A name and an address on the Holly Street Estate.

'This is where you live,' Jenkins tells him. 'And the name there, that's your older brother, all right?'

Simeon nods. The name on the piece of paper is Clyde Crooks.

'Clyde the snide,' Jenkins snorts, starting the engine. 'Crooks by name.'

Simeon says nothing.

They drive to the police vehicle compound in Enfield. It's not far from the reservoir, Chingford on the other side bathing in the winter sun.

'You can come up here on your holidays one day,' Jenkins laughs.

At the desk, Jenkins explains to the duty officer that young Simeon is Clyde Crooks' little brother, here to pick up Clyde's car, which was impounded after Clyde's unfortunate arrest twelve months ago for possession.

'He's out now,' Jenkins says happily. 'Just the three months for old Clyde.'

The duty officer processes the paperwork and hands over the keys. 'Drive carefully,' he winks.

In the pound, they locate the car.

No MOT, no insurance, no road tax, and the police compound tag is tied to the front windscreen wiper. Despite his best efforts, Simeon finds that this tag will not come off. Jenkins hands him the keys.

'Battery's flat,' Jenkins tells him. 'I'll give you a jump and then you'll be away.'

Simeon climbs into the driver's seat. The car is pretty grimy inside and it smells. Jenkins lifts the bonnet and attaches jump leads. In a moment, Simeon feels the engine rattle throatily, then turn over, then thrum.

Jenkins puts his head in the window. 'Whatever you do,' he laughs, 'don't stall!'

Simeon is more worried about being pulled over.

Jenkins hands Simeon an envelope. 'Put this in the glove compartment, all right.'

Simeon takes the envelope, which isn't heavy especially but feels thickly packed.

'Now,' Jenkins says. 'I want to see you do it.'

Simeon does as he's told. He notices that Jenkins is wearing *his* driving gloves.

'Good lad. Now get yourself over to the Holly Street Estate and park as close to it as you can on the Queensbridge Road.'

Simeon nods.

'We'll meet you there.' Jenkins slaps the bonnet. 'Bon voyage!'

The drive to Dalston is uneventful enough. Late-morning traffic on a schoolday, Simeon supposes.

As a rule of thumb, Simeon will do his best to avoid the Holly Street Estate specifically and Queensbridge Road more generally, with its blacked-out drug pub on the corner and kids sitting on walls ready to give the elders a nod when someone they don't know appears.

Simeon finds a spot and parks without stalling. Does a neat job of it too.

Out his window, he spots the sign by the road that announces he's arrived safely at the Holly Street Estate. In spray-can paint across the map of the towers and the corridors, is the word SHIT.

That's been there a few years, Simeon thinks.

Given the state of the rest of the place, there ain't a great deal of value in washing it off, Simeon thinks. He exits the car and wonders what to do with the keys. More pressingly, he wonders where he can wait for Jenkins without getting buttoned. He doesn't want to be hanging about on the street like a lemon for longer than he can help it.

He looks up and down the road, which feels quiet but isn't, and decides that the best course of action is to open the bonnet of the motor and examine the engine for a bit.

Simeon doesn't know a lot about engines, but this one doesn't exactly look like it's in the prime of its life. Then again, it got him here from Enfield, so it's not all bad news.

A police van chunters past and stops. It might be the first time Simeon has ever been happy to see one. A moment later, Jenkins pulls up just behind. He clocks Simeon and comes over.

'You got the keys, son?'

Simeon nods.

Jenkins clicks his fingers. 'Here, give them to me.'

Simeon does what he's told.

Jenkins opens the driver's door and pulls down the sun visor. He pops the keys on it and then pushes it back up and closes the door.

Jenkins jerks his thumb at his own car. 'You go and wait in mine. You know where to find the keys!' Laughing.

Simeon does what he's told.

He winds down the passenger window. Watches Jenkins chat to the uniforms in the van. Simeon knows a Territorial Support Group unit when he sees one. They get themselves kitted up and ready for something.

A few minutes later, a man of about thirty leaves the estate.

As he steps onto Queensbridge Road, the uniforms pounce.

They grab this man by the neck and by the arms.

They drag this man along the street.

They throw this man into the back of the van.

Simeon hears shouting and screaming. Simeon hears this man shouting that they've got the wrong brother.

Simeon hears one of the uniforms shouting something about how this man didn't get long enough from the judge last time.

Jenkins looking on.

The back doors of the van are wide open.

Simeon sees the uniforms kick and punch this man again and again.

Simeon sees the uniforms pull off this man's clothes and throw them into the street.

Simeon sees the uniforms drag this man naked from the back of the van. They throw a rough-looking blanket at him, laughing as he tries to cover himself up.

Simeon hears: 'This your car, is it, Clyde old chap?'

Clyde Crooks shouting, begging, crying. Clyde Crooks shouting, 'I haven't seen this car for over a year, it's been with you lot!'

'You sure about that, Clyde?'

'I don't even have the keys, for fuck's sake.' Pleading, now, sobbing, through blood and tears and snot, Clyde Crooks says, 'They're at my mum's, I swear.'

Simeon notes that the young lookouts and the elders from the pub are, from a safe distance, watching this scene very closely.

Simeon sees Jenkins lean into the car and pull the envelope from the glove compartment. He holds the envelope in the air, showing it to the uniforms – and anyone else who might be watching.

Jenkins opens the envelope and pulls out a newspaper. 'Yesterday's,' he announces.

He pulls out a matchbox and opens it.

'Bingo,' he says. 'Clyde old boy, get dressed, you're coming with us.'

Clyde Crooks is bundled back into the van. Jenkins beckons Simeon over with a wave. He tells him he'll give him a lift home in a minute.

Simeon nods.

6

Mistletoe and wine

December

One of the brothers brings a Christmas tree to the house.

'For your gran, you know, and for you too,' he tells Simeon. 'You'll have to do the mistletoe and wine yourself.' Laughing. 'Have a good one, yeah.'

Jenkins gives Simeon a 'well-earned Christmas bonus'.

'Get yourself a nice big turkey or whatever it is you lot eat this time of year.'

Simeon thinks Jenkins can afford it. He's been keeping a closer eye on the comings and goings in the safe since Noble first came round. Simeon reckons Jenkins is taking home upward of two grand a week.

Business is booming. Office hours – as Simeon likes to call the times of the week when they're available to their customers – are busy, constantly. The wholesale distribution element is in what the brothers like to call 'an exponential market growth paradigm'.

Simeon thinks the East London Logistics delivery vehicles are getting bigger. And they're taking a lot longer to load and unload. Simeon reckons his Christmas bonus is well-earned.

'One last job before the festivities,' Jenkins tells Simeon. 'We need one of your regular customers, but someone who goes elsewhere when your shop is closed, you get my drift?'

Simeon nods.

'One of my lot will be here for office hours next week. All you do is give whoever is there the nod when the right client comes along, and they'll do the rest.'

'OK.'

The next week, Noble's there for the last job before Christmas. Office hours are as busy as ever.

'Christmas rush,' Noble jokes. 'Stocking up for the holidays.'

But it's not really funny, Simeon thinks, as everyone is buying about twice as much as they usually do. And that can't be good.

Eventually Simeon sees the right sort of client. A twitchy enough addict, he'll do what he's told but smart enough to get himself from A to B without any aggro and reasonably well turned out most days.

So Simeon gives Noble the nod.

Noble follows the bloke off the estate and that's all there is to it.

The following week, the twitchy bloke doesn't show up at all, which is surprising for two reasons. Firstly, 'cos he always turns up. Secondly, 'cos it's the last office hours for a while.

A few of the regulars always hang around and chat a little bit after making their purchases and Simeon doesn't mind as long as they're not using anywhere near the house or causing any bother at all.

He sees that two of them are chatting happily one morning and he goes over and asks if the twitchy bloke is all right, if they've heard anything.

The two fellas exchange a look.

One of them says, 'He's been taken in, nicked.'

Simeon nods. It's always possible, he thinks.

'He got pulled by Babylon last week and they asked him for the names of his dealers.'

Simeon nods.

'Babylon wanted the dealers for themselves.' Another look is exchanged. 'Not 'cos they aiming to bring them in, mind. No, they want them to supply drugs to themselves, to Babylon.'

Simeon nods again. 'And?' he says.

'He didn't give them no names, so they done planted him.'

Simeon nods.

'Fourth offence, not a short stretch.' The fella doing the talking sniffs. 'He won't be round here for a while.'

Simeon wishes the two fellas a happy Christmas and goes back inside.

New Year's Eve: Simeon and his gran listen to the prime minister's New Year Message.

Simeon thinks she's got a nice voice, Mrs Thatcher.

'We stand on the threshold of a new decade, which will itself lead us into a new century,' she says. 'It is a time to look forward with hope and optimism to the limitless opportunities which lie ahead.'

'Hear, hear,' says Simeon's gran.

'Our policies of freedom and enterprise have produced a decade of solid achievement,' says Mrs Thatcher. 'They draw inspiration from principles which are timeless and soundly based because they respond to the hopes and ambitions of the human spirit.'

Simeon waits for his gran to say something, but instead she nods her head and murmurs encouragement as if she's there, in the audience, watching it live, Simeon thinks.

'We will continue to extend ownership. Water privatisation is the latest – huge – success creating over two and a half million shareholders. Wider ownership of shares and homes is giving power and wealth to those who never dreamed of it.'

Simeon sips at his mug of hot spiced rum.

Soon, he thinks, he'll be in bed, asleep, and tomorrow it'll be a new year and it'll all lurch back into gear and there won't be time for these sorts of reflections.

'We have reawakened in Britain her self-esteem. We intend to continue to build a Britain that is free, prosperous, generous and secure.'

7

Swings and roundabouts

January

Simeon and Shaun sit in the back seat of Jenkins' car, Noble in the front. Shaun's got his Walkman on but Simeon's listening to Jenkins and Noble discussing the 'order of play'.

The other two detectives – the fat one and the greasy one – are in a car behind. There are two vans with a few uniforms in them waiting at the meet, wherever that is and whatever that entails. Simeon doesn't have the foggiest, which is why he's listening so carefully. Though they might as well be speaking in code, he thinks.

'You got those warrants then?' Jenkins is asking.

Noble saying, 'By warrants you mean the photocopies you left on my desk?'

'Them, yeah.'

Noble pats the inside pocket of his leather jacket.

'Good,' Jenkins says. 'We'll only need five minutes, so it don't matter if they realise they're snide.'

'Five minutes?'

'Yeah, we already know where it all is.'

'How?'

Jenkins winks. 'My man.'

'Marlon?'

Jenkins puts a finger to his lips theatrically. 'Now, now, see no evil, speak no evil.'

Noble nods to himself meaningfully and sniffs. 'Regardless,' he says. 'These moody warrants—'

'What about them?'

'Well,' Noble says slowly. 'It don't much matter that they ain't legit if the thing on them we're saying we're after is actually on the premises.'

Jenkins guffaws. 'I am unclear as to your meaning there, son.'

'I mean—' Noble smiles and shakes his head. 'Never mind. I've read the small print.'

'Good.' Jenkins roars. 'Then you're definitely classroom-ready, old chap!'

Simeon doesn't know where they're going, and he doesn't know what they're going to do when they get there.

What he does know is that after whatever happens happens, he's taking something in one of the vans back to his gaff, and Shaun's taking something in the other van back to that restaurant where he works.

Stopped at a traffic light near London Fields, Jenkins looks over his shoulder. 'Right, you two, time to shape up.'

Shaun removes his headphones. Simeon swallows.

Noble says, 'We're going into a Caribbean establishment on Cambridge Heath Road.' He smiles. 'It's a deli, very modern.'

'It's a shop with a café,' Jenkins says.

'That's what I said.'

'You called it a deli, whatever that is. It's a shop with a café.'

Noble shakes his head. 'It's an establishment that serves products both on and off the premises.' Jenkins opens his mouth to speak, and Noble raises a finger. 'The point is there are customers but there is also a clientele in attendance.'

The lights change and Jenkins turns left without indicating.

'So,' Noble goes on, 'you two will wait by the door. Don't come in, we don't need your faces seen, but don't let anyone else out, all right?'

Simeon nods and looks at Shaun, whose eyes are red and blank.

'There'll be uniforms doing the crowd control, so this is just a heads-up.'

'Yeah,' Jenkins says. 'Don't fret or nothing.'

'We'll do what we do, and then you two go your merry ways and everyone's happy.'

'Except the cunts in the shop, of course,' Jenkins mutters. 'Or the café.'

'It's a *deli*.'

Jenkins stares into the rear-view mirror. 'Couple of minutes, look sharp.'

Noble gets on the radio to coordinate the vans.

Simeon and Shaun exchange a look. Simeon thinks about saying something but then thinks better of it and keeps his mouth shut.

Jenkins jams the car roughly into a parking spot in front of what Simeon imagines is the establishment. There's the sound of sirens and the vans pull up and block traffic.

Jenkins, Noble and the uniforms pile in. Simeon and Shaun wait at the door as instructed.

Simeon hears Jenkins shouting about a warrant to search the place for stolen lighters.

He hears someone with a gruff voice complain noisily at this.

He hears what he thinks is this same person being restrained.

Next, Simeon hears the sound of things being overturned and broken.

Shaun looks at Simeon. Deadpan, he says, 'I wonder what they'll find.'

Simeon smiles and laughs to himself. He thinks, who am I kidding I don't know what I'm doing here.

Shaun nods at the vans. 'At least we're getting a lift after.'

Simeon risks a peer inside the door.

The search is going full pelt, everyone getting stuck in.

A couple of large West Indian men shake their heads and click their tongues and kiss their teeth, apparently very aggrieved at the intrusion, Simeon thinks. He decides to withdraw before they notice him.

A small crowd gathers across the road. Men with beer bottles and attitudes making their feelings clear. Some kids on bikes. A couple of the uniforms step towards them, palms raised and shrugging, explaining they're just doing their job. Coming back across the road, under their breaths, chuckling to themselves, Simeon hears them muttering something about Yardie cunts.

Under different circumstances one or two members of this crowd might have ended up in the back of one of the vans with a boot on their neck and fresh drugs on their person. Swings and roundabouts.

'Here,' Shaun says. 'They're coming out.'

The uniforms load boxes into the two vans. Jenkins comes out looking flustered and sweaty, tie all over the place, hair unstuck. He points at one of the vans and then at Simeon.

'You're in that one,' he says. 'Now off you trot.'

Simeon looks at Shaun and nods farewell.

'Be lucky,' Shaun says quietly.

Back at the house, Simeon unpacks the van. The uniforms don't bother helping none, just stay where they are, smoking. Simeon carries the boxes upstairs. He opens the boxes one by one. He empties the boxes one by one. He places many packages of drugs into the safe. When he's finished, he goes downstairs to find Noble having a cup of tea with his gran.

'You all right, son?' Noble asks.

Simeon nods, tells Noble that he is all right, yeah.

'Good,' Noble decides. Struggling a bit, he climbs out of the armchair he's in. To Simeon's gran, he says, 'I must do that little job now, but ta very much for the tea, it was just what the doctor ordered.'

Noble gives Simeon a wink and heads upstairs.

Once he's left, Simeon goes up to his room and opens the safe.

Everything is just as he left it.

8

The long arm of the law

February

One of the brothers comes round with an old banger in tow, driven by some lackey. The engine just about turns over and it's a bit rusty, but it works.

'You can use this for a bit, Simeon old son,' he says. 'There's a vegetable knife in the glove compartment in lieu of a functioning screwdriver, should you find you need it.'

Simeon nods.

'Take your gran up west or something. Special treat.'

Simeon thinks this is a good idea and proposes a shopping trip at the weekend.

They visit Selfridges and buy some new clothes. They go to John Lewis and Simeon gets his gran the fanciest new kitchen appliances. They have lunch in a hotel in Marylebone. Then tea and cake just off Park Lane.

'You're spoiling me, Simeon!'

'Special treat, Gran,' Simeon says simply.

As it starts to get dark, they head home.

They go through Dalston Junction and follow Dalston Lane bearing left. There's a stationary police van blocking the road, lights flashing.

Simeon swallows. 'Don't worry, Gran,' he says. 'Probably just traffic duty.'

A WPC peers in the passenger side window at Simeon's gran. She indicates grumpily that she should get out. Simeon's gran, caught off guard and nervous, struggles with the door.

'I can't mek it work,' she tells Simeon. 'It's stuck!'

The WPC loses patience and yanks the door open herself. 'Out!' she says.

But Simeon's gran is not exactly nimble for her age, and she can't quite lever herself up and out of the seat.

The WPC leans in and grabs Simeon's gran by the arm and gives her a tug.

Simeon is out his door and round the car in seconds. Before he can help his gran, three uniformed Territorial Support Group officers are on him. They drag him along the road and throw him into the back of the van.

The van rocks as the three uniforms climb in after Simeon.

'All right, Sambo,' says one. 'That was threatening behaviour and assaulting an officer.'

'And a *woman* officer, no less,' says another. 'You snide little cunt.'

Simeon takes a deep breath.

They punch him three times in the face, and his nose fills with blood.

They slap him around the face. Simeon loses count of the number of times. His lip splits and he tastes blood.

He is pushed to the floor of the van, and he is kicked three times in the stomach, in the ribs, the breath knocked out of him. He hears the crack of boot on bone. It takes a moment to realise that it's his bone, his body breaking.

Simeon can hear his gran crying. He hears the WPC saying something about an offensive weapon in the glove compartment. Simeon closes his eyes. He is left alone, the doors closed.

The van moves off.

At Dalston nick, Simeon is strip-searched and left half-naked in a cell. Later, two officers hold him against the cell door and take turns hitting him.

They tell Simeon that he is being charged with causing actual bodily to two of the officers in the van and with possessing an offensive weapon.

Later, the duty officer comes round with a tray of food, which he tips onto the cell floor. Simeon calls after him. 'Wait, please,' he says. 'Jenkins. You need to tell DI Dave Jenkins that I'm here.'

The duty officer narrows his eyes. 'You what?'

'I work for Jenkins,' Simeon says, gasping. 'You got to believe me.'

'You work for him, like his snout?'

'In a manner of speaking,' Simeon manages. 'Please.'

The duty officer nods.

A few hours later, the cell door opens, and Jenkins comes in. 'Get your things, Simeon,' he says. 'The long arm of the law is letting you go.'

Outside the nick, Jenkins tells Simeon that the charges have been dropped. 'But that motor you were in had dodgy plates, so there's that. Looking at a fine, I expect. There'll be a notice in the post.'

Simeon nods.

Jenkins sniffs. He leans in close enough Simeon can smell the coffee on his wet breath. 'That wasn't too clever of you, telling tales on me like that,' Jenkins says. 'Don't you ever tell anyone you work for me again.'

Simeon nods, feeling bruised, hopeless.

He takes a deep breath and tells Jenkins about Noble and his telephone.

Jenkins grins. 'Well, well,' he says. 'When did this happen?'

'The other day.'

He watches Jenkins do some mental calculations and then nod.

'Simeon, my son, that is what we might call your get-out-of-jail-free card.' Jenkins sniffs. 'And as far as your arrangement with Noble is concerned, nothing changes.'

Simeon nods.

PART FIVE

White Riot

March 1990

On Thursday March 8th, 1990, Hackney Council met at the Town Hall to set its Poll Tax charge for the financial year 1990/91. The Hackney Against the Poll Tax Federation (HAPTF) organised a mass lobby of the meeting. An estimated 5,000 people attended the demonstration outside the Town Hall which developed into a confrontation between police and protesters with many people injured and 57 arrested.

A Peoples' Account of the Hackney Anti-Poll Tax Demonstration on March 8th 1990

'That this House notes the urban disorder that took place in Hackney on Thursday 8th March, that at least 38 people were arrested and there was violence and looting and that the people of Hackney are united in condemning the disorder and looting; but further notes that the blame for this disorder ultimately lies with the Government and its unjust Poll Tax; notes that very large numbers of Hackney residents will not be able to pay this tax; and further notes that in the matter of the Poll Tax the people of Hackney know who the real Urban Terrorist is.'

Early Day Motion from Diane Abbott in Parliament

ITN reporter
Can I just ask you, if I may, your reaction to the events last night in Hackney?
Mrs Thatcher
In a democracy the way is to debate in Parliament, the legislation has been through Parliament, and anything that is intimidatory or violent is absolutely flatly contradictory to democracy. People can demonstrate, of course they can. They should do so peacefully.

1

The criminalisation of protest

Jon's got clippings from some of the week's newspaper headlines spread across his desk. It makes for quite a collage:

POLL TAX MOB LOOTS SHOPS
Sun
MOB RULE
Today
LOOTERS ON RAMPAGE
Daily Mirror
POLICE BATON-CHARGE POLL TAX PROTESTERS
Independent
PM BLAMES MILITANCY ON LABOUR
Guardian
THATCHER HITS AT MILITANT OVER POLL TAX
The Times
A TAX OF DERISION: ATTACKS OF HATE …
Hackney Gazette

Jon had a ringside seat, of course.

It was a fairly textbook event, Jon thinks, all told.

The Hackney Against the Poll Tax Federation 'organising' a rally outside the town hall. A scaffolding barrier on the steps and police all around the place. Territorial Support Group vans parked round the back, waiting for the fun, no doubt. Lower-floor windows boarded up, private security guards with dogs patrolling the building, and only certain members of the public allowed into what should have been an open, public meeting.

Things get late, early.

First off, the Joint Shop Stewards Committee fails to deliver on their promise of a public address system. The HAPTF find a megaphone for the speeches, which don't last long. It's hard to understand someone yelling into a megaphone when there's three and a half thousand people chanting.

Then the anarchists and the squatters turn up and head to the front. The pushing and the shoving start, fruit and empty beer cans thrown at the police line, which is when the Territorial Support Group units announce themselves and form up by the town hall steps.

After that the arrests begin and then the fighting.

A bloke climbs onto the balcony above the town hall's main entrance with a banner, white letters on a black sheet:

PAY NO
POLL TAX

He's up there for about half an hour.

More and more TSG arrive. The crowd throbbing and bobbing out onto Mare Street, the fighting and the arrests full steam ahead.

A sit-down on Mare Street to stop the traffic.

Poor old Glenys Kinnock arriving for the International Women's Day festival at the Hackney Empire didn't time it especially well. A dozen or so masked demonstrators kicking her car and shouting at her.

The police kettle the demonstrators away from the town hall.

Not long after this, a group of about two hundred are into the Narroway with ripped-up paving stones, smashing shop windows and setting fire to the bins.

A brick dropped from the railway bridge lands on the head of a WPC, who is, fortunately, wearing a helmet.

Hackney Police Station is next. Windows smashed and the entrance quickly locked and secured. A police car turns up and a PC and a WPC get out, which is a mistake.

The crowd chase them off and overturn their vehicle.

Mounted police come charging out the station and the crowd disperses. Reinforcements arrive and everyone decides to call it an evening.

Jon sighs. He looks at the *Daily Express* on his desk, Thatcher saying:

'It is precisely the type of violence we have seen before at Grunwick, in the coal strike and at Wapping, and it is the negation of democracy.'

'The criminalisation of protest, Jon, is what it is,' Godfrey tells Jon. 'Plain and simple. Police state and all that.'

'I don't know, Godfrey.'

'I do, Jon. It has been a Thatcher government hallmark, and nowhere clearer than in the lead-up to the implementation of the poll tax.'

Jon, again, sighs.

Godfrey goes on, 'Our friends at the Hackney Community Defence Association are quite right when they say, and I quote.'

'You quote?'

'A draft memo at this stage.'

Jon nods. 'Right.'

'Anyway, I quote: "The criminalisation of protest is a political strategy by which the government, police, courts and media combine to portray demonstrators as criminals engaged in illegal activity."'

'Hence the high number of wrongful arrests.'

'Exactly!'

Jon sighs for a third time.

He knows that the arrests made outside the town hall – outside his *office*, for God's sake – will be for affray, for criminal damage, for the assault of an officer. And he also knows that there will be innocent people charged with these heinous acts. It's what happens when there's a ruck with the police: there's a ruck, and people get caught up in it, people who have done nothing wrong except exercise their right to legitimate protest.

Which is exactly Godfrey's point, of course.

'And the really clever thing,' Godfrey says, 'is that if the defendant loses his case, he is sentenced for a criminal act that just so happened to have taken place at a political protest.'

Jon nods and smiles wearily. 'And if that defendant wins,' he says, 'it's a failure of legal process, nothing to do with politics.'

'Bullseye,' Godfrey says, pretending to clap. 'Got it in one.'

Later, Jon reflects on the reality: non-payment.

Fighting with the police isn't going to get anyone anywhere. Non-compliance might work though. And Jon will be the one dealing with the fallout. He certainly can't be seen to encourage it.

Though, of course, he would. Of course he would.

Hackney Council's poll tax is set at £499.

In terms of balancing the books, this includes £10 million cuts in services.

And these cuts include the closing down of the George Sylvester Sports Centre and the Media Resources Centre, 100 redundancies thanks to a 15 per cent cut in grants to the voluntary sector, and further cuts in education, social services and environmental services.

It's not really a great deal, is it, Jon thinks, overall. But everyone knows that already.

Exhausted and pessimistic, he returns home.

The kids, mercifully, are in bed. Jackie is in the kitchen with a cousin or other, white wine on the go. Jon waves from the top of the stairs. He shrugs off his coat and hangs it on the banister. He takes his briefcase to his desk and pulls out his file on Riverside Close. He lays it on the desk and looks at it for a moment. For months now, most evenings, he has been chasing a paper trail, trying to discover exactly who owns the houses on the estate. He opens the file and reminds himself of his progress. He has a hand-drawn map of the units. When he finds an answer – an *owner* – he writes the name of the owner next to the house on the map. Invariably, the name he writes is the name of a company rather than the name of a person. He still has a few to go. He hasn't been back to the estate since November, and that was a strange visit, everywhere empty except that one place and there was something about the lad there that felt a bit off. Jon didn't find a name or tenancy agreement. And there haven't been any complaints about a lack of water since well before November. He supposes there wouldn't be with no one living there. But there is someone living there! John, again, sighs. He studies his map half-heartedly, his finger tracing the lines. It's been a long day, and the days are only going to get longer. He smiles. Give yourself a night off, he thinks. With Jackie's cousin there it takes the pressure off a bit, they might even have a nice time. He goes downstairs, fetches himself a glass.

2

Solo

Suzi stands on the street outside Solid Bond Studios, looking in. It's closed and there's no sign of anyone about. She turned up on the off-chance, wondering what Paul Weller is doing, how he's taken the news that The Style Council are no more after Polydor refused to release the *Modernism* album.

She called ahead and got the office manager, Carl.

'Bit cheeky, Suzi,' is all he said. 'Not very stylish of you chasing a story like that. I won't tell him, and we'll leave it there, all right.'

But Suzi couldn't leave it there.

She tried Keith, over the phone, and she could pretty much hear him shaking his head, the oh no no no *no*, Suze, leave me out of this, timbre of the voice leaving *her* in no doubt at all of Keith's position.

So here Suzi is, alone and damp on a wet day in March, and she's starting to feel a little silly about it. What exactly she expected is no longer clear. It felt like she had to do something, so she got on a bus and here Suzi is.

She sighs and thinks about packing it in to go to a pub round the corner that she knows and have a bit of a think about her next moves. She's digging in her bag for her camera thinking she might as well get a shot of the place when there's the sound of footsteps on the gravel and she turns.

A man wearing a blue security uniform appears and points at the door. 'It's closed, love,' he says. 'No one been here for a while.'

Suzi nods. 'Thanks, I was just—'

The man nods sympathetically. 'There's been a few of you about, his fans.'

'Oh, no, I'm—'

He smiles now. 'It's OK, I understand. Nothing wrong with wanting to pay your respects, as it were.'

'What do you mean?'

'They're selling it, the studio, I mean.'

'Selling it?'

The man leans in conspiratorially. 'They might need the money, I suppose.'

Suzi nods. 'That's a shame.'

'It is.'

'Any idea who they're selling it to?'

A quick shake of the head. 'None.' Then: 'I think he's going solo.'

Suzi nods again. She lifts her camera from her bag, raises an eyebrow. 'Can I take a photograph of you.' She points at the studio entrance. 'Standing in front, I mean.'

The man gives her a suspicious look.

'I'm a photographer,' Suzi says quickly. 'I used to take pictures of *him*, in fact.'

The man beams at this. 'Oh, well, you should've said.' He straightens up, shoulders back. 'Don't mind if I do.'

Suzi grins. She gestures with a nod. 'Just turn to the right a touch, would you?'

Later, in the pub round the corner, sitting at the bar, Suzi thinks that she's gone solo too, effectively. She didn't have much choice.

The last six months or so, she hasn't exactly been inundated. She hasn't exactly got around, has she, hasn't exactly been sociable.

Since the big Acid House piece in the summer, she's wondered if she's not become something of a busted flush.

More than one commissioning editor has told her that she might have bitten off more than she could chew with that one. That, what was it, she went undercover with some rave outfit and now she's telling the world there's political discontent in the air?

More than one commissioning editor has nicknamed her, with not a little irony, the indie Lee Miller.

Perhaps she saw the end of The Style Council as a way back in, use her inside track to get the real story.

She knows the nickname Weller would have given her for doing that. 'Tabloid' Suzi Scialfa.

The rave scene left her behind quite happily, and Suzi's been adrift, she thinks now, not attached to anything, not championing anything, treading water, and not even really scouring the horizon as she does so.

She put all her anger and all her energy into that piece.

Everything she felt about Noble too.

All the sadness and all the despair with everything she's *done*, it's all there in the prose in a righteous fury.

Sometimes she's surprised they published it at all.

Then again 'Death of a Party' was a catchy title, she was pleased with that. It captured the zeitgeist, even if whatever the zeitgeist was is now over.

Perhaps people don't like to be told that they're not cool anymore, maybe that was the problem.

She finishes her drink and signals for another.

There's a paper on the bar and she flicks through the first few pages of it, all about the various anti-poll tax demonstrations that are happening across the country, about the big one planned for the end of the month.

She thinks that of course she'll be there. She's never missed one like it.

She thinks about Noble, who's also not been in touch since her report on the party back in July. She wonders why. He can't be giving her the swerve too!

It's come to that, then, she's sunk this low: feeling neglected by her blackmailer, a pathetic state of play in anyone's book.

Perhaps it's time to do something with all that information she has documented, all that cash she has in that building society account, all those transcripts and recordings.

Suzi sighs.

She thanks the barman for her second gin and tonic and pays for it.

She examines her diary.

She's due in Camden in a couple of hours to see a band at the Falcon that her friends at Food Records are about to sign. The band's called Seymour, apparently, though they're trying to persuade them to change the name to Blur.

I'll go and do that, Suzi thinks. It'll be fun.

3

Wiretap

After the baby goes down and Lea drifts off on the sofa – or in the bath or in bed – Noble spends his evenings listening to the conversations that take place on Simeon's telephone. He's got Jenkins telling Marlon to set it up for the day of the poll tax demonstration in or around Trafalgar Square. What *it* is exactly, Noble ain't clear. Then Marlon telling Jenkins that it's done, set up, time and place, and that he, Marlon, will be there to facilitate the exchange. Later Noble has Jenkins telling Simeon he'll be meeting Marlon on the west side of Trafalgar Square at the big protest at 4 p.m. sharp and that he better not be late, and he should bring his pal Shaun with him too. Noble thinks about this. He'll talk to Parker, get him to be there too, keep an eye. If Parker doesn't know Shaun's going, Noble will make sure he does. That should persuade him, his girlfriend's little cousin, Noble knows all about that. Par for the course. Next time Noble sees Jenkins he tells him there's word of something brewing on the day of the protest and Jenkins tells Noble not to worry, he's got it covered.

4

Babydaddy

Once again, the day seems to have gotten away from Parker without him doing much more than running an errand and giving his baby girl a little cuddle. Tending to Carolyn as best he can.

Months have gone by when he ain't done much, it seems.

It don't matter. He's happy. He's not going anywhere, he reasons. This job is long-term.

Then Noble leaves word.

'Old Bill Stewart has passed on, son. There's a little memorial. Come along.'

'Do I have a choice?'

'No, you ain't, not really.'

Parker chews this over for a bit but knows he'll be there, course he will.

The wake goes off without incident. Back room of the Samuel Pepys next to the Hackney Empire. A select group, bit shadowy, Hendon and the Yard, no one introducing themselves or nothing and probably for the best. A few whiskies raised and pints on trays. Alan's there, from way back when, 1978. He knows better than to acknowledge Parker beyond the faintest of nods. An age ago, back when Parker was starting out, makes him feel old, really.

Parker thinks back to old Bill's spam-faced demeanour, that sand-paper voice, the pin-pricked, red-eyed, twisted look he got when he had the hump with you.

In the early days, old Bill taught Parker something useful.

Have a joke ready, have a *story* to tell.

Old Bill's regular story was a good one from a long line of anecdotes he'd filed away upstairs in the old canister, what he called that big and nasty brain of his.

'Try this one for size,' Bill told Parker. 'A mate of mine has gone to the doctor. "I'm having a few problems with the lady wife," he says. The doctor gives him a look. "What sort of problems?" "You know, in the boudoir." The doctor nods at this. "Performance issues, is it? Unlucky." "Well," my mate goes, "I can't barely make it onto the bandstand let alone perform." The doctor likes this formulation and smiles. "I've got just the thing for you," he says. "A pill, but it ain't cheap. They're three score each. Four hours of pleasure, though, pretty good bang for your buck, as it were." My mate considers this. "Go on then, I'll try one."'

Parker remembers already smiling by this bit. 'Dirty joke then, Bill?'

'Hang about,' Bill said. 'Patience, son. It's all about how you tell them.'

Parker nodded.

Old Bill continued. 'So my mate's gone and taken one. But disaster strikes! His missus has gone out shopping for the day! She won't be back for a good long time, certainly not within the next four hours. So he's called the doctor and told him about the predicament he's in. The doctor has a think. "Right," he says. "Is there anyone else in the house?" And my mate tells him, "Yeah, the au pair's here." "What's she like?" asks the doctor. "She's nineteen with big tits." "You'll have to do it with her," the doctor says. "Tell her it's a medical emergency." My mate's nodding at this, working it out. He says, "Thing is, doc, they ain't cheap, like you said. And it seems like an awful waste, I can get it up for the au pair without one."'

Parker chuckling to himself about this. About old Bill's roar of laughter after the punchline.

He never used the joke himself, never felt it was quite the right occasion for it. But it was a good point: know your audience and get them to like you and to trust you. Parker's done plenty of that, and he'll keep on doing plenty of that while he needs to.

He helps himself to another pint. He's feeling the drink a bit, as he would after all those sleepless nights and early starts. It feels good to cut loose a little, even at a secret wake that no one's admitting to attending.

He slides into a seat in the main bar away from the mourners. He'll finish this and then head home. Carolyn and the baby will be napping now if all is going to plan, Shaun out at college, Parker might get a bit of shut-eye himself if he's lucky.

Noble sees Parker sitting alone at a table. He takes a couple of glasses of whisky off the bar and puts one down in front of him.

'Irish,' Noble says.

Parker looks up and smiles. 'Aren't I the lucky boy?'

Noble sits down. 'I need a word, son.'

Parker nods. 'How's the family, guv?'

'Golden.' He smiles. 'Best thing that ever happened to me.'

'Oh yeah?'

'Yeah.' Noble nodding now, thinking that yeah, it's true, it really is.

'It's been a while, guv.'

'It has.'

'You've been busy, I gather.'

'What you heard?'

Parker shakes his head. 'Nothing specific.'

'What then?'

'Just that Jenkins and his associates have been getting around.'

Noble sniffs and adjusts himself in his seat. 'That's fair enough, I suppose.'

'There's talk at the HCDA of putting together an investigation next year.'

'Oh yeah?'

Parker nods. 'Police acquirement of drugs, police drug supplying, protection from prosecution, fabrication of evidence.'

Noble thinks, this is what getting involved looks like then. Though next year is a long way off. 'Anything about a council house on Riverside Close?'

'No, why?'

Noble shakes his head. 'Don't matter. You just tell me if there is.'

Parker nods. 'You got what you need yet?'

'Nearly there.'

Which is true.

The fact is Noble is involved in wiretapping and surveillance and for the first time is officially doing what he's been doing for years: gathering evidence of police crime and corruption.

So, yes, nearly there.

He's likely got what he needs, but it can't hurt to have a little bit extra, just in case.

But Parker doesn't require any of that, so Noble keeps it to himself.

He's left Parker out of it, largely – if his evidence is needed in any inquiry, it'll compromise his identity and blow his cover. Noble feels generous about this, keeping Parker's nose clean for him.

Parker sips his whisky and grimaces. 'I shouldn't have more than two of these, ever.'

Noble laughs. 'You're looking well, son.'

'Yeah, thanks.' Parker smiles. 'You too, considering. How old is he now then?'

'Not even six weeks.'

'Lea all right?'

Noble nods. 'She's doing great. C-section it was, you know, so she ain't exactly out jogging yet, but she's good.' He pauses for a moment. 'She's happy. We're happy.'

'I'm pleased for you, guv.'

'Cheers.'

Parker raises a glass. 'To family.'

'To family.'

They sit in silence for a moment, Noble again thinking about Parker's future, what it means to tell a man that's that, time to move on now, it's over.

It's not like Parker's got an office job, not so easy to pack your desk up into a box and be on your way.

He should get to the point.

Tell Parker what he needs to know and give him the rest later.

Step by bloody step.

'Listen,' Noble says. 'Two things, right.'

'OK.'

Noble glances around the pub, checking no one's watching. A couple of old geezers at the bar with toothless grins and halves of mild in front of them is about it.

'First thing is the protest on Saturday.'

'The poll tax demo?'

'That's the one.'

'OK.'

'I'm going to be there and so are you.'

'In what capacity, guv?'

'Never you mind what I'm doing there, but you're going to keep an eye on your old mate Marlon.'

'Am I now?'

'Yeah, you are.'

'Why?'

'It don't matter.'

'I don't know, guv.'

Noble nods. 'If you need further incentive, Parker, your other friend Simeon will be there.' Noble pauses for a moment. 'And he's been working with that kid, Shaun, who I believe you also know.'

Noble watches as Parker does his best to keep a straight face. He almost manages it, Noble thinks.

'Working?' Parker says.

'You know Marlon.'

Parker nods. 'Well, that's the thing, guv, I never really got to know Marlon all that well.'

Noble smiles. 'Look, it's simple, I need you there, eyes and ears. A meeting has been arranged, some sort of exchange, and I want to know what exactly is being exchanged.'

Parker nods.

Noble says, 'Go with them. You're a chaperone again. You've done it before. Let Marlon know you're going. Propose an outing.' Ironically, Noble adds, 'God knows we all want to show her ladyship she's wrong on this one.'

Parker nods.

Noble stands. 'You can swing that, can you?'

Parker says that he can.

Noble swallows his whisky. 'I'll be in touch morning of, so be around.'

Parker nods again. 'I think I'll stay here, finish my drink in peace,' he says.

'You do that, son.'

Noble nods towards the wake. 'I'll just go and say my goodbyes.'

Parker laughs grimly. 'I should probably give that a miss.'

Noble smiles. 'That's the spirit,' he says.

Parker's a little wobbly from the booze when he gets home and he's yawning on top of that, suddenly he's absolutely cream-crackered, his eyes hot and prickly, his mouth dry.

He trips on the step and his key glances off the latch, refuses to go in a couple of times, in fact, so he takes a moment and has a good deep breath, let's a bit of air in, and he feels immediately better for it, restored.

He didn't tell Carolyn where he was going, of course not, but he did mention a mate and a drink so he's not in the sort of state to prompt any questions. The keys feel hot in his hands. I'm not going anywhere, he thinks, this will last. He has another deep breath, for luck. This will last, I'm not going anywhere.

After his deep breath, Parker manages the key and opens the door.

He's sucking on a mint and reaches into his pocket for a fresh one then takes off his coat.

In the living room, Shaun has the baby in his arms, holding her like he's scared he might drop her, Carolyn next to him, beaming. The baby is making little noises with her lips and they're cooing over her, quietly.

Carolyn has brushed her hair and pushed it back behind a hairband and she's wearing tracksuit bottoms and a big cardigan that's wrapped around her. Her eyes are tired-looking, but she's scrubbed her face and put some cream on it and she's smiling, she looks so happy, Parker thinks, exhausted, yeah, but happy, like it's deep down inside her this happiness, that it's taken root.

They both look up as Parker makes his presence known.

He smiles sloppily. 'Did she sleep?'

Carolyn nods and smiles. 'She did.'

'Did you?'

Another smile. 'I tried.'

Parker nods. 'Sleep when baby sleeps, right, that's what they say.'

'I just wanted some time for me, so I took a bath, moisturised.'

'Well, you smell terrific, darling.'

Shaun says, 'Ah, thanks, hero.'

'Don't be cheeky, son.'

'You eaten?' Carolyn asks.

Parker sniffs. 'Of a manner, yeah.'

'Hmm.'

He looks at Shaun. 'I wanted to ask you something.'

'Yeah?'

'Saturday, the big protest, you up for that?'

Shaun's eyes flick from Parker to Carolyn and back again.

'If that's all right, love,' Parker says to Carolyn. 'Be good for him.' Nodding at Shaun. 'Get a bit political, you know.'

Carolyn smiles. 'Course. You two should go, you're right, it's important.'

'Nice one,' Parker says, rubbing his hands together. 'That's decided then.'

'Yeah,' Shaun says. 'All right.'

'We may not make it to south London,' Parker says. 'What with the baby and my nascent parental responsibilities.' Laughing at this. 'But we'll get to Trafalgar Square and have a good look at the scene, all right.'

'Yeah,' Shaun says again. 'All right.'

'Cushty,' Parker says grinning. 'Now hand over my daughter.'

Parker thinking he's kept Shaun out of trouble before and that he's happy to make a habit of it.

He's family now, after all.

Later, Parker gives Marlon a bell to suggest a day out at the protest, bit of a laugh, and Marlon tells him, yeah, why not, I'll be in Trafalgar Square.

5

Legal and above board

Friday afternoon and Jon has reached a conclusion.

The planning applications that Jon has examined demonstrate that Jon is complicit in his role as Borough Solicitor in the ethically questionable manner of the sale of the units on Riverside Close by Hackney Council.

What is also clear from the paper trail is that many of these sales were funded thanks to loans from a company called Start Capital. When these loans defaulted, Start Capital took ownership of the units before selling them on to multiple offshore shell companies. A detail of the loans is that they were written off on condition that the sellers' shares in Thames Water were transferred to Start Capital.

A jaunt to Companies House reveals Start Capital's relationship to Compliance Ltd, which in turn shines a light on Compliance Ltd's involvement in the Leaside Project.

A planning committee meeting earlier in the day is where it all comes together: the greenlighting of an application that Jon will soon sign off on. A Compliance Ltd subsidiary will take ownership of the Riverside Close land, on top of its prior ownership of the units on it. Public consultation rendered, therefore, irrelevant. The application indicates that these units will make way for an extension of the Leaside Project with significant foreign investment, a certain amount of which will go directly towards filling the council's coffers.

The planning committee and, by extension, the council, Jon understands, is unconcerned by all this activity as it is legal and above board.

Jon notes that the topographical land survey states definitively in the section on geotechnical engineering that there are no impediments to development in terms of soil, rock and groundwater. Individual surveys carried out on the units report no concerns regarding water access current or historical.

6

Finger

In light of ongoing conversations with your Scotland Yard big hitter, you tell Terry that the brothers need to vacate the unit on Riverside Close.

'Time to pull the plug,' you say. 'We need to offer it up. They can find somewhere else.'

Terry nods. 'Anywhere in mind?'

You shake your head. 'Wherever suits the market. They're protected, for the time being at least.'

Terry nods. 'Easily arranged.'

You nod. 'That lad they've got working for them, their middleman to the Stoke Newington lot.'

Terry nods.

'Put him somewhere safe, far away from prying eyes.'

'OK.'

'We might need him to corroborate certain allegations pertaining to our friends from the Met. Sooner rather than later.'

Terry says, 'And the grandmother?'

'Her as well.'

Terry nods.

'Timeline to be confirmed but won't be long. The Leaside Project extension is ready to go. Another reason we need to clear that last unit.'

Terry nods.

'Where there is discord may we bring harmony.'

'Sorry?'

'Nothing, Terry, just thinking out loud.'

7

Harmony

Saturday, 31 March 1990, 'The Demo', Anti-Poll Tax Demonstration

Jon wakes slowly then all at once. There's a crack in the curtains and a bright slice of light gets right in his eyes. It looks like we'll be lucky with the weather, though, he thinks.

Jackie rolls over. 'You sure you want to go today?' she asks.

Jon swallows and rubs at his eyes. 'Yeah, I'm sure. I think I should.'

'You probably shouldn't.'

Jon laughs. 'I know, but you know.'

Jackie nods. 'I think so.'

'I'll take the boy, like we talked about. It'll be good for him.'

'You be careful, though, all right.'

'There'll be a lot of families, don't worry.'

'Easy to say.'

'Yeah, I know.'

Jon thinks that not too long ago, Jackie would have been with them.

'I'd come, you know,' she says then. 'But it wouldn't be fair on Lizzie, it's best we stay put.'

Jon smiles. 'I know you would.' He sighs. 'I better get cracking if we're going to get down to Kennington Park for kick-off.'

'I'll drive you to Angel tube, shall I?' Jackie says. 'That'll make it a bit easier.'

Jon smiles. 'That would be great, love, thank you.'

'And tomorrow we'll do something together, just the family.'

'Yes please.'

'Good. I'll have a little think about what.'

Jon coughs and sniffs. He licks his lips, which feel cracked and dry. He turns to Jackie and gives her cheek a quick kiss. He breathes in the smell of her for a moment. 'I'll get cracking then.'

He eases himself out of bed and takes the stairs down to the boy's room a little gingerly, hand on the banister. He nudges the door open and crosses the room. He opens the curtains. The boy groans and yawns and then sits up.

'Dad?'

'I'll make you a cup of tea and a bit of breakfast,' Jon says. 'Get yourself up and put some clothes on. It's going to be warm!'

Jon washes his hair in the sink and gets dressed. They all have bacon sandwiches at the kitchen table, Jon packs a few supplies into his backpack, and off they go.

Jon's a bit twitchy in the car, if he's honest.

They get out at the top of Essex Road and head towards the tube.

The boy having to walk-jog-walk to keep up.

There's plenty of placards about already, most of them obediently bobbing into the station, disappearing down the escalators.

Socialist Worker's Break the Tory Poll Tax, Don't Collect, Don't Pay is prominent.

Also, *Militant*'s Pay NO Poll Tax, of course.

But don't talk to Jon about left-wing politics these days unless you want short shrift.

Jon's had enough of the blame game, the Trots did this, the TUC did that, making a virtue of marginalisation, never building consensus, never building a mass movement that might have popular political clout, might take the fight to these concentrations of wealth and power we're supposedly against.

If there's one thing the last twelve years have demonstrated to Jon with utter clarity, it's that the usual left-wing infighting is about as productive as the proverbial box of frogs.

Waiting for the train to arrive, the boy asks him the last time Jon did anything like this.

Jon smiles. 'You were there.'

'I was there?'

'You weren't even six months old, but we took you.'

'What was it?'

'The carnival against racism in Victoria Park, I'm sure we've told you, probably a few times.'

'I don't remember.'

But he's smiling, Jon sees.

'Tell me again, Dad.'

Jon checks the tube map on the wall behind him. 'We'll get off at Kennington and then walk down to the park. That's probably better than going to Oval. I expect it'll be busier there.'

'I expect so.'

'Come on,' Jon says, taking the boy's arm and pointing. 'Let's get down to the end of the platform, it's a lot quieter by the look of it.'

Soon, the hiss and huff of the wind in the tunnel, the tracks singing as the train arrives.

They stand in the middle of a busy carriage.

'Tell me again, Dad, about the carnival.'

Jon smiles. 'All right, let's see what you can remember.'

And as he's telling the boy about that day in Victoria Park, about X-Ray Spex and Steel Pulse, about The Clash and The Tom Robinson Band, Jon notices a few people listening in, one or two nods. A couple of around Jon's age smile and mouth that they remember it well.

'What was the main song again, Dad?'

'Well, I was a big Steel Pulse fan, so I'd say "Ku Klux Clan".'

'And The Clash? What about The Clash?'

And a handful of people call out all at once, '"White Riot"!'

The boy – Joe, Jon's son, all of twelve years old, twelve! Where did *that* go? – looks up at Jon with a big, warm grin, his eyes full of love and pride, yes, pride, that's what Jon's seeing and Jon pulls him close and says, 'Come here, you,' and time somehow dissolves then and his neat haircut is suddenly frayed and curly, ringlets everywhere, and the smell of him is powerful again, his features softer and Jon gets that familiar feeling he has from time to time with his kids, the emotion overwhelming, the emotion he feels both hopeful and yet frightening, and it occurs to him that there'll be a day, one day, when he won't hold his son in quite the same way that he's holding him now.

Most people pile out at Kennington tube.

Jon thinks, yep, that was the right place to get off, and we'll do a nice little loop now on our route.

They shuffle out into the sunlight, Jon's hand on the boy's neck.

Down the road and into the park, nearly midday and it's filling up already.

In among the branches, high up over the grass, there are hundreds of raised white placards with black text dotted with the red and yellow flags of the youth campaigns and the Anti-Nazi League, the odd homemade banner, a white sheet draped between two bits of wood with the words:

**UP YOUR
BUM**

In red paint.

A big orange flag at the head of the march:

LAMBETH AGAINST THE POLL TAX

The boy nudges Jon and points at another one, higher up, great long poles lifted into the blue sky by a few cheerful-looking thugs:

**BIKERS
AGAINST
POLL TAX**

Jon hands the boy a bottle of water and a cheese sandwich wrapped in cling film. 'Here, let's have this now before we set out.'

'Thanks, Dad.'

Jon smiles and unwraps his own sandwich, digs into his bag for a packet of crisps. He looks at his watch. They'll be heading up to Trafalgar Square in about half an hour.

'Let's sit down for a bit,' Jon says. 'It'll be a long walk when we get going!'

The atmosphere is really very good, Jon thinks, everyone smiling.

The sunshine definitely helps.

Parker manages a few hours' kip on the sofa after the baby ends up in bed with Carolyn, not an unusual outcome, of course. Wrapped in a blanket and tired, Carolyn hands her over to him and Parker makes space and cradles her in his arms.

'I'll have a shower and get myself sorted before you go,' Carolyn tells him.

Parker smiles. 'I'll pop out and pick up something for your lunch,' he says. 'A little treat for you while we're speaking truth to power.'

Carolyn makes an ironic, unimpressed face at this proposal before disappearing into the bathroom.

'What do you reckon, eh?' Parker says to his little girl. He smiles, tickles her under her tiny little chin. 'No, thought not,' he says, kissing her lightly on her forehead.

Half an hour later and Parker is in a phone box that smells of piss and animal. He dials his number for Noble and hears the beep. Then he hangs up and waits outside where it smells only of piss.

A few minutes later and the phone rings and Parker steps back inside and answers it.

'Right,' Noble says. 'Here's the plan.'

He tells Parker to find him in Trafalgar Square at four o'clock in the afternoon, west side.

'All right,' Parker says.

'At that point I'll know better what's next.'

'Right you are.'

'You squared it with that lad Shaun, did you?'

'I did. He'll be with me.'

'Beautiful. I'll see you later.'

Noble hangs up.

Parker crosses the road and goes into Granny's Caribbean Takeaway and picks up a boxed lunch for Carolyn.

At home, Carolyn and the baby are both asleep in bed.

They look identical, Parker thinks with a smile, both sets of arms thrown back, both of their heads off to the left, both breathing softly but noisily.

Parker backs out and gently closes the door.

He places the food on the kitchen table and leaves a little note, signs off Big Daddy, just for a laugh.

Shaun's on the sofa in his coat watching the news.

'You about ready, son?' Parker asks.

Shaun nods.

'Come on then, let's get a wriggle on.'

Outside the flat, Shaun says, 'That kid, Simeon, you remember him, I said he could come with us. Is that all right?'

Parker sniffs, pretends to consider this for a moment. 'Yeah, course it's all right,' he says, smiling. 'We meeting him there or what?'

Shaun points. 'Bus stop.' Shaun checks his watch. 'In about five minutes.'

'Oh, I see, you made the arrangements then.'

'No,' Shaun says quickly. 'He's going whether we're there or not.'

'That's not very polite.'

'I mean—'

Parker lifts a palm. 'Shaun, son, I am simply extracting the Michael, so please worry not your little head.'

'All right, sorry.'

'That's better.'

Simeon's waiting at the Clapton Pond bus stop, which feels busier than normal, Parker thinks.

'We'll get the thirty-eight to Tottenham Court Road,' Parker informs the lads. 'Walk down from there.'

He notices that Simeon and Shaun do seem rather chummy.

'Your girlfriend not coming?' Parker asks Shaun.

Shaun shakes his head. 'Her uncle won't let her.'

'No?'

'He thinks there might be trouble.'

'And what do you think, Simeon?' Parker asks.

'I don't know,' Simeon says.

'Effusive as ever, then,' Parker jokes. 'The bus will be here in a minute, shape up.'

It's an institution, the number 38 bus, Parker thinks admiringly as they pass through Islington.

No other way, really, of getting from Clapton up west and beyond.

The 55 is a torturous route, the traffic on Hackney Road and then through Old Street always a nightmare, and the North London line isn't any use to anyone except hippies and schoolkids.

Installed upstairs at the back of the 38, the smokers coughing and yellow-fingered, Parker assesses the view of Sadlers Wells, Finsbury Town Hall, Exmouth Market –

It's an aspirational area, he thinks.

Even the estates look a bit tidier than in the east, though that's as likely to be cosmetic as much as anything else.

More private owners, Parker supposes, yuppie money, meaning more to spend on the amenities and fewer drug addicts in the stairwells.

Parker likes the look of a Regency townhouse, if he's honest, though the state of some of them is a shame, not sure they pass much muster, the scaffolding looking a bit raw, climbing frames for the local tykes.

On the streets, there are placards and banners carried by earnest-looking types in urban outdoor gear, sensible shoes and backpacks, water bottles strapped to the sides, tramping along in groups of two and three, heading towards Trafalgar Square.

The bus stops on Roseberry Avenue opposite a primary school. Protestors trickle past. The bus doesn't move for a few minutes. Parker, as usual, twitchy with impatience at the vagaries of London's public transport system. Shaun and Simeon sharing the headphones of a Walkman, nodding away together. Parker stands and pokes his head down the stairs. Nothing doing, where's the conductor when you need him? The driver kills the engine. The ding of the bell, then a voice shouting something about a change in destination, this bus will terminate here.

Parker nudges Shaun.

'Time to get off and walk, it appears,' he tells him.

Shaun nods and the three of them bounce down the stairs and off the back of the bus onto the street.

Suzi has resolved to document the day's events through a series of eyewitness accounts.

She'll take pictures and record words, and it'll form the basis of a piece. She doesn't want to just stand there and gawp, she wants some interaction. These sorts of things in the past, she'd have gone with Keith, of course, and it'd be a day out as much as anything else, a bit of a beano, as he'd put it.

She doesn't really feel like having a good time, if she's honest with herself, it's not about *that*, this time.

No, she decides, this is the right thing to do.

Why not, she thinks, tell a side of the story – and there will be a story, she's sure of that – the rest of the media will likely ignore. She'll anonymise the quotes and let the photos speak for themselves, no commentary.

She takes herself down to south London nice and early and gets to work. She approaches a couple with Anti-Nazi League and Rock Against Racism badges on their donkey jackets. Suzi points at their lapels and gestures with her camera, asking their permission. They smile and pose. They start speaking, others join in, form an orderly queue, laughing then serious.

Suzi snaps and records, records and snaps:

The atmosphere on arriving at Kennington Park is like a carnival. Bands are playing, the sun is hot, thousands of people out to demonstrate their united opposition to the poll tax.

The anarchists are raggier than ever. The demonstration is leisurely with no heavy police or militant (stewarding) presence.

Suzi jots down soundbites and observations, her Dictaphone on then off then on again, frames photographs of people and banners and flags and trees and stewards and police and empty buses and traffic jams:

The demonstration is simply massive, enormous, a sea of people filling up and overflowing out of Kennington Park. And the atmosphere is wonderful. People are happy, but this isn't an empty, superficial happiness. This is happiness based on strength and power. And it is happiness that grows and develops as people realise the sheer size of the demonstration and thus of the whole movement against the poll tax. The collective is growing, flexing its muscles for the first time in years. No more individualised, atomised discontent. No more feelings of powerless anger. This is it: thousands and thousands of people out on the streets, angry and strong.

Suzi feels energised and involved, it's contagious, all this righteousness.

But she pulls back a touch, tries to create some emotional distance, some objectivity, snaps and records, records and snaps. It's not too hard to find people who are ready to talk to her:

Some of us are working, some of us on the dole, some on housing benefit, some squatting because they can't afford to pay for a reasonable home, others because there aren't any homes available, some folks have worked all their lives to provide for their families, some have never been able to find work. We all have something in common – we are all working class, and in today's wonderful British society we have become part of the growing, but powerful underclass. The poll tax is another financial burden on us, like all the other benefit and welfare cuts we've experienced, particularly in recent years. We've got no money left to pay now, but nobody seems to listen or care.

Even when Hackney went up, a few points were knocked off the Stock Exchange and rumours of Thatcher's resignation started to flow. This is going to show the government and the councils what a fight they've got on their hands, this is where everybody will be together in the centre of 'power', this is going to be the big one.

Suzi missed the Hackney protest, it happened too quick: by the time Suzi realised that she should be there, it was all over. Not a pretty sight, the aftermath in the Narroway, what with all the broken glass and the charred remains of rubbish in piles of ash dotted about the street. At least that's what she thought it looked like in her photographs, only half-joking.

She has her camera, and she has her notebook, and she has her Dictaphone:

Try to get out of the park and there's a huge sea of people in the way, trickling out like sand in an hourglass and pushing its way into this mass, a large group of scruffy anarchos from God knows where (a soap manufacturer's nightmare) banging drums and tins and anything else to hand.

She drifts over to the park exit before the procession to Trafalgar Square really gets under way.

She snaps some of these scruffy anarchos forcing open the park's main gates, allowing this sea of protestors through much more quickly now that they're not forced through the smaller side exits.

Suzi sees straight away that this means the march is split over both sides of the road.

Suzi follows, thinking the police and the stewards are going to have their work cut out keeping everyone in formation.

She hears someone say that there couldn't have been one this big since CND and the muesli types came up from the suburbs to be all moral with everyone, and Suzi smiles and writes this down.

Jon spots a group of families, parents and kids and other relatives it looks like, and they settle into a steady pace with them up towards the river, the boy close, his eyes darting, taking it all in, blinking at the noise but smiling too.

'It's a bit like going to football, isn't it, Dad?'

Jon smiles. 'Yeah, maybe, first half at home and everyone happy.'

They watch a little boy in a green tracksuit and an I LOVE ILEA badge struggling along, dragging a placard in one hand, a great big Mr Whippy in the other, ice cream smeared across his face.

There are quite a few paunches out enjoying the sun, lads with shirts round waists, hands gripping cans of Skol lager, a whiff of the old jazz cigarette as they barrel past, chanting something about Maggie taking it up the arse, Jon pulling the boy closer, laughing to himself, some wag asking loudly how the fuck do they know that to a few cheers.

Crossing Lambeth Bridge, the buzz seems to intensify, the whistles and horns louder and more insistent, the odd cow bell, someone yelling into a megaphone, Big Ben and the Houses of Parliament dignified and handsome in the hazy March sun.

You've got to give them that, Jon thinks, credit where it's due, our political headquarters do look the part.

On the other side of the bridge, the police try to take an anarchist flag from someone and there are a few scuffles.

A pensioner holds a placard with an amateurish painting of Thatcher's neck in a noose, THATCHER'S NIGHTMARE written underneath it, and under that:

CAN'T PAY
WON'T PAY

STUFF
THE POLL TAX

His granddaughter has a little yellow placard of her own:

MY
MUM
CAN'T
PAY

At the end of Whitehall, a line of police blocks the road, and the crowd is diverted towards Embankment.

Jon sees there are rows of mounted police, ominously still and waiting.

'Come on,' he says to the boy, picking up the pace, concerned now. 'Let's get up to the square.'

Parker surveys Trafalgar Square from the north side like a conquering hero, which is apt, he thinks to himself, cleverly.

It's heaving.

Tony Benn has not long relinquished the microphone and there's a palpable energy emanating from the ground up thanks to his rabble-rousing performance.

There's a load of crusties up some scaffolding waving banners and sort of dancing, Parker notes.

There are police lines and horses not too close to the action and vans parked not far away, but Parker reckons at this stage it's only your regular plods about, the TSUs and the riot gear must be safely stowed for now.

He puts his hand to his forehead and scans the crowd, the landmarks.

Marlon will be waiting close to the equestrian statue of Charles I, so he said anyway.

'Considered the central point of the city,' he explained. 'I respect your history, hero, it's like a pilgrimage.' Laughing away, he was. 'X marks the spot!'

Well, Parker can't see him from where he's standing, but he can see the best route.

There's a bit of movement down on Whitehall, near Downing Street, Parker thinks, a bit of dust in the air, a low hubbub, but it ain't clear it's any more than thousands and thousands of people traipsing up the road at the same time.

'Chaps,' Parker instructs, 'we're going straight across, divide the Red Sea.'

Shaun shaking his head, smiling.

Parker extends an arm. 'To the horse! As one! Charge!'

Suzi records someone saying that the police in the lines look incredibly smug.

At the Ministry of Defence opposite Downing Street, Suzi gets chatting to a couple who look very much like they might be old hands at this sort of event.

Nice bit of greenery to sit down and see if anything happens here, they tell her, indicating she should join them and have a bit of a rest.

They point and talk and Suzi records:

By the line of coppers protecting Downing Street is a group of about 200 people who are pushing and shouting and occasionally throwing cans and bits of placard.

There is no ammo in Whitehall, they tell Suzi.

There's a smell of burning and Suzi sees a flag off the Cenotaph is on fire. The couple that she's sitting with, and everyone around them, cheer.

Someone who seems to know the couple barges his way over to them.

The Old Bill went and redirected half of the march down the back of the Ministry of Defence, this person is saying breathlessly.

And who should be at the head of this little unpoliced and unstewarded bit of the march but some people with a Class War banner, this person is saying. And they take it down the side of the MOD and back onto Whitehall to huge cheers from the crowd.

A coup for Class War! Dancing a little jig now, this man.

The couple are laughing at him and Suzi snaps photographs of them and their friend.

Look, they say, a crush is developing.

Suzi nods.

Some of the peaceful protesters are starting to panic.

8

Discord

Whitehall, 3.28 p.m.

Noble thinking, here we are again then –

Thinking, it's all a bit different this time, a bit different from 1978 and Rock Against Racism and the Anti-Nazi League, not many riot police about in Trafalgar Square *then*, was there?

It's all a bit different today, he thinks, buried in a crowd at the bottom end of Whitehall.

Where's all the singing? he's thinking. Where's all the music?

Where are all the black and brown faces –

He's thinking –

Whitehall riot

This poll tax has really got people riled up.

Maggie, Maggie, Maggie

He hears.

Here we are again then.

He hears –

Out, Out, Out

Shouldering his way north. Thousands of people, people everywhere. Thousands and thousands of riled-up people, yelling.

Placards and posters –

Can't pay, won't pay

Unions and anarchists, the loony left –

Outside the Ministry of Defence, in front of Monty's statue, families picnicking on the green, which is nice.

Noble ain't here to protest, shouldering his way north.

He doesn't have especially complex economic opinions on the poll tax, though he supposes he doesn't much like the principle of the thing, the scrapping and capping of rates, the implementation of a *community charge*, what a misnomer.

He's not keen on this Tory arrogance, Mrs Thatcher banging on about rolling back the frontiers of socialism –

The choice of language feels a little archaic, in Noble's mind, a little too eastern bloc.

'Every time I hear people squeal,' said Nicholas Ridley, minister responsible for the introduction of the poll tax, 'I know we are right.'

Well, they're squealing today, Noble concedes.

Nicholas 'Not in my backyard' Ridley is getting a bit of stick off of the crowd. Couldn't happen to a nicer Tory cunt, Noble thinks.

But Noble ain't here to protest.

There's never any point, he thinks. He's learned, over the years, that protest gets you squarely fuck all.

For now, he's just a bloke trying to walk up the road.

Which ain't easy as there's a sit-in at Downing Street and Noble's stuck.

Don't Pay, Don't Collect

Double row of barriers in the middle of Whitehall, uniforms three deep, missiles and militants –

Bog Off Thatcher

This is only going one way, Noble thinks.

Twenty-five minutes and he's due to meet Parker. Better get a move on.

Suzi squeezes her way up Whitehall, still taking photographs, still documenting:

The horses charge the crowd and push it behind the MOD building.

Immediately a small barricade is built out of building rubbish from skips in the yard.

A roll of barbed wire is dragged across the top of the barricade.

The mounted cops don't charge again.

The MOD windows start to get trashed.

Suzi snaps and Suzi records.

The noise is by now overwhelming.

The air is thick with the smell of sweat and burning rubber.

She is wired tight and feels the crowd roiling with anger.

Trafalgar Square.

Simeon and Shaun are a little way ahead of Parker.

They are deep in conversation and ploughing through the crowd towards Marlon, oblivious to what Parker has noticed, which is a change in mood and vibe, and Parker has slowed down a touch to scope the scene.

Parker sees that people are moving in lines.

He hears the rising volume of confusion and anger.

He sees dust is kicking up and he can smell smoke.

He listens as someone says the portacabins on Grand Buildings have been set on fire.

He feels a ripple through the crowd, people turning in panic, pushing to get past him, yelling and scared.

Parker sees a police van drive straight through the crowd, which scatters.

People are running and falling and scrambling away from the van, and Parker jumps back as Simeon and Shaun jump forward, and they're further away from him, separated by a churning scrum of bodies, and Parker catches Shaun's eye from across this churning scrum and points he should keep going, get across the square and find Marlon, Parker will be right behind.

*

Whitehall.

Noble can feel that thrum of violence, that shift in the crowd.

It happens quickly.

Noble sees uniforms lining up on the grass opposite Downing Street.

Noble sees these uniforms wade into the crowd, pushing half the crowd north and half the crowd south, parting the crowd with truncheons and fists, a thick blue line straight across the middle of Whitehall, helmet-faced, shield-chested.

Noble pushes hard himself, north, makes it, the crowd divided, the uniforms in the middle, crowing.

Pay no poll tax

The sit-down protestors struggle to their feet, try to escape the boots and the knees, trampled and kicked, handcuffs and blood.

Noble sees bricks, bottles, iron bars –

Traffic cones and street signs.

Arrests by police snatch squads.

Sticks and stones and broken bones.

Break the Tory poll tax

Noble skirts the edges.

At the top of Whitehall, riot police and horses.

Batons and shields.

Noble sees it all coming and he edges round the crowd as the police move down Whitehall.

Noble inching up towards the theatre, where a peaceful group are sheltering.

The police charge, batons flailing, fanning out across the road, Noble pinned against a billboard advertising a play –

Run for Your Wife

Noble thinking, wryly, I bloody would if I could.

He sees, across the road:

PIZZALAND

Windows smashed, neon cracked –

Noble is pinned by a young police constable.

Noble looks this young police constable in the face.

Noble pulls his warrant card.

He sees that this police constable is confused and that he has panic in his eyes.

Noble nods.

The police constable, shaking, lets him go.

Noble looks again at his watch.

Five minutes.

He hopes Parker has the lad Shaun with him, though the state of it all going off, Christ knows if Noble will find either of them.

Suzi enters Trafalgar Square as the crowd scatters.

Barriers fall and the first line of police is forced to retreat, frightened-looking bobbies in their helmets waving their truncheons to no real effect as missiles pour down on them.

Suzi sees a police car with its back window missing, traffic cones bouncing off it, a man dressed in black running at it with a makeshift shield in one hand and a scaffolding pole in the other, which he smashes through the driver's window. The car gathers speed, protestors leaping out of its way as it accelerates towards the west end.

Suzi takes a series of photographs as four riot vans drive into the crowd.

More than a dozen people surround a police van and attack it with poles and rocks and pieces of wood, bricking the windows and shoving metal barriers underneath the wheels to stop it moving. The protective grille over the front window is removed and used as a battering ram.

Police snatch squads in riot gear, helmets and shields, batons and radios, charge at parts of the crowd, pinning anyone they can wrestle to the floor.

Suzi takes photographs of a man forced to the ground, his jacket over his head.

She takes a step back, pulls out her Dictaphone and speaks:

People high up in scaffolding, chanting 'No Poll Tax, No Poll Tax' to the heavy, sharp metallic beat of scaffold pole against scaffold pole. Then poles, braces, concrete rain down onto the police.

Police have a man in a headlock bleeding from a wound above his eye.

Smoke billows from South Africa House and the crowd cheers.

Protestors throw stones and bricks at the police line.

Suzi sees what they don't see: mounted police in hi-vis jackets trotting up behind them.

9

Pay No Poll Tax

Jon grips the boy's hand and pulls him up Whitehall, pressed against the shops, noise and projectiles flying around them, the boy in floods, Jon's heart thumping away, his feet crunching through broken glass, his arm protecting the boy's head. Police marching towards them, police marching away from them, crowds of people running, running at the police line, running away from it. Jon ducks right down over the boy, lifts his jacket up over his head, and they're scuttling along like crabs quickly as they can safely move, and he's saying to the boy, over and over, it's all right, it's all right, I'm right here, it's all right. Jon looks up and sees a man and a woman ahead looking at him and the boy, concerned, and they're pointing, this man and this woman, pointing in the direction of the Strand and they're yelling at Jon to move quicker and Jon stops, looks around, sees there is a lull for a moment in the chaos and he picks Joe up and he tells him to wrap his legs around him and keep his head down, and Jon feels the heft of his son and he pulls his neck into his own and he turns side-on so that Joe is away from the melee and Jon puts one foot in front of the other and then the other foot in front of the first and he pushes, his legs aching, his arms aching, and he yells and he moves, he moves and he yells, he pushes past Apollo Food and Wines whose windows are put in and people are clearing the glass and fetching drinks from inside, handing out cans and bottles and cheering and Jon yells again and he runs, and he staggers, the boy in his arms, onto the Strand and away from the mob, away from the crowd and away from the chaos, away from the flames and smoke billowing out from a building site, Jon looking up to see a shirtless man covered in tattoos halfway up a lamppost waving a Pay No Poll Tax placard, and Jon keeps running, staggering and running until they are past Charing Cross Station, and a policeman spots him, looks him in the eye, and Jon sees panic in this policeman's face, and he points and he waves and Jon staggers down Villiers Street towards the river, and he doesn't stop until they reach Embankment Gardens, and they go in and Jon puts down his son and they hold each other, trembling, Jon on his knees, and they sob, they sob, Jon telling his son, it's all right, it's all right, I'm right here.

10

Snatch squad

Trafalgar Square.

Parker is jammed in tight among a group of men who are all moving in different directions at the same time.

He's dropped the shoulder and squeezed, made himself small, made himself big, pushed and wriggled, done the breaststroke, but it's slow going.

Shaun and Simeon have made better progress.

Parker has his eye on them, and he sees them approach Marlon, and he sees Marlon point towards the West End, make for them to follow him and the three of them move off quickly up Cockspur Street.

Parker shoves himself through and runs after them.

He sees Marlon slow down, look left and right and then disappear into the crowd.

He sees Shaun and Simeon realise that Marlon is no longer with them.

From the crowd, Parker sees four men in hoods, their faces covered, spring out at Shaun and Simeon, four men in black hoods and white trainers, scarves round faces, broken placards, sticks and bricks in their hands –

Shaun and Simeon run.

The four men run.

Parker runs.

Parker thinking, what the fuck is happening and where the fuck is Noble.

The crowd swelling behind him.

*

Suzi steps forward to take a photograph, and the mounted police charge into the crowd and the crowd disperse and Suzi sees a woman fall, sees this woman fall under the horses, sees this woman kicked and stamped on by the police horses, and sees two men dive in, dive under the horses and pull this woman out, and she is standing and she is shaking, and the two men are shouting at her, shouting, are you OK, are you OK, and Suzi snaps and snaps and she feels a hand on her neck and feels her camera pulled from her hands, pulled from around her neck, and she sees her camera thrown to the ground, watches as it breaks, and then her arms are gripped and she is pulled away from the ground and her hands are restrained and she is told, you're under arrest, get in the van, and Suzi is pushed towards the back of a van and then pushed inside it, and she falls onto the floor of the van and feels herself held and pulled upright by a man and a woman who tell her, snatch squad but you're safe now, and she looks up and the man is bleeding and the woman puts her arms around Suzi and the door is slammed and they're moving, and Suzi closes her eyes and thinks, stay still, don't move, it's going to be all right.

11

Rogue

Noble breaks the line, into Trafalgar Square, left –

And he clocks Parker, and Parker sees him, and Parker nods, and Parker points –

And Noble's thinking, here we are again and what am I doing here, *really,* what am I *doing* here, thinking of Lea and the baby at home, watching on the television, thinking, they won't know I'm all right, thinking, I will be all right, nodding at Parker –

I will be all right.

Parker barrelling west round Trafalgar Square, head down, Noble thinking –

I will be all right.

Round and round, fighting against the crowd –

The crowd shouting, watch out and fuck off –

Parker arrowing west along Pall Mall.

Noble following, not running, not walking, head down, arms up.

Ahead of Parker, Noble sees movement, movement away from the crowd, three maybe four figures running.

Parker north into St James Square and west again onto King Street, following –

Noble next.

Noble turns, stops, the street empty, wind blowing newspaper and rubbish, Parker turning to Noble, Parker shaking his head –

Parker disappears left into an alley.

Noble hesitates. I will be all right.

Noble follows.

He sees Parker standing in a piss-stinking alley, Parker standing over a body, a body leaking blood, Parker kneeling –

Noble looks up.

Voices and footsteps fade, four figures in hoods vanishing down the alley and out –

Noble clocks the name of the alley: Angel Court.

Noble thinking, was this the exchange? Noble thinking, where the fuck is Simeon?

Noble notes the CCTV camera, ducks his head, gets in what he thinks must be a blind spot.

Parker has his hand on Shaun's neck trying to stop the blood but it ain't working he can feel Shaun literally slipping through his fingers, Shaun is coughing and gurgling and shaking and there is fear in his eyes, his twitching eyes, his face draining of colour and Parker looks up and sees Noble and yells at him to call an ambulance.

'Go, now!' Parker yells. 'Call an ambulance.'

Noble turns and leaves the alley and then stops.

Shaun, he thinks.

He takes a breath.

He takes another breath.

His mind buzzes. His body aches.

He studies the street, which is quiet, no one around.

The noise from Trafalgar Square is big, but feels distant, a world away, suddenly.

Noble nods to himself and makes a decision.

He goes back into the alley.

He sees that Parker is cradling Shaun's head now.

A bloody knife on the ground.

He sees that Shaun's eyes have closed and that his breathing is ragged, faint.

Parker is stricken. 'Well?' he says.

Noble nods. 'On its way,' he lies. 'But with what's going on it might be a while.'

Parker yelling, 'Fuuuuck!'

Noble gets down on his haunches, looks Parker in the eye. 'When it arrives, you can't be here, son.'

'What do you mean?'

'You can't be here, you're a ghost.' Noble spelling it out. 'You get questioned, you get *nicked*, well, there ain't nothing we can do for you, not for something like this.'

Parker shakes his head, tears in his eyes, cradling Shaun, Shaun whose life is leaving him, leaving him, leaving –

He points. 'They went down there.'

Noble nods. 'I saw them go. What about Simeon?'

Parker shakes his head, his eyes wide. 'I don't know.'

'There ain't no good you can do being here, son,' Noble says. He puts a hand on Parker's arm. 'He's gone, son, come on. He's gone.'

Noble eases Shaun's head from Parker's arms onto the pavement.

He helps Parker up. He smoothes down his coat.

He looks Parker in the eye. 'There ain't much time, but you need to listen to me carefully.'

Parker nods.

'This is it, OK, end of operation. It's time to come in, you understand?'

Parker nods.

'This is a clean extraction. No going back.'

Parker nods.

'You know where the safe house is, the debrief venue?'

Parker nods.

'You go there right now, and you don't look behind you until you've arrived.'

Parker nods.

'There'll be someone waiting. I'll come and see you tomorrow.'

Parker nods.

Parker runs. Unsteadily.

Must be in shock, Noble thinks.

Noble examines Shaun.

He checks his hands, and he checks the knife, and he checks the perimeter, touching nothing.

He works out his story.

He was at the march on a reconnaissance job.

He observed an unconnected suspected attack and gave chase.

He discovered the body alone.

He secured the scene. He made the call and waited.

He turns to exit the alleyway and find a phone box.

'All right, Chance.'

Jenkins –

Jenkins.

'I always fancied you were a snide, Noble.'

Noble points at Shaun. 'And this?'

'Don't be soppy,' Jenkins says. '*This* is a mistake. They were supposed to do Simeon. Where is he, by the way?'

Noble shakes his head.

'Oh well, he'll turn up.' Jenkins grins. 'Always does. Anyway, I expect you knew that already given you've been listening in for a while now.'

Noble runs his tongue over his teeth. 'What're you saying, Dave?'

'Collusion in a criminal drugs conspiracy run out of a council house, a dead boy who is a known associate of an informant who was assisting me in breaking that conspiracy, one who is now at large and in danger.'

Noble sniffs, says nothing.

'I can go on.'

Noble nods.

'You keep your gob shut, Chance, and it's all sweet.'

Noble nods.

Jenkins grins. 'Go home, Patrick. See your lady wife, your beautiful baby boy. You've your responsibilities to consider.'

Noble nods. He hears sirens. He'll be protected, he thinks. There's plenty of evidence.

He licks his lips and leaves.

12

Resolution

Mrs Thatcher is watching the television.

Michael Buerk reading the news on BBC1 at 9.30 p.m.:

'There's been serious rioting tonight in central London,' says Michael Buerk. 'More than a hundred people have been injured after a mass demonstration against the poll tax ended in violence. Trafalgar Square's been turned into a battleground. Cars have been destroyed. Shops have been looted. And more than three hundred arrested in London's night of riots. The trouble is still going on. The police say fifty of their officers are in hospital and twenty of their horses have been hurt. Tonight, they accused a minority of around three thousand of the demonstrators of launching a ferocious and sustained attack on them.'

She switches off the television and pours herself a whisky, feeling only one thing.

13

Stay in your lane

They've got Suzi in West End Central police station.

She's sharing a holding cell with the couple in the van, who are sleeping now, it's been a few hours since they were brought in.

Suzi overhears excited voices in another cell, someone saying:

'St Martin's Lane, mate. Three cars idly overturned, completely on their roofs, wheels swinging in the air. And, oh what a glorious sight, a Porsche utterly burnt out.'

She thinks that she'll remember that one, add it to her archive of the day, not that there will be any photographs of course.

Later, an officer appears and tells Suzi that she's free to go.

Suzi's given her things back and she walks quickly out the door, nervous someone will stop her and tell her that in fact, no, she's not free to go at all.

Outside: Noble, his hands in the pockets of his leather jacket.

Suzi stands still, mouth open, for a long moment, then shakes her head.

'All right, Suzi,' Noble says. He offers her a cigarette. 'Want one?'

Suzi nods and takes the packet.

'Light?'

'Please.'

Suzi takes out another cigarette, hands it to Noble, pops the packet into her bag.

'I've given up anyway,' Noble says, lighting it.

They smoke quietly for a bit.

Eventually, Suzi asks, 'Are you going to tell me that this is all thanks to you then?'

Noble smiles. 'In a manner of speaking.'

'A manner of speaking?'

'Yeah.'

Suzi pulls hard on her cigarette, exhales out the corner of her mouth. 'Go on then, I'm listening.'

'Your name,' Noble says, 'is on a list.'

'A list.'

'A list that means if you're ever nicked, I'm informed. And then I can come and get you out, whatever it is they say you've done.'

'And for what do I deserve that privilege?'

'Oh, I think you know why, Suzi.'

Suzi sniffs and nods. 'I expect I do.'

She thinks of all the things she's done for Noble over the years. She likely does deserve some special treatment now and again.

She smiles grimly, shakes her head.

Noble drops his cigarette and stamps on it. 'Point is, Suzi, you'll always be on that list.' He breathes out slowly. 'Whatever happens, you'll always be on that list.'

Suzi nods. 'And?'

Noble smiles. 'That's not a threat, Suzi, it's reassurance.'

'Of what exactly?'

'Well, let's just say you stay in your lane, Suzi, and no one will ever bother you again.'

'No one's bothering me now.'

Noble nods. 'You're right, no one is bothering you now.'

'Is *that* a threat?'

Noble laughs. 'It ain't, no. All I'm saying is that what's happened is all in the past, and so long as it stays there everyone's happy.'

Suzi finishes her cigarette. She gives Noble a hard look. 'I should be going.'

'Stick to writing about music, Suzi, bit of advice. You know, going forward.'

Suzi nods.

At home, on the kitchen table, she lays out her notes and her recordings and her building society statements and anything else she has that proves she has been an instrument of the state.

She pours herself a glass of wine and sits down.

She's tired and rolls her neck, stretches her toes.

The money's quite good, she thinks, examining the statements.

It'd buy her some time and space, let her do the work she wants to do.

On Monday, she'll withdraw it.

She bags everything up and takes it downstairs and outside into the backyard.

Noble can't know that she's been gathering this evidence.

But she's not doing this for him, she's doing it for herself.

She places the bag on the rusting barbecue and sets fire to it with her lighter.

She watches it melt and smoulder, spark into flame.

SEVEN MONTHS LATER

PART SIX

Exit Ghost

RESIGNATION ACTION PLAN: 22 NOVEMBER 1990

0730	Prime Minister conveys her decision to AT and PHM
0735	Prime Minister clears press statement
0740	AT informs Palace, agrees statement and time for Audience
0740	PHM tells Mr. Hurd and Mr. Major of her decision
0745	AT warns Treasury and Bank
0830–0900	Questions briefing
0900	Cabinet
	Prime Minister informs Cabinet of her decision
	Telephone messages from Private Office to inform
	– Mr. Speaker
	– Mr. Kinnock
	– Mr. Ashdown
	– Mr. Molyneaux
	shortly before statement issued
	Political office informs Mr. Onslow
0930c	Statement issued
1015	Cabinet concludes
1015	Sign personal messages to President Bush, President Gorbachev, EC and G7 leaders plus Gulf leaders
1030–1240	Speechwriting
1200	Nominations close
1235	Depart for Audience
1245	Audience
1300	Return to No. 10

1

Things can only get better

November 1990.

Ayeleen. I'm seeing Carolyn quite a lot these days. I bump into her and the baby, she sometimes comes into the shop where I work now that Uncle Ahmet has taken me out of the restaurant, for good it seems. It's a nice little deli by Clapton Pond, full of fresh foods and imported stuff, and everyone always tells me that it's much better than the offie that was there before, no drunks hanging around outside, more like what you get in smarter parts of town.

Carolyn looks well, I think, and I tell her, course I do, every time I see her. The baby is growing, smiling and gurgling and all chirpy-looking. Carolyn has a determined expression on her face, like she's a bit colder than she was, and who can blame her? Shaun's dead and Parker's disappeared. How do you live with that exactly? What do you do with that?

After Shaun died, my uncle and my mother decided that the best thing for me would be to leave London, leave all this mess behind, leave this place for somewhere safer, somewhere nicer.

They never told me this exactly, though, they never spelled it out. They wanted me to make my own mind up, but this is what they wanted me to decide to do.

What they *really* wanted me to do was go to Turkey and live with family over there, but I never even entertained that idea. Lauren and me, we talked about uni somewhere else maybe, but it never happened.

Uncle has got a point.

In the last few months there's been more violence. They're calling Lower Clapton Road Murder Mile now. Ever since Shaun was killed there's been an ongoing tit-for-tat conflict, about drugs of course, Stoke Newington and Clapton and Homerton at each other's throats. And it all happens in and around Chimes, the nightclub on the Lea Bridge Roundabout, just a few doors down from the restaurant, really.

That boy Simeon was shot just outside, only a few weeks after Shaun, sitting in a parked car when a motorbike pulled up and two kids in helmets and masks fired six shots through the window.

Lauren heard that he's still in a coma, that they got him in the leg and in the shoulder and the chest, but he's still alive, for now. It's been months.

Rumours about him and Shaun and what they were getting up to. I didn't know about it, and it makes me sad to think of Shaun like that. The story is he was forced into it, that it all goes back to before he even knew me properly, back to Tottenham, even.

There was a friend of his at the funeral, Anton, who came to talk to me. I was too upset to chat, and I never saw him again, but there was something about him that makes me think I should, like he knew the real Shaun, the Shaun I knew, the Shaun Carolyn knew, I suppose.

Lauren told me that some copper was round the restaurant asking a few questions, some bloke called Noble, she said. Uncle was friendly and helpful – nothing to tell. Anyway, that man Marlon hasn't been around since Shaun, and the copper's not been back since neither and that was ages ago.

Thing is I don't want to live in Hackney anymore, but I don't know anything else.

Uncle is adamant we're on to a winner, that it's changing, new people with money coming to live here, but I don't see that when I look out the window.

'We'll go abroad, Leen,' Lauren says. 'Once we've graduated, let's do that.'

I think it's a good idea and I smile.

Let's do that, I think.

*

December 1990, Scotland Yard.

Noble's in for yet another debrief.

'With her ladyship's departure,' Young is saying, 'we don't yet know which way the wind will blow.'

'No, guv?'

'No.' Young smiles, a faraway look crosses his face for a long moment. 'She was …' He's smiling, wistfully. 'She was *particular* about who she entrusted with certain *dealings*.' He nods. 'Yes. That's it.'

Noble says nothing.

'And we don't yet know how her successor will want to, well, proceed.'

Noble nods. He thinks, why doesn't he just say his name?

'Your work though, Noble, sterling, you know that.' Another smile. 'As ever, as always.'

'Thank you, guv.'

'We'll be able to get one or two of them thanks to your evidence.'

'One or two of them?'

'The media is sniffing around, and we'll have to give them a story.'

'But—'

'And the MP for Hackney South – Sedgemore, I think – he brought it up in parliament, so we'll have to do something about that too.'

'I thought—'

'A Police Complaints Authority-supervised anti-corruption inquiry, I think. Some wag has suggested a code name, quite funny, given the context.'

Noble open-mouthed. A public relations exercise is what it sounds like, which he thinks is not funny at all.

'Operation Jackpot.'

'OK.'

'Your undercover, you got him out?'

'Yes, he's, well, he's elsewhere.'

'Good. So long as his new alias isn't Salman Rushdie, he'll be fine!'

Talking of humour, Noble's not sure how clever a fatwa joke is neither, under the circs.

'We'll need all the intel he gathered on the Hackney Community Defence Association organised, archived, you up to that?'

Noble nods.

'Those telephone conversations of yours, they're inadmissible, of course.'

Noble smiles defeatedly. 'Of course they are.'

Young narrows his eyes. 'You don't look thrilled by what I'm telling you, Detective Constable.'

'No, guv, I—'

Young waves this away. 'Nature of the job, Noble. You've banked a lot of goodwill, let's call it that.'

Noble nods. He thinks, don't piss on my shoes and tell me it's raining.

He notes the open tabloid on Young's desk.

He glimpses a photo of Tony Adams, who's off inside for a bit after driving pissed into a garden wall.

There's another photo on the same page: those two dozy birds who got done shifting heroin out of Bangkok, looking glum in a Thai jail, and they'll be going away for considerably longer than the Arsenal captain, that's for sure.

'So, what next then, Detective Constable, is I suppose the pertinent question.'

'It is, guv.'

'You're a family man now.'

Noble nods.

'I'd have thought you might want a bit of stability in your work, a bit less time in the field, as it were.'

'That might be nice, guv.'

Noble thinking, Christ, that would be nice.

'I thought a job for you here, with me. *For* me.'

'A desk job, guv?'

'A desk not far from where you sit now, Noble. Nine to five.' Young chuckles. 'Well, almost nine to five, there will be the odd black-tie event, I expect.'

'I better take myself shopping then.'

'Very good. You'll think about it?'

Noble shakes his head. 'No, I don't need to. I'd like it.'

'Good man.' Young points at the door. 'She'll handle it from here. Have a couple of weeks off and you'll start first Monday in January.'

Noble nods.

On his way home, Noble stops at a florist and buys a big bunch of something seasonal that looks very pretty. Next, he ducks into a sports shop and gets a teddy bear and a little football, a junior West Ham shirt for luck. Then, the fancy off-licence for a bottle of Champagne and a family-sized bag of Spanish crisps.

And that's that, he thinks, smiling.

September 1993.

Suzi's got her Dictaphone on.

Paul Weller's talking nine to the dozen in a west London pub, ostensibly promoting his new LP, *Wild Wood*, which looks like it's going to re-establish him back at the top of the pop game.

Not that he's sticking to any kind of a script.

'I mainly just like listening to music. It still inspires me; I still get something from it, a very personal thing I can't put into words. It's the only thing that really excites me, to be honest. And it worries me sometimes, because it does feel like I've got a very one-dimensional life. It all just seems to revolve around music. But that's the way it is. I've accepted it.'

Suzi nodding and smiling, happy to be here with him, to listen.

'I'll get the drinks in,' she says, and Paul Weller throws his pint back, grinning in agreement.

Suzi brings over a tray and they get stuck in.

'I'm a very individual, very private person,' Paul Weller says.

Suzi nods. 'What about Red Wedge?' she asks. 'What happened with all that?'

Paul Weller gives Suzi a look as if to say you know perfectly well what happened, darling, but all right then.

'I don't like the idea of carrying a card,' he says. 'The Wedge thing escalated from when a lot of artists, including us, were doing benefits and someone decided to pull it all together. I felt uneasy about getting involved but I did, and did the best I could. I thought we were exploited by the Labour Party. Around that time they wound down the Young Socialists and said that the Wedge would take the YS's place. But it shouldn't have been down to us. I felt we were manipulated. And on the road we met a lot of local Labour Party people who I just didn't believe in; they were more showbiz than the people on the tour bus. I've got a real mistrust for a lot of politicians, and I wouldn't get involved again. I should have stuck with my original instincts.'

Suzi reminds Paul Weller that she helped make some of the introductions, Annajoy David and Billy Bragg –

'Billy's a very persuasive person, a very amiable, likeable person, and he's genuine, very into what he does,' Paul Weller says. 'He was aware of what I distrusted, and he doesn't defend it either, but he sees the ultimate aim as much greater, and he's probably right. Before the Wedge, The Style Council had done a lot independently, raised a lot of money in benefits. But after the Wedge we were so disillusioned it all stopped. We were totally cynical about all of it.'

Not really a surprise, Suzi thinks.

All that media noise surrounding it and Maggie won by a landslide, the whole thing looking a little quaint now, she reflects, a little amateur hour in dungarees and beads, though the shows were fantastic, the Council really tight.

They were a great live band, until the Albert Hall show, though Suzi enjoyed herself.

'The last serious thing I did was *Confessions of a Pop Group*,' Paul Weller says, talking now about the end of The Style Council. 'Which most people fucking hated, but I thought was really good.'

Suzi thought it was really good too.

She wrote about it, of course, reappraised it, assigned it misunderstood masterpiece status.

'It didn't matter what we did or said, nothing would change.'

Is what Paul Weller said about it all, later.

Words Suzi still takes very much to heart.

It didn't matter what she did or said, nothing would change.

'It was a bad time, a low time,' Paul Weller goes on. Selling Solid Bond, starting again. 'It did me good, helped me come back down to earth a little bit. The turning point for me was writing "Into Tomorrow" on my first solo album.'

Suzi smiles, feels the warmth of Paul Weller's presence, the promise of the afternoon's drinking, where they'll go next, her new fella coming out to join them later, Keith too, back in the Weller fold and he and Suzi something like old friends, all very grown up.

Suzi feels content. Suzi's felt content for a while now.

'When I was a kid and had just started to play guitar, all I wanted to be was in a pop group, successful and make records. And I don't see a thing wrong in that, really, I just got sidetracked.'

Yeah, Suzi thinks, tell me about it. Sidetracked for about twelve years.

March 1994, the River Lea.

Saturday lunchtime and Jon and the boy and Lizzie are out on their bikes. The last time the three of them went on a bike ride, two of the bikes were an awful lot smaller.

They've crossed Millfield's Park, pootled along the canal past the Prince of Wales and over the little footbridge up to the marshes, stopping to watch a little weekend football.

Jon turns away from the 'action' for a moment to look at Riverside Close on the other side of the canal.

The Leaside Project is almost complete.

There are vast computer-generated images of wholesome family happiness, of wildlife and water, a statement attesting to the affordable housing to be found within this stunning new purpose-built development in the heart of the east London regeneration, offering contemporary living at its finest, seamlessly blending indoor and outdoor spaces, the ideal home for modern eco-living.

Jon wonders if H. is to be found basking in a unit.

Unlikely.

About as unlikely as the taps not working, Jon thinks.

Jon wonders how many H2Owners will be resident.

He shakes his head and turns back to the football.

Jon left all this behind after the poll tax riot.

Immersed in community charge non-compliance cases, he understood that he couldn't go on as Borough Solicitor, asked to sign off on things that compromise his sense of morality.

A month or so after the riot, he put out a few feelers.

It didn't take long before he took a job as a private solicitor.

He'll always be able to support his family now.

The bonuses alone are outrageous.

'Come on,' he says to his kids, swinging a leg over his bike. 'I'll race you to your mother.'

Jackie –

Jackie.

Waiting for them at the Robin Hood or will be by the time they get there.

The love of his life.

There's a priority, Jon thinks, and it's your family.

There might not be any other way to look at it.

You do what you can.

Jon does.

Things can only get better.

*

Years later, Dalston.

Parker – a baseball cap pulled low on his head – stands on the site of the Four Aces Club where poor old unfortunate Trevor used to go back in the days when Trevor was Parker's snout, and the club catered to his sort of clientele.

Not there anymore then, the club, Parker thinks.

Walking around Hackney for the first time in many years, Parker thinks that a lot of things aren't there anymore. And quite a lot of new things are there instead.

He has a brochure in his hand for a luxury development of 550 apartments, the five blocks named:

Labyrinth Tower, Dunbar Tower and Collins Tower (after Four Aces co-founders Newton Dunbar and Sir Collins), Marley House and Wonder House.

The Four Aces became Club Labrynth.

In 1998 it closed down, Hackney Council exercising its right to a compulsory repossession of the premises.

Ten years later the building is demolished.

There were trees planted in the club's garden in memory of those who died in the New Cross fire.

These trees are cut down.

Parker looks on at the empty space across the road from where he stands and remembers what Newton Dunbar himself said about it:

'They called it Dunbar Tower without consulting me.'

Parker remembers Trevor.

Parker remembers Marlon.

Parker remembers Simeon.

Parker remembers Shaun.

Parker remembers Carolyn.

Parker remembers –

Parker has no right to remember her.

Parker will always be dead to her.

Which is how it will end –

Acknowledgements

True Blue is a work of fiction based on, and woven around, fact. Much of this fact is recognisable in terms of certain names, places, statistics, institutions, events, documents, laws and policy, which have been adapted and, in some cases, changed for dramatic purposes. I grew up in Hackney; this experience accounts for much of the information, and many of the anecdotes, in the novel. Friends, family, colleagues, associates and contemporary media outlets all informed the writing of the novel, both directly and indirectly. Most of all, and as with *White Riot* and *Red Menace*, I want to thank the people who were there for their accounts of what they did.

Equally, and as per *White Riot* and *Red Menace*: much has been written about this period; I am grateful to the writers who have gone before. Once again, I made extensive use of the exhaustive online archives of the wonderful *Radical History of Hackney*; the *Hackney Gazette*, too, and again, was an invaluable resource; where documents from these resources are quoted, it is listed in the Notes section that follows. John Eden's illuminating article for *Datacide* magazine remains essential reading and an inspiration. The *Undercover Policing Inquiry* hosts an archive of documents relating to the spycops scandal at ucpi.org.uk that is important, fascinating and terrifying. Internet resources are cited in the Notes section where appropriate. I made use of the online archive of the Margaret Thatcher Foundation, at margaretthatcher.org, which catalogues everything she ever uttered in public, as well as private papers and declassified documents. The Special Branch Files Project is an extraordinary resource, 'a live-archive of declassified files focussing on the surveillance of political activists and campaigners'. The National Archives produced certain significant documents, details in the Bibliography and Notes.

The police officers in the novel and their actions are entirely fictional.

Simeon is a fictional character and all interactions that he has are wholly imagined. Elements of his story and experiences were inspired by certain details from the pamphlets 'Fighting the Lawmen' and 'A Crime is a Crime is a Crime' (see Bibliography for details), specifically, aspects from the miscarriages of justice detailed in articles collated in the pamphlet pertaining to Glenford Lewis and Clint Nelson, articles which describe horrific acts of police violence and corruption against innocent men.

Jon Davies is a fictional character. All interactions he has with characters in the novel are wholly imagined.

Parker is a fictional character; the Undercover Policing Inquiry has demonstrated that spycops were placed in activist groups in Hackney.

Whilst certain Acid House promoters, bands, the music and the magazines in the text are real, my characters Suzi and Keith are fictional and therefore the portrayal of their work and their interactions with those real people and groups is wholly imagined. Suzi and Keith's interactions with Paul Weller and members of The Style Council and associates are fictional. The influence of Paul Weller and The Style Council on this novel is far-reaching and I'd like to thank them, sincerely. I want to thank, again, Wayne Anthony for permission to quote from his memoir.

Please see the Bibliography and Notes sections for further detail.

Bibliography

Non-Fiction books

Anonymous, *Poll Tax Riot: 10 Hours that Shook Trafalgar Square* (Acab Press, 1990)

Anthony, Wayne, *Class of 88* (Virgin Books, 1998)

Beckett, Andy, *Promised You a Miracle: Why 1980–1982 Made Modern Britain* (Allen Lane, 2015)

Beckett, Andy, *When the Lights Went Out: Britain in the Seventies* (Faber & Faber, 2009)

Blackman, Rick, *Babylon's Burning: Music, Subcultures and Anti-Fascism in Britain 1958–2020* (Bookmarks Publications, 2021)

Bloom, Clive, *Violent London: 2000 Years of Riots, Rebels, and Revolts* (Palgrave Macmillan, 2010)

Butler, Tim with Robson, Garry, *London Calling: The Middle Classes and the Re-making of Inner London* (Berg, 2003)

Carroll, Rory, *Killing Thatcher: The IRA, the Manhunt, and the Long War with The Crown* (Mudlark, 2023)

Evans, Rob & Lewis, Paul, *Undercover: The True Story of Britain's Secret Police* (Faber & Faber, 2013)

Gillard, Michael, *Legacy: Gangsters, Corruption and the London Olympics* (Bloomsbury Reader, 2019)

Gillett, Ed, *Party Lines: Dance Music and the Making of Modern Britain* (Picador, 2023)

Hannah, Simon, *Can't Pay, Won't Pay: The Fight to Stop the Poll Tax* (Pluto Press, 2020)

Independent Committee of Inquiry, *Policing in Hackney 1945–1984* (Karia Press, 1989)

Kessler, Ted, *Paper Cuts: How I destroyed the British Music Press and Other Misadventures* (White Rabbit, 2022)

McLean, Donna, *Small Town Girl* (Hodder & Stoughton, 2021)

McSmith, Andy, *No Such Thing as Society: Britain in the Turmoil of the 1980s* (Constable, 2010)

Miles, Barry, *London Calling: A Countercultural History of London since 1945* (Atlantic Books, 2011)

Morton, James, *Bent Coppers: A Survey of Police Corruption* (Warner Books, 1994)

Munn, Iain, *Mr Cool's Dream: A Complete History of The Style Council* (A Wholepoint Publication, 2011)

Rachel, Daniel, *Too Much Too Young, The 2 Tone Records Story: Rude Boys, Racism and the Soundtrack of a Generation* (White Rabbit, 2023)

Rachel, Daniel, *Walls Come Tumbling Down: The Music and Politics of Rock Against Racism, 2 Tone and Red Wedge* (Picador, 2016)

Reynolds, Simon, *Energy Flash: A Journey through Rave Music and Dance Culture* (Faber & Faber, 2013)

Robinson, Simon, *Can't Pay, Won't Pay: A Short History of the Anti-Poll Tax Struggle 1987–1993* (Thinkwell Books, 2023)

Sandbrook, Dominic, *Who Dares Wins, Britain, 1979–1982* (Penguin, 2019)

Sandbrook, Dominic, *Seasons in the Sun: The Battle for Britain 1974–1979* (Penguin, 2013)

Sinclair, Iain, *Lights Out for the Territory* (Penguin, 2003)

Sinclair, Iain, *Hackney, That Rose-Red Empire* (Penguin, 2009)

Stewart, Graham, *Bang! A History of Britain in the 1980s* (Atlantic Books, 2013)

Thatcher, Margaret, *The Autobiography* (Harper Press, first published as *The Downing Street Years*, 1993, and *The Path to Power*, 1995)

Turner, Alwyn W., *Rejoice! Rejoice! Britain in the 1980s* (Aurum Press, 2008)

Turner, Alwyn W., *Crisis? What Crisis? Britain in the 1970s* (Aurum Press, 2008)

Widgery, David, *Beating Time: Riot 'n' Race 'n' Rock and Roll* (Chatto & Windus, 1986)

Articles

'The Right to Buy' by Andy Beckett, *Guardian*, 26 August 2015

'How a Married Undercover Cop Having Sex with Activists Killed a Climate Movement' by Geoff Dembicki, *Vice*, 18 January 2022

'Inside Feltham: Why London's Young Offender Institution is one of the scariest prisons in Britain' by Archie Bland, *Independent*, 4 September 2013

'"Music shouted louder than racism": the pioneering Black nightclub born in far-right east London' by Daniel Dylan Wray, *Guardian*, 25 July 2023

'They Hate Us, We Hate Them – Resisting Police Corruption and Violence in Hackney in the 1980s and 1990s' by John Eden, *Datacide* Magazine

'So why DID rocker Paul Weller decide to cover one of the all-time seminal house tracks…?' by Editor, *909Originals: The Stories behind the music*, 4 October 2017

'Police spy: "I thought, how would they feel about their son's name being used"' by Rob Evans and Paul Lewis, *Guardian*, 3 February 2013

Special Demonstration Squad: unit which vanished into undercover world' by Rob Evans, *Guardian*, 24 July 2014

'Met deputy too busy for questions on spy officer's relationship with woman' by Rob Evans, *Guardian*, 16 March 2021

'"Spy cops' filed reports on Diane Abbott's anti-racism campaigning", inquiry told' by Rob Evans, *Guardian*, 3 July 2024

'Party Music' by Simon Frith and John Street, *Marxism Today*, June 1986

'Legacy In The Dust: The Four Aces Story: a film by Winstan Whitter – Interview with the Director' by Bryony Hegarty, *Louder than War*, 13 July 2016

'Thatcher's War on Acid House' by Michael Holden, *Vice*, 9 April 2013

'"Finding liberation somewhere else": acid house, Thatcherism and the present-day parallels' by Aaron Levitt, an interview with Bill Brewster about then and now, *Stamp the Wax*, 27 November 2018

'Secrets and lies: untangling the UK "spy cops" scandal' by Paul Lewis and Rob Evans, *Guardian*, 28 October 2020

'Last Man Standing' by Paul Lester, *Uncut*, via http://www.wellerworld.co.uk/Uncut.html

'I was engaged to an undercover police officer' by Donna McLean, *Guardian*, 29 January 2021

'I helped to privatise England's water firms. But it's government inaction that wrecked them' by John Nelson, *Guardian*, 8 July 2023

'Sold down the river: England's broken water industry is a case study in the dangers of dogmatic privatisation. It is time to rethink our ownership model' by New Statesman, *New Statesman*, 10 April 2024

'The Style Council Modernism: A New Decade' by Jon O'Brien, *Classic Pop*, 19 October 2023

'Andrew Weatherall: lone swordsman who cut new shapes for British music' by Alexis Petridis, *Guardian*, 17 February 2020

'Cheap sales, debt and foreign takeovers: how privatisation changed the water industry' by Nils Pratley, *Guardian*, 10 July 2024

'Modernism Vs. Classicism: Paul Weller Interviewed' by Valerie Siebert, *The Quietus*, 30 June 2014

'The Tottenham 3: the legacy of the Broadwater Farm riot' by Natalie Smith, *The Justice Gap*, 13 July 2018

'Paul Weller: "Most people dislike me anyway… it can only get better"' by Mat Snow, *Guardian*, 16 April 2014, a reprinting of a *Q* article from 1993

'Weatherall Report 1', *The Face*, archive material reproduced online, https://theface.com/archive/andrew-weatherall-tribute-primal-scream-boys-own-scream-dream-diaries-archive

'I was abused by an undercover policeman. But how far up did the deceit go?' by Kate Wilson, *Guardian*, 21 September 2018

'A Man Escaped: The Style Council's Confessions Of A Pop Group 30 Years On' by Lois Wilson, *The Quietus*, 3 July 2018

'It's Still Mrs. Thatcher's Britain' by James Wood, *New Yorker*, 25 November 2019

Documents

'A Crime is a Crime a Crime: Graham Smith interviewed by Ken Fero', transcript, 2001, http://www.uncarved.org/blog/wp-content/uploads/2009/03/colin-roach-a-crime-is-a-crime-is-a-crime.pdf

'Hackney Against the Poll Tax Federation Newsletter' May 1990, Hackney Museum Archive

'A Crime is a Crime a Crime: A Short report on Police Crime in Hackney' pamphlet by the Hackney Community Defence Association, November 1991

'A People's Account of the Hackney anti-Poll Tax demonstration on March 8th 1990' pamphlet by the Hackney Community Defence Association, 3 August 1990

'Fighting the Lawmen' pamphlet by the Hackney Community Defence Association, 8 October 1992

'On the Border of a Police State' pamphlet by the Hackney Community Defence Association with the Hackney Trade Union Support Unit, September 1993

'Hackney's Acid House Party Hysteria', The Radical History of Hackney:

https://hackneyhistory.wordpress.com/2022/04/09/hackneys-acid-house-party-hysteria-1988/

https://www.youtube.com/watch?v=jTKTGTQit3A&t=3s

New Year Message, 31 December 1989, Message, Margaret Thatcher Foundation

Speech to Conservative Local Government Conference, 4 March 1989, Margaret Thatcher Foundation

Speech to Conservative Central Council, 18 March 1989, Margaret Thatcher Foundation

National Archives, Resignation Action Plan 22 November 1990, 901122 No.10 mnt RESIG ACTION PLAN PREM19-3213 f215

National Archives, PREM 19/2724, Department of the Environment, letter, 5 October 1989

National Archives, PREM 19/2724, Privy Council office, letter, 27 November 1989

National Archives, PREM 19/2724, 10 Downing Street, letter from the Principal Private Secretary, 6 November 1989

National Archives, PREM 19/2724, Note to PM, ACID HOUSE PARTIES, 12 October 1989

National Archives, Bernard Ingham, Water Privatisation, September 14, 1989, 890914 Ingham mnt for Gray WATER PRIVATISATION PREM19-3846 f377

National Archives, Chris Patten, Memo to Prime Minister, 12 September 1989, 890912 Patten mnt for MT WATER PRIVATISATION PREM19-3846 f379

National Archives, John Redwood, letter to 10 Downing Street, 28 February 1989, 7972652F72A54D1884F75701978DE819

'Who Killed Michael Ferreira? Part One', The Radical History of Hackney: https://hackneyhistory.wordpress.com/2022/01/06/who-killed-michael-ferreira-part-one/

'Who Killed Michael Ferreira? Part Two', The Radical History of Hackney: https://hackneyhistory.wordpress.com/2022/01/14/who-killed-michael-ferreira-part-two/

'Police Crime: A Constitutional Perspective' by Graham Richard Smith, Thesis submitted for degree of Doctor of Philosophy, Faculty of Laws, University College London, June 1998

'The Legacy of the Stoke Newington Scandal' by Graham Smith, Paper submitted for publication by Police Science and Management: January 1999

Film/television/media

'1990: Chaos, Carnage & Bloodshed in Poll Tax Riots' from the ITN Archive, https://www.youtube.com/watch?v=I4QQN2aqeKA

Babylon by Franco Rossi (1980)

BBC1 1 January 1989 Late Evening News, https://www.youtube.com/watch?app=desktop&v=vB3O1gbhIc8

Michael Buerk with BBC News reports on Poll Tax riots in London, 31 March 1990, https://www.youtube.com/watch?v=ckLcsFMhiXo

Bent Coppers: Crossing the Line of Duty (3-part BBC series) by Todd Austin (2021)

boys own snub tv andrew weatherall terry farley pete heller bocca juniors, https://www.youtube.com/watch?v=_vqf9DDHqUg

Interview with Robert Fearon aka Ribs from UNITY SOUND SYSTEM on 20 February 2002, from the sleeve notes to the Honest Jon compilation album *Watch How the People Dancing: Unity Sounds from the London Dancehall, 1986–1989*

London Poll Tax Riots of 1990 https://www.youtube.com/watch?v=IeFS6So6w8c

People's Account (1985) by Milton Bryan, Ceddo Film and Video Workshop, with support from Channel 4 and the GLC, but never shown on British Television: 'the Independent Broadcasting Authority (IBA) objected to the description of the police as racist, lawless terrorists, and to the description of the riot as a legitimate act of self-defence' https://the-lcva.co.uk/videos/59787f52e811330af43ebb2a

Small Axe (5-part BBC series) by Steve McQueen (2020)

The Eighty Eight Podcast #13 Genesis'88 Leaside Rd 1988

The Style Council – Royal Albert Hall – 04-07-89 https://www.youtube.com/watch?v=7tkcPYaUYoc

Uprising (3-part BBC series) by Steve McQueen (2021)

Yardie by Idris Elba (2019)

Notes

5	'They Call Her Cleopatra Wong' tagline quotes from original film posters, via https://www.imdb.com/title/tt0077343/
11	The depiction of the attack of Michael Ferreira draws from 'Who Killed Michael Ferreira? Part One', The Radical History of Hackney: https://hackneyhistory.wordpress.com/2022/01/06/who-killed-michael-ferreira-part-one/
12	To contribute to authenticity in terms of language used at the time, certain lines of police questioning quote and/or adapt the play 'Who Killed Michael Ferreira?' written collectively by a group of school children in Tower Hamlets under the supervision of Chris Searle, text from 'Who Killed Michael Ferreira? Part Two', The Radical History of Hackney: https://hackneyhistory.wordpress.com/2022/01/14/who-killed-michael-ferreira-part-two/

Here are the lines in question:

What do you lot want?

What have you been up to?

Yeah – what's going on?

Hold your horses, I want to know exactly what's going on here.

Shut up – now first of all, give us your names and addresses.

Keep quiet son, we'll attend to you in a minute. I've got to take a statement first.

Where was this?

Did you recognise any of them?

What's going on here?

These boys have been starting trouble.

Watch your language with me, sonny. Now have you lot been in any trouble before?

So you started a fight eh? Picked on some white boys eh? Then you got the worst of it and come here with your lies about other kids?

Be very careful son. Now what time did this so-called attack occur?

Oh yeah? And what were you little boys doing out at that time of night?

Just answer the questions.

A likely story.

I don't want no lip from you Sambo. Now what street did this happen on?

What street's this then?

Who do you think you're bloody swearing at? Up against the wall! You too, up against the wall!

There's nothing wrong with him, just a bloody scratch – you can't have us on.

Look, the quicker you tell us what happened, the quicker your mate will see a doctor.

So where were you when he got stabbed?

Have you been in trouble with the police before?

You could have been out nicking tonight for all we know.

15 Biographical information on Michael Ferreira from 'Who Killed Michael Ferreira? Part One', The Radical History of Hackney: https://hackneyhistory.wordpress.com/2022/01/06/who-killed-michael-ferreira-part-one/

16 The Jackal Run, certain details from 'Police spy: "I thought, how would they feel about their son's name being used"' Evans and Lewis, *Guardian*, 3 February 2013

16 Timeline, details from hearing at Highbury magistrates; and extract from *Hackney People's Press*, from 'Who Killed Michael Ferreira? Part One', The Radical History of Hackney: https://hackneyhistory.wordpress.com/2022/01/06/who-killed-michael-ferreira-part-one/ While this section draws on the historical record, Parker's involvement is entirely fictional.

23 *Hackney Gazette* quotations, 'Hackney's Acid House Party Hysteria', The Radical History of Hackney: https://hackneyhistory.wordpress.com/2022/04/09/hackneys-acid-house-party-hysteria-1988/

24 Genesis Chapter III poster based on original: https://opensea.io/assets/ethereum/0x495f947276749ce646f68ac8c248420045cb7b5e/11381574941909146410362809906095775346628784383507059180766899460534884630616

34 Incident involving Dennis Bovell is based on Gillett, *Party Lines*, pp. 25–7

41 'I went from listening to "United" by Throbbing Gristle to dancing

in a field to "Josephine". Which gives you some idea what a powerful drug ecstasy is.' Andrew Weatherall quote, *Guardian*, 17 February 2020

42   *Boy's Own* fanzine and the term 'acid ted' and its derogatory meaning, Reynolds, *Energy Flash*, p. 104

44   Wayne Anthony's anecdote quotes Anthony, *Class of 88*, pp. 27–8. Anthony and Tony Colston-Hayter organised warehouse parties as Genesis-Sunset in Hackney, and I quote from and refer to Anthony's brilliant memoir; Suzi, Parker and Marlon's interactions with them – and other real-life associates – are entirely imagined, fictional.

44   Handwritten note and related, Anthony, *Class of 88*, p. 27

52   Dialogue from the promoters based on and quotes Anthony, *Class of 88*, pp. 36–7, specifically:
This is a genuine music business showcase for invited guests only
We have provided fire-extinguishers, illuminated EXIT signs, and crash barriers
We have made sure fire regulations are implemented and anything flammable has been removed or sprayed with fire-resistant chemicals
We have one thousand especially invited guests from the world's music industry, ranging from celebrities to major record company MDs. Stepping on our toes could lead to massive law suits and huge compensation fines
We have legal rights to be on the property with the landlord's full blessing
In fact, we are quite within our rights to ask you to leave the building and only return with a court order or warrant

53   The descriptive details of the warehouse both inside and outside drawn from classof88.co.uk and The Eighty Eight Podcast #13 Genesis'88 Leaside Rd 1988 https://www.youtube.com/watch?v=jTKTGTQit3A&t=3s

53   'Can You Party' anecdote, Gillett, *Party Lines*, p. 89

58   Soul II Soul reference, Jazzie B and Lloyd Bradley quotes, Gillett, *Party Lines*, p. 32

59   Three golden rules of venue management, off the record, right? No blacks, no Pakis, no sportswear, Gillett, *Party Lines*, p. 19

60   They're planning some kind of party. We don't want it and I'm sure it's not safe. Have a look. It's down to you. Anthony, *Class of 88*, p. 38

60   Everything seems fine to me, says the fire officer. As far as I'm concerned, they can have their party. Anthony, *Class of 88*, p. 39

69   Excerpts from Margaret Thatcher's New Year Message, 31 December 1988, https://www.margaretthatcher.org/document/107426

70   Denis Thatcher quotes and details regarding the Oval and his gin and cigarette regime, Wood, *New Yorker*, 25 November 2019

71   major green initiative. National Archives, Chris Patten, Memo to Prime Minister, 12 September 1989, 890912 Patten mnt for MT WATER PRIVATISATION PREM19-3846 f379

71   Food is just as much a basic commodity and not even Labour are suggesting that there should be government bread and jam. National Archives, Bernard Ingham, 890914 Ingham mnt for Gray WATER PRIVATISATION PREM19-3846 f377

75   Mrs Thatcher has warned against a revenge attack on those responsible for the Pan Am disaster. As the search for evidence continued, the police denied her husband's accusation they'd taken too long to deal with the bodies.

75   And in Rio de Janeiro, over a hundred New Year revellers are drowned or missing after a pleasure boat sinks. BBC1 1 January 1989 Late Evening News, https://www.youtube.com/watch?app=desktop&v=vB3O1gbhIc8

81   Keith's speech on strands of house music is based on, and quotes, Reynolds, *Energy Flash*, p. 62 and p. 66

83   Andrew Weatherall quote, boys own snub tv andrew weatherall terry farley pete heller bocca juniors, https://www.youtube.com/watch?v=_vqf9DDHqUg

84   Attempted robbery of the warehouse party based on, in part, Anthony, *Class of 88*, p. 41

86   Certain details and anecdotes of Feltham prison, Bland, *Independent*, 4 September 2013

92   Certain passages here in Noble's recollections reference and quote *White Riot*

99   Mrs Thatcher's policies are now essentially irreversible; 'capitalism with a human face', Robinson, *Can't Pay, Won't Pay*, p. 22

100   Godfrey Heaven's war with local authorities, Robinson, *Can't Pay, Won't Pay*, p. 35

100   Quote from Conservative Manifesto, 1987, Turner, *Rejoice! Rejoice!*, p. 432

100   Shortest suicide note in history, ibid.

102   Descriptions of music performances and videos from Top of the Pops are Suzi's own, programme broadcast 16.02.1989, BBC 1

103   Suzi quote reviews of 'Promised Land' cited in Munn, *Mr Cool's Dream*, section: February 1989

104   Paul Weller quote in *The Face* cited in Munn, *Mr Cool's Dream*, section: April 1988

104   Paul Weller quote with which Suzi ends her piece, from 'So why DID Paul Weller decide to cover one of the all time seminal house tracks …?' https://909originals.com/2017/10/04/so-why-did-rocker-paul-weller-decide-to-cover-one-of-the-all-time-seminal-house-tracks-february-1989/

105   Details on the police operation and arrests after the Broadwater Farm uprising from Smith, *The Justice Gap*, 13 July 2018

109   1 January 1989 is the day the Hackney Community Defence Association start to monitor cases of injustice in the Hackney and Stoke Newington divisions of the Metropolitan Police, HCDA, 'A Crime is a Crime is a Crime', November 1991, https://hackneyhistory.wordpress.com/2015/05/26/a-crime-is-a-crime-is-a-crime-on-the-crimes-of-hackney-police-1991/

109   First case of police criminal violence taken up by the HCDA from an incident on 15 January. Civil action proceedings taken out against the Metropolitan Police almost immediately. Ibid.

110   Veered off the road, crashed through the railings and ended in a pond, *Guardian*, 20/02/92, via HCDA, 'A Crime is a Crime is a Crime', November 1991, https://hackneyhistory.wordpress.com/2015/05/26/a-crime-is-a-crime-is-a-crime-on-the-crimes-of-hackney-police-1991/

110   Details of Trevor Monerville's initial arrest and consequences, from 'Fighting the Lawmen' pamphlet by the Hackney Community Defence Association, 8 October 1992, https://hackneyhistory.wordpress.com/hcda/fighting-the-lawmen/

111   Details of subsequent arrests and consequences, *Guardian*, 20/02/92,

via HCDA, 'A Crime is a Crime is a Crime', November 1991, https:// hackneyhistory.wordpress.com/2015/05/26/a-crime-is-a-crime-is-a-crime-on-the-crimes-of-hackney-police-1991/

114   Suzi's descriptions of how Genesis Sunset found new premises and secured them, including the Special Projects Department Manager text, Anthony, *Class of 88*, pp. 42–3. Suzi's interactions with Genesis Sunset are entirely fictional.

116   The Genesis Sunset membership scheme and 'hype' text, Anthony, *Class of 88*, pp. 42–3. Suzi's interactions with Genesis Sunset are entirely fictional.

129   Paolo Hewitt quotes from 'So why DID rocker Paul Weller decide to cover one of the all-time seminal house tracks …?' by Editor, *909Originals: The Stories behind the music*, 4 October 2017

177   Suzi's piece on *Confessions of a Pop Group* quotes articles in *The Quietus* (see Bibliography, 'Modernism Vs. Classicism' and 'A Man Escaped')

180   *Iron Lady, Iron Fist*, references and quotes from the following sources:
PMQs, 4 May 1989
National Archives, PREM 19/2724, Department of the Environment, letter, 5 October 1989
National Archives, PREM 19/2724, Privy Council office, letter, 27 November 1989
National Archives, PREM 19/2724, 10 Downing Street, letter from the Principal Private Secretary, 6 November 1989
National Archives, PREM 19/2724, Note to PM, ACID HOUSE PARTIES, 12 October 1989

196   Quotes 'Hackney Against the Poll Tax Federation Newsletter', May 1990

196   as any kind of progressive instrument of wealth distribution, Hannah, *Can't Pay, Won't Pay*, p. 13

210   Jon's recollections of his visit to the Land Registry reference and quote *Red Menace*

218   Details from the Hackney Show line-up from https://www.phatmedia.co.uk/flyers/event/hackney-show-1989

236   The 1 July party is fictional, but certain dialogues/interactions are based on Anthony, *Class of 88*, pp. 98–9, specifically:

Are you the organiser of this event?

You're under arrest and coming with me

You can't arrest me. What are the charges? This is a perfectly legitimate event.

You're still legally under arrest, mind, and in serious trouble. But you get in there and tell them to stop the music and pack up all the equipment

Fuck the Old Bill, let's stand firm and confront the bastards

It's not about resorting to violence. It's about love. It's about loving our comrades

248   Suzi's descriptions of the crowd's response to The Style Council's performance at the Royal Albert Hall (see Bibliography)

249   Bill Brewster quote from Levitt, 'Finding liberation somewhere else'

278   'Hissing Sid' is Sidney Cooke, a convicted child molester and murderer and leader of the Dirty Dozen paedophile ring, described by the *Guardian* in 1991 as 'Britain's most notorious paedophile'

292   Quotes New Year Message, 31 December 1989, Message Margaret Thatcher Foundation

303   Newspaper headlines from 'A People's Account of the Hackney anti-Poll Tax demonstration on March 8th 1990' pamphlet by the Hackney Community Defence Association

304   Jon's description and contextualisation of the Hackney anti-Poll Tax demonstration is based on details from 'A People's Account of the Hackney anti-Poll Tax demonstration on March 8th 1990' pamphlet by the Hackney Community Defence Association, specifically the 'Chronology of events'

315   Bill Stewart's joke that Parker remembers is an old one and has featured before in a novel, *The Information* by Martin Amis (page 15 in the Kindle edition, 'Scozzy' telling the joke to '13'). I think Amis gets the telling of it slightly wrong (specifically not using the present perfect tense in places) so I've rectified that but essentially nicked the idea from him.

325   Certain details of the Poll Tax demonstration from contemporary news outlets, personal experience, and other media sources (see Bibliography for details)

332   Suzi's documenting of the day quotes from Anonymous, *Poll Tax Riot*. In the preface to the main text, it states: 'This pamphlet is

anti-copyright and can be freely reproduced by any revolutionary group. But copyright protects it from being used by journalists, rich bastards, etc.' Suzi's stated aim is to tell a story that the mainstream media will likely ignore. I quote this text in good faith, to tell parts of the story that the pamphlet depicts. I think it's important to document faithfully this alternative history, one that is so often suppressed by the mainstream, conservative media.

Here are the sections from the text that I quote from, using Suzi as a fictional conduit:

The atmosphere on arriving at Kennington Park is like a carnival. Bands are playing, the sun is hot, thousands of people out to demonstrate their united opposition to the Poll Tax (p. 5)

the anarchists, who are raggier than ever. The demonstration is leisurely with no heavy police or Militant (stewarding) presence (p. 15)

The demonstration was simply massive, enormous, a sea of people filling up and overflowing out of Kennington Park. And the atmosphere was wonderful: like a carnival. People were happy, but this wasn't an empty, superficial happiness. This was happiness based on strength and power. And it was happiness that grew and developed as people realised the sheer size of the demonstration and thus of the whole movement against the Poll Tax. The collective was growing, flexing its muscles for the first time in years. No more individualised, atomised discontent. No more feelings of powerless anger. This was it: thousands and thousands of people out on the streets, angry and strong (p. 33)

Some of us were working, some of us on the dole, some on housing benefit, some squatting because they couldn't afford to pay for a reasonable home, others because there aren't any homes available, some folks had worked all their lives to provide for their families, some had never been able to find work. We all had something in common - we were all working class, and in today's wonderful British society we had become part of the growing, but powerful underclass. The Poll Tax was another financial burden to us, like all the other benefit and welfare cuts we've experienced, particularly in recent years. We've got no money left to pay now though, but nobody seems to listen or care (p. 53)

Even when Hackney went up, a few points were knocked off the Stock Exchange and rumours of Thatcher's resignation started to flow. [This] was going to show the government and the councils what a fight they've got on their hands, this was where everybody would be together in the centre of 'power', this was going to be the big one (p. 57)

Try to get out of the park and there's a huge sea of people in the way, trickling out like sand in an hour glass and pushing its way into this mass a large group of scruffy anarchos from god knows where (a soap manufacturers' nightmare) banging drums and tins and anything else to hand (p. 27)

337 Nice bit of greenery to sit down and see if anything happens. By the line of coppers protecting Downing Street is a group of about 200 people who are [pushing and] shouting and occasionally throwing cans and bits of placard. (p. 9)

and who should be at the head of this little unpoliced and unstewarded bit of the march but some people with a Class War banner who promptly take it down the side of the M.O.D. and back on to Whitehall to huge cheers from the crowd, a coup for Class War! (p. 28)

a crush is developing. Some of the peaceful protesters panic (p. 15)

340 Nicholas Ridley quotation, Robinson, *Can't Pay, Won't Pay*, p. 12

340 Suzi as conduit, as above:
Immediately a small barricade is built out of building rubbish from skips in the yard. A roll of barbed wire is dragged across the top of the barricade. The mounted cops don't charge again. The M.O.D. windows start to get trashed (p. 10)

344 Suzi as conduit, as above:
People high up in the scaffolding, chanting 'No Poll Tax, No Poll Tax' to the heavy, sharp metallic beat of scaffold pole against scaffold pole. Then all of a sudden poles, braces, concrete rained down on to the cops (p. 59)

354 Michael Buerk quoted from https://www.youtube.com/watch?v=ckLcsFMhiXo

355 Suzi as conduit, as above:
St. Martin's Lane. Three cars idly overturned, completely on their

roofs, wheels swinging in the air. And, oh what a glorious sight, a Porsche utterly burnt out (p. 42)

363   National Archives, Resignation Action Plan 22 November 1990, 901122 No.10 RESIG ACTION PLAN PREM19-3213 f215

368   Suzi's interview with Paul Weller quotes 'Paul Weller: "Most people dislike me anyway ... it can only get better"', by Mat Snow, *Guardian*, 16 April 2014, a reprinting of a Q article from 1993

With thanks to
Paul Engles, Will Francis, Nathaniel Alcaraz-Stapleton, Katharina Bielenberg and Piers Russell-Cobb
Lucy Caldwell
Jake Arnott, Daniel Rachel, Abir Mukherjee and Dominic Nolan
Deepa Anappara, Jessica Andrews, Jonathan Gibbs and Rebecca Tamás
Martha, Lucian and Louise